ZOMBIES
AND SHIT

CARLTON MELLICK III

DEADITE PRESS
Portland, OR

DEADITE PRESS
an imprint of Eraserhead Press

ERASERHEAD PRESS
205 NE BRYANT
PORTLAND, OR 97211

WWW.ERASERHEADPRESS.COM

ISBN: 1-936383-19-5

AUTHOR'S NOTE

"*Braaaaaaaiinss* ...and shit."

Every zombie fan has a plan for what they would do in order to survive the zombie apocalypse...you know, if it were to actually happen someday. My plan is to put my brain into a robot body. It doesn't matter what it looks like, as long as it has tank treads for legs, laser cannons for arms, and can fly. Then I would be like a robotic superhero of the zombie apocalypse. I would carry around a battle axe and wear an american flag cape, fighting zombie hordes and rescuing survivors from malls and farm houses. It would be awesome. But I guess it would also be kind of lonely, because I'd be the only robot in the wasteland and who wants to be friends with a robot? Still, it's kind of a cool idea...

I've been obsessed with zombie movies my entire life and I believe I might have one of the largest zombie movie collections in the world, it includes some movies that are so rare that the only other people who own copies of the movies are the people who made them.

My collection started back when I used to bootleg zombie movies for a living. When I was 21 and trying to make it as a writer, I was able to write full-time because I bootlegged zombie movies on the side. Then I started a company called Crappy Homemade Zombie movies, where I sold unreleased backyard zombie movies through bootleg distribution channels. It was a fun way to make a living. Most writers are happy to quit their day jobs once their writing careers take off, but once mine took off I was actually kind of sad to quit.

"Zombies and Shit" is my thank you letter to the zombie genre. If it weren't for those zombie movies I probably wouldn't have a writing career today. However, I have been hesitating to write a zombie book for quite a long time. So many zombie movies and zombie books come out these days that it seems unnecessary to unleash yet another zombie novel onto the reading public. But I wrote one anyway, for the fun of it.

However, I decided not to go with the Romero style of zombies. Instead, I did the Return of the Living Dead style of zombies. Nobody does the sludgy brain-eating indestructible Return of the Living Dead zombies in literature. I don't know why. They should. Return of the Living Dead is fucking awesome. And it's punk as hell. And it was also the first zombie movie I saw as a kid.

It is pretty obvious that this book was inspired by the Return of the Living Dead movies (well, at least 1 and 3). It was also inspired (in small ways) by zombie video games like Resident Evil and Left 4 Dead, as well as zombie books by Brian Keene. But probably the biggest influence for this book is the book/movie/manga Battle Royale. I have always loved the "elimination match" plot line. It's something I've always wanted to do.

"20 people go in, only one comes out..."

This book is an elimination match story set in the zombie apocalypse, which is something I've always wanted to read. They say you should write what you want to read, so that's what I've done. It was the most fun I've had writing a book in a long time. I hope you enjoy it.

- Carlton Mellick III 10/10/10 4:08pm

INTRODUCTION
AND
SHIT

As far as trends go, I think most of us can agree that zombies should pretty much be done. They've had their fifteen minutes in the pop-culture spotlight, and now the marketplace is saturated. The time has come for the dead to die off again, and come shambling back a decade from now, with new life and purpose, to eat the hell out of a new generation.

Except this isn't happening.

And it used to be my fault.

But now the blame falls squarely on Carlton Mellick.

Let me explain. In case you've been living under a rock or in a coma for the last decade, most critics and media-watchers agree that the current uber-zombie craze in pop culture (books, movies, comic books, television, video games, board games, card games, role-playing games, trading cards, toys, clothing, food, tattoos, philosophy, music, college courses, etc.) is at least partially my fault.

A decade ago, the publication of my first novel, *The Rising*, coincided with the release of a movie called *28 Days Later*. Both *The Rising* and *28 Days Later* featured different kinds of zombies, which was okay with most people, since nobody else had done much with zombies for the decade leading up to the book and movie's releases. Both were big hits. *City of the Dead*, my sequel to *The Rising*, followed soon after, and so did a lot of other books and movies and comics. And they haven't gone away. Indeed, there seem to be more of them than ever. There are now publishing companies that publish nothing but zombie literature and authors who write about nothing but the living dead.

I had a chance to do the same. In truth, I could have probably made a very good living (i.e. a lot more money than what I make now) doing for zombies what Anne Rice and Laurell K. Hamilton did for vampires, and just written zombie novels, but doing so didn't appeal to me. I didn't want to be typecast. I didn't want to become 'The Zombie Guy'. Occasionally, I would write about zombies. I tried my hand at the traditional "Romero-style" undead (with *Dead Sea*) and returned to the world of *The Rising* with a collection of thirty-two original short stories that all took place in that world, called *The Rising: Selected Scenes From the End of the World*. After that, I decided I was really burned out on them. Upon reflection, though, I wasn't so much burned out as I was written-out. I didn't want to just repeat the same story over and over again (which is the risk any author or filmmaker runs when dealing with zombies—or any other genre trope). There are only so many things you can do with the dead, and I felt I'd done them all. Much of what I read and saw from my peers seemed to be treading the same old ground. Oh, don't get me wrong. There were some good stories. Some great stories, in fact. But they weren't anything new. We'd seen it all before.

Recently, after several years of refusing to write anything about zombies, I returned to sub-genre for three projects: a novella (*The Rising: Deliverance*), a novel (*Entombed*), and an ongoing comic book series (*The Last Zombie*). The only reason I agreed to do them was because I felt they were something different than what we'd all done before. *The Rising: Deliverance* is a prequel that focuses heavily on characters and not on zombies. In *Entombed*, the zombies appear only briefly (a handful of pages) before the story focuses on a group of survivors who are safe from the zombies but not each other.

And *The Last Zombie* takes place after the zombie apocalypse is over, and focuses on humanity's efforts to rebuild.

Still, the majority of what is still being published is material that just re-treads and recycles the same old plotlines. And as a result, I predicted readers would soon grow bored, and then zombies would go away for a while until somebody younger and smarter came along and figured out a way to revitalize them. I figured this would take about ten years.

I was wrong.

Fucking Carlton did it in the here and now.

It would be easy to dismiss *Zombies and Shit* as nothing more than a fun, entertaining, literary distraction. And if you want to look at it as just that and nothing more, there's no harm in doing so, because the book is fun and it is entertaining. Hell, it's fucking exhilarating—a tight, breakneck narrative and lots of awesome ultra-violence and quirky, distinct characters.

But it is the setting that really sets this book apart, and thus, not only elevates it above any other zombie novel currently on the market (including my own), but also instills that new blood and new idea I was talking about before. And the bitch is, the whole thing is so deceptively simple. Carlton simply changed the location. Gone is the familiar shopping mall or island or skyscraper or any of the other genre tropes. Instead, we have a dark, dystopic, post-apocalyptic future. Think *Mad Max* or *Battle Royale*… with zombies.

How fucking genius is that?

Throw in some wild futuristic technology, a bit of Carlton's trademark social commentary (this time focusing on our society's reality television addiction and Warhol's fifteen minutes of fame), and a plot that literally leaves you guessing until the end, and you've got a hit. You've got a classic. You've got an addition to the zombie canon that, twenty years from now, will be just as influential on the next generation as Romero's original trilogy and Skipp & Spector's *Book of the Dead* anthologies were on our generation.

If you love zombies, you'll love this book. But more importantly, if you're sick of zombies—if you want them to go the fuck away now—then you will love this book. Why? Because it will remind you of what you loved about them in the first place, before they became overdone clichés that saturated the marketplace.

And in either case, you can blame Carlton Mellick.

Empathize
Brian Keene
Somewhere in rural Pennsylvania
June 2011

ZIPPO

SCAVY

POPCORN

BRICK

HAROON

XIU

GOGO

HEINZ

ALONZO

NEMESIS

ORO

JUNKO

WENDY

BOSCO

ADRIANA

VINE

LEE

RAINBOW CAT

LAURENCE

CHARLIE

CHARLIE

Charlie rolls over in his sleep and spoons his wife lying next to him. He burrows his face into the back of her neck and inhales the scent of cinnamon and motorcycle grease. His eyes still closed, he takes a deeper smell of her hair and recognizes the odor of cloves mixed with river clay. Her hair is soft against his nose. He wonders why she has such soft hair. Rainbow Cat, his wife, normally has very crusty dreadlocks that are itchy against his nose. With his lips pressed against her bare neck, it feels as if she doesn't have dreadlocks at all. It feels more like she has a short pixie haircut.

As he rubs his arm against the front of her body, he wonders if this is actually his wife at all. His hand is cupped around a large plump breast, yet his wife is nearly flat-chested. Her waist and hips are soft and curvy, yet his wife's body is knotty with muscle from working in the fields. When the woman moans, it is deep and smooth, not high and coarse. This is definitely not his wife.

Charlie opens his eyes. He feels groggy, drugged. His muscles are so relaxed that he only just realizes that he's been fully clothed this whole time, lying on a hard concrete floor. He pushes himself up and looks at the woman next to him. She's an Asian woman with short dyed-blonde hair, someone he's never seen before in his life. She's wearing jeans and a white tank top. Her mouth is open against the pavement, a puddle of drool below the corner of her lip. In her

13

sleep, she grabs his arm and pulls it back against her chest, hugging it like a teddy bear.

Leaning awkwardly against the sleeping woman with his arm in her grasp, he takes a look around the dimly lit room. It seems to be the lobby of an old abandoned hotel or office building. Dust-coated couches and chairs can be seen through the stripes of light coming from the boarded up windows. Debris from the partially-collapsed ceiling litters the reception area.

There are other people sleeping on the floor all around him, almost two dozen of them. Most of them look to be real scumbags: vagrants, gutter punks, junkies, whores. Charlie wonders how the hell he got there. The last thing he remembers is having drinks with his wife. It was their five year anniversary, the first day in months they were able to afford to go for a night on the town. He remembers having some drinks and then waiting to be served. He remembers the owner of the establishment giving them each a couple of free drinks.

The only thing that makes sense to him would be if he'd gotten too drunk to walk home and passed out in a nearby abandoned building. It isn't rare for abandoned buildings to be filled with lowlifes these days. It also isn't uncommon for him to pass out in public places after a night of heavy drinking. But what is strange is the drugged feeling in his brain, his numb mouth and tongue. If he did some kind of drug while he was drunk, Rainbow is probably pissed off at him right now. He promised her he would never do any kind of drug ever again. She might have even kicked him out of their apartment. Perhaps that's why he's sleeping in a place like this.

He looks down at the Asian woman snuggling his arm. She's probably a prostitute. Charlie might have even slept with her last night for all he knows. Rainbow isn't with him, thankfully. He hopes she arrived safely to their apartment last night and has no recollection of what happened to them the night before. Otherwise, he might have just fucked up their marriage for good.

For a hippy, Rainbow Cat is a very angry and unforgiving human being. She's also materialistic, snobbish, and high maintenance. He told her he was done with pills and hookers. If this is what happened that would be the end of it. She wouldn't take him back this time.

Charlie tries to slip his arm away from the sleeping woman, but she only hugs it tighter. He tries to rip it away and she digs her fingernails into his arm. When the fingernails draw blood, he cries out, waking her. Her black eyes pop open and point up at him. As he hovers a foot above her, he sees the shocked look on her face. She is just as surprised and confused to be there as he is. He can tell that she too has no idea where she is or why she is there.

Still holding his arm, she glares at Charlie. Then she grinds her teeth and digs her nails deeper into his arm, as if she thinks he is the person responsible for bringing her there.

The woman is about to go for his eyes when they hear somebody yell, "What the fuck!"

They turn their heads to see a young punk with a tall yellow mohawk standing on the other side of the room.

"Where the hell are we?" he says. "What the fuck is going on and shit?"

A punk girl, one with pink spiky hair, gasps and looks around frantically. More people begin to wake up, all of them just as surprised to be there as Charlie.

"Why am I on the floor?" cries a shivering prostitute, no older than sixteen.

"You've got to be shitting me," says a large black homeless man with a beard and mud-coated hoody.

Charlie looks down at the Asian woman and their eyes meet. The white tank top she's wearing is moist with sweat. Because she's not wearing a bra, Charlie can clearly see her dark nipples

"Get the fuck off me," she yells, then kicks him to the floor.

When Charlie gets up, he watches the angry woman storm away from him, covering her breasts with folded arms. She pushes through the shoulder of a muscle-bound punk with a white flat top and a hot pink half-shirt.

"I've been drugged," says a voluptuous punk girl with green hair. "I can taste it."

"Yeah, me too, and shit," says the yellow mohawk punk. "What the fuck!" He kicks a piece of rubble across the concrete floor.

Everyone in the room has now woken, pulling themselves slowly to their feet, rubbing their groggy eyes. All of them except for one: a girl in the corner. A tall, bony girl with blonde dreadlocks.

"Rainbow?" Charlie says.

He goes to her and turns her over. It is his wife. She rubs her eyes open and smiles at Charlie.

"There you are," she says, touching her index finger sloppily to his lower lip.

15

The Asian woman looks over at Charlie with a sneer, feeling dirty for snuggling with a married man while his wife was in the same room, even if it was an accident. She shakes her head and stares out of a crack in the boarded up window.

When Rainbow Cat looks around and notices the unfamiliar surroundings, she leaps to her feet, and yells, "Oh god."

The hippy girl looks around the room in a panic. When Charlie tries to hug her to him, she pushes him away.

"This has got to be some kind of mistake," she says. "This isn't the way it was supposed to happen."

The Asian girl looks over at Charlie and says in a calm, serious tone, "You better shut her mouth right now."

"I can't be here," Rainbow cries. "I can't be here!"

"Shut her up or I'll snap her neck," says the Asian woman, without raising her voice.

Charlie can tell by the look in her eyes that she's serious, so he calms down his wife. The Asian woman's eyes return to the window, peering at something in the distance.

"Where the fuck are we and shit?" says the yellow mohawk punk, as Charlie passes him to go to the window. The punk follows him.

Standing over the Asian woman's shoulder, Charlie peers out of the window. Outside is a vast city of collapsing vine-ridden skyscrapers and rubble. A wasteland. The building they are in is an old hotel, with a security wall around the perimeter.

The punk's jaw drops when he sees the city. It is one of the ancient ones, the kind of city that they have only seen in old pictures and books.

"We're on the mainland," says the punk, "in the middle of the damned Red Zone!"

"Impossible," Charlie says. "How did we get all the way out here?"

The punk's mohawk quivers. "Look around and shit! We're not on the island anymore. It's obviously the damned Red Zone!"

The Asian woman glares up at the punk. The look in her cold dark eyes is enough to shut him up. She peers at Charlie and puts her long black-painted fingernail to her lips, then points to a figure on the other side of the yard.

When Charlie looks, he sees a naked man staggering through the weed-coated parking lot. His skin has melted off of his body, his face nothing but a skull buried in fluffy pink meat, his intestines wrapped around his neck like a scarf. He's a walking corpse, moaning with every step he takes.

"We *are* in the Red Zone, aren't we?" Charlie asks.

The Asian woman nods. "Right in the middle."

"How is that even possible?" Charlie asks. "That's hundreds of miles away from the island. How could we have possibly gotten here?"

"We were put here," she says.

"For what reason?" he asks. "To play some kind of joke on us?"

"Something like that," she says.

When the young prostitute with the dark red hair looks out of the window and sees the zombie, she screams.

"What the fuck is that!" she cries. "What is it doing here!"

The zombie hears the prostitute and looks over at her. Sunflowers are growing out of its hollow skull like weeds. A tongue coils out of its black teeth.

"Brains…" it says, then approaches the building.

When the prostitute's eyes meet with the zombie's, she covers her mouth and backs away. The zombie shuffles forward like bags of garbage spilling from a dump truck.

"It's a fucking zombie!" says the yellow mohawk punk, almost excitedly.

Everyone runs to the window to see it for themselves, but once they get a glimpse of it they all back off.

Charlie looks back at his wife, sitting on the floor, curled around her knees, shaking her head. He goes to her. "Do you know what's going on?" he asks.

She looks up at him with tears in her eyes.

"I'm so sorry…" she says.

He holds her close to him, her tears tickling his cheeks.

A voice comes over the intercom system. The building has long been without electricity, so Charlie is confused by how it is functional.

The voice says: "Welcome, contestants!" It's the voice of an overly excited young woman with a Japanese accent. "I hope you slept well! I'm sure you're all wondering what has happened to you and why you have come to be in the middle of the Red Zone. But, for you, I have super great news! All twenty of you have been randomly selected to participate in the hit television series, *Zombie Survival!* The Platinum Quadrant's favorite reality game show, number one!"

"I knew it," says the Asian woman.

The voice continues: "Most of you are probably unaware of this show, because citizens of the Copper Quadrant such as yourselves do not have the luxury of television. But it is the most electrifying entertainment on TV, guaranteed! If you do a good job and win the game, first prize will be citizenship in the Silver Quadrant, with certified passports to the Gold and Platinum Quadrants. However, there can be only one winner. Losers will be left for dead in the Red Zone."

"This can't be," says an obese man of Italian descent. "I'm not a citizen of the goddamned Copper Quadrant. I'm from Silver. I was just visiting my dumbshit nephew!"

The Asian woman hushes him.

The voice continues: "If you will all make your way up to Room 222, you will find your supplies. Each of you have been left a backpack including survival gear and a unique weapon personalized to your estimated fighting capabilities! The backpacks are electronically locked and will not unlock until you have left the safety of the barricaded hotel. I recommend you go upstairs and claim your pack immediately. If you stay in the lobby for too long you are likely to gain some unwanted attention."

The punks rush up the stairs and go for room 222. Everyone follows. Charlie is the last one upstairs, waiting for Rainbow to stop crying and get to her feet.

"Braaains!" the zombie yells through the glass.

Looking behind him on the way up the stairs, Charlie examines the zombie banging on the boarded window trying to get in. It rips at the boards with its claws, a cracking sound splits through the wood but the plank remains in its place… for now. Charlie gets a good look at the sunflowers growing out of its empty eye socket and out the top of its hollow skull. Its mulched brain must have acted like fertilizer for the flowers, its head like a pot. He wonders how the thing can think without a mind in its head.

It's been seventeen years since Charlie has seen a zombie. Back when he was a kid, he lived in one of the many fortified cities along the coasts of the mainland. Back then, he saw zombies every day, through the barrier, in the wasteland. The dead were constantly trying to get into the city and the living were always reinforcing their perimeters to keep them out. Every capable human was responsible for guarding the perimeter. Charlie's father was no exception.

"There are so many of them out there, like an ocean," his father used to say when they would stare at the zombie wasteland from the top of the guard tower.

His father was fascinated with the walking dead. He thought of them as almost beautiful, like works of art.

He handed Charlie his machine gun and had him look through the scope. While zooming in, Charlie saw a black sludge-covered skeleton creeping down a street. Its eyes bulged out of the sockets, its skeletal teeth in a wide smile. Its black flesh melted from its body. The thing looked comical in its bumbling state. It made Charlie laugh.

"What is it?" his father asked.

"It's funny," young Charlie said. "The zombie looks funny."

Then he looked again at its bulging googly eyes and laughed harder.

His father patted him on the back. "Yeah, perhaps they are a bit funny. From a distance."

Eventually, civilization moved off of the mainland completely. They built protected cities on islands, on oil rigs, on aircraft carriers. Most of Charlie's generation have it pretty good compared to those who had to survive the zombie apocalypse that began over fifty years ago. Very few people have to fight for their lives on a day to day basis anymore, especially those in the upper-class Platinum Quadrant of Neo New York.

The twenty contestants squeezed into the small hotel room on the second floor. Lying along the wall were twenty bags. They weren't all backpacks. Some were duffel bags, some were purse-sized packs, some were large mountaineer packs. Charlie guessed the size had something to do with the weapon included within. A good weapon would be a huge advantage, but lugging around a large pack would not.

The voice came over the intercom: "Your packs will also include a map of the area with the pickup point marked by an X. You have three days to arrive at the designated pickup zone, but remember brave contestants: the remote control helicopter only has room for one passenger. If more than one person tries to board the craft, it will not take off. If all of you fail to arrive by 3pm on the third day, all of you will be left behind. If you want to win you will not only have to fight the zombies, you will also have to fight each other."

Rainbow hugs Charlie, her dreadlocks wrapping around his body like itchy tentacles. His eyes widen at the thought of only one of them getting out of there alive.

"There is only one rule: do not break the cameras," the voice says.

Then, outside the window, a floating spherical device about the size of a coconut rises to eyelevel. The lens on its front films the contestants, broadcasting their alarmed expressions to all the fat wealthy families watching at home in the Platinum Quadrant.

"The cameras are equipped to defend themselves against contestants as well as the walking dead. If you do happen to break one of them it will cause an explosion capable of killing all contestants within a 50 yard radius. This is the only rule we enforce. So, whatever you do, don't mess with the cameras."

"You mean like this?" The yellow mohawked punk kicks the glass right in front of the floating camera ball.

The device flies backward at the movement. The other punks burst into laughter. He flips off the camera and then shows it his bare ass. A couple of the other punks join in, flipping off the camera, hollering at it. A scantily dressed green-haired punk slut flashes her boobs at the camera and then spits.

The voice continues, unaware of the vulgar display happening before the camera, "So, good luck brave contestants! You can work as a team for a while if you like, or go solo right from the start. But remember, there can only be one survivor. I also recommend getting a move on as soon as you have your packs. The barricade around the hotel was only designed to last for a few hours, max."

When the voice is finished, the obese Italian man steps forward and speaks at the camera through the window. "My name is Alonzo Fisichella. I am a citizen of the Silver Quadrant, not the Copper Quadrant. I do not belong here. I have connections to people in both the Gold and Platinum Quadrants. I am not a scumbag lowlife like the rest of these people. Just look up my credentials. I should be exempt from this. You have to come pick me up!"

The camera hovered. It did not speak back to him.

"Answer me, you bitch!" Alonzo says to the intercom system.

The Asian woman says, "It's just an automated message. You're not going to get a response."

"How the hell do you know that?" Alonzo asks.

The Asian woman takes a breath. "Because I was the one who recorded it."

All eyes lock on her.

Charlie and the other contestants listen to the Asian woman's story. She introduces herself as Junko. It was five years ago when Junko recorded the message, back when she was a younger, more naïve girl, who was viewed as a typical empty-headed large-breasted sex object hired on to be the spokesperson for the Zombie Survival reality television series. That is, until she quit and led a protest against the show last year. After that, she had been deemed unemployable in the Platinum, Gold, and Silver Quadrants. She had to move to Copper with the hard laborers and the vagrant scum of the island. She knew it was only a matter of time before she was chosen as a contestant for the show herself.

"I know how this game works," she says. "It's all about sticking together and working as a team, not dividing apart. The people who go solo, no matter how tough they are, never make it to the end."

"But there can only be one winner?" asks the muscle-bound punk guy with the flattop and pink half-shirt.

"Very few people ever actually make it as far as the helicopter," she says. "Most games don't have winners at all. Don't think of this as a competition. Think of it as survival."

"How many winners have there been?" Charlie asks.

"Out of the ten games that have been played so far?" Junko blinks. "Only two, and one of those was infected and had to be eliminated by the time she got back to the island."

"So there's no hope?" Rainbow Cat asks. "We're done for?"

The large bearded vagrant steps forward and pulls the hood from his head to reveal a short black mohawk.

"There's always hope," he says, "if we stick together."

Then he gives a thumbs up and smiles a big dumb smile, his bright white teeth contrasting with his unwashed skin.

Each of the bags has a name tag on it. The big black vagrant, Laurence, calls out the names written on the bag and hands it to the appropriate contestant. This is also how the contestants are introduced to each other.

There is already one team that has formed: the seven punks.

They either know each other from before the contest, or already made fast friends. There's Scavy, the punk with the yellow mohawk, Brick, the large muscular punk with a platinum blond flattop and pink half-shirt, Gogo, the busty green-haired punk slut, Popcorn, the short punk girl with the spiky pink hair, Xiu, a Chilean punk girl with a black mohawk, Zippo, a skinny punk guy with an aviator helmet and goggles, Vine, a quiet punk guy with black hair, a black surgical mask, and a black spiked-leather outfit.

Bosco, a skinny redneck with a comb-over and facial features that can only be described as goblin-like, tries to team up with the punks, but they won't have him. They don't trust anyone who isn't a punk.

"This is going to kick ass and shit!" Scavy says, and his punk army raises their fists with him.

To these guys, this is nothing but a game, even if their lives are at stake.

"Shouldn't we all stick together?" Charlie asks Junko.

Junko is busy trying to pick the lock on her duffel bag.

Charlie leans into her field of vision. "You said we needed to work as a team in order to survive."

She turns to him, "Large teams draw too much attention. Splitting up into three or four smaller teams is preferable. I wouldn't want any of those punks on my team, anyway. They're unpredictable."

"Who's on our team then?" Charlie asks.

Junko looks at Charlie with an annoyed expression. "Who said I wanted you on my team?"

Charlie steps back. "I just thought…"

"Actually," Junko says, "if you get rid of your bitch I'll take you along."

"What?" Rainbow cries.

"You're Charles Hudson, aren't you?" Junko asks. "The writer?"

Charlie smiles. No matter how accomplished of a writer he is, he always appreciates being recognized.

"Yeah, or at least I *was*," he says. "Until the Platinum Quadrant decided fiction wasn't worthwhile anymore. I've been a poor nobody in the Copper Quadrant ever since."

"I've read some of your books," she says. "You have a clever mind. I could use clever."

"But what about my wife?" he asks, hugging Rainbow to his waist.

"For starters," she says, "she'll slow us down. She's dead weight.

Secondly, couples never make it very far in this game. They always get themselves killed by risking their necks to save each other. Thirdly, trust is the most important thing I need from a teammate. If I can't trust you then I don't want you."

"But why can't you trust us?" Charlie asks.

"I can probably trust you," Junko says. "I just don't trust her."

Charlie looks at Rainbow with her confused puppydog face, then back at Junko. "Why don't you trust my wife?"

Junko glares at the hippy girl. "Because she's the reason you've been chosen as a contestant for this show."

Rainbow bursts into tears when Charlie looks back at her. He doesn't know what the Asian woman is talking about, but based on Rainbow's reaction whatever she is saying is likely the truth.

"What do you mean?" Charlie asks.

Junko tells him about how the producers of *Zombie Survival* pay a reward to any citizen who recommends a good candidate for the show. She can tell that Rainbow recommended her own husband for the show, expecting to retire from the reward money. Charlie's celebrity status would make him an interesting contestant to the people watching back home.

"But you had no idea the producers never intended to pay, did you?" Junko tells his wife. "You might have heard rumors about the show and the reward, but you didn't know that your only payment would be to share the fate of your husband. That's what they always do."

Charlie notices a floating camera ball above Junko's shoulder, filming their conversation. Rainbow looks at Charlie with red watery eyes.

"Is this true?" he asks.

Rainbow nods her head and looks away.

"You didn't have a job and we needed the money," she says, her back to him. "I was sick of being the one who pays for everything all the time. I was sick of taking care of you."

"You did it just for money? On our five year anniversary?"

"You owed it to me," she says. "I work so hard to buy your food, pay your rent, support your alcohol addiction."

"I hardly drink anymore!"

"This was the only way I could get that money back."

"But, it's just money," Charlie says. "I've only been unemployed for the past ten months. When I was a novelist and we lived in the Gold Quadrant, you didn't have to work for over three years!"

"I know!" she says, her eyes no longer tearing with sadness but with anger. "That's why you owe it to me! You took that life away from me and I want it back!"

"I loved you..." Charlie says.

Her anger subsides.

"*Loved?*" she says. "You don't love me anymore?"

"What the hell do you think?" he says to her, the camera zooming in on his face. "You sentenced me to death just because you were tired of paying the bills yourself. How the hell do you expect me to feel?"

"But they sent me here, too," she cries. "We're in this together now."

He shakes his head. "You're in this alone."

Her lips quiver and then open as if to argue back, but she can't find the right words. She turns and runs down the hall, to another room, collapsing on a mattress that crumbles to dust beneath her.

Adriana, the young prostitute, looks out of the window at the urban wasteland below. The zombie with the sunflowers in its skull is attracting the attention of other zombies. There are three more of them now, and five more headed in the direction of the hotel from down the street. Their soggy green and black flesh drips from their limbs. Some of them have debris melded into their flesh, as if they had been lying in the rubble of the wasteland for over a decade, waiting for humans to return. Like the sunflower zombie, some of them grow weeds, moss, or vines from their rotten flesh.

"Braaaaiiins..."

The girl steps away from the window, just in case the zombies look up. She wouldn't want to excite them too much.

"So what the fuck are we going to do?" Bosco says. "The bitch said we only have three hours max before this place becomes unsafe."

Junko scowls at him for calling her a *bitch*, even if she does agree that she was a bitch in that past life.

"And the sooner we get out the better our chances," Laurence says.

Adriana looks out of the window again and sees a dozen more zombies approaching. And beyond them, in the distance, there is at least a dozen more.

"I'm not going anywhere," Adriana says, her voice quivering as she scrunches her puffy short skirt.

They look at her.

"You can't just stay here," Junko says.

Alonzo steps forward. "I'm staying, too. I wouldn't last ten minutes out there in my condition." He jiggles fifty pounds of belly fat to prove his point.

"I agree," another man says from the back of the room. He steps forward, a blond man wearing a black suit and leather overcoat. Charlie and Junko hadn't noticed him before. They only know his name from the tag on his enormous mountaineer pack that reads: Heinz.

"I think staying back might be a worthwhile strategy," says Heinz. His voice has a snobbish upper class tone to it, as if he thinks he is speaking to a group of inferior peasants. "If we lure all of the dead in the vicinity to one place, such as this building, they would be much easier to kill."

"Don't you understand what it takes to kill just one of those things?" Junko says.

"Of course," says Heinz. "It will not be too difficult of a task."

Junko shakes her head. "You're crazy."

"I think he could be right," another man says. Haroon, a young man of Indian descent, who is wearing perhaps the nicest clothing in the room.

Junko says, "You all have to know that staying here is suicide. I've seen it happen every time. Every season, there's always somebody too afraid to leave the starting point. They never last long."

"Yeah, what the hell is wrong with you pussies?" Scavy says.

"That's not what I mean," Haroon says. "I think we should forget about the helicopter. Only one of us can survive that way. If we work together I think we can all survive."

"How's that?" Bosco asks.

"I've been studying the map," Haroon says. "In order to get to the helicopter, we'd have to go through the most dangerous parts of the city. But what if we were to skip the helicopter and go for a boat?"

"Is it possible?" Alonzo asks.

Haroon holds up his map and points to a blue line along the bottom. "There's a harbor along the river here. It's farther than the helicopter but we'd travel through less dangerous territory. If we find a boat we can sail it downstream to the ocean. Then we'd be home free."

"That's never going to work," Junko says. "It seems close on the map but it is nearly three times the distance of the helicopter. There's no way anyone could survive out there for that long. And even if you happened to survive the trip and find a boat it would be over fifty years old. It's not going to be sail-worthy after rotting in disrepair for so long."

"Maybe we can find a plane at an airport to get us home?" Adriana says.

"Or find an armored vehicle that could take us out of the Red Zone," Alonzo says.

Junko groans and shakes her head at all of them.

"We're talking fifty years!" Junko says, knocking on her head. "Do you know what happens to machinery, boats, and buildings after fifty years?"

Nobody answers.

"They become useless," Charlie says. "She's right. Our only option is to go for the helicopter."

"But then only one of us will survive," Haroon says.

"You don't understand," Junko says. "We'll be lucky if even one of us survives. Last season not a single person lasted beyond the first day."

"Then why bother?" Adriana says. "We might as well kill ourselves now."

Junko shrugs. She doesn't really have a good answer for her. But Laurence steps forward and answers for her. "Because if we're gonna die, we're not gonna die like chumps."

Then he punches his large fist into his palm.

The punks cheer him.

Junko goes to Charlie.

"So, are you going to join me," she asks, "and leave the bitch behind?"

"Yeah," he says, without making eye contact. "I'm with you."

Junko smiles at him. "Good. Forget all about her and you might actually last awhile."

Charlie wipes his tears away, tries to toughen up.

"So who else should we team up with?" he asks.

Junko looks around the room. She points at the black man with the mohawk and the guy he is talking to, an ex-soldier turned vagrant named Lee. "Them."

"They can be trusted?"

She nods. "I'm a good judge of character."

"Who else?"

"I think I can trust that Haroon guy," Junko says. "But he's an idiot if he thinks he can actually get out of the wasteland by anything other than helicopter."

"He seems okay. That all?"

Junko looks around the room, then nods.

"Yeah, the rest are either worthless or scumbags or both."

Charlie says, "Then let's talk to the three that are worthwhile."

As Junko introduces herself to Laurence and Lee, Charlie grinds his fist at the thought of Rainbow betraying him like that. He knew she was on the selfish side, he knew she hated the idea of living in the Copper Quadrant, and he knew money was important to her. But what he didn't know was how little of importance he was to her.

Rainbow was a hippy from the Gold Quadrant. She lived in relative luxury since as long as she could remember. As a rich spoiled girl whose parents paid for everything, she was able to spend her time reading, smoking pot, protesting, painting, promoting peace and happiness, smoking pot, dancing, sun-bathing, and smoking pot. There were a lot of hippies in the Gold Quadrant. There were very few in the Silver and Copper Quadrants, because people were too busy working their asses off for just the bare essentials of survival.

When Charlie and Rainbow first met, it was at the university.

"What are you reading?" Charlie asked her.

Rainbow looked up from her picnic blanket to see the strange man staring down on her, blocking the sunlight.

"Charles Hudson," she said, folding her legs, her wet grassy toes resting on top of a cucumber sandwich.

"What are you reading that crap for?" he said. "There were much better books written before Z-Day."

"But I like his books," she said. "I relate to them. He's the only good writer since the apocalypse."

Charlie smiled and stretched his back at her. "I don't know, I think he's kind of a douchebag. Just look at his author photo. Total douche."

Then he walked away.

"Asshole," Rainbow said.

She hated when people said crap about her favorite author. Just because he was a popular contemporary writer, that didn't make him terrible. Most of the classics were originally bestsellers, written by the popular contemporary writers of their time. Just because Charles Hudson wasn't dead yet and had yet to withstand the test of time, that didn't mean he wasn't going to.

She muttered to herself, "You look more like a douchebag than Charles Hudson."

Then she turned to the bio page and looked at his author photo. Then she looked back at Charlie, who was walking casually through the park with his hands in his pockets. Charlie was wearing the same green antique army coat as the author in the photo.

She chased Charlie down and walked beside him, looking at his face and holding his book up as reference. Although he was younger in the photo, had less meat on his bones, and was clean shaven, she could see they were the same person.

"You're him, aren't you?" she asked. "Charles Hudson."

Charlie smiled. "I was wondering if you'd notice."

"Why didn't you tell me!" she said. "You're my favorite author!"

"If I'm your favorite author," he said, "you're not reading the right books."

"I've read a lot," Rainbow said, then licked her upper lip. "You're the only author that really speaks to me."

"But there's a whole library full of books by masters of the craft," he said, pointing at the university library on the other side of the park. "Those are the all-time greatest works of literature, written by geniuses. I'm no a master. I'm no genius. I'm not even smart, really. I've just been writing stories my whole life, since I was a kid, as a way to escape our shitty reality."

"But I can relate to that," she said, swinging her dreads over her shoulder to make sure they weren't blocking her cleavage. "I can't relate to some masterful genius from a completely different era telling stories about a world I never knew. You write about our lives now, in Neo New York."

"But those other books are brilliant works of art."

"I don't care if they are brilliant. I care about emotion. You make me smile, laugh, cry, fear, fall in love. That's what is important."

Charlie smiled at her. She smiled at him. He noticed she was sucking in her stomach, arching her back, pushing out her breasts so that they wouldn't look so small.

"What's your name?" he asked her.

"Cathy," she said. Then she leaned in, pressed her cheek against his, and said in a gentle voice, "But you can call me Rainbow Cat." Her lips so close they tickled his earlobe when she spoke.

He was used to the flirtatious advances of his female readers. His past six girlfriends were all young pretty fans. They were the only girls he was interested in, because even though he liked to make light of his writing talents all he really wanted was to have his ego stroked as much as possible. Compliments meant so much more when they were coming out of the lips of a beautiful woman.

By the next morning, they had already had sex three times. Rainbow was aggressive with her sexuality, gluttonous with it. She knew what she wanted, and she wanted it all right then and there. Charlie liked that about her. The more she wanted him, the better he felt about himself as a writer. She didn't know him, personally. She only knew his work. So for him to see her crave him sexually so bad meant that it was his art that she wanted to fuck. She wanted to lick his art, press her body against his art, feel his art inside of her. As an artist, it was like an ego blowjob, and he loved every second of it.

But she didn't just want to make love to him, she wanted to possess him. It wasn't long before she dropped out of college and moved in with him. It wasn't long before she convinced him to marry her.

They were happy together. Rainbow was happy that her favorite author now belonged to her, both physically and mentally, and he was happy to be with this pretty young girl who loved his work so much that she was willing to dedicate her life to him because of it. For each of them, it was a perfect arrangement. But it didn't last.

When the last fiction publishing company in Neo New York went out of business, Charlie was no longer an author. With no college education, neither Charlie nor Rainbow could get jobs in the Gold Quadrant. They were downgraded to the Silver Quadrant and eventually ended up in the ghetto of Copper.

Rainbow still believed in her husband. At least she did when they first moved into the Copper Quadrant. She told him that she would take care of them from then on. All he had to worry about was his writing.

"Your work is what is important," she said. "Someday a new publishing company will go into business. When that happens, you'll have several manuscripts ready to go. Then we'll be rich again."

Charlie agreed, but he wasn't as optimistic as she was. It was difficult for him to get back into writing. He became more interested in drinking, sulking around the house. He started taking pills, getting high on Waste, and sleeping around with prostitutes. But Rainbow helped him out of his despair. She told him that she would leave him if he didn't quit taking drugs or ease up on the drinking.

To get back at him for sleeping with prostitutes, she told him he had to write ten pages a day, every single day. If he was short a single page, a single paragraph, she would go out and fuck a random guy that night. Sometimes he met his goal, sometimes he didn't. She always made good on her promise, even if she wasn't in the mood that night. If he didn't write a single sentence, even if he happened to be sick, she wouldn't even come home that night. She would let some strange guy pick her up, then sleep in his bed with him, snuggle him, kiss the back of his neck as he slept, until it was time for her to go to work the next day.

Even though he wasn't making any money, Rainbow Cat made him a better, more responsible writer for doing this to him. He thought she was a total bitch for it, but because she was a bitch she had helped him through a hard time. He believed she was a bitch to him because she loved him.

He still can't believe she would sell him out to this television show, just for the sake of money. And on their anniversary, of all days, which wasn't just to celebrate five years of marriage but also to celebrate the completion of his newest novel. It wasn't only his newest, but also the greatest book he had ever written. His masterpiece. The book that he would be remembered for more than anything else he's ever written.

The last thing he remembers from their anniversary dinner, before the drugs in their drinks took effect, was telling her who the book was dedicated to.

The inscription on the manuscript page read:
To my Rainbow Cat, for always believing in me.

BRICK

The number of zombies outside of the hotel is rising. The undead are breaking the wooden barrier into splinters. Some are puking green radioactive vomit across the walls, others are dripping black oily fluids on the sun-burnt pavement.

"We need to get going pretty soon," Junko says to Charlie.

They have separated from the others and are now in a private hotel room, trying to plan their escape. Haroon and Lee are in the room, leaning against a dresser. Laurence is also there, pointing at the path.

"I say we head straight through there," Laurence says, while pointing at the widest street in sight. "It might be the most wide-open but it has the least amount of obstacles. We'll be able to run faster."

"No," Junko says. "You want to put obstacles between you and them. They can run pretty fast, but they are terrible climbers. We should go over the wall. They won't be able to follow us over and it'll take them a good hour to figure out how to get around. I've seen it before."

"How far away do we have to get before our packs open?" Lee asks through his scruffy gray beard. By his tipsy posture, Charlie assumes that the old man is drunk even though he couldn't possibly have any alcohol on him.

"Don't bother with them until we get over the wall and find safety," Junko says. "Focus on running. Trying to fight them will only slow us down."

"When should we leave?" Charlie asks.

"Right now," Junko says.

Once the five of them arrive in the lobby, they notice that the seven punks have the same idea. The punks are ready to go, their eyes lit with excitement. The other people in the room don't seem to be as organized. Charlie can't tell if they are all one group, several small groups, or if they all plan to go solo. Rainbow is the only person who isn't in the lobby. She must still be hiding up in a room somewhere.

The zombies are ripping boards from the windows and scratching against the glass. One of them is missing flesh from the tips of its fingers, causing a screeching noise as its finger bones scrape across the glass.

Scavy looks closely at one of the zombies. It is a female corpse who looks like she had been an exotic dancer in her past life, wearing fishnet stockings and a withered black corset. Her breasts are hanging out of her ripped open shirt. Scavy can see the saline implants through holes in her breast meat, where chunks of flesh had been bitten away.

The female zombie locks eyes with Scavy and says, "Braains!"

Then she thrashes harder against the boards. It's as if looking him in the eyes made her more hungry, as if she could see his brains through his pupils.

"Hey, this one's kind of hot!" Scavy says to his friends, pointing at the ex-stripper zombie.

His friend, Brick, laughs and wiggles his tongue at her through the glass.

"Braains," she says, staring Scavy in the eyes. "Let me eat your brains!"

Charlie notices that she is salivating.

"Brains!" she cries.

Brick and Scavy pretend to squeeze her breasts through the glass. This only works up the zombie even more.

"Need!" she cries. "Need your brains! Now!"

Junko pushes the punks away from the window. "Don't tease them. You'll only make them hungrier."

The punks don't seem to care.

"Are they intelligent?" Charlie asks Junko. "I've never heard them say anything but *brains* before… even when I was a kid and saw them all the time."

"It depends on how much of their minds are still intact," Junko says. "Most of their minds have been destroyed. Some of them, especially the freshly turned ones, can have entire conversations with you."

"So you can reason with them? Convince them to let us go? They must understand what it's like to be human."

Junko laughs and shakes her head. "Even the most intelligent zombies are like junkies going through a massive withdrawal. All they need to get their fix is to feed on the electrical impulses in your nervous system. If you want to convince junkies not to shoot up anymore, it's not going to happen while you're waving a bunch of free Waste in front of their faces."

"But what if you tried to reason with them from a distance, over an intercom?" Charlie asks. "Maybe if you take the Waste out of their faces it wouldn't be a problem."

"Clever," Junko says. "But a useless idea."

"I wonder if the more intelligent ones have conversations with each other," Charlie says, "when humans aren't around to drive them brain-crazy."

"Brain-crazy?" Junko asks.

"It's a term I use in my novels to explain zombie behavior around living beings."

"Hmmm…" She scrunches her eyes at him. "No wonder why people don't take your books seriously."

He shrugs. "I was never trying to be taken seriously."

"Are you ready to do this?" Junko asks.

Charlie looks behind him to check with Lee, Haroon, and Laurence. They nod their heads. Laurence smiles and gives him a thumbs up through his black leather glove.

"Let's do it," Charlie says.

The punks crowd the front entrance, wanting to be the first ones out. As they pry the boards from the front door, all of the zombies in the yard become attracted to the sound and gather on the other side.

"How are we gonna get through them?" Bosco says.

"We should leave through another entrance," Haroon says, inching away.

Before the punks get the boards down, the door splinters apart and a hole opens up on the top half.

"Braains!" a zombie's face says through the hole.

All the punks back away except for Brick and the pink-haired girl, Popcorn. They try to hold the door in place as it is ripped apart.

"Help us!" Popcorn yells.

The group scatters. Some of them run to the east side of the building, some run to the west. All of the punks leave their two friends, except for Scavy.

"Leave it," Scavy yells at them. "Come on!"

Brick and Popcorn won't let go of the door.

"You go first," Brick tells the girl, flexing his enormous weightlifter muscles. "I've got this."

Popcorn says, "You sure?"

"Yeah!" he says.

Popcorn bites her lip and eases away from the door. But just before she can get back far enough, a skeletal hand reaches through the hole and grabs her by the arm.

"It's got me!" she cries.

Scavy grabs her by the other hand and tries to pull her away, but its grip is too strong.

"Brains!" the zombie says, black sludge pouring out from between its teeth.

Then radioactive vomit sprays out of its mouth and covers Brick and Popcorn.

"Get back," Junko says to Charlie and her crew.

Charlie and the others back away from the vomit puddle on the floor as it bubbles and steams. Brick cries out as it burns his flesh like acid. Steam rises from the green slime on the right side of his face. As it drips into his eyes, it bleaches the color out of his right eyeball.

"If you get that shit on your skin you'll be infected," Junko says. "Let's get out of here. These guys are done for."

Junko takes off to the west side of the building, Charlie and the others follow after.

Rainbow Cat misses Charlie by three seconds as she comes downstairs with her bag over her shoulder, still wiping tears from her eyes. She sees that everybody has already gone except for the three punks in the entryway.

Popcorn screams as the zombie's bony claws dig into her skin. Scavy yanks on her arm with all of his strength and the zombie's claws are ripped out of her flesh. When he feels the release, he thinks she is free. But then there is another tug and Popcorn is pulled closer to the door.

When Rainbow approaches them, she sees that the zombie no longer has a grip on her arm. Instead, there is a thin red rope attached to her wrist that the zombie is holding on to. When she gets a closer look, Rainbow realizes that it isn't a rope. It is the girl's tendon.

Popcorn's cries hit a high pitch as the zombie reels the girl in closer to the hole in the door, using her tendon like a fishing line.

"Braains!"

Brick lets go of the door with one hand and grabs hold of her tendon, holding it from being pulled further through the hole. But without using his full strength to hold the barrier, the door crumbles open. The zombies pour inside.

When Junko and Charlie get to the side entrance, the door is already wide open.

"Let's do this," Laurence says behind them.

Junko looks back to make sure they are all with her.

"Where's Haroon?" she asks.

They look back.

"He was behind Lee," Charlie says.

Lee, in the back, just shrugs at them.

"We'll have to go on without him," she says.

When they exit the building, they run under a camera ball hovering overhead, ready to follow them through the wasteland. Up ahead, they see the tail-ends of other contestants running across the yard, dodging the zombie horde. Three of the punks who had ditched their friends are in the lead. Led by the Chilean female punk, Xiu, they weave quickly through the horde like cocaine-driven football players.

Bosco, the bony redneck, is in the back, not having as much luck. He gets cornered by five of them.

"Help me, goddamnit!" Bosco yells, as Junko and her crew run past him.

Charlie considers throwing some rocks or debris at the zombies to knock them away from the redneck, but Junko knows what he's thinking and snaps him out of it.

"Leave him," she says.

Charlie takes his eyes off of Bosco and focuses on his own survival. They run past two zombies with outstretched arms. One soggy corpse hisses at them, bubbles gurgling out of its throat as if it had been soaking at the bottom of a pool for the past decade.

There are only about a dozen on this side of the building, but they move pretty fast. Charlie and Junko run through six of them just before they squeeze together, blocking the path between them and their teammates.

Junko keeps moving, but Charlie looks back. Four of the zombies grab Laurence and pull him to the ground. Behind him, Lee turns around and runs in the opposite direction, heading for a collapsed section of the wall by the south side of the building.

"Keep going," Laurence says to Charlie. "I got this."

Charlie turns and continues after Junko.

They get around to the front of the building and arrive at the wall they had originally planned to go over. Charlie acts as a ladder to get Junko up the wall, then she lowers her arms to pull him up. Charlie notices that despite Junko's 4'11 height and soft flesh that doesn't appear to have an ounce of muscle, the Asian girl is surprisingly strong. She pulls him up with little effort.

At the top of the wall, the two of them look back at Laurence. Zombies are piling on top of him.

"He doesn't stand a chance," Junko says. "Come on."

She turns to drop down on the other side, but Charlie stops her. "Wait."

They look at the pile of zombies and see movement coming from beneath. Then the entire pile lifts from the ground as Laurence stands. The man is massive, Charlie knows, but with those baggy clothes covering up every inch of his skin he wasn't sure how much of him was fat and how much was muscle. As the corpses are thrown across the yard, Charlie imagines he is all muscle under those rags. He must be two or three times the size of Brick, and Brick looks like one of the old time professional wrestlers.

Laurence punches one of them in the stomach so hard that his fist bursts through its rotten soggy organs. But that doesn't stop the creature. With his fist stuck inside of it, the thing goes for Laurence's

36

skull with its claws. It shrieks in his face and widens its fingers. But before it reaches him, Laurence stomps down on the creature's knee, breaking its leg. The zombie crumples to the ground.

As the zombies return to their feet, Laurence punches them with his leather-gloved fists, knocking them back down. Then he pauses and turns to Charlie and Junko. He gives them a thumbs up and a big smile.

"Not a problem," he says. "Give me a minute to take care of these suckas."

Charlie looks back at Junko. She examines the vagrant carefully. The zombies have yet to lay a scratch on him. His clothes are covered in their rancid goo, but none of it has gotten on his skin. He's not infected. Junko agrees that they should wait for him.

Beyond Laurence, Charlie sees Lee escaping through the south wall. Bosco does not appear to be dead, but he's no longer in the place they had last seen him. He must have made it out of there somehow. On the other side of the wall, deeper into the city, the three punks are running down the street, dodging corpses and jumping rubble. Even though they are punks, they move like trained soldiers, their minds focused.

Beyond them, in the distance, there is machine gun fire. Charlie isn't sure where it is coming from, but somewhere out there contestants are already fighting their way toward the helicopter.

Brick runs from the hotel entrance toward the perimeter, leaving his friends inside to fend for themselves against the zombies. Then Scavy runs out of the hotel, carrying Popcorn at his side, her blood leaking out of her arm and from a fresh bite-wound on the back of her neck, just below the skull. Zombies exit the hotel, chasing after them.

And in the back of the crowd is Rainbow Cat. From the wall, Charlie can see his wife running for her life. He wonders how he'll feel if the zombies kill her right in front of him. He wonders if he'll feel sorry for her or feel satisfaction that she got what she deserved. He wonders if he'll feel anything at all.

"They're doomed," Junko says. "If that punk kid ditches his girlfriend he might stand a chance, but the other two are already infected."

Charlie can see how the vomit on Brick's face and Popcorn's chest has eaten away at their flesh like acid. Brick's cheek is dripping from his face like a long bloodhound jowl. His right eyeball is pure white and poking slightly out of the socket.

Far ahead of the others, Brick runs until he makes it through the perimeter into the city street. Once he gets there, his long duffel bag makes a beeping noise as it unlocks. He doesn't continue running from there. He drops the bag and opens it up, digging for his weapon.

Charlie watches as Brick pulls out a large two-handed sledge-hammer. He leaves his bag on the ground and runs back to his friends to help them out, raising the enormous hammer over his head like he's ready to chop wood with an axe.

Brick and Scavy had been friends for several years, ever since Brick had become a punk. Not many sub-cultures from the old world had survived, but the punk culture was stronger than ever. It had nothing to do with music anymore. It was all about attitude and style. Punks embraced the post-apocalyptic lifestyle. They raged against the authority of Neo New York. They despised the greedy scum living in the Platinum Quadrant.

Brick was born one of the rich kids in Platinum, but the Platinum Quadrant had strict rules for their youth. Three strikes and you're kicked out. Brick was a troubled kid. He enjoyed breaking into other people's apartments and stealing their stuff, just for fun. He enjoyed ditching class and getting drunk in his room while his parents were off shopping for new golfing outfits.

Eventually, he was caught shoplifting one of the brand new televisions that had finally come back into production for the first time since the collapse of the old world. It was the third strike, and he was out. His parents disowned him. A rich kid thrown into the Copper Quadrant was like throwing a sheep to the wolves.

Brick was beaten every day. Any money that he made from working on the docks was stolen by one of the many punk gangs that prowled Copper. In order to defend himself, Brick worked out everyday. He had to toughen himself up. By working on the docks, he was able to steal fish that put plenty of protein in his diet. By the time he was seventeen, he was one of the most muscular men in the Quadrant.

He became friends with Scavy the day Scavy and his crew tried to mug him. They asked for his money, but Brick told him no. When they got violent, Brick didn't back down. He beat one of the punks unconscious with his bare fists. He dislocated one of their shoulders. He sent another running off into the alleyway. No matter how many came at him, he wouldn't give in.

Eventually, they hit him in the back of the head with a two-by-four, then took his money and left him face down in the mud. But Scavy was impressed. Not just because the guy stood up to his entire gang, but because he did it to hold onto a lousy ten dollar bill.

The next day Scavy asked him to join his gang. All by himself, he approached him while he was at his job, loading boxes on the dock in his gray uniform covered in fish guts.

"Why do you bother working this shit job for shit pay?" Scavy asked.

"It's all I've got," Brick replied.

"Do you know each fish here sells for $10 each in the Platinum Quadrant?" Scavy said. "That's as much as you make in a day."

Brick knew how much things cost in Platinum. He didn't need some punk reminding him.

"Get lost," Brick said.

"You know how much I make in a day?" Scavy said.

Brick continued loading boxes onto a cart.

"$500 a day, minimum," Scavy said.

"Bullshit," Brick said.

"Okay, not me personally. That's how much my crew makes. We split it up evenly and shit."

"What is it that you do to make that much money?"

"We take it," Scavy said with a smile. "From the stupid."

"You took money from me," Brick said. "Are you calling me stupid?"

Scavy laughed.

"In this world, it is survival of the fittest," Scavy said. "The strong prey on the weak. The weak are left to suffer."

"So?"

"Do you want to be on the bottom of the food chain?" Scavy said. "Or do you want to fight your way to the top and shit?"

Brick dropped a box and it smashed on the ground, dozens of dead fish oozing out in the mud by his feet. He decided to leave the fish where they lay.

"Honestly, I'd rather fight my way to the top," Brick said. ". . . and shit."

As Brick runs through the yard with his sledgehammer in hand, he thinks back on how much better his life had become once he joined up with Scavy. No more working his ass off for shit pay. No more getting beat down by every punk who confronted him on the street. Scavy gave him a new family and a new life. And even if it wasn't as luxurious of a lifestyle as he had when he was a kid, it was still a hell of a lot more fun.

Brick smiles as he swings his sledgehammer at the first zombie to get in his path. His eyes light up with glee as its skull explodes on impact.

Charlie notices that there is something unusual about Brick's weapon. It's not shaped like a usual sledgehammer. Instead of a rectangular shape, the head of the sledgehammer is shaped like two fists, one on each side. When Brick slams the hammer into the next zombie's face, it is as if he is crushing open its jaw with knuckles made of high carbon steel.

As Scavy and Popcorn pass him, Brick gets in the path between the zombies and his friends. He raises his double-fisted sledgehammer over his head and charges straight into the horde.

Although he thinks of him as a brother, Brick isn't fighting for the sake of Scavy. He's fighting for the sake of Scavy's girlfriend, Popcorn. Even though the gang believes his girlfriend is that slut Gogo, Brick has been in love with Popcorn since the day they first met.

"This is Brick," Scavy said to Popcorn as they entered her apartment. "He's my new muscle and shit."

As they approached her, Brick checked out the thin little punk girl as she painted her toenails pink. She had pink spiky hair, pink tattoos, and she was draped across the couch wearing nothing but pink panties.

When she noticed he was checking her out, she said, "Hey, think fast."

Then she threw a baseball at him. He didn't lift his hands in time to catch it and the thing hit him right in the diaphragm at full speed. With the wind knocked out of him, Brick leaned over and gasped, trying to catch his breath. It hurt more than the two-by-four that had hit him in the back of the head a couple days prior.

When he looked up at her, Popcorn was laughing, her pointy breasts shaking at him like children pointing their fingers.

"He's slow," she said. "Sure you want another dumbass in the gang?"

When Brick looked up at her, their eyes met. She smiled at him with her bright pink lips. It was love at first sight.

For the next year, Brick and Popcorn were fucking behind Scavy's back. She said that she loved him, but he wasn't so sure. She said she wasn't a one man girl, that she could love both of them at the same time. Even though he didn't like it, Popcorn convinced him that it was for the best.

"If I was with just you I would get bored too easily," she told Brick. "This way our relationship will last much longer."

Plus, she thought it was fun sneaking around behind Scavy's back. Brick didn't know it at the time, but she was also sneaking behind his back and sleeping with a couple of other guys in the gang. She also slept with Brick's faux-girlfriend Gogo from time to time, but Brick already knew about that. Everyone in the gang slept with Gogo.

The night before they were abducted, Popcorn was going to tell him that she and Scavy were breaking up. She was bored with Scavy who had also lost interest in her. She decided that she was willing to give Brick a try for a while, as her number one.

But she never got the chance to tell Brick about it. Scavy's apartment was gassed while they were drinking beers and playing cards. The producers of *Zombie Survival* got the lot of them. The last thing Brick remembers was his face hitting the floor next to Popcorn's pink combat boots, as men in gasmasks flooded the room.

Popcorn looked back at Brick as he caved in a zombie's ribcage with his double-fisted sledgehammer. She could tell he was doing it for her, even though she never got a chance to tell him he's now her main boyfriend.

She pulls away from Scavy and yells back at him, "I love you, Brick!"

Brick turns around. His pink half-shirt covered in zombie goo.

"You're my number one!" she says.

Brick smiles wide at her, as the right side of his face slips off of his head to reveal the white of his skull. His right eye drops out of its socket and lands next to his pink combat boot.

Popcorn didn't realize he was wearing the combat boots she had stolen for him until just now. When she first got them for him, he said he didn't want to wear them because he would get shit from the other guys. They already gave him shit for wearing pink shirts from time to time. He didn't want to make it any worse.

Popcorn covers her mouth when she sees the boots. They looked withered and old, as if he's been wearing them all the time, when nobody else was looking.

Brick turns back to the zombie horde and uses the last of his strength to fight them off, breaking their faces open with his steel fists.

Charlie helps Scavy climb up the wall, and then Scavy lifts up Popcorn.

"We can take the guy," Junko says. "But the girl is infected. Get rid of her."

"She's fine," Scavy says, crouching on the wall like a cat. "Don't worry about it."

Junko is about to push the both of them off of the wall, when a scream echoes through the yard. They look over to see Rainbow Cat has been tackled by the zombie with the sunflowers growing out of its head. It crawls slowly over her, toward her brain.

"Bitch will get what she deserves," Junko says to Charlie.

But when she looks over at the writer, she doesn't see a look of satisfaction across his face. She sees a look of horror.

"I'm going after her," Charlie says.

He leaves his bag and stands up, balancing himself on the top of the wall.

"You've got to be kidding me!" Junko says. "After what she did to you?"

"I know she deserves it," Charlie says. "But I can't just let her die."

Then he walks carefully along the top of the wall to get closer to his wife. A few zombies on the ground follow him below, trying to jump up to reach his feet like snapping turtles.

"Fuck," Junko says.

Charlie leaps off of the wall, over the heads of the zombies, and lands on his hands and feet. He gets up and runs before the zombies even turn around.

Rainbow screams as the zombie bites down onto her skull, to get at her brain. Its jaw closes down on her head, but misses her flesh. It can't get through her dreadlocks. When it tries to eat her brain again, all it gets is a mouthful of hair-tentacles.

Charlie kicks the zombie in the face, sunflower petals exploding into the air. He pulls Rainbow to her feet and leads her back to Junko and the others, several zombies following close behind.

Before Junko can help the hippy bitch up the wall, a loud bang vibrates the bricks beneath her feet. She looks over at Laurence. Somehow, the wall next to him has collapsed and a dozen more zombies are pouring into the yard with them. They get between Laurence and the others. He has to fall back, in the wrong direction.

"Laurence," Junko yells.

"Forget about me," Laurence says. "I'll catch up with you all later!"

Then he heads to the south, running over the zombie he had earlier crippled, like a tank.

The zombies close in around Charlie as he pushes Rainbow up the wall. When she's at the top, Junko lowers her arm for Charlie to grab.

"Braains!" Charlie hears all around him as he takes Junko's hand.

Before he makes it up, the zombies grab him by his lower section. They pull him back. Rainbow grabs Charlie's other hand and tugs on him.

"Charlie!" Rainbow cries.

They pull him out of the zombies' grasp and get him to the top of the wall. He stands up and looks down. The zombie horde fills the area below them, leaving not an inch of ground.

"Fuck," Charlie says. "That was close."

He looks over at Rainbow Cat.

"You came back for me," she says, tears in her eyes. "Even after what I did to you."

He shakes his head. "I couldn't let you die. I still love you, no matter what you did."

"Brains!" the zombies yell from below.

"I'm so sorry," Rainbow says, burying her eyes in his chest. "I'm so sorry."

"Forget about it," Charlie says. "If we're going to die we'll die together."

Rainbow nods her head. "Okay. As long as we're together."

As she leans in to kiss her husband, his legs break out from under him. Her lips hit nothing but air. Charlie falls from the wall, into the crowd of zombies below.

"No!" Junko yells, trying to catch him. She reaches out just a second too late.

Charlie screams as they bite into his skull and limbs, trying to get to the neural tissue. From inside of the horde below, Brick licks the blood off of his double-fisted sledgehammer. His eyes lock with Popcorn's.

"Brains," he says to her.

Popcorn shakes her head at the sight of her zombiefied boyfriend and jumps down to the other side of the wall.

As they chew through Charlie's flesh, Rainbow reaches down to him. When he sees her through his twitching eyes, Charlie reaches out for her.

"I love you," Rainbow cries, his fingers too far out of reach to meet hers.

"I love you, too," Charlie says with a bloody smile. "…you bitch."

The tips of their fingers touch for a brief moment, just barely. Then his body is ripped into eight different pieces.

"No…" Rainbow says, still reaching out for his hand as his arm is taken away from his body.

Junko pulls her back, but Rainbow won't budge. She won't take her eyes off of her husband's severed head as it is pulled through the crowd.

"Let's go!" Junko yells.

Rainbow finally turns away when a zombie cracks open Charlie's skull like an egg, to get at the runny brains within.

They jump down on the other side of the wall, and run down the street to get as far away from the horde as they possibly can. Junko shakes her head at herself as she runs, realizing that none of the people she is with now are people she would have chosen to team up with. She's stuck with a useless bitch who backstabbed her own husband and two punks, one who's infected and one who's a complete idiot. Still, she knows it's better than going on alone. Those who go solo from the start never make it very far.

RAINBOW CAT

The last thing Rainbow Cat wanted was for her husband to die so soon in the game. If she wasn't there she knows he would have lasted much longer, perhaps even made it all the way to the end. He had ingenuity, charisma, strategy. He would have been a perfect hero for the show, the one everyone rooted for back home in Platinum. But then he had to go and get himself killed rescuing her.

"That idiot," she says, as they run into an alley to get off the main drag.

Rainbow lied about her reason for getting Charlie on the *Zombie Survival* reality game show. She didn't do it for the money. She did it because she wanted people to read Charlie's new book. Even though he was her favorite writer, she felt his books had gotten worse and worse ever since his first major success. The four books he published while they were living together in the Gold Quadrant were borderline crap. They didn't have that raw emotion as his early books did. It didn't seem like he was even trying anymore. For all she knows, his publishing company might have gone out of business just because people were no longer interested in their bestselling author.

But things changed after he was sent to the Copper Quadrant. He stopped writing for the money and started writing for the art. That is when he had created the greatest book Rainbow had ever read. A book about a couple struggling to make ends meet in the ghetto of Copper. It was a story about love and despair, isolation and hope. It was a story that everyone in Neo New York *had* to read. The kind of book that would change the way people think about how they live their lives.

She tried to figure out ways to get people interested in Charles Hudson again. She had sent letters to his old publisher, sent a duplicate of his manuscript that she typed up herself during breaks at work, but she never received a response. His manuscript was returned unopened.

That's when she came up with the idea of getting him on *Zombie Survival*. She had heard the rumors of this popular television show. The people in the upper quadrants were obsessed with it and idolized the contestants more than any other celebrities. She knew if Charlie was on Zombie Survival he would capture the attention of the public again. He would become a bigger celebrity than he had ever been before. And she knew the public would demand his books come back into print. Then his final masterpiece would be published and it would solidify him as a great voice in the history of literature.

She believes it would have all worked out perfectly, but her plan backfired. When she was also brought onto Zombie Survival as a contestant, everything got fucked. She was the one who was supposed to negotiate the publication of his last book after he had been killed. She was supposed to dedicate the rest of her life making sure that Charles Hudson was remembered. But without her, it is likely that nobody is going to know that his last manuscript ever existed. Not only that, but because of her Charlie was one of the first contestants eliminated. She doubts any of the viewers will care about him now that he's gotten killed off so quickly.

She wishes she would have been the one to get killed off instead of Charlie. Once she realized she had been brought onto the show, she came up with a backup plan. She was going to let the audience perceive her as the bad guy, Charlie's horrible wife. They would have felt sorry for him and empathized with him as a victimized hero-type. Then the audience would have relished in Rainbow's death, she would play the role of the bitch who got what she deserved. As long as Charlie was cheered on by the audience, there would be a renewed interest in his work. Perhaps they would even find his final masterpiece at some point, locked away in their apartment.

But now Charlie is dead and she has to come up with a new plan. As Rainbow runs down the alley, leaping over ancient garbage cans and cat skeletons, she decides that her new plan is to be the winner of the *Zombie Survival* reality game show. With that kind of celebrity status, she will be able to direct the attention of the masses on her husband's work. She can explain why she betrayed him. She can explain how her husband's book is so good that it was worth sending him to his death just so that it could be read by the world. Then his masterpiece will be published. Then he will be remembered as the greatest writer of their generation.

But first, she has to win the game. If she can win then it will all work out fine. The only thing she will regret is that Charlie died thinking she sent him to his death for the sake of money, when in reality she sent him to his death because she loved him so much.

If Charlie were still alive and found out the reason behind Rainbow's betrayal, he would have said, "You didn't send me to my death because you loved me, you sent me to my death because you loved my books."

Then, after a long pause, Rainbow would have said, "I don't understand the difference."

Junko leads them to an isolated area in the parking garage of an old grocery store. They duck behind a wall of scrap metal, which looks to have once been several wrecked vehicles that have rusted together into one giant slab the size of a garbage truck. There is a ten foot buffer between Popcorn and the others. Nobody wants to get near her.

"Let's see what we got," Junko says, kneeling down to unlock her duffel bag.

The others sit down and place their bags into their laps, as they catch their breaths. A camera ball floats over their heads, panning across their powwow. Revealing each of the contestants' weapons is one of the viewers' favorite moments of the show.

Scavy unzips his bag first and pulls out two rods, one with a long jagged blade attached to it. He holds them up to the camera, as if giving his audience what they want to see.

"What the hell are these?" Scavy says. "I wanted a fucking machine gun and shit."

Junko looks over at his weapon.

"You screw them together," she says. "It's an ancient Japanese naginata spear."

"A spear?" Scavy says. "They said the weapons would be personalized to our fighting capabilities. Why would I get a spear?"

Junko shrugs. "Because the blade matches your mohawk?"

"I'm totally a machine gun kind of guy," Scavy says.

Junko's eyes light up when she spots the weapon in her bag.

"Well, they got mine right," Junko says, pulling a chainsaw out of her bag. "I'm totally a chainsaw kind of girl."

It is a custom-designed chainsaw built specifically for the game. It is long, thin, and lightweight, created to strap onto her right arm.

"Chainsaw arm!" Scavy says. "You lucky bitch!"

Rainbow Cat is the most disappointed in her weapon. With her thumb and index finger she lifts it out of her purse-sized bag by the handle, holding it like a dead rat by its tail.

"A dagger?" she whines.

They look at her.

"That's it?" Scavy says. "Just a knife?"

Junko chuckles. "They did that on purpose."

"Why?"

"You got a dagger because you stabbed your husband in the back," Junko says. "The people back home are probably laughing their asses off right now."

"That's bullshit," Rainbow says. "How am I going to get any-where with this?"

"All you really need is something to cut them off when they grab you," Junko says. "A lightweight weapon has its advantage. You'll be able to run faster and it won't give you a false sense of security."

Rainbow pulls up her skirt and straps the dagger around her thigh.

Junko continues, "Too many people get killed off early on in the game by thinking their weapon is powerful enough to take on a whole horde head-on. The people who get the furthest are those who don't stay and fight, but run away. Avoiding confrontations is best way to survive."

When Popcorn pulls a 9mm handgun out of her bag, Junko snags it away from her.

"Hey!" Popcorn cries, reaching out to take back her gun.

Junko dodges her hand and digs ammo clips out of her bag, then places them into her own. "You don't get a weapon. You're infected."

"I'm fine!" Popcorn says.

Then her tendon slides out of her wrist and lands in her lap.

Junko snorts and spits. "I doubt it." Then she points at Popcorn's shirt.

The zombie puke had burnt through her clothing and eaten away a few layers of her skin above her cleavage. Popcorn pouts as she looks down at her chest. To her, it just looks like a really bad sunburn.

"Who gets the extra bag?" Scavy says, looking down at Charlie's duffel bag next to Junko.

"Take it," Junko says.

Rainbow jumps in. "Hey, he was my husband! I should be the one to take it."

Scavy unzips the long duffel bag and pulls out a black rectangular case. When he opens it, he finds an M24 sniper rifle.

"Fuck yeah!" Scavy says.

Junko shakes her head. "That'll be useless."

"No, it won't," Scavy says. "It kicks ass and shit."

"It'll only slow you down. The only use you'd have for it is shooting zombies from a distance, but if you see zombies in the distance you're better off sneaking around them."

"If it's useless, then why'd they give it to Charlie?"

"Because the producers saw him as a strategist," Junko says. "Somebody who would fight from a distance, from an advantage point."

"I'm a good strategist," Scavy says.

Junko laughs and tries to take the rifle away from him. Scavy pushes her back.

"No, I'm taking it! I don't care what you say."

"Fine, but you'll regret it," Junko says.

"No, I won't," Scavy says. "Besides…" He holds it up to his shoulder and peers through the scope. "How else are we going to take out the competition?"

"We need to move on," Junko says. "This is the most crucial part of the game. We need to cover as much ground as possible."

"What's with this pussy crap?" Scavy is holding up his middle finger to her while he speaks. "I don't want to just run away. I want to kill some fucking zombies and shit."

"Then you will die," she says.

"I don't give a fuck," Scavy says. "As long as I have fun with it. Besides, they're not even that tough."

"Not tough?"

"Back at the hotel, almost everyone got out alive and they weren't even armed yet. Once Brick got his hammer he was able to take out eight of those things like they were nothing."

Junko points her chainsaw at his face.

"You don't understand," she says. "The zombies in this area haven't been in hunting mode for decades. They've been in hibernation and are just now waking up. Over four million infected people lived in the area we have to cover, and by the end of today they will all have woken up. They'll know we're here and every single one of them will be coming for us."

"Four million?" Scavy says, his rifle shrinking toward the ground.

Junko nods. "And they're all waking up as we sit here wasting time."

After Junko says that, there is a bang in the wall of meshed vehicles behind Popcorn. They turn around. Another bang.

"Let's go," Junko says, pulling her bag over her shoulder.

The others go to investigate the noise.

"Forget it," she says. "Let's go!"

A zombie bursts out of the mound of rusted metal and charges for Scavy. Most of it is black and charred. Car parts have been fused with its flesh: a steering wheel is jutting out of its shoulder, a muffler is melded into its left leg, rusted engine parts run down its abdomen. Junko guesses that the creature had been hibernating in there for a long time, before the vehicles had decomposed together into one lump.

"Braains..." it says in a deep, barely-audible growl.

The girls get away from it, but Scavy doesn't back down. He swings the rifle over his shoulder and points his spear at it. The thing stumbles awkwardly forward, tripping on its muffler-fused leg.

When Scavy swings his naginata spear, his gun strap falls off of his shoulder and lands on his wrist, weighing down his arm too much for an effective attack. The blade misses the zombie's chest by a foot. The creature raises its arms as it comes closer.

"Forget it, come on!" Junko yells.

"Braains."

Scavy drops the rifle and swings the spear at its neck to cut off its head, but the blade bounces off of the steering wheel. The zombie grabs the shaft of the spear before Scavy can make another attack. The punk kid pulls back, but the skeletal fingers have too strong of a grip. He can't pull it free.

Junko shakes her head and sighs. Then she turns on her chainsaw arm, revs it up.

"From now on, you listen to me," Junko says as she cuts the arms off of the zombie.

Scavy pulls back. The zombie's arms are still attached to the shaft of the spear.

"Now come on," Junko says, and turns to run.

Scavy picks up his rifle. Then he looks up at the skeleton hands attached to his spear, wondering how the hell he should take them off.

"Braains," the zombie says.

Scavy shrugs and continues on, leaving the arms still attached to the weapon.

ALONZO

Alonzo finishes boarding up the stairwell to the second floor of the hotel. He decided not to leave with the others. He stayed back, where it was safe. After he saw the writer, Charles Hudson, ripped into pieces from the second floor window, he knew he couldn't go out there. He just couldn't.

"Will that hold?" Adriana says.

He looks over at her, the hammer shaking in his hands. "It better."

They had found extra wood, hammers, and plenty of nails in Housekeeping. The *Zombie Survival* work crew, who had dropped them off and boarded up the building for them, must have ditched their leftover barricade supplies in there. Alonzo made good use of them.

"There's only two stairwells we have to worry about," Alonzo says, then collapses against a wall to catch his breath. "Plus, I don't think they realize we're still up here. They went after everyone else."

"What about Heinz?"

"He's on the roof," Alonzo says, breathing so hard he can hardly speak. He pulls off his coat to reveal massive sweat stains under his armpits. Adriana cringes when she sees them. She's not used to being around fat people.

"Should we go up there with him?" she asks.

He shakes his head. "In a minute. I need a break." Then he holds his chest to make sure he's not going to have a heart attack.

There aren't really any fat people in the Copper Quadrant. There isn't enough food or money to fatten anyone up. The Silver Quadrant, where Alonzo is from, is full of fat lazy people. The Gold and Platinum Quadrants also have some fat people, but most of them are wealthy enough to hire personal trainers or get their excess weight removed surgically.

Alonzo had been fat since he was a kid. Unlike most people who grew up post Z-Day, he never had to struggle for survival. He had it easy. His father was the foreman of an oil rig when Z-Day hit the mainland. While the majority of the population was being transformed into brain-eating undead mutants, his father was safe at sea. It was hard to get by at first, but nothing compared to the turmoil taking place everywhere else in the world.

Eventually, when society began to rebuild itself, his father was in an excellent position for trade. He traded oil for food and supplies to the walled cities on the mainland that were still around during that time, and eventually to the people in Neo New York as it was being constructed and populated. He took charge of other oil rigs in the region and built an empire. He married and had children. When his parents passed away, Alonzo and his brother inherited the family business. They didn't have to want for anything for most of their lives.

Eight years ago, the government of Neo New York bought him out of the business and so they decided to retire on the island. He started out in the Gold Quadrant, but ended up in Silver as he realized he was blowing through his money fast. His brother, who had a wife and kids, went through his cut of the money faster and ended up in the Copper Quadrant in just a couple of years. Because they were newcomers to the island, they couldn't get jobs. Neo New York was overpopulated as it was, so one way to discourage immigration was to encourage companies to hire employees based on residency. Once Alonzo's money ran out, he wouldn't be able to earn any more legally. That's why Alonzo decided to start earning money by illegal means.

"I want you to come work for me," Alonzo asked his nephew, the night before he was abducted. "I've got a little business going in Silver and could use your help."

Tony, his nephew, was nineteen. A scrawny little good for nothing punk who made next to nothing as a tattooist.

"What kind of business?" Tony asked, mopping blood off the floor of his shop from when two of his punk customers got into a knife fight earlier in the day.

Alonzo sat down on a homemade stool barely strong enough to hold his fat ass off the ground. "Waste."

"You want me to sell drugs?" Tony asked.

Alonzo laughed. "No, I'd sell it in Silver. There ain't no fucking money in Copper. I want you to make it."

"I don't do illegal shit," Tony said.

"Nothing's illegal in Copper," Alonzo said.

Tony took off his sweat-stained shirt, revealing a collage of black sunflower tattoos. "Even if I agreed, how the hell would I get the stuff from Copper to Silver? They'd never let me through the barrier without a pass and they don't issue passes to anybody. I don't even know how you managed to get one."

"I've got my connections," Alonzo said. "I've already arranged to have it smuggled through the produce shipments."

Tony put his mop in a doorless closet. "I don't know, Uncle Alonzo. My shop's doing fine. I'm the top tattoo artist in Copper. Most of my clients are assholes, but they respect me."

"But you make shit," Alonzo said. "You knocked up that whore girlfriend of yours. You need to make some real money if you're going to raise a kid."

"I'll do it my way," Tony said. "If I'm going to be a dad, I need to do honest work."

"Honest work?" Alonzo said. "You sound like your idiot father."

Tony glared at him when he said that. It was too soon to say shit about his father. "Find somebody else."

"But you're family," Alonzo said. "Believe it or not, I care about what happens to you. You've been the closest thing I've had to a son. I want to see you living better. If business goes well I might even be able to get you citizenship in Silver."

"I'm sorry, Uncle," he replied.

Alonzo stood up. "You're starting to piss me off, kid."

"What do you want me to say? I don't want to work with you. The answer is no."

"Do you want to raise your kid in this dump?" Alonzo said, getting in his nephew's face. "Do you want to end up like your dumbfuck father? Knifed in an alley by some punk over pocket change?"

"Don't you fucking talk about him like that, Uncle Alonzo."

Tony's eyes were burning red.

"I'm just trying to look out for you, ya moron," Alonzo yelled. "If you want to end up like my idiot brother then go right ahead. Have a kid with some bitch when you got no money. See what happens once the slut gets sick of you and takes off, leaving you to raise the brat on your own. You'll slave away for the rest of your life keeping your kid fed, then one day you'll find a knife in your guts. Because, like your father, you were too much of a dumbfuck to make the right decisions."

Then Tony punched Alonzo in the stomach with all of his strength. Alonzo slumped over and gasped, nearly puking out his breakfast of smoked halibut and poached eggs. Tony didn't say anything. He stepped away from his uncle and started putting away his inks.

"Fine, if that's how you want it…" Alonzo held his stomach and caught his breath. Then he unfolded a jackknife and cut his nephew's throat while his back was turned. "I don't need a worthless fuck like you anyway."

Tony's eyes widened as his blood gushed down his black sunflower tattoos. His body landed on the floor, in the spot he had just mopped.

"Stupid little shit," Alonzo said, folding up the knife.

He didn't even bat an eye as he passed his nephew's pregnant girlfriend on the street outside of the tattoo shop. He just spit on the ground by her feet and walked on.

When they get to the roof of the hotel, Adriana and Alonzo see Heinz peering over the edge, tying shreds of ancient bedsheets into a rope. Heinz's suit and coat are perfectly clean, despite being a resident of the Copper District. His trench coat flutters in the cool breeze as he stares up at the violent clouds that smother the sky around them. The sound of moaning zombies echoes through the yard. A camera ball hovers by his head.

"What are you doing?" Alonzo asks.

Heinz finishes his sheet-rope and looks over at the obese man.

"Give me your bag," Heinz says.

Heinz lifts up his backpack. "Why?"

"It's the smallest." Heinz snatches it out of his hand and ties the end of the rope to the straps. "Get back."

After the fat man and the teen prostitute back away, Heinz runs like a pole-vaulter and tosses the backpack over the edge of the roof. It goes over the zombies, past the yard, and lands outside of the perimeter. The electronic lock beeps off.

Then Heinz reels the backpack in with the rope, pulling it up to them. He hands it back to Alonzo. When Alonzo opens it, he pulls out his weapon: a .45 caliber revolver.

Alonzo smiles. He likes the way it feels in his hand. Then he looks down at Heinz's enormous mountaineering pack.

"How are you going to toss that big thing all the way over there?"

"I won't." Heinz pulls his blond bangs out of his eye. "I'll have to find another way." He holds out his hand to Adriana's pack. "Now you."

When the second bag is thrown, it doesn't make it quite as far. As Heinz reels it back up, the movement catches the attention of a zombie and it lunges on top of the pack. Heinz tugs and the bag yanks free of the zombie's grasp, but now it is covered in purple slime-meat.

Five more zombies go for the bag, they grab at it, fight over it. The rope goes loose as a knot in the rope comes undone. The bag is lost.

Before the trio back away from the edge of the roof, the zombies look up to see where the sheet-rope is falling from. When they see the three contestants, their mouths begin to salivate a green fluid.

"Fresh brains!"

The zombies rush toward the building, a dozen more of them follow suit. In the distance, zombies recently woken from hibernation are heading their way.

Heinz turns to Alonzo. "Go downstairs and hold them off." Then to Adriana. "Reinforce those doors. I'll be there in a minute."

"Who the fuck says you can boss me around, pal?" Alonzo says.

"You're the only one with a gun," Heinz says. "Use it if you want to live."

Alonzo looks over at the door leading downstairs. His gun is shaking in his hands. He doesn't want to go down there.

"I'll be there in a minute," Heinz says, raising his tone to him, his shiny pronounced forehead reflecting the fat man's scared bulgy face back at him.

Growing up on an oil rig, Alonzo hadn't seen many zombies in his life. The only time he had ever seen one was when he was a kid, the one that killed his little sister.

They thought they were safe. They had hundreds of miles of ocean between them and any landmass inhabited by the living dead. But one of them still got to them. Nobody is sure how it happened. The crew of the rig assumed it had been caught up in a riptide and was pulled out to sea or came up from the bottom of the ocean, from some kind of sunken ship.

Little Alonzo had heard stories about the walking dead, but he didn't know what to expect. He had seen dead bodies before, but never anything like the creature that crawled on board that night.

He awoke to his sister's screams across the hall. He was used to her nightmares. She would wake up screaming regularly, after having dreams about their house sinking into the sea, or about Father's ship getting sunk by an infected whale while he was off on business. Alonzo always went to her room to comfort her. If he didn't she would keep the whole ship awake all night.

When he left his room, he noticed the trail of black slime in the corridor leading into his sister's cabin. The zombie had skipped his brother's room and all of the other rooms along the way. It had chosen the one cabin that had left its door open. Alonzo's little sister was too scared to sleep with her door shut.

The zombie was eating his sister's brains out of her skull as young Alonzo entered her cabin. The thing was like a skeleton with gray patches of flesh dangling from the bones. Its chest was covered in barnacles and seaweed. Tiny fish were flapping around in its hollow chest, half-filled with water. A crab crawled across its shoulder and disappeared into its neck. Its eyeballs were like that of a sea slugs'.

His sister was no longer moving. The zombie flopped her corpse around like a doll as it ferociously tore the meat out of her split-open head. It gurgled and hissed as it consumed her. The image drilled a hole into young Alonzo's mind. An image that he was never able to get rid of. After the adults came running to his screams, and pulverized the zombie's bones under the bottoms of fire extinguishers, Alonzo understood the horror that his parents had been trying to keep from him. He prayed he would never have to face a creature like that ever again.

When Alonzo gets downstairs, the zombies are already banging on one of the boarded doors.

"Get some more wood on there," he tells Adriana.

The teenager looks at him with a terrified face.

"Don't think about it, just do it," he says. "I'll cover you."

She runs to the wood. Her hands shaking hard as the door rumbles next to her. When she pounds a nail with the hammer, her strikes are timid and sloppy, causing the nail to drop from her fingers.

Alonzo looks to his right, through a hotel room window. He sees a swarm of zombies running through the street toward the building. Three times as many as had earlier attacked. Beyond them, in the distance, he sees explosions erupting from street corners, as if some contestant out there is trying to fight off the zombie horde with a grenade launcher.

When he sees the chaos outside of the window, his gun hand begins to quiver. He imagines the zombie he saw that night inside of his sister's bedroom. Now he imagines a hundred of them, all outside, all of them coming to get him. Ever since that day as a kid, he has been having nightmares that zombies are coming to get him. Now he is living that nightmare. Looking down at the gun in his hand, he contemplates pointing it at himself in order to wake up.

Heinz finishes knotting a second sheet-rope. He breaks a power line with a piece of brick and attaches it to a satellite dish on a higher section of the roof. Then he ties the sheet-rope to a strap on his giant mountaineer pack and snaps the other strap around the power line. He lets the pack go.

The zombies swarm the yard below as the pack slides down the power line. When it hits the edge of the rooftop of the next building, the locking mechanism beeps off. Then Heinz pulls the pack back up the power line with the sheet-rope.

He can hear a commotion of smashing and banging noises in the hotel rooms below as the zombies fill the building. He doesn't have much faith in the defense capabilities of a fat slob and a childish whore, but he hopes they can hold back the creatures long enough for him to put his plan into action.

Alonzo stands behind Adriana and points his gun at the door, his pockets filled with extra ammunition. He can see the young girl's ass cleavage hanging out of her tight vinyl shorts. Her shiny mounds point up at him like she's begging him to take her from behind as she hammers boards on top of the other boards. He licks his lips with his cracked dry tongue.

Adriana didn't know it, but Alonzo was there last night when she was selected as a contestant for *Zombie Survival*. After he had murdered his nephew, Alonzo was in a rotten mood and needed some cheering up. He had to find a new business partner and had no idea where to look. The next morning, he planned to figure that out. But that night, he was going to release some stress.

The prostitutes in Copper were numerous. They were cheap as hell and wouldn't object to anything the client wanted them to do. What Alonzo was most interested in was the underage prostitutes. In Copper, the prostitutes came in any age you wanted. Girls in their prime, girls on the mature side, girls in their teens, and girls who haven't even gone through puberty yet. The only age group that wasn't available were elderly women, just because the people in Copper didn't live long enough to make it into their golden years.

A lot of girls end up in prostitution when they're kids because their parents decide they can't afford to raise them anymore and toss them out into the streets. Prostitution is the only job a kid can get in Copper, so that's where the majority of them end up.

Adriana is a typical case. She lost her mother when she was nine and went right into whoring herself on the streets. By ten she was addicted to Waste. By eleven she had lost all sense of self worth. By thirteen she had her first abortion. By fifteen she was chosen to be a contestant on the *Zombie Survival* reality game show.

The producers of the show bring at least a few prostitutes into every season. They add an element of sex appeal that viewers at home can't get enough of. Viewers love to see prostitutes trading sex for protection. They love to see their slutty little bodies torn apart by the undead. There's no shortage of whores in the Copper Quadrant, so they never fail to make it onto the show. They have even thought about maybe doing an all-hooker season of *Zombie Survival* at some point in the future.

Alonzo saw Adriana in an alley as he prowled the redlight district. She was giving some guy a blowjob behind a ten-foot pile of refuse. He knew he should have minded his own business, but Alonzo decided he would check it out. He could tell the girl was young. He thought she might have even been thirteen, which was the age he was looking for. He was hoping she would be willing to give him a blowjob after she was through with the other guy.

Standing with a smug smile on his face, Alonzo watched as the man came inside of her baby-soft lips. The man moaned slightly through his white goatee.

"There you go, my darling," said the man, his penis still dangling in front of her face. "How does it taste?"

Adriana stared up at the man with her cheeks full of his gunk.

"Swirl it around on your tongue," said the man, petting her dark red hair behind her ears, as if she were a kitty, or perhaps his daughter.

She did as he asked.

"That tastes good, doesn't it?" he said. Then he used his hand to nod her head for him, as she continued swirling his cum around in her mouth.

Alonzo noticed that the man with the white goatee looked too clean to be from Copper. His clothes were too nice. His hair was too neat. He looked more like somebody from the Gold or Platinum Quadrant.

"Now swallow it," he said. "Swallow it for me."

She gulped it down dramatically for him, lifting her throat closer to his face so that he could hear it go down. She liked to please clients like this man. The only clients she respected were the ones who treated her like she was a worthless piece of shit.

"Good girl," he said to her, stroking her hair. "That's my good little girl. Daddy's proud of you."

Alonzo was getting a little too creeped out while watching this. He was pretty sure this was all just an act to get the man off, but Alonzo couldn't stop imagining that he really was her father.

Before he turned around, men in white masks came out from the other side of the alley and grabbed Adriana from behind. She tried to scream, but they put a rag of chloroform over her mouth. Her muffled cries didn't last long before she was out.

As Alonzo backed away, he kicked a whiskey bottle with the heel of his shoe, sending it clanging against the asphalt.

The man with the white goatee looked up at Alonzo.

"Take him, too," he said, as he zipped up his fly.

The men in white chased after Alonzo. He ran across the street toward a strip bar, but the door he chose was the back entrance. It was locked from the other side. The men in white tackled him against the door and put the chloroform over his mouth. He slammed his fists against the door, but the music inside was too loud, the men inside were too focused on bouncing naked breasts.

Alonzo is so focused on Adriana's tight little ass that he doesn't notice the wood of the door cracking apart. Before Adriana can hammer in the last nail, a hand bursts through the door and grabs her by the hair. She screams.

"Braains!" says the zombie as it pushes its head through the hole in the door.

Alonzo fires his .45, throwing his arm back with the recoil, but blowing the right half of the zombie's face clean off. This doesn't faze the zombie, though. It continues to pull Adriana up by the hair. Alonzo grips the pistol tighter this time and fires again, just before the creature bites into the girl's skull. The bullet shatters its lower jaw into dusty fragments. The zombie's eyes roll around with confusion as the teeth of its upper jaw taps against her forehead, not sure why its not able to bite into her.

Adriana hammers at the zombie's hand, thrashing to get the thing to let go. She smashes melted flesh off its arm, but the bony fingers have a tight grip.

Heinz opens his mountaineering pack and pulls out his large, heavy weapon. He takes out the map, flashlight, and a canteen of water, and tosses the rest of the contents over the side.

He straightens his blond hair and looks down at the massive horde of zombies gathered below. Their eyes stare in his direction, like an audience gathering to hear him speak.

The camera ball pans around him as he juts his chin into the air.

"Help me!" Adriana cries.

Alonzo fires the .45 again, but misses the zombie. Instead, the bullet goes through a board, exploding a new hole in the door. The hole splinters apart and another zombie's hand reaches through it, grabbing her by the arm that holds the hammer.

"You idiot!" she screams. "Get them off of me you fucker!"

Alonzo comes in closer to get a better shot. He raises the gun up to the zombie's head and fires.

Heinz removes his trench coat and tosses it over the side. Then he straps fuel canisters to his back, nuzzles a hose around his hip to the handle of the flamethrower's igniter. And flicks the igniter switch, sparking the flame to life at the tip of the nozzle.

The camera ball circles around to his side and pauses on the swastika armband strapped around the upper sleeve of his black suit.

He raises out his left hand and sieg heil's the cloudy heavens above him. Electricity sparks through the clouds. Then he squeezes the trigger on the flamethrower and bathes the zombie horde in a rain of fire.

Alonzo's bullet shatters the zombie's arm at the shoulder, freeing Adriana's hair. She pulls herself back, but the other zombie has her by the wrist. It twists her arm sideways, digging its claws into her. She cries out and drops the hammer.

Another zombie gets its arms through at the bottom of the door and grabs her by the ankle. Alonzo shoots and blows apart a zombie's neck, knocking its head off its spine. The skull dangles by a rope of meat, still snapping its jaws in Adriana's direction.

As Alonzo reloads his revolver, slamming noises rattle the door to the other stairwell.

"Shit." Alonzo snaps the revolver's cylinder back into place. "They're coming in from over there, too."

Heinz showers the zombie crowd with flames. Shrieking balls of fire run in circles below him. Their dried up flesh burns quickly, reducing them to quivering smoldering blobs in the dirt.

He can hear the screams of Adriana and Alonzo beneath him, as he inhales the scent of his burning enemies. Flakes of ash sail through the breeze like a ballet of black butterflies.

His lips curl into a smile as the ash twirls around him and the flames dance from his fingertips.

A zombie pulls Adriana's head up to the hole in the door and bites the back of her neck. She shrieks at Alonzo, but the sight of the zombie biting into her freezes up the fat man. His gun begins to shake and he can't get himself to pull the trigger.

The zombie pulls back, ripping flesh from her neck. A large red centipede coils out of the wound. It takes Alonzo a moment to realize that the thing squirming inside of the zombie's mouth isn't a centipede, but the girl's spinal column. Her lower body goes limp, but by the look in her face Alonzo can tell that she's still alive. Her eyes wide and mouth dropped open in shock as the zombie tugs on her spinal cord with its teeth like a dog playing a game of tug-of-war.

When the back of Adriana's skull tears open, Alonzo screams. It isn't the prostitute that he sees anymore. It is his little sister, being eaten before him once again. The girl's brain is yanked out of the back of her skull, and dangles from the end of the spinal cord in the zombie's foaming jaws.

Alonzo turns and runs toward the stairwell to the roof, but before he gets there the barricaded door on the other side of the hall breaks open. The hallway fills with the undead, blocking his path. He turns around and the door by Adriana's corpse splinters open, the dead piling through over her body.

Dodging into the closest hotel room, he locks the door behind him, then pushes a crumbling dresser in front of it.

When the zombies burst through the stairwell onto the roof, Heinz whips around and covers them in flames. Smoke fills the rooftop as the hotel catches fire. A camera ball films the first floor of the hotel, as flaming zombies run through the lobby, catching the building on fire.

Alonzo looks out the window and sees the smoke pouring up from the ground. He considers jumping down from the second floor, but the mass of burning bodies in the yard below look like Hell on Earth to him.

He points the gun at the door as it breaks open. Smoke and zombies shuffle over the dresser, two of them on fire. He shoots them in their chests and heads, but they keep coming toward him. A bullet blows a zombie's hand off of its wrist as it reaches out for him.

"Braains!" the zombies groan, as they close in on him.

With the hotel up in flames, Heinz's job is done. He had attracted all the zombies in the vicinity to him, got them to enter the hotel, then burned it down. Fire is the most effective weapon against the undead. It is the only thing that can ultimately destroy them. He is pleased with the weapon that the producers of *Zombie Survival* had chosen for him. It will help ensure a victory for the leader of the Fifth Reich.

He walks through the smoldering corpses that crawl across the roof on their bellies.

One of them reaches out for him and whimpers, "Braaains!"

He steps on its head with his leather boot, crushing its skull into a pile of charcoal, as he walks to the power line he had used for his backpack. Wrapping his arm around the cord and gripping his other wrist, he slides down the wire and drops down next to Adriana's pack. He scoops it over his shoulder, then walks casually out of the yard down the rubble-filled streets.

When he looks back, he sees the hotel being swallowed by the flames. He doesn't know if Alonzo and Adriana are still alive in there, nor does he care. They served their purpose and are of no further use to him. They just saved him the trouble of having to kill them later.

As Alonzo's revolver clicks empty, the zombies grab him and tear into his flesh. They suck the nerves out of his skin like angel hair spaghetti, the sensation of their chewing sends jolts of electrical pain through his body.

The zombie with the sunflowers growing out of its skull grabs Alonzo by the throat. Its flesh is now burned and blackened, the flowers charred to a crisp. When Alonzo sees the burnt sunflowers, he zones out. He doesn't see it as a zombie anymore. Through the smoke, he sees the creature as his nephew, Tony. Fresh blood runs down Tony's chest, over his black sunflower tattoos.

"You said I was like a son to you," Tony says to him.

Alonzo shakes his head. "You got what you deserved, punk!"

"All I wanted was to raise my kid honestly, like my father raised me."

"Your father was a damned idiot!"

Tony's mouth stretches open so wide that his lower jaw touches his chest. Then he bites his uncle's skull open.

"And I'm also a damned idiot for thinking you could have been any different!" Alonzo says, as Tony chews on a meaty strip of his brain.

POPCORN

Junko, Scavy, Popcorn, and Rainbow Cat are on top of a high-rise downtown, scanning the area. They needed the high vantage point to see which path would be safest through the city. But all the streets look the same. All are packed with the living dead. They use the sniper scope to look farther into the distance, but there are zombies everywhere.

"They're waking up way too soon," Junko says. "We should have been mostly clear for at least until the late afternoon."

"So what do we do?" Rainbow asks.

"We need to keep moving," Junko says. "It's bad now but it is only going to get worse. Much worse."

A few blocks away, explosions erupt along the street, blowing up sections of the zombie horde.

"That's what is doing it," Junko says, pointing at the explosions. "That asshole's being too loud. He's waking them up."

Then they see the man who is causing the explosions. The old ex-military vagrant staggers down the street, tossing grenades at the zombies around him.

"That guy is punk as fuck!" Scavy says.

The old man heads toward the door of a building across the street from him. He tosses a grenade and it blows some of them apart, but

67

then the rest of the undead close in on him, grab him by the arms. He pulls them with him, trying desperately to get through the door of the building, but they won't let go, biting into his arms and shoulder.

He tries throwing another grenade but it lands only a few feet away. Lee's grenade blows the zombies into pieces across the asphalt, but takes him out with them. His body flies though the glass door of an ancient city tavern.

"Well, that's the end of that guy," Scavy says, chuckling.

Junko frowns. "At least he won't wake any more of the dead."

Rainbow Cat looks down at the street immediately below them, and sees three of the other punks—Xiu, Zippo, and Vine—running through the zombie crowd. Vine leads the way, shooting out their knee caps with an AK-47 as they run. They don't even bother going for the head. They just want to cripple them enough so that they can run past.

"Your friends look like they're doing alright," Rainbow says to Scavy.

Scavy looks down at the other punks. "Oh yeah, those guys."

"They're good," Junko says. "How long have you known them?"

Scavy shrugs. "I don't know. I just met those guys."

"You mean they're not part of your gang?" Junko asks.

"No," Scavy says. "I just thought they looked cool so I let them join my crew. Never seen them before today. I don't think they even speak English."

Junko looks down at the trio of punks and examines them carefully. They move in formation, like trained soldiers. Xiu, their leader, tosses a throwing axe at one of them and dismembers both of its arms before it can latch onto Zippo's back.

"Those aren't ordinary street punks," Junko says, as the axe boomerangs back to Xiu's hand. "They're merc punks."

Junko knew the ratings for *Zombie Survival* had been going down. The past couple of seasons were very disappointing for fans and many of them were so outraged that they almost got the producer of the show, Wayne "The Wiz" Rizla, fired by the network. The show was becoming repetitive and boring. Last season, all the contestants died on the first day. Most of them were killed before even getting out of the safe house. Wayne was choosing too many weak, boring contestants. Just the same old vagrants, hookers, and street punks. The network said he had to do better than that. He had to get some contestants who would actually last long enough to make it to the helicopter.

Junko knew Wayne had chosen her for the show to help with ratings. He knew audiences would love to see the old host of Zombie Survival on the show herself. But she knew throwing on celebrities like Charlie and herself would not be enough to save his job. He had to get some badass zombie killers. There's no better zombie killer than a merc punk.

While most of the human population stays as far away from the mainland as they can get, there are small bands of scavengers who live in ships along the coast of the mainland like pirates. When Z-day struck, many people survived not by fortifying themselves in bunkers or walled communities, but by constantly moving. They were post-apocalyptic biker gangs who kept on the road, stopping only to fill up on gas and supplies. They never stayed in one place long enough for the zombies to gather in a number they couldn't handle.

Eventually, gas had become an issue. It was a limited resource that spoiled quickly. They knew it wouldn't last them forever. So they went out to sea, living on sailboats instead of armored vehicles. They sail up and down the coasts of the Americas, stopping on the mainland to kill zombies and scavenge for food. For several generations, these punk pirates of the apocalypse have been surviving out there on the outskirts of the Red Zone. They even have their own culture they have developed over the years.

Over the past decade, the government of Neo New York had been hiring them as mercenaries to recover technology and important artifacts from the mainland. That's why they're called merc punks. Although they look and dress very similar to that of common street punks like Scavy and Popcorn, merc punks are a hell of a lot more dangerous.

"This is going to be even harder than I thought it would," Junko tells them. "Our competitors have been doing this kind of thing since the day they learned how to walk."

Scavy looks back at Popcorn. She is sitting against a wall on the other side of the roof, quivering. Her skin is white. She doesn't look good at all. At first, he thinks she could just be going through Waste withdrawal. But he can tell that's not it. Junko was right, Popcorn is infected.

Scavy had known Popcorn since they were kids. Both of them were living on the streets, abandoned by their parents, running with the same gang. If you're abandoned by your parents in the Copper Quadrant you have two options: whore yourself or sell Waste. They chose the latter.

Popcorn was the weirdest chick Scavy knew. She was unpredictable, destructive, and always on high energy. They were never really romantically involved at first, even though they did hook up from time to time. She dated a lot of his friends but he wasn't really interested in her in that way. He thought the pink mohawk she had back then was pretty cute, but he mostly just thought she was cool to hang out with.

He clearly remembers the first day they met. He was walking along the beach in his bare feet, squishing the sand between his toes, watching the waves hitting the shore. The one thing he liked about Copper was that he had the beach. The people in the upper quadrants couldn't walk in the sand if they wanted to. They were walled up in the center of the island. A lot of those people haven't even seen the ocean through their tall barriers.

Sure the beach was littered with broken glass, medical waste, and all the other trash the rich people dumped into the ocean, but he still felt privileged to visit the beach whenever he wanted.

As he walked past the vagrant shacks that lined the beach, he saw a teenaged pink-mohawked girl about his age. She was trying to break down the door of one of the shacks, kicking it in with her pink combat boot.

"What are you doing?" Scavy asked.

She didn't stop kicking the door.

"Robbing the shack?" Scavy said. "You know they don't have shit in there, right?"

She shrugged at him and then kicked the door open. But once the door was open, she didn't enter. She just went to the next shack and started kicking that door in.

"Why are you kicking in doors?" Scavy asked her.

She shrugged. "Just for fun."

Scavy liked that answer.

"Can I help?" he asked.

"Sure," she said.

They went from shack to shack, kicking doors down. A couple of hobos stumbled out of their shacks and slurred drunken obscenities at them. The punks just laughed and continued kicking.

One door Popcorn kicked splintered on impact and Popcorn's

boot went through the middle. She burst into laughter when some hobo on the other side grabbed her leg.

"Damn punks!" cried the hobo on the other side of the door. "I'll fuck you, fucking punks!"

Then the homeless guy twisted Popcorn's leg, as if he was trying to twist it off. Popcorn just giggled at him and grabbed Scavy by the shoulder.

"Help!" she cried, then laughed.

Scavy grabbed her under the arms and pulled, then pushed off against the door with his foot. The door opened and hit the hobo and the face, causing him to let go. They both ran off, laughing, then hid under the dock and did some lines of Waste.

Once they were high, Scavy asked, "What's your name?"

"Poppy," she said. "But some people call me Popcorn."

They became good friends after that. They used to go out and wreak havoc on the neighborhoods. Scavy would steal a crate of fish from the docks and then they would throw them at strippers in the redlight district. Poppy would sleep with the local tattooist to get them both free tattoos. Then they would shit in crates of produce that was to get shipped to the upper quadrants. She was Scavy's kind of person.

One of Popcorn's favorite things to do was spray paint pictures on the wall separating Copper and Silver, usually of muscular women with pink mohawks sneering and flipping the middle finger. They would have dialog bubbles that were supposed to be insulting, but never quite hit their mark. Stuff like: "Silver Sucks!" or "Fuck off, filthy scum!" or "think fast, fuckers!" which is one that really made no sense to anyone else except for Scavy and Poppy.

Popcorn was a huge fan of the "think fast" game. Whenever Scavy wasn't looking, she would say "think fast!" and then throw an apple or a rock at him. Sometimes he would catch the object, sometimes he wouldn't. Scavy knew that when Poppy said "think fast" trouble was coming.

One day, while they were doing lines of Waste, Poppy said, "Think fast!" and then stabbed a knife through Scavy's hand, nailing it to the table.

Scavy just looked at the knife in his hand and back up at Popcorn who had a goofy "I totally got you" look on her face. "What the fuck!" Scavy yelled, his blood mixing with the lines of Waste on the table.

"You're too slow," she said, then snorted one of the lines with his blood in it.

Scavy tried to pull the knife out of his hand, but it was jammed into the table pretty good. He just sighed and shook his head at Poppy, his blood on her nostril. When you're friends with a crazy unpredictable bitch, you've got to take the good with the bad.

They started dating, for a while, but both of them knew that wasn't going to stick. Popcorn wasn't the type to get serious with anyone for very long. She just gets bored too easily. But Scavy relates to that. He's the exact same way.

A couple of days ago, Scavy told her, "So I think we should break up and shit."

And all she did was shrug, and said, "Yeah, sure. You wanna do a line?"

"Yeah."

And that was it.

As Scavy watches Popcorn shiver and spit, he taps the bottom of his spear against the concrete roof. Junko notices that he's finally come to terms with his friend's condition. She goes to him.

"We have to take care of her," Junko says, holding up the 9mm. "Before she changes."

Scavy nods a few too many times. "Yeah, okay."

"I'll do it if you want," Junko says.

"No, I'll do it," Scavy says, reaching for the gun.

"Make sure she doesn't see it coming," Junko says, blocking the sight of the handoff from his girlfriend. "It'll be easier for her that way."

"Yeah. Easier."

"Shoot her before she even knows what's going on."

"Yeah, I can do that."

"Okay," Junko says, and pats him on the shoulder. "I'm sorry…"

Then he turns to Popcorn. He takes a deep breath and points the gun at her. A smile appears on his face as he gets a funny idea for how to handle this.

"Hey, Poppy," he says.

She looks up at him.

"Think fast."

Then he shoots her in the face.

"What the fuck, Scavy?" Popcorn says to him, as blood drips from the bullet hole in her forehead.

The other three just stare at her.

"Umm…" Scavy leans over to Junko. "She didn't die."

Popcorn wipes her forehead and then looks at the blood on her fingers. "You think that's funny, asshole?"

"She's already turned," Junko says, taking the handgun from the punk and pointing it at the punk chick.

Poppy looks behind her at the blood on the wall, then she stands up and goes to them. "You're such a dick."

"Stay back!" Junko says.

Popcorn stops. Junko isn't sure if she even knows what is going on.

"Why isn't she trying to eat our brains?" Rainbow asks.

Junko shakes her head. "I have no idea."

Scavy knows why she isn't hungry for brains. It's because Popcorn doesn't get hungry for anything. Ever since he knew her she has been that way. She had done so much Waste growing up that it had destroyed the nervous tissue in her stomach and through much of her body. She could eat all she wanted and never feel the sensation of being full or she could starve herself for weeks and never get hungry.

That was why she was so skinny. She didn't ever get hungry for food. She never even had cravings for food. The act of eating to her was just chewing a flavorless substance and then depositing it inside of her body. If she didn't get weak and tired from lack of food she would have just stopped eating altogether. Now that she's a zombie, it's not any different.

"So what do we do?" Rainbow asks.

"We can't take her with us," Junko says.

"But I'm fine," Popcorn says.

73

"We don't know if you're going to stay fine," Junko says. "And, besides, you're still infectious."

Popcorn sticks her pinky finger in her bullet hole and then pulls it out again, then smiles as if the act is amusing.

"But it would be cruel to just leave her here…" Scavy says.

Junko says, "You put a bullet in her head like it was a joke, but you think leaving her is cruel?"

"I don't want her coming with us," Rainbow says.

"Well, I think she should," Scavy says.

"Two to one," Junko says. "She stays. Trust me, it's for the best."

They look at her smelling the brain blood on her finger. She tastes it. The taste of brain makes her cringe.

"Besides," Junko says. "She's a zombie now. All the other zombies will treat her like one of them and leave her alone. She'll most likely survive longer than any of us."

"Hey, yeah," Scavy says. "That's kind of fucking badass. She'll be like the queen of the zombies."

"But I don't want to be the queen of the zombies," Popcorn says. "I want to kill zombies, with you."

Scavy shakes his head. "We've got to go on without you."

"This is bullshit," she says.

"Come on." Scavy puts his arm around her shoulder. "It's going to be awesome. You'll have the entire wasteland to yourself. You can wreck shit up all you want."

"What if I start to rot like the others?" she says. "I don't want to be just bones and slime."

"Fuck it," he says. "Just have fun with it."

"But I don't want to be alone."

Scavy looks back at the others who are waiting for him to leave. Junko looks so impatient that she might punch the camera ball floating next to her.

"What about Brick?" Scavy says. "He's a zombie too, now. Maybe the two of you can hook up again and rule the wasteland together. That is, unless you have a problem with his looks being uglier than usual."

Poppy laughs. "Well, half his face is gone, but he did look pretty hot in those pink combat boots."

"That's the spirit," Scavy says.

"Let's go," Junko yells. "Now."

"I got to go," Scavy says.

He hugs her and steps back.

"I should eat your ass for leaving me like this," she says.

"Say hi to Brick for me."

Popcorn waves to him as he goes, her bloody tendon dangling from her wrist, swaying back and forth. Then she looks out across the wasteland, imagining it as her new kingdom.

Before Scavy enters the building, he calls out to her. "Hey, Poppy."

She looks back.

"You look pretty hot with that bullet hole in your head."

She flips him off.

He smiles, then follows after the others.

LEE

Lee pushes a squirming zombie torso off of him. Its sludgy head and limbs had been blown away by the grenade, coating the barroom floor in ground meat. The living corpse absorbed most of the blast, but Lee didn't get away unscathed. The blast took off flesh from the right side of his head, including his right ear. Both of his legs are mangled. He can't feel anything in his left arm. There are also large shards of glass buried in his back.

The corpses outside of the dilapidated tavern are in much worse shape than he is. The grenades he had tossed blew many of them into pieces. All of them are still alive, worming across the ground, pulling themselves by finger bones. The only one still standing wanders the street with nothing but a mass of pulpy soup for a head.

Pulling himself up by his one good arm, Lee goes behind the bar of the old tavern. Most of the shelves have rotted away, breaking bottles on the floor below. But the bottom shelf is still standing and holds a single bottle of 55 year old sour mash Kentucky bourbon.

Lee's eyes light up.

"Hello, beautiful," he says to the bottle, before breaking it open and taking a swig.

He plops himself down on a wrought iron barstool and exhales the smooth whiskey fumes.

"Braains," belches a severed zombie head on the bar next to him.

"Cheers to that," Lee says, and taps the zombie's forehead with the bottle, like a toast. Then he takes another swig.

When Lee separated from Junko and the others, he had only one goal in mind: he wanted to get drunk. He knew there was no way he was going to win the contest. He didn't even want to win. Lee was fucking old and ready to die. Life is shit when you're a 65-year-old homeless war veteran abandoned by your society. There's nothing he wanted more than to just throw in the towel and die already. If he had the guts he would have hung himself years ago.

Bosco was the only other contestant he had run into after leaving the yard of the hotel. The young redneck was hanging from a fire escape with zombies grabbing at his ankles. He called out to Lee for help but the old man wasn't stopping for anything. He waved good-bye to the screaming man and just took off down an alley.

When he opened his pack, he groaned at the sight of grenades. There were almost twenty of them, but they were heavy and not the type of weapon that he could use at close range. With all of those years of zombie-fighting experience, he knew that close-range defense is what matters most.

He crossed a park, waking three of the undead sleeping there. They were half-submerged in the dirt, covered in grass and weeds. One of them couldn't get up due to the roots of trees that had grown through its abdomen. He lost the other two that chased him by ducking into a liquor store. As the corpses passed, Lee watched them through a broken window: two dirt-coated skeletons whose flesh looked to be made of chewed-up clay. Their mouths and throats were so filled with mud and weeds that their voices came out of holes in their necks when they tried to say *brains*.

When Lee turned around, what he saw was pure heaven. Lined up before him were shelves upon shelves of spiced rum, potato vodka, pear brandy, orange cognac, single malt scotch, and every other liquor he could possibly dream of. And it was old world liquor, not the cheap shit that people pass off as liquor these days in Neo New York. It was made back when people cared about the quality of their wines, their foods, their cigars. People lived well and died old. Their lives didn't revolve around fighting every single day just to stay alive.

Lee had grown up in this era, before the zombie apocalypse. He lived in the suburbs with his upper middleclass family. This period of his life he remembers well. He remembers playing basketball with his best friends, picking flowers for his first girlfriend, watching television with his parents. But he doesn't remember much of Z-Day. It was like a distant dream, a time when everyone was in a constant state of shock as the chaos swept in around them. One day he was scribbling notes to his girlfriend during math class, and the next everyone he knew was dead and he was being evacuated by fire truck to the only safe zone in Kansas.

Then he went from safe zone to safe zone. Each one either fell to the zombies or ran out of supplies and had to be evacuated. After surviving for eight months with random strangers whose faces changed on a weekly basis, he eventually ended up in a fortified city along the Gulf of Mexico that would become his home for the next twenty years.

Like most male refugees with no family to take care of him, Lee was immediately drafted into the local army. Despite the fact that he was still a teenager, he was expected to defend their city from the hordes of undead surrounding their settlement. At first, Lee was proud of his job. The city's population was over 2,000. He wanted to do his part to keep all of those people alive. But so many of his fellow soldiers died. Even the trained soldiers were little match for the indestructible undead. Lee realized that it was unlikely that he would live long enough to see adulthood.

In the first year after Z-Day, there were over 150 fortified cities like this one in America. By the next year, there were only 57. The year after that, there were only 22. By the time the island of Neo new York was constructed and the entire continent was undergoing evacuation, only 6 cities were still standing and most of those had populations that had dwindled into the low hundreds.

The worst part was when Lee realized that the people he was giving his life to protect were a bunch of selfish assholes who didn't give a shit about him. They lived in comfort and safety, while he risked his life to hold back all the undead who tried to break through the barricade. The citizens despised the soldiers so much that they separated them from their society. The soldiers became third class citizens. They weren't allowed in most parts of town and spent most of their time in the barracks, in the guard towers, or patrolling the city walls. Lee saw this as a form of slavery. His superior officers, who did have full rights as citizens, saw this as just following orders.

He knew that the only way he could be integrated into society was if he became an officer. He did his best to rise through the ranks, but could never get past the rank of sergeant. This rank meant that he was more commonly put into dangerous situations and had far more responsibilities than lower ranked soldiers, but without the benefits of being an officer.

The only time Lee was truly happy was when he led scavenging missions. Once a month he would take a team of six soldiers in an armored vehicle into the Red Zone for several days, picking up canned food, tools, machine parts, and everything else that could be useful. They had to fight their way through zombie hordes to get from store to store. Part of the reason Lee liked these missions was the absolute freedom he had. He wasn't a slave to his superior officers, he was a ruler of the wasteland. But the main reason he loved going on these missions was that he was able to drink. In old convenience stores or bars, Lee and his men took the liquor for themselves. They barricaded themselves in old garages and drank themselves stupid. It was the only time the soldiers were ever able to enjoy their lives.

In the old liquor store Lee went for two bottles of single malt scotch. When he was a soldier on missions, good single malt scotch was in high demand among the fat upper class citizens of their city. But when he was in charge of the missions, the best bottles of scotch would never make it back to home base. He would drink them with his men.

Lee opened a bottle and took a swig. Then smiled. He had not tasted something so wonderful in a very long time. When he looked down at the label, he recognized the brand. It was a bottle of Talisker 1994 Manager's Choice, double-matured in a sherry cask.

Talisker reminded him of his old friend, Timothy. This guy was his right hand man on many a mission. Not because he was a great shot or a good soldier, but because he knew how to track down the best liquor. Lee wasn't sure if it was because he had good logic when it came to guessing locations of taverns on city maps or if he was just a lucky bastard, but that guy was always able to track down a cache of liquor bottles no matter how well-scavenged of a region they were in.

"You're supposed to drink the worm," Timothy said to Lee as he held up the bottle of mescal.

"What kind of worm is it?" Lee put his eye close to the bottle.

"It's a butterfly larvae, actually," Timothy said. "It's supposed to make the tequila taste better."

"Are you sure they weren't just put in there by Mexicans to see if they could get gringos to eat worms?"

"Of course they were, but that's not the point," Timothy said. "The point is you're a pussy if you don't drink the worm."

"Oh…"

Lee took a drink from the bottle. His face cringed as the harsh liquor burned his throat.

"The worm isn't working," he said, holding back a cough. "This stuff tastes like shit."

"Of course it does, there's a fucking worm in there." Then Timothy laughed and took a swig of Talisker.

Lee stared at the worm in the bottle. He could swear the thing had a little human face that was staring back at him. He knew that it was impossible for insects to become infected with the zombie virus, but he could swear the worm in there was alive and watching him. He decided to put the cap back on and save the rest for the upper class.

Then Timothy poured him four fingers of Talisker.

Lee drank half the bottle in less than five minutes. He didn't know how long he was going to last in the game and he wanted to make sure he was good and drunk as soon as possible.

A camera ball followed him as he walked down the street, chugging the bottle of scotch. He flipped off the camera and then stuck his finger up his nose. Lee hated the upper class. He always did. When he was relocated to Neo New York, it was no different. They put him with the rest of the trash in the Copper Quadrant, outside of the city gates, separated from the rest of society. He had given thirty years of his life protecting the assholes and once they moved to Neo New York they didn't need him anymore and tossed him aside.

Copper was filled with old soldiers with similar stories. Living in homemade shacks down by the beach, living off of crabs and seagulls, shitting in holes in the sand. They drank the worst swill on the island that was made in orange rusted garbage cans. It tasted like urine-flavored rubbing alcohol and quickly turned their livers into blackened husks.

Lee decided that he would not put on a show for the fat cats. His final act would be to get drunk and die a very boring death. No going out in a blaze of glory for Lee. He was going to just let those zombie bastards take him without a fight.

So he walked casually down the street, drinking from his bottle. When the two clay-fleshed zombies came after him, Lee just tossed a grenade over his shoulder and blew them into pieces.

Staggering down the road, Lee tossed more grenades at the zombies as they approached him. The explosions completely disabled the corpses. The grenades might not have killed many of the undead, but they did blow all of their legs out from under them. The zombies weren't able to catch up to him even if he was walking so slowly.

"Fuck you, bastards," Lee said to the camera. "I gave all you rich sons of bitches the best years of my life. You know what you gave me? Nothing."

He paused to take another swig and throw another grenade.

"You know why all of you assholes are still alive? It's because of me. I kept all of you safe and sound while you sat on your fat asses eating all the food I risked my neck scavenging for you. And how the fuck do you thank me? You put me on this fucking show. You feed me to the zombies I protected you from since I was fourteen years old."

The sound of the grenades was waking the dead in the surrounding buildings. The number of zombies that were coming after him was increasing dramatically.

"But you know what I have that you don't?" Lee raised his bottle to the camera. "I've got a sixty year old bottle of single malt scotch whiskey. Not a single one of you will ever have a liquor of this quality, not ever in your lives. No matter how rich you are. No matter how many mercs you send into the Red Zone. You're never going to find a bottle quite as nice as this."

Then Lee finished off the bottle right there in front of the camera.

"I'm living the high life," he said, pulling out the second bottle of scotch.

But before Lee could break it open, a thin red laser beam shot out of the camera ball and shattered the bottle, splashing the liquor all over him.

The camera eyed the whiskey-drenched Lee as if it were laughing at him.

"Fuck you, you fat dirty pigs!" he growled at the camera. Then flipped it off.

With his liquor gone, Lee went looking for something else to drink. He went from store to store, wishing he had Timothy's alcohol intuition. In the center of downtown, he saw a tavern at the end of an intersection.

"Bingo," he said to the bar.

But before he could get inside the place, the group of zombies had caught up to him and he accidentally blew himself up.

Bleeding from his legs and face, Lee takes a sip of the sour mash. It's not as flavorful as the scotch but it's just as smooth. The camera ball floating next to him zooms in on his wound. A piece of shrapnel juts from his temple. He's so drunk that he can hardly feel the chunk of metal pressed against his brain.

"I'll never forgive you fuckers," Lee says to the camera. "I'll never forgive you for what you did to Timothy."

When the fortified city on the Gulf of Mexico was evacuated, not everybody was allowed to leave. There were only so many people who were allowed to move to the island of Neo New York. Over two hundred soldiers were left behind to fend for themselves. They weren't left with any food, supplies, or weapons to defend themselves with. They weren't even left with the proper tools necessary to keep the barricade up. They were left to die. Timothy was one of them.

"I'm going to stay, too," Lee told Timothy the day he was supposed to evacuate. "It will be better here than on that shitty island with all those assholes."

"Nah," Timothy said. "You should get out of here. You're one of the lucky twenty percent."

"It's bullshit they had us draw straws. None of the citizens had to draw straws."

"Forget about it. That's just the way things are."

"I'm not going to forget about it. I'm going to stay. We can scavenge the Red Zone like we used to. Only now everything we find we can keep for ourselves."

"They didn't leave us with any weapons or vehicles. Going into the Red Zone now would be suicide."

"We'll get new vehicles. We'll get new weapons."

Timothy just shook his head. "Lee…"

"We can live better than we ever did before."

"Lee." Timothy raised his voice. "We aren't going to survive the night."

Lee looked behind him at the men with guns aimed at the soldiers that were being left behind. He knew that the main reason they were letting twenty percent of the soldiers come with them was so that they would protect them from those who were staying behind. Besides Lee, every single one of them were ready to kill their own friends in order to keep their seat on the boat.

"Forget about us and get out of here." Then Timothy walked away, leaving Lee standing there in front the row of armed men.

As Lee drinks from his bottle, a new horde of zombies closes in on the bar, attracted to the noise of the last explosion. He doesn't pay them any attention as he drinks his whiskey and thinks back on the day he left Timothy.

As his ship was setting sail, he saw that the soldiers left behind didn't bother putting up a fight for survival. They just opened the gates and let the creatures in, welcoming their demise. Lee saw nothing but a blank stare on Timothy's face as the zombies opened up his skull and chewed out his brain.

Just as his friends did on that day, Lee welcomes zombie teeth to his flesh. He sips his whiskey as they grab him by the shoulders and bite into his neck. The camera ball zooms in to get a good look at Lee's face as he is eaten. The old soldier tries to ignore the zooming sounds of the camera, but they are too irritating to tune out.

Lee looks into the camera with a sneer. Black slime oozes from a zombie's face down his chest. His blood sprays out of him across the bar, into his drink. Then he pulls something out of his pocket and holds it up to the camera.

"How fast can you fly, little bird?" the old man says to the camera, as he flicks the pin of the grenade across the bar.

When the camera sees the grenade in his hand, it flies backward. Lee smirks as it flees for safety yet refuses to miss the shot of Lee's death. Just before the camera escapes the tavern, Lee tosses the grenade and it bounces off the side of the camera's protective casing. Then the grenade explodes and smashes the camera against the wall.

Lee smiles wide as the bomb inside of the camera goes off. The bar becomes a flash of white light. Then Lee, the zombies, and the entire city block disappear into a cloud of fire.

HAROON

Haroon rushes through the streets, avoiding the undead, trying desperately to find *her*.

He swears that he saw her among the group of contestants back at the hotel, but he only caught a glimpse of her during the escape. She's good at blending into crowds, so it's very possible she was with them the whole time without him noticing. If she is a contestant he must find her. She could save him. She could save them all.

His hand grips tightly to his weapon: a spiked club. It's not exactly a club, more like a child-sized aluminum baseball bat, embedded with several metal studs, then painted black. He uses it to club zombies out of his way. He doesn't use it to fight the undead. All he needs it for is to bat away reaching claws and biting mouths. Because of its smallish size, it's lightweight and swings fast.

All he needs to do is run and keep an eye out for *her*. Once he finds her, she'll be all the protection he'll need. He wonders why she didn't come to him back in the hotel. There's no way she wouldn't have recognized him. Perhaps she was just overwhelmed by the situation and her new environment. In her entire life, she had not seen much of the world—only the secret underground chambers beneath the Platinum Quadrant. He wasn't even sure if she had seen the sun before. It makes sense that she would have been so overwhelmed that she wouldn't have been paying attention to the people surrounding her.

If he can't find her right away it would be good for him to find other people to team up with. He got separated from Junko's group when he thought he'd seen *her*. Even though he wanted the group to stick together, he had to go after the woman to verify whether or not it was really her, but she got away too quickly. She jumped out of a hotel window and raced out of there so fast it was like a blurred ghost darting through the yard and disappearing into the shadows of the wasteland beyond. When he went back to find the others, they had already gone on without him.

Right now, if he wants to survive he must seek out other people. Perhaps they will help him find the woman he's after and together they can find a different way out of the Red Zone, rather than competing for the one seat available on the helicopter. Unfortunately, most of the people are far ahead of him.

After an hour of searching, Haroon comes across another contestant. He hears a commotion coming a few blocks east and takes an alley to investigate. Crouching down and peering around a corner, he sees a crowd of flaming zombies crumbling to the ground. Beyond them, he sees Heinz marching through the street with his flamethrower in hand, burning down every living corpse that gets in his way.

When he sees how well the tall blond man seems to be doing against the undead, Haroon decides he would be the perfect person to team up with. Haroon stands up and heads toward the man, running to catch up to him.

A black leathery hand reaches out from an open door and grabs him by the arm. It pulls him into the shadows. Haroon opens his mouth to cry out to Heinz for help, but another leathery hand covers his mouth. His scream is muffled.

"Be quiet, fool," says the attacker.

Haroon turns around to face the man who had grabbed him. At first, he just sees a large black form. Then he realizes that the large form is Laurence.

Laurence holds up his leather gloved hands to show that he means no harm.

"What did you do that for?" Haroon says.

"I was trying to save your sorry ass," Laurence says. "You were

86

thinking of making friends with that scumbag out there, weren't you?"

Haroon nods.

"Let me show you something." Laurence has Haroon look out of the window at Heinz's clothing. He points at the swastika armband. "You see that symbol on his arm there? That means he's not interested in making friends with you. It means he's a racist nazi piece of trash." Then he pulls Haroon back inside.

"I don't understand," Haroon says.

"Trust me," Laurence says. "That guy's no good. You're better off alone than going with him. If you want to team up with somebody you can team up with me. I won't let you down."

Laurence gives him a thumbs up.

Haroon decides to believe Laurence, even though he's never heard of nazis before. After Z-Day, a lot of Earth's history had become lost and forgotten. The horrible events of the past paled in comparison to present day life. Although the schools in the Gold and Platinum Quadrants have been getting into teaching history over the past few years, the majority of the citizens of Neo New York just don't know much about the old world. Most kids are assigned a career and then trained specifically for that position. Construction workers are raised to learn the skills to work construction. A farmer is raised to learn how to farm. They might also learn how to read and do basic math, but that's about it. History just isn't taught, perhaps because most people are trying very hard to forget the past.

When the two men enter the street to head back toward the alleyway, Haroon looks back at Heinz. The tall Aryan man is burning a zombie, a look of sadist pleasure stretches across his face. The zombie shrieks as it is burned. Upon closer inspection, Haroon notices that the zombie is Brick.

Zombie Brick cries in agony until he crumbles to ash. Then Heinz grabs the punk's double-fisted sledgehammer from the ground, drapes it over his shoulder, and continues marching down the street.

As they backtrack through the alleyway, trying to get as much distance between them and Heinz as possible, Haroon notices Laurence is unarmed. He has his backpack slung over his shoulder, but otherwise he's empty-handed.

"What weapon did you get?" Haroon asks, holding up his spiked club.

Laurence shakes his head. "Didn't get one."

"What?" he asks. "Everybody gets a weapon. You had to have gotten something."

"Nope," Laurence says.

"Give me your bag."

Laurence hands it over. They duck into an old coffee shop, making sure no zombies are following them. In a back room, Haroon empties the pack across a table. He spreads out the items and examines each one. Every item he has is exactly the same as the items Haroon has in his pack, minus a weapon.

"You're right, there's nothing," Haroon says. "Why the hell did they screw you like this?"

"Well, I'm not exactly unarmed. My whole body is one giant weapon." Laurence punches his fist through the plaster wall next to him to prove his point. "I think they just wanted to make it fair to the other contestants."

Then Laurence smiles.

"Still, they should have given you something. Brass knuckles, nunchucks, something."

Laurence shakes his head. "I don't need any of that. I can kill zombies with my bare hands just fine."

Then Haroon notices something unusual about one of the items on the table: the map. It doesn't look quite right. It's much bulkier than the map he received in his own pack. Haroon picks it up and unfolds it. Inside, there are several sheets of paper.

"What's that?" Laurence asks.

Haroon holds them up for inspection. "Blueprints."

Laurence leans over the Indian man's shoulder. "What kind of blueprints?"

"I'm not exactly sure," Haroon says. "I think they are instructions on how to build a weapon."

"Build a weapon? They expect me to build my own weapon when everyone else gets their weapons fully constructed? Who do they think I am, MacGyver?"

Haroon has no idea who MacGyver is.

"By the looks of this, I bet it's an incredibly powerful weapon," Haroon says. "Perhaps too powerful to give to any contestant right at the start."

"Hmmm.... Maybe you're right. And they gave it to me because they knew I'd be the contestant most likely to survive unarmed long enough to build the thing. Only one problem..."

"What's that?"

"Finding these parts to make it. I have no idea what most of them even are."

Haroon scans the list.

"Then you're lucky you ran into me," Haroon says. "This kind of thing is my specialty."

Haroon was a top researcher who worked on classified projects for the government of Neo New York. He was registered as a citizen of the Platinum Quadrant, but he had never once stepped foot in Platinum. He lived in an underground research facility with over fifty other scientists. Each scientist was a specialist in their field, educated from childhood to fill a unique position. Haroon was trained to become a weapons engineer.

Bullets are effective against living beings, but against the undead they are not as much so. Haroon worked on developing weapons that would be more effective against the undead. There was a division that focused on freezing weapons and another that focused on particle beam weapons, but Haroon's division focused on self-recharging weapons. The kind that could have an unlimited power source, without the risk of running out of ammunition.

The most significant item produced by Haroon was the solar-powered shotgun. It was still years away from being perfected, but the basics were there. The big problem was that its range was only ten feet and it took an entire hour to recharge. It also didn't do as much damage as an ordinary shotgun. One ten-foot shot per hour was not nearly as effective as a standard shotgun. But he promised his superiors that with time he could develop a weapon as powerful as a shotgun, one that would never run out of shells or need to be reloaded. All a soldier would have to do is put it in the sunlight for one hour every couple of days and the ammunition would be unlimited.

Of course, Haroon failed to deliver on his promise. Lucky for him, he could never be fired from his job for failing to deliver. The worst that could happen to him was reassignment. His best friend in his division, Terry, was responsible for blowing their boss's right index finger off, and all he got was reassigned to the genetics division. He might have been mopping floors and washing toilets, but he still had a job. Since they put so much work into training their researchers, they don't just get rid of them unless they absolutely have to. A person would have to commit murder or high treason in order to lose their position. But if that were to occur the person wouldn't be fired, they would be executed, imprisoned, or worse: put on *Zombie Survival*.

This is how Haroon was chosen for Zombie Survival. He committed an act of high treason. He never heard of the show in the underground facility—researchers didn't have the luxury of television—so Haroon had no idea this could have possibly been his punishment. For six months, he waited in his cell for execution, but it never came. They were holding him there until the next season of the show.

Haroon is thankful they gave him a fighting chance. As long as he's alive, there is still hope. It is also nice to be outside in the sunlight after so many years underground. Even if he is going to die, at least he's able to see the sun again. He did have a sunroof in his lab for testing weapons, but it was only one square foot of light which just wasn't the same as being out in the open.

And if *she* is really out here with him, everything will work out perfectly.

Laurence and Haroon go from building to building, searching for the components listed in the blueprint. Some of them aren't easy to get, but most of them are obtainable at any grocery store. If only they can find one.

"You sure we'll be able to build that thing?" Laurence asks.

"Positive."

They move in the direction of the helicopter marked on their maps, picking up items as they go. Because they aren't firing guns, the zombies aren't as attracted to them as the other contestants.

"Back at the hotel," Laurence begins, "you said that you wanted us all to go for a boat instead of the helicopter. That way we all could make it out alive."

"Yeah," Haroon says. "I still believe it's possible. The Asian girl was right, most of the boats would not be useable, but I'm sure we could find at least one boat that would work. Hell, we could probably even make our own."

"I like the way you think," Laurence says. "There's always another way. That's what I've always said. Just because the Man says there's only one way to survive, that doesn't mean it's the only way. Once we get this gun together, I say we collect Junko and whoever else we can, then head for the river."

"Sounds like a plan," Haroon says.

"It's a plan and a half."

All Haroon has to do is build this weapon and find *her*, and he knows the plan will succeed. Then they can all get out of there without having to kill each other.

JUNKO

Junko, Scavy, and Rainbow Cat race down a city street, trying to cover as much ground as possible. Unfortunately, there are too many zombies awake already for them to get very far. They go down one street and their path is blocked by a crowd of undead. They go around to another road and run into another crowd of zombies. They take so many detours that they seem to be getting farther away from their goal, rather than closer.

"We have to fight our way through them," Scavy says. "This pussy running bullshit is getting us nowhere."

The camera ball floating behind them makes beeping noises as if it agrees with Scavy, annoyed that they aren't giving it any interesting footage. The camera's operator, sitting safely behind a computer hundreds of miles away, must be bored out of his mind.

"Trust me," Junko says. "We want to avoid a fight with them at all costs. Shooting them will only attract more. Melee fighting is only useful when you're up against one of them at a time, not a crowd. We just need to keep moving, even if it's in the wrong direction."

"Bullshit!" Scavy says. "Those badass merc punks fought their way through crowds no problem."

"You're not a merc punk."

Scavy shuts up at that comment. He really wishes he was a merc

92

punk. They seem tough as fuck. He wishes he would have joined up with them rather than Junko and the hippy.

Once they run into yet another zombie mob blocking their path, Scavy says, "Fuck it," and charges forward.

"What the hell are you doing!" Junko yells.

The camera ball quickly follows Scavy, as if excited the viewers will finally get to see some action.

"I'm sick of going around them," he says, holding up his naginata spear like a lance. "I'm going straight through."

He lets out a battle cry and all of the zombies turn their attention to him.

"Braains…" they moan as they stagger toward him.

"Get back here, you dumbfuck!" Junko yells.

Junko stomps her foot and glares over at Rainbow Cat. The hippy girl rolls her eyes. Junko groans loudly and then races after the idiot.

"The only good part about being put on this fucking show," Scavy says, just as he reaches the first zombie, "is being able to kill shit."

Then he swings the blade of his spear at the attacking corpse with all of his strength, the blade cuts through the zombie's neck and decapitates it. The head flies over his shoulder and rolls down the street toward Rainbow Cat.

But the zombie continues its attack. Green sludge spews out of the corpse's neck hole as it wraps its claws around Scavy's shoulders. Even though it no longer has a head, it's stump of a neck still tries to get at Scavy's brain, as if desperately hoping that there might be a way to slurp the brain into its neck hole.

"Don't let that green shit touch you!" Junko yells at Scavy. "It's infectious."

Scavy pushes away at the headless corpse with the shaft of his spear, as the green sauce geysers in his direction. Then two other zombies grab him by the elbow and neck, going for his brain. The punk thrashes around to prevent them from getting a good bite, but the thrashing causes the green sludge to get onto his clothes.

One of the zombies that has a hold of him is incredibly sloggy and melted. It has dozens of pennies, nickels, and quarters embedded into its flesh, as if it had been hibernating in a wishing fountain for the past few decades. When it opens its mouth to groan, several coins trickle out of its mouth like a slot machine. Scavy laughs at the sight. He wonders if the zombie had swallowed all of those coins in order to eat the brains of all of those tiny metal presidents.

As the coin zombie widens its jaws around Scavy's ear, Junko smashes its face with the base of her chainsaw arm. Coins fly into the air as it tumbles away from the punk. Then she revs her chainsaw and severs the arms off of the headless zombie and kicks him away. Scavy shoves the third zombie off of him.

Eight more zombies come at them, and Junko charges forward. In a spinning motion, she ducks under their reaching arms and slashes their Achilles tendons. They drop. Before they can grab her from the ground, she runs at the other four. She jumps at one of them and decapitates it, then leaps at another and its head goes rolling. One at a time, she cuts off their heads. Once their heads are off, she goes for their ankles.

When she has incapacitated all of the undead, she turns to the others. "What are you waiting for? Come on!"

Scavy and Rainbow Cat stare at her with wide open mouths.

"That was fucking awesome!" Scavy says, squirming zombie bodies all around him.

"Let's go," she says, turning off her chainsaw. "The noise is going to attract ten times as many of those things." Then she turns and runs.

Rainbow Cat and Scavy follow after her, jumping over the zombie arms that reach blindly across the asphalt. Up ahead, they see a dozen more of the undead coming straight for them.

"Fuck," Junko groans, as she revs her chainsaw back into life. "I was hoping to avoid this shit."

Junko knows exactly what she's doing out there, because she had fully prepared herself for this competition. In the history of *Zombie Survival*, she was the first contestant to actually know she was going to be selected for the show beforehand. The second she had become blacklisted by employers in the Platinum, Gold, and Silver districts, she knew that it was done for a single purpose: so she would be forced to move to Copper and become eligible for the Zombie Survival contestant selection. And she knew who was responsible for getting her on that blacklist: her old boss, Wayne "The Wiz" Rizla.

She had met Wayne when she was seventeen years old. He was the judge of a beauty pageant she was participating in. She remembers the way his creepy eyes wouldn't look anywhere else but on her body. She remembers him licking his crusty too-red lips behind his too-white goatee.

Back then she had long black hair, perfect ladylike posture, and a glowing artificial smile. Her mother encouraged her to focus on being beautiful. If she was beautiful she could marry a rich man and live in the Gold or Platinum Quadrant. If she was beautiful she would be too valuable to be discarded by society into the ghettos of Copper. So her mother made sure she wore the latest fashions, took good care of her nails and hair, learned the art of makeup application, and developed an attractive personality: innocent, joyful, pure. And her mother always put her in beauty pageants. She wanted her daughter's beauty on display for all the rich men to see.

Even though her daughter was underage, her mother encouraged her to flirt with older wealthy men. When Wayne "The Wiz" Rizla introduced himself to her after she had come in third place in the pageant (the worst she had ever placed since she was ten), she could feel her mother's eyes telling her: "Don't fuck this up. He's interested in you. Smile. Flash your eyelashes. Arch your back. Stick out your cleavage."

But Junko was more creeped out by him than any man she had ever met. She just couldn't flirt with him.

"Hi there," he said, rubbing his white goatee. "My name is Wayne, but people call me The Wiz."

Junko cowered beneath him, her back slouching, her eyes glancing at the ground, her teeth chewing nervously on the inside of her cheek. She could see her mother glaring at her from across the room for not flirting properly with the older man. Junko wasn't presenting herself at all in the way that her mother had taught her. Junko knew that she would be punished by her mother for coming in third place, but if she could attract the affection of this older man perhaps she would be forgiven. She wouldn't have to seriously form a relationship with the man, just give the impression to her mother that he was a potential suitor.

Junko widened her eyes and opened up her body to him, flirting with her neck and smile. She asks, "Why do they call you *The Wiz*?"

Wayne leaned in and spoke directly into her ear with his rough deep voice, "Because I make magic happen."

When he pulled away he laughed, as if that was supposed to be a joke. Junko laughed with him. She knows to always laugh at a man's jokes even if she isn't sure whether or not he told a joke.

"I'm looking for a young pretty face for a new show I'm working on," Wayne said. "I think you'd be perfect."

"A show?" Junko asked. "Like a play?"

"No, a television show," Wayne said. "Do you know what a television show is?"

Junko shook her head, but kept her fake smile beamed in his direction.

"You will soon enough. Television is finally coming to the island and the show I'm working on will be the biggest hit series of all time."

"And you want me to be a part of it?" Junko asked, her excited tone of voice was actually genuine this time.

"I want you to be the star," he said.

Then Junko's fake smile became a real one.

Junko leads her crew into an abandoned building to escape the zombie fight. They don't bother barricading the door and allow the zombies to pile in after them. Instead, they zigzag through corridors until they lose them. Then they jump into the pitch-black stairwell. They seem to have also lost the camera ball that was following them.

Rainbow Cat ruffles through her pack for her flashlight, but Junko says, "Leave your lights off."

Feeling their way up the steps, they pray they don't run into any corpses. But Junko feels safer knowing that the zombies are even more blind in the dark than they are and have a difficulty with stairs.

They continue climbing, stepping in sticky fluids and tripping over rubble, but they don't run into any bodies... that they know of.

A wave of relief rushes over Rainbow Cat when they leave the stairwell onto a random floor. The offices here are dimly lit, but the little amount of light they have is enough to know exactly what's around them. They choose a well-lit office with a large window, then lock the door behind them.

"Just keep your voice down," Junko whispers, "and they're not going to find us."

They drop to the ground and catch their breaths. When Junko gets a good look at the green slime on Scavy's clothes, she says, "Did you get that shit on you?"

Scavy looks down. "Guess so."

"Take 'em off!" she whispers. "Now!"

She helps him carefully remove his shirt and pants, repeatedly calling him a *dumb fuck* for letting this happen.

"Did it get on your skin?" she asks. "If it's soaked into your skin and into your bloodstream you're dead."

When he is down to his underwear, Junko examines every inch

of his skin for the green substance. She pulls him up to the window to be absolutely certain.

"I don't see anything," Scavy says.

Junko frowns. "You look fine, but from now on you listen to me."

"You've got it," Scavy says.

The punk has a new found respect for Junko ever since he saw her take down all of those zombies. He could hardly stand up to just one, but she made short work of nearly a dozen of them.

"You kicked ass out there," he says. "Have you fought zombies before?"

Junko shakes her head.

She says, "No, but I've worked for this show long enough to know which attacks are most effective."

Then she lies back to rest for a few minutes, getting off her feet so that they won't blister.

"I also know what mistakes not to make," she says with her eyes closed. "Like the mistake you made back there. If you want to survive you will listen to me from now on. I won't bail you out next time."

After a long pause, Rainbow Cat asks, "How was it?"

"What?" Junko asks.

"Working on the show?"

It was fun at first. Junko liked being treated like a celebrity, even though she was just a host for the show. The real stars were the people who fought and died for everyone's amusement. Junko was just the pretty face and cheerful voice that introduced each episode of the season. She liked being pretty for a living. Her mother loved it even more, because her daughter was not just a pretty face but also a major sex symbol. There was no way Junko wasn't going to end up marrying a very wealthy man.

Then she grew up and the novelty of being a celebrity wore off. Her mother died from choking on a wine cork, and her influence died with her. The desire to marry a wealthy man faded, because she already had plenty of money. She always knew the show she worked for was brutal and cruel, but she was raised to accept these things as normal, just as all children in the upper class districts were.

But one day she was asked on a date by a handsome young man with emerald green eyes. She fell in love with him the first time she looked into those deep eyes.

"How can you do it?" he asked her, over dinner. "How can you work for that horrible show?"

Junko smiled and shrugged. "It's my job."

"But it's so cruel," he said. "Those people are being sent to their death for our amusement."

"But people die everyday," she said. "The world is a cruel place. That's just the way it is."

Then he said a single word, one that she never thought to use in her privileged life.

He said, "*Why?*"

Junko was taken aback.

"Why does it have to be that way?" he asked. "Why does the world have to be so cruel?"

"The living dead took over," she said. "They turned society into a dog-eat-dog world. We have to do what we do in order to survive."

"That's no excuse at all," he said. "Our government has all the resources necessary to make life better for everyone in Neo New York. Instead it chooses to make life even better for the privileged few, while making life even worse for the unfortunate lower class citizens."

"But most of those people are criminals," she said. "They rape and murder each other. They do drugs. They prostitute their children. Maybe the show is cruel, but if anybody deserves it it's those people."

"I can't believe you said that," he said. "Nobody deserves that kind of fate. Those people are just victims of circumstance. They would have turned out no different than you or I if our government spread out its resources to everyone evenly."

Junko was confused by his statement.

"That's stupid," she said, then took a big bite of salmon.

"Compassion is stupid?" he asked.

Junko continued chewing her salmon with a full cheek. She saw anger in his beautiful green eyes. She regretted arguing with him. If only she lied he might have liked her better.

"You're so beautiful," he said, standing up from the table. "But only on the outside."

Then he left the restaurant.

The next season of the show, she recognized one of the contestants by his emerald green eyes. The rest of his face she didn't recognized. He looked like he had gone through hard times in the Copper Quadrant. When she asked her boss, The Wiz, what his story was, he told her that he was an idiot. He was a wealthy fiction publisher who had decided to close down his company, move to the Copper Quadrant, and give away all of his money to the people who lived there.

"Why would he do that?" Junko asked him.

Wayne's white goatee fluffed out as he smiled. "He did it out of protest. He said he was disgusted by our way of life in Platinum, so he refused to live here anymore. Can you believe the moron?"

The next day, when Junko saw the young man with the emerald eyes die in uptown Scottsdale, Arizona, his head torn open by crispy sun-burnt zombies, she left the television station mortified. It was the first time a contestant had been somebody she knew. She had seen violent deaths so much since she started hosting Zombie Survival that she had become desensitized to it, but it was different with him. His emerald green eyes lying on the sidewalk next to his corpse was an image she couldn't get out of her head. She went to a bar and drank until morning.

Although she was under contract to finish the season, she wanted to quit right then and there. But she had no choice but to finish it. She did such a bland job hosting the show that Wayne was happy to get rid of her.

"You're getting too old anyway." Those were the last words he ever said to her.

Wayne would have just left her alone had she just left the show, but she didn't think quitting was enough. She wanted to get the show cancelled. She led protests against the show, she spent much of her savings on a smear campaign against the television show. She also wrote a book about her experience on the show and gave tons of copies away for free. Eventually, she ran out of money and needed to find work, but she had been blacklisted. She was forced to move to Copper.

The second she stepped foot in Copper, she knew Wayne was going to put her on the next season's show. The negative publicity was not something he was going to just ignore. He would have his revenge.

So Junko trained every day. She did the military exercises. She studied previous episodes of the show. She practiced every possible weapon, from guns to swords. If Wayne put her on the show, she wasn't going to give him the satisfaction of watching her die. She was going to win it.

Then, once she gets back to the island, she's going to use her new passport to visit the Platinum Quadrant. Then Wayne "The Wiz" Rizla is going to die.

Scavy runs across the street naked except for his underwear and boots—the metal of the sniper rifle cold against his bare skin—following Junko and Rainbow Cat to a place where he can get some new clothing. The camera ball they had lost in the zombie fight finds them and chases after the trio.

"What's this place?" Scavy asks, as they enter a dark windowless building. He closes the door before the camera ball can squeeze in behind them.

Junko is too busy digging out her flashlight to respond. She flicks it on and moves deeper into the black, to get far away from the entrance.

When Scavy turns on his flashlight, the beam brightens the face of a melty white zombie only inches away from him. The zombie's hand raised to his face. Scavy shrieks and lowers his naginata spear into its head.

The zombie doesn't fall. It doesn't even move, frozen in place.

Junko goes over to the punk, "Shut the hell up."

Scavy points at the zombie to show Junko why he screamed, but then he notices that the zombie doesn't look much like a zombie.

"It's just wax," Junko says, pulling the spear out of the wax head. "We're in a wax museum."

The wax figure had been sculpted after Adolf Hitler, but over the decades the figure had melted into an unrecognizable blob. Adolf's arm was raised in a sieg heil, but now the fingers had melted into gnarly curls. They look around at many other melted figures surrounding them.

"What did they use wax museums for?" Scavy asks.

"They made sculptures of celebrities and famous historical figures, probably so the public could pretend to meet them in person. Those clothes are real, though. If you can get them off of the sculpture you can wear them."

Scavy nods and points at Hitler. "Who was this guy?"

"I believe he was one of America's greatest presidents," Junko says. "The one who freed the slaves."

"Cool. I'll wear his clothes then."

As Scavy uses the blade of his spear to cut the melted wax off of the sculpture, Junko and Rainbow Cat patrol the area.

"We should get thicker layers of clothing for ourselves as well,"

Junko says. "We at least need some gloves."

All of the melted figures standing around them makes Rainbow Cat feel as if they're in the middle of a zombie horde. Their faces are sagging in distorted ways, mouths stretched open, eyes popping out, necks melted away completely so that chins sink into chests or heads twist into awkward angles. In ways they are even more horrifying to Rainbow than the zombies.

She looks at one of the sculptures: a pirate man whose dreadlocks have melted and curled so much over time that he looks like a medusa. The sign below the sculpture reads, "Captain Jack Sparrow." Bites have been taken out of the back of his head, as if a zombie had at one time thought he was a real person and tried to eat his brain.

"These clothes are all waxy," Scavy yells, as he tries on the uniform.

Junko hushes him and then whispers back, "That's good. The more water resistant the better."

They get gloves from other figures: a Michael Jackson sculpture, a Darth Vader sculpture, and a Mork from Ork sculpture. Junko takes the Darth Vader gloves for herself.

"The gloves will make fighting a little more difficult," Junko says, "but being able to push zombies off of you without getting infected is more important than any weapon."

Once every inch of their skin below the neck is covered up, they head back toward the entrance. But something of interest has captured Rainbow's attention.

"What's that?" she asks Junko.

It is a wax sculpture of a cyborg dog.

"Was it from a science-fiction television show?" Rainbow asks, approaching the soggy animal sculpture.

Junko looks carefully at the animal near Rainbow. It is a large black German shepherd inside of a metal exo-skeleton. Long metal talons protrude from its paws, and mounted on its back are miniature Gatling guns and rocket launchers.

When Rainbow Cat leans down to look into the dog's eyes, she says, "It looks so fake."

"Back away from that thing," Junko tells her.

"Why?" Rainbow says.

She backs away once the wax sculpture begins to growl.

"It's not fake," Junko says.

Then the creature lunges at Rainbow.

Junko pulls out her 9mm and fires at the dog's snarling face, bits of tooth and eye spray over its snout as it barks ferociously. It ceases its attack, giving Rainbow Cat a chance to get away.

As Rainbow gets behind Junko, the Gatling gun on the dog's back spins at them.

"Get down!" Junko cries, and the trio drops to the floor.

The gun whirrs, but no bullets are fired.

"It doesn't have any ammo," Junko says, as they get back to their feet. "Get it!"

Then she charges the creature, revving her chainsaw. The creature charges at her, then jumps in the air with its blade-like talons spread, aiming for her throat.

She cuts its head off in midair. When the headless body lands, it keeps charging forward. It runs past Scavy and Rainbow Cat, piling straight into a display of the cast of M.A.S.H. and attacks the set with its blade-like claws.

As the body of the cybernetic zombie dog rips apart a wax sculpture of Alan Alda, Scavy looks down on the severed dog head. It bites rapidly at the air and licks the pavement with its black tongue. Inside of its neck, there are wires and gears moving within the oozing flesh as if they're a natural part of the animal's body.

"I thought you said we should always run away from the zombies," Scavy says. "But you fought that thing head on."

"There's no running away from those things," Junko says, wiping blood off her chainsaw with a Doctor Who scarf. "They're just way too fast."

"So we get to fight these things when we come across them?" Scavy asks, excitedly.

"Not if we can avoid it," Junko says. "If we run into one that's fully armed we're all dead."

"What are they?" asks Rainbow Cat.

"Mechjaws," Junko says. "You've never heard of them?"

They stare at her blankly.

"These things are responsible for the entire zombie outbreak, fifty years ago."

Mechjaws were built by the US military several years before the zombie outbreak. They were designed to be immortal killing machines that could replace humans on the battlefield. One mechjaw was worth a thousand soldiers. It could not be killed by bullets. It had no need for food or sleep. It could survive in any terrain. Its orders could be beamed directly into its head from satellite. They were furry machines of death.

But they didn't realize the serum designed to keep the animals alive could be transmitted by blood. They discovered this during their first field test. The first mechjaw was sent into the middle east to take out a terrorist cell. The researchers observing the test were pleased with the speed at which the mechjaw shot down each of its targets, but were then shocked by what it did to the corpses after they were all dead. The mechjaw ate all of their brains. Not their flesh, just their brains.

Then, like a virus, the chemical serum was transmitted to the dead terrorists. It brought them back to life and they became brain-eating monsters. The zombie outbreak was contained two days later and, despite the drawback, the project was considered a success.

The US military continued making mechjaws for several months until they learned that the outbreak had not been fully contained. A zombie foot had been left behind in the desert and was eventually eaten by a stray dog, which had become infected and bit a child who had become infected and bit his parents. Within a few days, the outbreak had spread throughout the Middle East and was already hitting Africa and Europe.

When news of the outbreak hit the U.S., the mechjaw project was cancelled. They were just about to salvage the mechjaw machinery and dispose of the organic material, when a group of militant animal rights activists broke into the mechjaw facility and released the dogs. Over two hundred mechjaws were unleashed on the east coast, killing and infecting every human in their path. With no orders to follow, they just followed their instincts: eat and destroy.

Z-Day, as the survivors called it, happened forty-eight hours after the mechjaws were released. That was the day practically every city on the planet had become under siege by the living dead. Some cities had it worse than others, but every city on the mainland was fighting for survival against the hordes of brain-eating undead.

The scientists who created the mechjaws had no idea what they had done. They never knew the serum would work on humans just as well as dogs. In later days, it was discovered that many species could be infected with the virus. It's mostly restricted to large mammals, from dogs to bears to elephants to pigs, as well as water-dwelling mammals such as whales and dolphins. Smaller mammals, such as rabbits and cats, are immune to the virus. Nobody has ever researched why the virus doesn't infect smaller mammals. If a cat is bitten by a zombie it does not become a zombie cat, it just dies. Some predict that it has to do with brain size, but that has never been proven.

Junko keeps her eyes on the mechjaw dismembering the wax Alan Alda, as she leads her companions toward the exit.

"We're going to be in trouble if there's more of those things in the city," Junko says.

"Do they usually kill a lot of the contestants in the show?" asks Rainbow.

"No," Junko says. "They've never been in the show before. Wayne always hoped to have mechjaws in the show, but no contestant has ever run into one. There are only a couple hundred of them on the entire continent."

"So you think we won't run into any more of them?" Rainbow asks.

When they step out of the door and check to see if the coast is clear, Junko runs into the floating camera ball that zooms in on her face.

"I hope so," Junko says, then she looks into the camera. "And it would piss the fuck out of Wayne if he knew the only mechjaw attack to ever be on Zombie Survival happened off-camera."

As they run down the street in their new extra-padded clothing, Scavy thinks about it for a minute. He's seen enough stray dogs in Copper to know something about their behavior.

"But don't dogs travel in packs?" he asks.

Junko freezes when she hears his words, then she turns to her left. Staring back at her is a pack of eight mechjaws, licking their scabby lips at her from the windows of a crumbling retro arcade.

"This time we run," Junko says.

But Scavy is the first one to take off down the street as the mechjaws' fully-loaded Gatling guns open fire.

GOGO

Gogo stands behind the doorway of a low income housing apartment building as a gang of Mexican zombies stagger by on the street outside. She holds a silenced submachine gun tight to her chest, waiting for the majority of them to pass. A camera ball floats impatiently behind her shoulder, focusing on her large breasts that barely fit into her sweaty ripped-up white shirt.

"Cerebros!" the Mexican zombies groan. "Cerreebrossss…"

She waits for the last zombie, the straggler. She hopes to shoot out its legs and pull it inside before the others notice. Because her weapon is silenced, the other zombies won't likely hear it.

Gogo didn't realize she had a silencer in her pack when she first left the hotel. She just ran for her life, opening fire on every zombie that got in her way. She was the first one out of the hotel and was far ahead of everyone else, but then she started to get lonely and decided to go back for her friends.

She went to a rooftop and ate some kind of fruit and protein bar. All of the rations the show gave to the contestants were in bar form. After she ate the bar, she realized she was still hungry and went for another. That's when she found the silencer. At first she didn't know what it was, until she realized it was a piece of her gun.

Gogo likes having the camera watch her. She holds the silencer like a dick between her breasts, rubbing it slightly up and down her sweaty cleavage. Unlike the other contestants, Gogo couldn't think of a better way to die than as a contestant on *Zombie Survival*. She likes the idea of being a star. It gets her off knowing that all the upper class men on the island are drooling over her body right now.

The last Mexican zombie in the line is a young tattooed living corpse, who was possibly a gang member in his previous life. As he passes the doorway, Gogo opens her skirt and stretches her thigh out into his view. Her black-painted fingernails caress up the fishnet stockings on her legs, beckoning him to come take a bite out of her.

The zombie turns to her, only seeing one leg and one hand moving beyond the doorway.

"¿Cerebros?" says the zombie, as it enters the building.

Gogo tosses a blanket over him and then wraps him up with an extension cord, binding not only his arms to his sides but also the blanket over his face and torso. Then she closes the door and shoots out the zombie's kneecaps with her silenced SMG. The other zombies hear their friend's cries as he hits the ground, but they don't come back for him.

Gogo smiles seductively at the camera. Then she leans close to the zombie's ear and says softly through the blanket, "Hey, living dead boy, wanna go for a ride?"

The zombie growls behind the cloth.

Gogo giggles flirtatiously and looks up at the camera ball.

"I'm going to give all of you a show you're never going to forget."

Then she drags the body into an apartment room and closes the door.

Gogo has had a zombie fetish for as long as she can remember. Necrophelia of any kind really turns her on, because the idea of sex with the dead (or living dead) seems so sick and twisted to her. She gets off on sick and twisted.

Her boyfriends were never into sick and twisted stuff. One time she was fucking Scavy while Brick was off fucking Popcorn somewhere, riding him reverse cowgirl. As she came, she took a huge dump right on Scavy's stomach. He saw the log ooze out of her ass onto the soft flesh below his belly button.

"What the fuck!" Scavy shouted.

Gogo laughed. "What?"

"You just shit on me and shit!"

"So?" she asked, as she pulled off of him and looked down at her log of feces.

"I was just about to come when you did that, you bitch," he said. "Get it the fuck off me!"

Gogo put her face up to it and sniffed at it. The odor was mild, but had strange hints of marijuana and red licorice. The heat coming off of it was warm against her face.

"Don't stare at it, get rid of it!" Scavy said.

Gogo continued smelling it and examining its textures and curves, like she had just created a work of art.

"It turns you on, doesn't it?" she asked.

"Fuck no."

"Then why are you still hard?"

She grabbed his cock and stroked it.

"It turns me on," she said.

"You're a fucking freak," Scavy said.

Then she grabbed a handful of her shit and wrapped it around his penis, masturbating him with her shit as if it were some kind of lubricant.

"Don't rub it on me!" Scavy cried.

"Tell me to stop and I will," she said, as she jerked him off.

Scavy couldn't get himself to tell her to stop. She was masterful at giving hand jobs. She used to give them professionally. Unlike himself and Popcorn, Gogo did go into prostitution rather than drug-dealing when she was young. But she wasn't just some common street whore, she was an exotic dancer who also sometimes slept with her customers for money. But she said she only did this for fun, when she was in the mood. The problem was she was always in the mood.

Just as Scavy started to get into the handjob and block out the smell of shit on his body, Gogo put his penis in her mouth.

"Oh, no…" Scavy cried, as he watched Gogo suck furiously on his shit-covered dick. "That's just nasty…"

After he came, Gogo swallowed her shit with his cum, and Scavy almost puked at the sight of it. He jumped out of bed and walked out of her apartment buck naked. He went a block down to the ocean and jumped in, trying to wash away her shit as well as the memory. He promised himself that he would never have sex with Gogo again.

Everyone in Scavy's crew had sex with Gogo several time and every single one of them had their own crazy story of some sick stunt she pulled on them:

Scavy had the shit story.

Popcorn had a story about Gogo wanting to be fucked by a gun that had been converted into a strap-on. It wasn't until after they both came that Popcorn learned that the gun strapped to her crotch had been loaded the whole time, with the safety off. If Popcorn had orgasmed just a little harder she would have put a bullet through Gogo's back.

Brick had a story about how Gogo once pretended she was a zombie while they were having sex. As she fucked him, Gogo scratched and bit him, trying to get to his brain. Brick almost thought she really was a zombie, because she used all of her strength when she scratched and bit him. She drew blood in several places. She put teeth marks on his skull. He had to hold her down to continue having sex with her, but she wouldn't stop trying to eat him alive while they screwed.

When she was done with her roleplaying, Brick asked, "Why'd you act like a zombie and scratch me up like that?"

Gogo lit a cigarette and shrugged. "I thought you'd like it. Personally, I've always wanted to have sex with a zombie."

"Why?"

"Because of the danger," Gogo said. "I bet having sex with something that's trying to kill you would be pretty intense."

As soon as Gogo learned that she was in the middle of the Red Zone, she knew she would have to test her fantasy to see if having sex with a zombie really was as intense as she imagined. And the fact that she had an audience only made it more appealing to her.

With the zombie strapped naked to an ancient bed and the camera ball hovering over the scene, Gogo removes her clothing slowly as if she's dancing for a group of horny old men at her strip club.

As she removes her shirt, she rubs her breasts and points them at the camera. She licks her nipples and sucks on her fingers, then touches the moisture between her legs. The camera zooms in at her elongated clit as it becomes erect. She hopes the size of her clitoris disturbs some of the viewers watching her. It always turns her on when guys become uncomfortable or intimidated by her clit size. It's not nearly as large as the smallest penis, but they can't help but see it as one. This awkwardness drives her wild. It almost always makes her want to force the guy into giving her oral sex.

When his friends were about to have sex with Gogo, he'd always tell them, "Don't show any fear. If she can tell you're nervous around it, she will make you give it oral sex."

Gogo strokes her monster clit for the camera, then turns to her undead lover. Her green hair brushes against the corpse's writhing soggy body—collecting patches of brown sludge—as she climbs on top of it. The smell of rancid chicken hits her nostrils and she inhales deeply.

"You're a dirty boy," Gogo says. "I like dirty boys."

"Cerebros!" cries the zombie.

She presses her tongue against a leathery mud-caked patch of flesh and slides it up to his torso. Weeds grow out of his lungs like chest hairs, tickling her lips as she kisses his nipple. A section of his skin is missing from his chest below the nipple, exposing the ribcage. She curls her tongue around a rib and then bites down on it.

The zombie growls. She can feel his growl vibrate through her upper jaw. She growls back and then tears the rib bone out of his chest. Then spits it onto his neck.

As she lies her weight on top of him, her breasts squishing into its oozing flesh, she brings her face closer to his. The zombie bites at her, snapping its jaws at the air between them.

"Cerebros! Cerebros! Cerebros!"

She bites the air back at him, flirtatiously. Then grabs him by the throat. She chokes the zombie so hard that no sound comes out of his mouth when he says *cerebros*. He thrashes to get out of her grip so that he can bite her hand, but once she uses both hands he's no longer able to resist. She turns his face to the side, leans in, and bites into his brain. The skull is so brittle that it's like she's biting into a soft-shelled crab.

Pulling out a long strip of brain, she lets go of his neck and has him watch. Black fluids dribble down her chin as she chews on his brain. She looks over at the camera seductively and swallows. Then licks her black lips.

"Cerebros!" cries the zombie.

"Brains!" cries Gogo.

She sits back and shoves her hand into his torso, pulls out some intestines, and rubs them on her breasts. The intestines are filled with decayed fifty-year-old brains and congealed blood. Dark reddish-brown in color, they smear like inky oatmeal against her skin.

"I want you," she tells the zombie. "I want to fuck you, my living dead boy."

She puts on a show for the camera, laying it on nice and thick to both arouse and disturb the people back home. She hopes they don't edit a single second out of her performance. She wants people to be watching this scene and talking about this scene for years after her death. She wants the producers of the show to know that they sent the right girl into the zombie wasteland. They chose the right girl to become a star.

As Gogo handles the zombie's cracked penis, she realizes it's not becoming hard. Even her masterful hands are not enough to arouse the living corpse.

"What the fuck?" she asks the zombie. Then she punches it in the chest. A cloud of dust rises into the air.

She examines his deformed penis. It is wrinkled and scaly. Brown fluids leak from a crack in its side. There are two large bulges in it, as if his rotten testicles had dropped out of his scrotum into his urethra and slid down the shaft halfway.

"We're going to have to make this hard somehow," she says.

Her eyes scan the room for something long and hard to prop it up with. She finds a long splinter of wood beneath an ancient dresser and brings it back to him. Holding it up to the camera and up to her lover, she gives them a good look at it. Thin and pointed at one end, but it gets thicker and flat toward the other end.

"This will probably do just fine," she says.

She lifts his shriveled piece of flesh and brings the sliver of wood to it, pressing its sharp point lightly against the head. Like a long fingernail, she caresses the zombie's penis with the splinter, scratching the side of the shaft. The splinter catches on a large blister and it pops, white fluid dribbles down its shaft like pre-cum.

The penis hole looks as if it had been sealed up a long time ago, so she has to reopen it by force. She points the tip of the splinter at the eye of the penis and then pokes it slowly inside. There is resistance, so she pushes harder. She grips his penis tightly with her other hand and then with all of her strength she stabs the long wooden spike through, creating a new hole.

The sound of tearing flesh as she jams the splinter deep into the zombie's dick. A geyser of yellow pus shoots out the top and brown mucus oozes over her fingers from the hole in the side.

"Yeah..." Gogo says, as the wood goes all the way in.

She feels his dick again.

"Now it's hard enough to fuck," she says to the camera.

She climbs on top of his body and stares the zombie in the eyes.

"Ready?" she asks it.

She looks down at her crotch as it lowers toward his erection.

Her eyes widen as she watches the gnarled blistered member disappear inside of her pussy.

"Oh yeah," she tells the zombie, in her very phony stripper voice.

She can feel the knots in his penis as she fucks it. She moans out loud, not caring if any other zombies hear. To be torn apart and eaten alive while fucking a zombie in front of a television audience is exactly how she wants to die.

"Brains!" she yells, fucking the zombie faster.

The zombie doesn't yell back, as if confused and frightened of Gogo.

"Brains!" she yells.

She grabs the zombie by the throat and twists his head into her face.

"Brains!" she yells again, then bites into the zombie's brains.

She eats the creature's gray matter as she fucks it, thrashing against him on the bed as if she's a zombie herself.

"Brains!"

Then the ancient bed collapses and she hears a tear. A look of concern crosses her face as she gulps down the chunk of brain in her mouth. She looks at the straps that are binding the corpse, hoping the tearing noise wasn't one of the knots breaking. But when she looks down, she notices the noise had come from the zombie's dick. It has been ripped off.

When Gogo stands up, the camera zooms in on the severed penis between her legs. She pulls out the ragged scabby piece of meat and holds it up, frowning at it.

"You wimpy little bitch!" she yells at the zombie, then tosses the dick in his face. "You ruined it!"

The zombie's tongue reaches out for the penis by his face. Gogo knows he's probably trying to eat it, just in case it happens to be a piece of brain, but she imagines the corpse just wants to lick her vaginal fluids off of his dick. She always liked guys who would lick her juices off of their fingers or her dildo, but it turned her on even more to think of a guy licking her vaginal fluids off of his own severed dick.

Gogo realizes that she's still turned on and needs to still get off somehow. If she can't fuck him now that his penis is missing and can't receive oral sex from him without her labia being bitten off, she decides she'll let him finger her into orgasm. Of course, since his body parts don't need to be attached to his body in order to function, she decides to cut off his arm.

The door bursts open as Gogo is fingering herself with the zombie's severed hand. She shrieks, then grabs the submachine gun next to her and points it at the intruder.

"Don't shoot," Popcorn says, standing in the doorway with her arms raised.

"Popcorn?" Gogo asks, staring at her pale-faced friend with the bullet hole in her forehead.

"Gogo?" Popcorn says, staring at her naked friend with a writhing zombie hand in her crotch.

Gogo puts her clothes back on and shamelessly explains in great detail what she was doing with the zombie tied to the bed. Then Popcorn tells her about what happened to her, and how she is now officially a zombie even though she doesn't feel all that different so far.

"That's kind of awesome," Gogo tells her. "I wish the same thing would happen to me."

"Well, after having sex with this corpse you're surely infected," Popcorn says. "We'll have to see what happens to you once you turn. You might be like me or you might become a ravenous mindless brain-eater."

"Either way," Gogo says, "I'm out of the contest. I guess it's just you and me in the zombie wasteland from here on out."

"Yep, just the two of us," Popcorn says. "The queens of the dead."

"It's going to be awesome!" Gogo says.

"Yeah…"

Gogo stares hungrily at Popcorn's head. At first, Popcorn thinks she's imagining what it would be like to eat her brain. But as Gogo licks her lips, Popcorn realizes that she's thinking of something sexual. She is imagining what it would be like to fuck the bullet hole in Popcorn's head with her elongated clit.

Popcorn realizes that she's not looking forward to spending the rest of her undead life all alone in the zombie wasteland with Gogo.

BOSCO

Bosco watches from the window of an office building as the zombie war dogs chase after Junko, Scavy, and Rainbow Cat. The dogs' Gatling guns roar at them, showering the streets with bullets. The noise of gunfire catches the attention of the living dead and the street becomes full of them. The trio finds themselves stuck between the pack of fully-armed mechjaws and a wall of the living dead.

Junko takes her crew straight into the mob, weaving through the soggy corpses. The zombies reach out for them, clawing at the air only inches away from them. If just one of them grabs Junko, that would be the end of it. There wouldn't be enough time to cut its limbs off before the mechjaws catch up. Luckily, most of the zombies' attentions are focused on the sounds of the Gatling guns and haven't noticed the three humans ducking through their crowd.

The mechjaws' bullets cut through the zombie horde, but the dead do not fall. This creates the perfect human shield between Junko's crew and the bullets. But the dogs are still closing in on them. They easily run through the mob of undead, knocking them down like dominos, shredding their corpses with their talon blades.

Bosco watches patiently to see which of the three will get killed first. Rainbow Cat is falling behind the other two. She chose a much denser path through the mob of corpses. He wonders if she will be the first to die. He really hopes not. He hopes Scavy is the first to die, because that asshole punk wouldn't let him join his crew. Though Junko also wouldn't let him join her crew. She wouldn't even make eye contact with him when he talked to her, pretended that he wasn't even there. He hopes that stuck up bitch gets what she deserves and dies painfully.

Back at the hotel, nobody wanted to join up with him, not even the other loners. Because he had to go on his own, he was nearly killed several times an hour. He was grabbed trying to climb a wall, he was cornered by a group of zombies, he was tripped by a legless zombie while trying to run away from a horde. If he had a friend with him none of these things would have been a problem. His friend could have easily helped him get over the wall or helped him fight their way out of a swarm. If only he had a friend.

Bosco has always been unlucky when it came to making friends. People just don't ever seem to like him. He somehow rubs them the wrong way. He's not sure why. He likes people. He likes to be around people. He's not shy. He's not an asshole. People just don't like him.

In the Copper Quadrant, Bosco worked in a sweat shop making dresses for women in the Silver and Gold Quadrants. His mother had taught him to sew growing up. A skill he thought he could use, but he never thought would become his trade.

He was the only male who worked on his floor. The other workers surrounding him were older women, the youngest of them was ten years older than him. Most of them were single mothers. None of them wanted anything to do with him. He thought they would be desperate enough to be interested in him, but they all turned him down when he asked them out on dates. He's not the most attractive man in the world, but he's not the ugliest either. He's in good shape and still has most of his teeth. But women just weren't interested in him. Outside of prostitutes, he had only slept with one woman in his life.

If he couldn't be with a woman he at least wanted to have friends, but even friends were impossible for him. Every day after work he would go to the local bar and try to make friends with the other regulars. Some of them thought he was gay and just coming on to them, because his approach to starting a conversation was too aggressive. Others thought he was boring and annoying. Others just wanted to be left alone. But, still, every day he went back to the bar trying to make a friend. At least just a drinking friend. But nobody, not even the bartender, wanted to have anything to do with him.

He doesn't care much that he was put on *Zombie Survival*. His life has always been shit. He wasn't expecting his life to get any better. Death has always appealed to him. All he wants is to not have to die alone. If only somebody would have let him join their group he would have gladly sacrificed himself for them.

His goal isn't to get to the helicopter and survive. His goal is just to find somebody/anybody to be with him when he dies.

As Junko and Scavy get further ahead of Rainbow Cat, one of the mechjaws launches a rocket. The explosion hits between Rainbow Cat and the others, blowing everyone off of their feet. The zombies absorb most of the blast, their body parts flying through the air, black sludge splashing across the pavement. Like a landslide, the front of a building crumbles into the horde. Rainbow Cat runs into a nearby department store to avoid the avalanche. It takes down two of the mechjaws and most of the crowd of zombies.

As Junko helps Scavy to his feet, the mechjaws climb up the rubble after them. They look back for Rainbow Cat, but she's nowhere to be seen, perhaps even buried under the wreckage. Before the mechjaws have a chance to open fire, they take off running.

Bosco sees Rainbow Cat hiding in the department store, looking out the window at her companions as they leave her behind. The zombies and mechjaws follow after.

A smile creeps up on Bosco's face, happy that Rainbow was left all alone. If he can get to her in time she'll have no choice but to let him join her.

"Now you will be mine," Bosco says to the hippy girl in the doorway of the department store, "my beautiful Rainbow."

Then he licks his finger and draws a heart in the window glass around Rainbow, as she cowers in the distance, lost, alone, and afraid.

Alone with only a dagger, Rainbow Cat realizes she needs to find a better weapon. Even though Junko had told her being able to run fast is more important than a weapon, Rainbow would feel a lot safer if she had a sword or a large club. She at least needs to find a better knife. The one she has seems better for stabbing than cutting, and she needs a weapon that will cut through limbs.

Rainbow explores the store. She doesn't require her flashlight because stripes of sunlight brighten the room. It is a five story building but so many floors and ceilings have collapsed, cracked apart, and fallen away, that sunlight reaches all the way down from the roof to the ground floor.

Mostly everything in here is useless from exposure to the elements. The clothing falls apart between her fingers. The wooden bars used as coat racks break in half when she pulls them off the wall. Even the metal parts from the display shelves are rusted and brittle. The building feels as if it could collapse at any moment, so she decides not to search upstairs. She'll have to go somewhere else. Hopefully she'll be able to catch up to Junko and Scavy later.

On her way out of the department store, she runs into a figure standing in the doorway, blocking her path.

As she raises her dagger, the figure's arms raise up.

"I'm not infected," says the figure.

Rainbow Cat steps forward to see Bosco. A bent smile creeps onto his face, an expression that is like he's both frowning and smiling at the same time. Rainbow steps back a little.

"I see you're all alone," Bosco tells her. "I'm all alone, too."

Bosco's tone of voice is one of sleaziness, even though he thinks he's speaking in a friendly unthreatening tone.

"Get out of my way," Rainbow says.

"I just want to help you," he says. "I just want us to team up. I can watch your back, you can watch mine."

"I already have a team."

"You don't need them anymore. I'll protect you from now on."

"I don't want to have anything to do with you."

Bosco raises his weapon, a machete.

"How can you say that?" Bosco asks her. "After all we've been through?"

Rainbow Cat is confused. "What do you mean? Do I know you?"

"How could you have forgotten me?" Bosco asks. "You have to remember me. You just have to."

"What the hell are you talking about?"

A tear falls down Bosco's cheek as he says, "We used to be lovers."

Although Rainbow Cat didn't recognize him until now, Bosco was one of the guys she had slept with in Copper to get back at her husband for skipping a day of writing. Charlie had spent the entire day in bed, feeling sorry for himself. He had not written a single word in a day. It didn't matter that his typewriter was out of ink and that he had food poisoning from the dumpster chicken she brought home the night before. He didn't meet his quota and she was going to make good on her promise.

She chose Bosco because he was the most pathetic-looking guy in the bar. Sleeping with strange men was not something she enjoyed. She only did it to piss off her husband, so she picked the most worthless pieces of scum to fuck. And because he had not written a single word, she had planned to spend the night with this total loser.

Bosco had never been able to pick up a girl at a bar, let alone get picked up himself. It was like a dream come true for him. There was finally someone who wanted him, who could maybe even love him. And she was far more beautiful than any woman he had seen before. Her tiny pink smile, her lioness hair, her thin muscled arms; she was absolute perfection to him. He fell in love with her immediately. Not just because she was young and attractive, but because she chose to spend time with *him* of all people.

The prostitutes he used to pay to sleep with him had two rules: no kissing on the mouth and no cuddling. No matter how much he offered to pay they refused to do those things with him. This was heartbreaking to Bosco, because those are the two things he cared about most. Sex wasn't that big of a deal to him. He wasn't very good at it due to problems with impotency and premature ejaculation. All he wanted was to be kissed by a woman, to hold one in his arms.

Rainbow Cat was the first woman he ever kissed. The first woman who slept in his arms. When she kissed him, she did it passionately, as if he was her whole world in that moment. They didn't just have sex, they made love. They drenched his bed with their passion. And after he came inside of her, she hugged her naked body to him.

He wrapped himself around her and she slept in his arms the entire night. For that one night, she belonged to him. But the next morning she was gone.

He looked for her everywhere after that day, imagining all sorts of excuses for why she had not stayed. He thought she obviously had feelings for him, that she loved him. A week later he learned she worked on one of the farms. But after following her home from work, he discovered that she was married to another man. A horrible man who could not possibly love her as much as he did.

The next time he met her alone in the bar, she didn't make eye contact with him. She left with somebody else that night. It was a large tattooed man with a blond beard. Dan was his name, a regular at the bar and a real shit head. Bosco tried to be friends with Dan once. He bought the guy a beer and Dan still refused to hang out with him. He thought Bosco was gay.

Rainbow didn't spend the night with Dan that night. She just let him fuck her against a dumpster in an alley a few blocks down. The way the large muscular man rammed himself into her body was disturbing to Bosco. Dan shoved her head in the trash and repeated said *how do you like that, bitch?* as he fucked her. After he came, Dan smacked her bare ass and left her sitting there naked and sore. She just wiped the slime out of her crotch, gathered her clothing, and went home as if nothing had happened.

On the way back to the bar, Bosco confronted Dan.

"What the fuck were you doing with my girl back there?" Bosco asked him.

Dan looked back with a confused face.

"You?" Dan asked, recognizing him. "Did you follow us you fucking pervert?"

"Yeah, and I saw what you did. Rainbow is my girl. I love her more than anyone ever could."

"You're her husband?"

"No, I'm her lover. I love her far more than her husband does."

"You're a fucking freak, dude. Get the fuck out of here."

Bosco got into his face.

"You don't understand," he said. "She belongs to me."

Dan looked down at the scrawny man. "Look, weirdo. You're starting to piss me off. If you don't—"

Before Dan could finish, Bosco stabbed him in the face with a broken beer bottle. Dan screamed and fell to the ground, a shard of glass stuck through his eyelid and buried deep into his eye socket. Then Bosco stabbed the bottle repeatedly in his face and chest, until

Dan was no longer moving and the bottle had shattered in his hand.

"She's my beautiful Rainbow," he said to the corpse, wiping the tears from his eyes.

After that day, Bosco stalked Rainbow. He followed her home from work and watched her sleeping with her husband through their apartment window at night. It wasn't often that she had sex with other men, but when she did Bosco didn't let them get away with it. He made sure they shared the same fate as that asshole Dan.

At night, Bosco fantasized about her body sleeping next to his. He wrapped himself around the pillow her head had slept on that night, and imagined it was her body against him. In his dreams, he would kiss her on the mouth and bury his nose deep in her blonde dreadlocked hair. They would make love and live inside of his bed like a tomb for all eternity.

Yesterday night, he had followed Rainbow and Charlie to the restaurant. He assumed Charlie was abusive to her, a horrible human being she wanted to have nothing to do with. That's why she cheated on him so much. Bosco wanted to help her escape her living hell of a relationship. He planned to kill her husband the next morning, while she was at work. He didn't want her to go through the anguish of seeing her husband's murdered body, so he planned to make it appear as if Charlie left her for another woman. Just imagining how happy she would be to get rid of him for good brought a smile to his lips.

But he never got the chance to kill him. At the restaurant, Bosco watched as Rainbow Cat and Charlie collapsed into their plates of food. Their wine had been drugged. Then a man with a white goatee stepped out of the kitchen and went to the couple. Other men in white masks came in from the street, picked up their bodies and brought them into the back. The restaurant was empty save for the manager who appeared to be friends or business partners of the man with the white goatee.

Bosco didn't know what was going on, but he knew his beautiful Rainbow was in trouble. He pulled a machete out from under his coat, the same weapon he had planned to kill Charlie with, and charged the man with the white goatee.

The men in white masks turned to Bosco as he ran screaming at them. They held out there hands to grab him, but he went in swinging. His machete cut one of their hands in half, split down the middle, spraying blood on the white suit. He chopped another one through the neck, nearly cutting his head off. Before he could get to the man with the white goatee, enough of them had grabbed him to pin him to the ground.

"Wayne," said one of the white-masked men, "who is this guy?"

"I have no idea," Wayne said, wiping his hands. "But I like him. Let's put him on the show."

They chloroformed Bosco, brought his body in the back, and dropped him on top of Charlie and Rainbow. He didn't know it through the drugs, but he had snuggled Rainbow Cat again that night, in the back of the helicopter, all the way to the Red Zone.

The producers decided to let him use his own machete in the game. It was the first time anybody had ever been allowed to use their own weapon in the show. When he woke up, Bosco was happy to see that Rainbow was with him. But he was not happy that she was with Charlie. He decided to bide his time, wait for the two of them to separate, wait for Charlie to be killed by the undead, wait to get Rainbow alone, then save her, then they could die together.

Everything had worked out perfectly for him... until he learned that Rainbow Cat had no idea who he was.

"That was a long time ago," Rainbow told him. "I normally don't think much about guys after I sleep with them."

"I've never stopped thinking about you."

Rainbow backs away. "That's a little strange..."

Bosco steps closer, with his machete reflecting beams of sunlight coming through the ceiling.

"I want you to win this, Rainbow," he said. "I want to do everything in my power to protect you and keep you safe. All I ask for in return is that you let me die in your arms."

As he opens his arms, as if to embrace her, Rainbow panics and runs away.

"Stop!" Bosco says.

He chases after her. "Get back here!"

She runs for an exit in the back of the department store. Angry at her for running away, he swings his machete in the air at her back to take out his frustration. He would never hurt her, but right now she's pissing him off. The sound of the machete swiping at the air behind her makes Rainbow Cat scream.

She trips over some rubble and falls face-first into the cement. Her eyes spin in a daze as she tries to get to her feet.

Bosco drops on top of her and wraps himself around her body. She goes for her dagger, but he pries it from her fingers and tosses it across the room. She kicks at him and screams, but her head is still spinning from the fall.

He snuggles her forcefully, hushing her.

"I'm not going to hurt you," he whispers into her ear. "I just want to cuddle with you. That's all I want before I die."

As her senses return, Rainbow realizes that this freak is snuggle-raping her. He spoons her in the pile of rubble, one arm pressed between her breasts, one leg lying over her legs. She pulls her hand out from under his snuggling arm, then elbows him in the face, breaking his nose

"Get off of me!" she says, wriggling out of his grip.

When she gets to her feet, she faces him.

"You're so disgusting!" she says.

Bosco stands up, holding his bloody nose.

"You don't mean that," he says. "I love you more than anything in the world."

She says, "I only fucked your ugly pathetic ass to get back at my husband. I figured it would piss him off if I fucked the biggest loser in the bar."

Bosco points the machete at her. "You don't mean that."

She spits at him. "Why the hell would I ever want to be with a loser like you?"

Bosco glares at her.

"You fucking bitch…" he says, angry tears ripping down his face. "I'll fucking kill you."

Rainbow bends her knees, getting ready to run away.

"Oh yeah?" Rainbow says. "Go ahead and try it."

Bosco raises the machete and charges her. She turns to run away, but after ten feet she leaps into the air, spins around like a butterfly, and kicks him in the face. His lower jaw dislocates and he falls to the ground. Rainbow gets into a fighting stance above him, ready to defend herself.

Bosco never knew, nor did her husband, nor did anyone in the Copper Quadrant, but Rainbow was an expert martial artist. Before she was with Charlie, she was in an abusive relationship. She had a boyfriend who used to beat her. A popular soccer player named Teddy who took a liking to her. This was before she had the dreadlocks, before she read Charles Hudson novels.

She liked him at first, because he was so adored by all the other girls. Then she discovered he was a total asshole. He was a bully and flirted with women behind her back. The first time he hit her was the day she tried to break up with him. He made her change her mind, physically. Then he started beating her all the time. He hit her whenever she raised her voice to him. He would throw her to the ground and kick her in the stomach if he found out she talked to another guy. If she refused to give him sex when he wanted it she would go home with blood stains on her clothing. She was too afraid to leave him, too afraid to tell anyone about what he was doing to her.

Then she started taking lessons in self-defense. She studied several books and practiced every moment she wasn't around him. The next time she told him she was dumping him, he wasn't able to lay a finger on her. He threw one punch and she broke his arm.

After that, she studied the martial arts for fun. It helped her build confidence and self-esteem, which is what she needed most after the weak cowering creature that Teddy had turned her into. But after she met Charlie, she quit all of her hobbies. She wanted to devote herself completely to his writing. The reason she decided not to tell her husband about her fighting skills was because she didn't want it to effect their relationship. She knew it might threaten his macho ego to know that his wife could kick his ass in under a minute. Plus, if Charlie ever did become abusive toward her, she wanted her ass-kicking skills to come as a surprise to him.

"I'll cut your fucking face off," Bosco says to Rainbow Cat, but she can hardly understand him with his dislocated jaw.

He swings his machete at her, aiming for her hips, but Rainbow catches him by the wrist and bends back his arm. He drops the machete. She punches him twice in the diaphragm, knees him in the stomach, and flips him over her shoulder into the dirt.

"Don't get up," she says to him with her foot in his back.

He doesn't get up.

As she walks away, she feels as though her skills have become pretty rusty, but they're still there. She's going to need them if she's going to be the one to win this competition.

Bosco retrieves his machete and charges her back, aiming to plant the blade directly in the center of her skull. When she turns around, the machete hits her in the throat. Bosco's eyes widen with regret when he sees the look of shock and sadness on her face.

He pulls out the machete and blood dribbles out of the wound. Rainbow grabs her neck wound, holding in the blood. Then she looks up at Bosco.

"I'm sorry," he says.

The blade didn't hit her jugular, so the wound isn't fatal. But the idea that he came only a centimeter away from ending her life fills Rainbow with rage.

She charges him.

Bosco holds out his machete to defend himself, but it takes Rainbow less than a second to grab his machete arm and break it at the elbow. A sliver of bone tears through the skin of his upper arm and he cries so loud that it attracts zombies in from the street. She stomps on his knee, dislocating it, and he falls to the ground in front of her.

She wraps herself around his back, snuggle-raping him in the same way he had done to her, and puts him in a tight headlock.

"Wait…" Bosco cries.

She flexes her muscled arms around his head, and slowly breaks his neck against her body.

"Don't…" Bosco says, just before the loud cracking sound.

His body goes limp in her arms.

She tears a piece of fabric from his clothing and wraps it around her throat to stop the bleeding.

"Braiiins," says a skeleton as it staggers toward her. Four more zombies follow close behind.

She picks up the machete and wipes her blood off of the blade, ready to hack these living corpses into pieces. Before she charges into battle, she looks back at Bosco's corpse. He looks even twice as pathetic now that he's dead. She has no pity for losers like him. They are a waste. She could never respect a man who loved her more than anything in the world. The kind of man she loved was one who put his ambitions above all relationships, like Charles Hudson did with his writing.

Rainbow realizes that she did end up giving Bosco what he wanted after all. When she broke his neck, he died in her arms. As she chops the head off the first zombie that comes toward her, she kicks herself for letting the pathetic asshole get his way. She wishes she would have just used the machete to slice open a major artery, and then left him there to bleed to death all alone.

LAURENCE

After they find all of the components necessary to build the weapon laid out in the blueprints, Laurence and Haroon look for a safe place to put them all together. They cross a street to a gas station and climb a ladder to get to the rooftop. Junko had told them that zombies were horrible climbers, so Haroon figures that's the safest place for them at the moment.

On the mold-coated roof, Haroon empties the pack. He spreads out all of the items in the black slime. Then unfolds the blueprints to figure out how to construct the thing.

Haroon knows his way around building weapons, so this isn't much of a challenge for him. He can tell it is some kind of gun. He puts together the barrel first, then the trigger and the power supply. In less than half an hour, the weapon is constructed: a mess of wires and cables formed into the shape of a rifle.

"What is it?" Laurence asks.

"It can't be…" Haroon says.

"What?"

Haroon examines closely.

"It's a completely different model than mine," Haroon says. "But they perfected it."

"Perfected what? Spit it out."

"My solar-powered shotgun," Haroon says. "This is it. The weapon I had been working on for years… But this thing looks like it could actually work."

"Let me see," Laurence says.

He picks up the weapon and aims it at a zombie in the distance. When he pulls the trigger, nothing happens.

"Brains!" the zombie yells at him from the distance.

"It doesn't work," Laurence says.

"No, it wouldn't. Not yet. The power supply needs to be charged up, in the sunlight."

"How long is it going to take? We don't have much sun left."

"I have no idea. We should wait at least an hour."

"Fine with me," Laurence says, reclining into a moldy puddle on the roof. "I could use a rest anyway."

Haroon places the rifle onto a ledge in the direct sunlight.

"You looked like MacGyver putting that thing together," Laurence says.

"MacGyver? You said that name earlier. Who the heck is Mac-Gyver?"

"Oh, he's an old television character who used to build laser cannons out of bubble gum and paperclips."

"You have a television? In Copper?"

"No, this was a long time ago. Back in the 1980's. I used to be on a show back then, too."

"The 1980's? You're not old enough to have been alive in the 1980's."

"I was."

"That's impossible."

Laurence grunts at the sky and says, "Nothing's impossible."

Then he tells Haroon his story.

Laurence's full name is Laurence Tureaud, but he was widely known by the name Mr. T.

Back in the 1980's, Mr. T was a television star and a cultural icon. Everybody loved him. He was the most badass motherfucker on television, the epitome of cool. But then he was diagnosed with terminal cancer. He spent several years coming to terms with his disease, fighting the cancer every step of they way so that he could spend as many years with his family as possible. But eventually, the disease got to the point where the doctors just couldn't do anything for him anymore.

The thought of losing Mr. T was just too much for America. A fundraiser was started to help keep the national hero alive. Although no money in the world could cure his cancer, enough money was raised to have him cryogenically frozen. So for sixty-three years, Mr. T has been suspended in time. He missed Z-Day and the apocalypse, he missed the 50 years of struggle the world had endured since then.

A couple of years ago, a scientist named Jacob Wyslen brought Mr. T back to life. He was a researcher who had a lab on a small island off the east coast. After Z-Day hit, several research stations were put together around the country, all of them with a mission to put an end to the zombie problem. After thirty years, Wyslen's was the only one that remained. He started with a staff of twenty scientists and soldiers, but these people didn't last very long. He sent them on dangerous missions into the Red Zone and very few of them came back alive. One day, he realized he was all alone.

Because he couldn't do his work all by himself, Wyslen decided to resurrect the people who were frozen in the storage. He went from chamber to chamber, trying to bring the bodies back to life. On all occasions, he failed... apart from one. He was able to resurrect Mr. T.

"This isn't the world Mr. T was expecting to come back to, Doc," he told Dr. Wyslen, as the doctor examined his motor functions.

"I can put you back if you want?" the old man said.

"No thanks," said Mr. T. "I would rather help you take down those dead things than live like a dead thing."

For months, Mr. T assisted the doctor with his research. He proved to be much more useful than the doctor had expected. Not only was he able to go on missions in the Red Zone and come back alive, he also proved intelligent enough to brainstorm theories with him.

"You see, Doc," Mr. T told him in the large empty cafeteria, "you're goin' about this all wrong. You can't just freeze the undead suckas. They crave brains, and the electrochemical impulses it sends out through the body. That means they must survive on these impulses. I say you work on a nerve gas that'll take out their whole nervous system. Do that and it's goodbye zombies."

"But nerve gas would also kill the surviving humans in the area," said Wyslen.

"There ain't nobody left alive out there. It's just zombies. Mr. T says gas the whole place and be done with them."

"But nerve gas is pretty useless out in the open. It would just dissipate in the atmosphere."

"How about putting a fumigation tent over the whole country? Then gas 'em."

The doctor laughed. "It would probably be easier to just drop some bombs."

Mr. T laughed with him. He said, "Now you're talking," and slapped the doctor on the back so hard he almost fell out of his chair.

The doctor didn't work on a nerve gas, but he did invent a sonic device that worked as a repellant for the undead. It was kind of a high-pitched vibration that drove zombies crazy, like a dog whistle.

Wyslen died before his work was completed. Before his death, he asked Mr. T to take his research and bring it to the island of Neo New York. He wanted Mr. T to assist the scientists there with completing his work. With some time and the right resources, his device could become the breakthrough invention that would finally solve the zombie problem for good.

"I'll make sure they finish your work," Mr. T told the doctor on his death bed. "Otherwise, they'll have to answer to Brick and Mortar."

"Brick and Mortar?" the doctor asked.

"Those are the new names for Mr. T's fists."

Doctor Wyslen laughed himself to sleep. He never woke up after that.

After an hour, Haroon's ready to test the weapon.

"Hopefully there's some zombies nearby so we can test it from safety," Haroon says.

When they go to the edge, they see a large horde surrounding the gas station.

"Braaiins!" the zombies yell when they see their heads popping up from the roof.

"You sure we're safe up here?" asks Mr. T.

"Junko said those things can't climb, so I figured this would be the safest place."

"Just because they can't climb doesn't mean they can't mob," Mr. T says. "If that shotgun thingy of yours don't work we might be trapped up here for good."

"Well, let's try it out," Haroon says. "Hopefully it works better than the one I created."

Haroon aims the weapon at the crowd of zombies below. When he pulls the trigger, a beam of energy shoots out of the barrel and shreds four of the walking corpses below.

Mr. T smiles. "It don't shoot like no shotgun, but it sure hits like one."

Haroon pumps the shotgun and fires again, blowing zombie limbs and body parts into the air. He shoots again. Then again. After thirty shots, the zombies are still coming at him, but he's not running out of bullets. Just as he always planned the solar-powered shotgun would work.

"You're pretty good with that thing," says Mr. T. "Even though it's technically supposed to be my weapon, I'll trade you for the club."

"You'd rather have the club?"

"That gun sure does the job well, but I'd rather have a weapon I can trust. The club will do just fine."

"Sure," Haroon says, then blasts the legs out from under another zombie.

When Mr. T arrived at the island of Neo New York, he was greeted only with hostility. The small sailboat he had taken from Dr. Wyslen's island was stopped a mile off shore by the NNY Coast Guard. Two ships pulled up alongside his boat and he was forced to allow them to board.

Six men with automatic rifles came aboard, all of the weapons pointed at his face. Mr. T raised his hands.

"Are you armed?" asked the Lieutenant.

"Mr. T don't need weapons to protect himself," said Mr. T.

"Are you alone?" the young officer asked Mr. T.

"Yeah."

After they searched his ship, the Lieutenant asked some more questions.

"Do you have business on the island or are you just looking for safe harbor?"

Mr. T responded, "I was sent by Dr. Jacob Wyslen of the Z-19 Project."

"Never heard of him."

"That's not my problem," Mr. T said. "He told me to give his research to the zombie research division on this island."

"Zombie research division?" The Lieutenant laughed. "We don't have a zombie research division."

"Then who's working on solving the living dead problem on the mainland?"

The soldiers look at each other with large smiles, then look back at Mr. T.

"They gave up on that decades ago," said the Lieutenant. "The zombie problem hasn't been a problem of ours for a very long time."

"Then you shouldn't have given up so easily," Mr. T said. "My friend Dr. Wyslen continued his research over the past fifty years until the day he died. He finally came up with something that just might be a solution to make the mainland safe again."

"And what solution might that be?"

"It's a kind of zombie repellent device. If I can get the right minds looking at this research, I believe this device can be constructed."

"It sounds like a load of bull," said the Lieutenant.

"You don't have to believe me. You just have to let me through. Leave the believing up to the scientists who might actually understand this jibber jabber."

"Fine," said the Lieutenant. "But your boat will be impounded. You'll have to ride with us."

"Whatever you say," said Mr. T. "Just as long as I get this research into the right hands."

When all of the zombies are writhing on the ground, Haroon and Mr. T climb down the ladder and continue on their way. In the distance, in every direction they look, there are hundreds of zombies staggering through the streets.

"More and more of those things are coming out," says Mr. T. "And it's going to be dark soon. We better find some shelter for the night if we ever want to see tomorrow."

Haroon contemplates the zombie numbers up ahead. Then he says, "We shouldn't find cover yet, not until it's dark. We have to make as much progress as possible if we're ever going to catch up to the others."

"I don't like it," says Mr. T, "but whatever you say."

"We shouldn't have too much of a problem now that we have this weapon on our side."

"I already told you, I don't trust that gun. It's a great invention, don't get me wrong, but it's not something Mr. T would rely on."

"It'll work just fine," Haroon says. "Trust me."

Mr. T nods. Then they move on, deeper into the city, deeper into the ocean of the living dead.

They didn't allow Mr. T to enter Platinum to meet with the top researchers who lived there. One of the scientists came out to meet him in Copper, and by the looks of it they sent the lowest ranking member of the staff.

The doctor asked to see Wyslen's documents and Mr. T handed them over.

After scanning through the pages for a few minutes, the young man said, "I'll have to show these to the higher ups to see what they think. Are you staying here?"

"Yeah," Mr. T said.

"Great. I'll keep in touch."

As the man walked back to the gates with Wyslen's research in his hands, Mr. T yelled out, "Tell them I've got a lot of ideas on how to get it operational. I worked closely with Dr. Wyslen for quite some time."

Then the gate closed behind the young scientist, then Mr. T went up to the gate and put his hands on the bars.

"And tell them if they don't make this happen they will have to answer to Brick and Mortar."

The man waved back at Mr. T without turning around.

He never heard from the scientist ever again and the Coast Guard never returned his boat, so he was left stranded in Copper with no home, no job, and nothing left to do. So he moved into an abandoned shack on the beach. It wasn't much but it was shelter. He started crabbing for food and would sometimes sell crabs at the market. People in Copper didn't have much money, so he didn't sell them for very much. Later, he taught the other beggars in his shantytown how to fish and crab, but after a while so many of them started doing it that there weren't enough crabs left to go around. Still, he was happy his vagrant friends were able to eat a little better.

One day, Mr. T saw a group of kids doing Waste under the peer. When he saw what they were doing, he charged right up to them and took the drugs out of their hands.

"What do you kids think you're doing?" asked Mr. T. "Do you know how bad drugs are for you? You should be thinking about your futures, not wasting it on this trash."

"Give it back, asshole!" said a ten year old street punk.

"You mouth off to me again and I'm gonna smack that mouth off your face," said Mr. T, pointing his finger at the punk. "Now, you kids can do anything with your lives. You don't need this to have fun." He holds the drugs up to them. "You should have fun by playing basketball or practicing guitar."

"Give it back, scumbag!" yelled a little 9-year-old girl with a shaved head.

"You're not getting it back," said Mr. T, raising his voice. "I'm trying to tell you how this stuff will get in the way of your dreams."

Then the little girl put out her cigarette on his forehead. Mr. T screamed and the kids grabbed their Waste out of his hands and took off running across the beach. Mr. T ran after them for ten yards before giving up. He kicked a pile of seaweed into the ocean.

"And what were you going to do if you caught up to them?" Lee asked Mr. T, sitting on the beach in front of him, drinking a cup of the snake piss the Copper Quadrant calls whiskey.

"I was going to teach them a lesson about drugs," said Mr. T.

"What for?" Lee said. "Those kids are prostitutes, thieves, and dealers. All they've got is drugs."

"If they got off of drugs who knows what they could do with their lives," Mr. T said.

"There's nothing they can do, Laurence. This is Copper. Once you're in Copper there's no moving up in the world. If you're born in the shit you die in the shit."

"I don't like you're attitude, Lee," said Mr. T. "There's always a hope for a better life. If the people in Copper just came together we could clean up this place. We could turn it into a clean, safe place for children to grow up in."

"How do you plan to do that?"

"Well, first of all, we get rid of the drug problem."

"What?" Lee laughed at him. "It can't be done."

"Don't you think there's a problem with drugs here?"

"Yeah, of course."

"Well, if there's a problem then there's got to be a solution." Mr. T punched his fists together, then said, "And that solution's name is Mr. T."

Haroon and Mr. T go a mile deep into the zombie-packed streets of downtown, blasting their way through the horde. The first zombie that comes up from behind, Mr. T attacks with his spiked club. The bat goes through the zombie's face and gets stuck in its mouth. The zombie bites down and thrashes it out of T's hand, then blindly runs in the opposite direction.

Weaponless, Mr. T looks down at his hands.

"And you said you could trust that weapon better than this?" Haroon asks, holding up his solar-powered shotgun.

Mr. T smiles.

"Just because I don't have a weapon," he says, "doesn't mean I'm not armed." Then he punches a zombie's head off of its shoulders.

The duo go a half mile farther down the street until there are so many zombies they come to a standstill. Haroon can only shoot them down quick enough to hold them back, not quick enough to enable them to move forward. The zombies come at them from all sides.

"They're coming in from behind," Haroon says. "Fall back, to the east."

"We got this!" Mr. T yells, throwing punches at the living dead coming at them.

"Fall back!"

"We got this!"

Haroon breaks away from Mr. T and runs down a side street to get away from the main horde. Mr. T doesn't follow. zombies fill the space between them.

"Come on," Haroon says, trying to shoot a path for his large friend.

But Mr. T keeps on fighting, no matter how bleak the situation looks.

Mr. T learned that the head of the drug trade was Tim Lion. He was the inventor of Waste, and he pretty much owned Copper. The moment he discovered that Tim Lion owned a club in the downtown area of the quadrant, Mr. T decided he was going to give the chump a visit.

He stormed into the club in his red jumpsuit, pushing strippers out of his way and knocking over platters of Waste that were carried by waitresses from table to table. He went straight for the big man in the back, the one in the green top hat.

Tim Lion was surrounded by armed men and naked women. He was drinking a cosmo and eating buttered lobster over pasta.

"Are you Tim Lion?" he asked the man. "Mr. T wants a word with him."

"Who the fuck is Mr. T?" Lion asked.

"You're looking at him, fool!"

The gangster was almost amused by Mr. T's forwardness. He decided to hear him out before he had his men kill him.

"Mr. T don't like the way you're selling drugs to kids," said Mr. T, leaning in as close as possible. "Scum like you give the good folks of Copper a bad name."

"Is this guy for real?" Lion asked.

"I'm going to clean up this town," said Mr. T. "Starting with you."

Tim Lion looked at his men and said, "Get rid of this idiot."

Mr. T clothes-lined one of his men over the back of his chair, and kicked over the table, spilling Lion's food and drink into his lap. The entire bar looked over at them.

"Kill this asshole!" Lion yelled.

Mr. T grabbed a man's wrist before he could draw his gun, then headbutted him, knocking him to the floor. As he raised his fist in Lion's direction, three gunshots rang out across the table. The bullets hit Mr. T square in the chest.

Mr. T continues punching zombies as they come at him, knocking them to the street.

Haroon fires at the zombies furiously. "I can't hold them off much longer."

"Just get out of here," Mr. T yells, tossing a zombie over his shoulder. "I'll be fine."

"I'm not leaving without you," Haroon says.

"I'll be fine," Mr. T says, raising his fist to punch out another zombie.

Before he could throw his punch, a zombie grabs Mr. T's fist and bites down on his arm.

"T!" Haroon yells, as the zombie's teeth break through the fabric of Mr. T's clothing.

Haroon turns and moves on. He knows his friend has to be infected now. There's no hope for him. Haroon has to go on by himself.

As Haroon disappears down the street, Mr. T gives the zombie on his arm a growling face. The zombie growls back, with his arm in its mouth.

"How come this guy isn't dead?" Tim Lion asked his men, as Mr. T still stood there in front of them with three bullets placed directly in his chest.

"He didn't even fall down," one of his men said. "That should have killed him."

Mr. T just glanced down at the holes in his red jumpsuit, then looked up at Tim Lion with a snarl on his face.

"I'm not just Mr. T, fool!" he said, ripping open his clothes to reveal a robot body made of gold-plated stainless steel. "I'm the motherfucking T-2000!"

The zombie's eyes roll with confusion as all of its teeth crumble out of its head. Mr. T throws the corpse to the ground and pulls off his hooded sweatshirt. His golden metal body glimmers in the twilit sky.

Then he swings his fist of steel through three zombies at once, their heads exploding into a splash of red soup.

When Mr. T was cryogenically frozen, they did not preserve his entire body. They only preserved his head. So before Doctor Jacob Wyslen resurrected him, he had built Mr. T a robot body. One that was powerful enough to go on missions into the Red Zone and still come back in one piece. He still had artificial organs and still had to eat, sleep, and breathe like a normal human, but Mr. T's new body was not made of flesh. It was made of steel.

When Wyslen showed Mr. T his new body in a mirror for the first time, Mr. T nodded in approval. Then he pointed at the numbers on the chest.

"T-2000?" Mr. T asked.

"That's the model number," Wyslen said. "The previous one I built was the S-1000. This is the first one that actually kept its host alive. There are several earlier models, but this is the best of them."

"Why did you build these things?"

"I used to think that the best way to survive in a world of the living dead was for mankind to exchange their flesh for machinery."

"That sounds almost as bad as becoming one of those dead things," said Mr. T.

"You're not happy with it?"

"I didn't say that, Doc. Living in a metal body is better than being dead with no body."

"Good."

Mr. T checked his metal musculature out in the mirror, noticing that his muscle size was even larger than his previous life.

"T-2000," Mr. T said to himself. "I like the ring to that." Then he looked more carefully at his hands. "But this drab metal color has got to go…"

"Oh?" asked the doctor. "We can paint it if you want."

"Not paint," said Mr. T, then he pointed at a mountain of gold jewelry in a crate near his cryogenic chamber. "Melt all that down. Mr. T's metal body needs some gold-plating."

Then he gave the doctor a big twinkling smile.

The T-2000 stood in front of Tim Lion in his men. Their mouths dropped open at the sight of him.

"Now do you want to promise to quit selling drugs, or is Mr. T gonna have to pound some sense into the lot of you?"

Machine guns opened fire on him as a response. The bullets ricocheted off of his body, sending sparks into the air. The T-2000 just swatted them away like mosquitoes.

Mr. T punched his fist through a gangster's chest, ripping his heart out through the backside. As the heart stopped beating in his golden hand, Mr. T said, "If you had a *real* heart you'd stop selling drugs to kids."

Then he used the gangster's corpse like a battering ram and drove its head through a bald man's stomach. The bald man puked up his guts as he died.

"All of these scumbags make me want to puke, too," Mr. T said to the dead gangster.

After the T-2000 dismembered and decapitated every last gangster in the club, filling the room with blood and gore, he went for the big man, Tim Lion, who was cowering on the floor in the corner, hiding under his green top hat.

"You better listen to the T-2000," he told the cowering drug lord. "Crime doesn't pay. And even if it does pay, there's taxes on that pay. And the T-2000 is the tax man, come to collect. And he makes sure you pay your taxes in full, on time. And you can't write off nothing, not even a company car."

"What the fuck are you talking about?" Tim Lion asked.

Mr. T thought about it and realized his metaphor had gotten a little too convoluted.

"Forget it," Mr. T said.

Then he ripped the man's brain out through the top of his top hat.

On the way back to his shack on the beach, Mr. T came across the group of kids who had been doing drugs under the peer.

The kids began to shrink and tremble as they saw his blood-coated gold metal body towering over them.

"Don't worry, kids," he said. "I took care of that drug pusher for you. Now you don't have to do drugs anymore. You're going to have a bright future."

Then he gave the kids a bright smile and a thumbs up.

The kids ran away.

As he continued down the street, whistling, a man with a white goatee stepped out of the shadows behind a strip club.

"I want him," the man said to his associates in white masks.

"Now?"

He shook his head. "Wait until he's at home, asleep. I wouldn't want to get any more of you killed after that last guy went psycho on us."

The men in white masks agreed, staring at the large metal man as he strutted happily down the street, envisioning a brighter tomorrow.

HEINZ

Heinz walks casually over charred corpses, heading toward the sound of two fellow contestants. It is the punk kid and that Japanese ex-host of the show. Their shoes are caked in thick meat mud as they trample over piles of mannequin limbs and cat skeletons, fleeing down the alleyway. Heinz hides behind a wall of charred yellow bricks, peeking out at them, ready to unleash a cloud of flames as they pass. But then he notices they are being chased by a pack of weaponized cyborg zombie dogs, snarling and thrashing and firing machinegun ammo. He decides it might be best to keep out of this fight.

Scavy and Junko collapse in a pile of blue flowers growing from black mulch behind a dumpster, catching their breaths.

"Did we lose them?" Junko asks.

Scavy looks back.

"They are chasing one of the floating cameras," he says, watching the mechjaws jumping up and snapping at a floating camera ball. The camera shoots lasers at their feet, trying to scare them away.

Junko laughs. She bets it really pisses off Wayne that his own cameras accidentally distracted the mechjaws long enough for her to escape.

"You think the hippy made it?" Scavy asks, stomping a blue flower into the concrete.

"Probably not," Junko says. "Even if she got away from the dogs and the collapsing building, there's no way a weak little rich girl like her could make it alone out there with only a dagger."

"So what do we do now?"

"It's almost dark," Junko says. "We should find shelter. Very few contestants who try to travel at night survive long."

"Where?" Scavy asks.

Junko points at a tall white castle-shaped building a few blocks down.

"There," she says. "The castle building. It should be safe there until dawn."

They get up and head for the white building, passing Heinz pressed up against a wall with his flamethrower pointed at the ground.

Heinz steps into the street.

"So you're going there, are you?" he says to their backs as they run into the distance. "I'll be sure to kill you there later, you Japanese trash."

Heinz hates the Japanese. He hates all races apart from the superior Aryan race, but the Japanese he hates most of all. That's why Junko is at the top of his hit list.

White people are a minority in Neo New York. The dominant race is Asian, mostly Japanese. After Z-Day, Japan was one of the last countries to be hit with the zombie outbreak and one of the first to learn about it. They had plenty of time to prepare themselves. They fortified their cities, they evacuated VIPs to secure islands in the Pacific, they loaded people onto ships and spread them out into the sea. Of course, none of their efforts worked out according to plan. Letting one infected person into a fortified city would wipe out most of the population within a couple of days. Loading up boats full of people and sending them out to sea keeps them from getting infected, but they're going to run out of food and supplies eventually. Though most of their population was wiped out, Japan still faired better than most countries.

It was the Japanese survivors that helped the American survivors build Neo New York. They had more resources and were better organized. When the class system was established for the construction of Neo New York, the Gold and Platinum Quadrants were populated with mostly Japanese survivors, whereas the Silver and Copper Quadrants were mostly American.

Heinz was born in Silver, in a German-American neighborhood. But as a teenager he was moved to Platinum when his father got a position at the new university that had opened up. It was very rare for entire families to be moved from Silver to Platinum, but they made some exceptions for university faculty. The high school Heinz attended was predominantly Japanese, with some Indian and Chinese students. The few students who were considered white were Jewish or half-Japanese. Heinz was the only blue-eyed blond kid in the school.

The other kids didn't like him. Not only because his eyes, skin, and hair were different, but because he was low class. He had come from Silver. He didn't belong. Because of his white skin, the kids called him Cum Face.

"How's it taste, Cum Face?" a Japanese kid told him as he shoved his face into a mound of dog shit. "Does it taste like home? Did you used to have to eat dog shit for lunch in Silver because your family was so poor?"

Heinz wanted to fight back, but that would only make it worse.

"Maybe we should put shit in your eyes, too, so they won't be blue anymore."

They rubbed shit in his hair, on his skin. Then the group of five Japanese boys kicked him repeatedly. When they were done, they laughed.

"It's a good look for you," one kid said. "You're not quite as ugly with shit all over you."

"From now on," said another, "you have to wear shit all the time. We're sick of looking at your ugly cum skin and snot-colored hair."

Another said, "If we see you and you're not wearing shit on your skin we'll kick your ass."

When Heinz arrived at home covered in shit, his father was displeased with him.

"You let those inferior slanty-eyed rodents do this to you?" his father yelled. "You are Aryan, the descendent of Germans. Have you no pride?"

"But there were five of them," Heinz said.

His father slapped him. "One Aryan is worth a hundred of them.

A million. You are racially superior to them."

His father lifted his shirt to reveal a large black swastika tattooed over his heart.

"Do you see this?" his father said, pointing at his tattoo. "This is a symbol of pride. One day you too will wear this symbol, if you prove worthy of it. You must never cower before such vermin. It is better to die than to shame your race in such a manner."

"I'm the only Aryan in the school," he said.

"One day that will change," his father said. "Until that day you must endure. You must show these scum what a true Aryan is made of. You will not show any weakness. You will prove the quality of your genes. You will show them your race is the master race. Is this clear?"

Heinz nodded and then his father helped him clean the shit off of his face.

Heinz freezes when he hears the sound of growling coming from behind him. He turns around slowly. A large mechjaw is facing him, pointing its Gatling gun at his chest.

"Nice doggy," Heinz says with a smile. The dog growls at him.

Heinz reaches into Adriana's pack and pulls out her weapon: a blowgun. Slowly, without making any sudden moves, he brings the blowgun close to his lips.

"It's okay." His voice calm and soothing. "No need to shoot."

Just as the Gatling gun is about to fire, whirring into motion, Heinz blows a dart into the dog's neck. The gun shuts off before any bullets come out. The dog's body twitches and then falls to the street, paralyzed.

"That's a good dog," Heinz says, placing the blowgun back into the bag.

The nerve toxin in the darts might not do any damage to the undead, but it numbs their muscles and nervous system for a short amount of time, immobilizing them. At first he thought the blowgun would be a useless weapon out here, but now that he's run into a mechjaw he sees how useful it can be.

Heinz kneels down to the undead dog. With his gloved hand, he pets the hair on its slimy head, staring into its black hungry eyes.

"Why aren't you covered in shit?" a Japanese bully asked Heinz the next time they saw him.

There were seven of them this time.

"We told you to wear shit from now on," said another. "Otherwise we'd kick your ass."

"I considered it," Heinz said. "But I decided not to."

Heinz changed directions to take a shortcut behind a shopping center. The bullies followed.

"Why not, Cum Face?"

"Because I didn't want to look like the lot of you," Heinz said.

Two of the bullies got in front of him so that he couldn't move forward anymore.

"What did you say, Cum Face? You saying our skin looks like shit?"

Heinz got in the kid's face. "You heard me, insect. Now get out of my way. I'm sick of looking at your filthy skin."

The kid punched Heinz in the eye. He was wearing an iron skull-shaped ring that cut open the puffy flesh around the Aryan's eyebrow. Heinz looked back at him, a thin trickle of blood on his cheek.

"Don't you dare ever touch me again with those disgusting hands," Heinz said.

The kid punched him again, causing more blood to erupt from his forehead.

"This is your last warning," Heinz said. "Do not touch me again."

The kid raised his arm to throw a third punch. Then Heinz stabbed him in the head with a crab fork. The boy screamed as blood squirted out of the hole on his forehead. Two boys tried to grab the Aryan, but he turned on them before they could pin him down.

Heinz stabbed the thin two-pronged fork into one of their eyes, scooping out the eyeball like a scallop from its shell. The kid dropped to the ground, shrieking. Then Heinz stabbed the other in the neck. This bully did not cry out. He stepped back, holding his neck. A look of horror crossed his face as blood geysered from his jugular over his fingers, showering the pavement and the other bullies.

When they saw this, all of the kids ran away, except for two: the leader with the hole in his forehead and the kid with the neck wound, bleeding to death by Heinz's feet.

"One day all of you cockroaches will fall to the master race,"

Heinz told the lead bully, flicking the eyeball off the crab fork.

The bully cried at Heinz, begging for mercy. The blood from his stab wound ran down his nose and mixed with his tears.

"I'm sorry," said the bully. "I'm so sorry."

As the bully's friend lay motionless in a puddle of blood, a horrible stench of feces filled the air. The kid had shit his pants after he died.

Heinz looked at the dead kid's ass.

"I want you to smear his shit all over your face and hair," Heinz said, impersonating the Japanese kid's voice. "If you don't I'll kick your ass."

The bully cried as he pulled handfuls of shit out his dead friend's pants and rubbed it on his skin and hair. The shit collected in the hole on his head, mixing with the blood and crumbs of skull.

"That is why your race is pitiful," Heinz said, bringing the crab fork to the kid's throat. "An Aryan would never disgrace himself like that, no matter what the cost."

Night falls and the streets fill with the living dead. A cloud covering blocks out all light from the moon and stars, drowning the city in black. The only thing that lights Heinz' way is the fire from his flamethrower and the burning corpses as they hit the ground.

The zombie mob stretches as far as he can see in all directions, a great sea of writhing molten flesh. The fifteen foot circle around Heinz is the only empty space that he can see for blocks.

In this close of a fight, Heinz discovers a major problem with using a flamethrower as his weapon: flaming zombies. After he burns them, they do not immediately fall to the ground. They continue shambling toward him with their flesh on fire, trying to wrap themselves around him. If the zombies get too close to the gas canisters on his back it is likely to cause an explosion.

Heinz has to switch between the flamethrower and Brick's double-fisted sledgehammer. Once he ignites the zombies and the flaming corpses come after him, he swings the sledge at their midsections and sends them hurling back into the crowd.

Up ahead, Heinz notices two small lights in the sky. When he focuses his vision, he can tell they are flashlights shining from the window of an office building a few blocks down. Somebody is camping out there for the night.

Heinz knows his fuel tank won't last for much longer if he continues using it at this rate. He'll have to move indoors as soon as possible. Perhaps whoever is camping up there in that building has a secure enough setup to last through the night. He decides to make that his destination. Whoever is up there, they will have to share their shelter with him if they want to live.

When Heinz returned home to his father covered in blood, his father was furious. Heinz proudly told him the story of how he stood up to those Japanese insects.

"You idiot," his father yelled. "You've ruined everything!"

Heinz didn't understand.

"I've spent twenty years trying to get to the position I am at now. There are only three other members of the Brotherhood who have infiltrated the Platinum Quadrant."

"The Brotherhood?"

"The Brotherhood of the Fifth Reich. Our mission is to take this island from those slanty-eyed rodents and convert this nation into a proud Aryan state, under Nazi control. We have people in key positions all over the island. When you were old enough, you too were supposed to play a crucial role in the uprising. Then you went and murdered the sons of important government officials."

"It was self-defense," Heinz said.

"It doesn't matter," his father said. "You don't have a future anymore. You can't stay here."

"Where will I go?"

"Pack your things," his father said. "I'm going to send you off of the island, to join the others."

"What others?"

"The rest of our forces," said his father. "The Fists of the Fifth Reich."

Heinz fights his way into the lobby of the building, the zombie mass flooding in behind him. The door to the stairwell is electronically locked. With his back against the wall, he has no other choice but to get through this way. He uses the sledgehammer on the window, which is just a thin strip of plexi-glass down the upper left side of the door. The first blow does nothing. The second swing creates a popping noise. Heinz turns around and blows fire at the mob as it closes in. With the third swing, he uses all of his strength. He won't have time for a fourth.

"Brains!" cries the mob of molten flesh reaching for him.

The glass breaks open. Heinz sticks his hand through the hole and opens the door from the inside. He enters and shuts the door behind him. The undead reach their arm through the slot, but likely aren't intelligent enough to get the door open.

Heinz climbs the stairs, using the tiny flame of his weapon to lead him through the dark. As he takes the first flight, he hears the sounds of the undead in the stairwell a few floors down. They are coming up from the underground parking levels, attracted to the echoes of his human footsteps.

The nazis claim there were five notable reichs in history. The Holy Roman Empire was the First Reich. The Great German Empire of 1871-1918 was the Second Reich. When Adolf Hitler was in power, he created the Third Reich which was the birth of Nazism. The Fourth Reich, formed by postwar neo-nazis, was an underground movement that attempted to bring nazi values back to the Aryan people. Now there is the Fifth Reich, which formed soon after Z-Day, after the fall of civilization.

It started with a group of neo-nazi skinheads who had survived in a bunker in Tennessee. They welcomed all survivors into their facility, but only Aryans who supported their ideals were allowed to join them. All others were fed to the undead for their amusement. They grew in numbers until they were able to embark on an exodus toward the coast, where they found their new home for the next forty years: a nuclear-powered aircraft carrier. And, like most nuclear-powered vessels of the time, it had enough uranium fuel in its reactors to last them for several decades.

After they cleared the ship of naval zombies and claimed it for their own, they named it the Fifth Reich.

Their mission was to redesign the new world in the way God had intended: a world dominated by the one true master race. They created a breeding program. Aryan women became breeding slaves whose only purpose was to bear their young. Only the purest, strongest, and most intelligent Aryans were allowed to breed with them. Heinz's father was born through this breeding program. He was bred to be a leader, a man who would one day bring their ideals to the people of Neo New York.

Heinz was delivered to the aircraft carrier by a small fishing boat, owned by brothers of the Fifth Reich living in Copper. On the boat ride over, Heinz imagined how majestic this colony of Aryans must be. A nation of proud, mighty white men. But when he arrived, it was not at all as he expected it to be. Things had changed greatly since the day his father had left the Brotherhood to infiltrate the island of Neo New York.

The people on the ship were starving and weak. They had long lost hope of ever taking the island. And worst of all, they were no longer proud of their race. Since the majority of them had never even met a member of another race, they didn't understand what was so special about their own. They didn't understand their own magnificence.

"What is wrong with these people?" Heinz asked the Captain of the ship. "They are weak and have no spirit in them. Do you call this an army?"

The Captain leaned back in his chair and put his shredded boots onto his desk.

"It hasn't been an army for a long time," said the Captain. "Not since I've been in charge of this ship. My predecessor was your grandfather, a stubborn idealistic fool who was so determined to build a grand army that he didn't realize that we didn't have the food and resources to support so many men. He overpopulated the ship. The men were starving, but your grandfather didn't care. All he cared about was preparing for a war that was never going to happen."

"What happened to him?"

"He was killed by his own men. After he cut their rations down to a fifth, his men couldn't take it anymore. They shot him dead one night while he was sleeping. As his second in command, I took over the ship. I promised these people we would focus entirely on our own survival and forget about the war. You might think those men out there are starving and weak, but they are much better off than they were five years ago."

Heinz slammed his fist on the table.

"Better off?" Heinz yelled. "They would be better off dead than the pathetic wretches they have become. Your men are the Fists of the Fifth Reich. They should have the intelligence to thrive even in the harshest of circumstances. If you were a proper leader you would

147

not have let this become of your men."

"What the fuck do you know, kid?" the Captain said. "Since birth you've lived in the luxury of the Platinum District. What do you know of hardship and survival? You've had everything you could possibly want."

"I have not lived long in Platinum. I was born in the slums of the Silver District."

The Captain laughed. "The slums of Silver? Any one of these men would kill the both of us just to live one year in Silver. Even the people in Copper have better lives than most of the men on this ship."

"It doesn't matter where I'm from," Heinz said. "I am Aryan and I will not allow my people to live like scum."

"Get out of my office," the Captain said. "I'm through talking to you. You'll learn soon enough."

"And you'll learn just what a true Aryan can do," Heinz said on the way out the door. "The Fists of the Fifth Reich will be strong once again. Stronger than ever before. I will make certain of that."

"Sure, kid. Just get the fuck out of here."

By the end of his first day on the ship, Heinz decided he would make it his mission to bring pride back to these fallen people. He would bring them out of the muck and restore them to the great people they were destined to be.

When Heinz arrives at the lighted floor of the office building, the door to the stairwell is wide open. He looks up ahead to see the lights coming from an office a few doors down. He shuts the door behind him, and creeps toward the sound of voices.

"You're making me sick," says a female voice.

Another female voice giggles and moans.

"It's so fucking hot," says the other voice.

"It's disgusting."

When Heinz peeks around the corner into the room, he finds two women in punk clothing. The one with the green hair is facing the other, completely naked with her hands in her crotch, her back arched. Upon closer inspection, Heinz realizes that the green-haired punk has a severed zombie head in her lap. All of its teeth have been removed so that it doesn't bite into her. She writhes and moans as the zombie licks and gums her clit and labia, trying to eat her flesh. Black slime leaks from the corpse's cheeks down the girl's inner thighs.

"Make me cum," Gogo tells the zombie head, then she licks her lips at the camera ball floating above them.

Popcorn is sitting on the floor, cringing at her friend's unsettling display. She watches as Gogo whimpers and sweats with ecstasy.

"Oh fuck," Gogo cries. "You don't know what you're missing."

As she comes closer to orgasm, Gogo shoves the head so hard into her crotch that the zombie's lower jaw breaks in half. She pulls the head beneath her body and presses all of her weight against it, crying out as she cums. The skull cracks open like an egg and her ass crushes it flat against the seat of the chair.

When Gogo stands up, stretching and rubbing the zombie goo covering her buttocks, she looks down at the remains of the zombie head. It is now just a puddle of bone and slimy meat on the chair. One of its eyeballs rolls to the side of the mush to stare at Gogo as she rubs its liquid flesh up her crotch to her breasts.

"That was amazing," she tells the remains of her undead lover.

Popcorn drops her face into her hand and groans. It was bad enough her friend had sex with that corpse, but rubbing its rancid jellied flesh on her body goes too far. That smell is going to linger. Popcorn doesn't know if she's going to be able to handle being around Gogo for very long. When Popcorn takes her hand away from her eyes, she sees a man standing in the doorway over Gogo's shoulder.

Heinz steps into the office with a look of disgust and rage on his face. When Gogo turns around to him, she goes for her submachine gun on the desk. Heinz kicks her in the chest and she falls back. He casually takes the machine gun from the desk and points it at them.

"You filthy whores," Heinz says to them. "How can you degrade yourselves in this manner?"

Gogo laughs at him. Heinz steps forward and backhand slaps her so hard she falls to the ground. While the nazi isn't looking, Popcorn flats her bangs into her face so that the guy doesn't see the bullet hole in her head.

"My eyes tell me that you are Aryan women. Perhaps your ancestry is not Nordic or Germanic, but you look at least Celtic or Anglo-Saxon."

The girls have no idea what he's talking about. Those raised in Copper are usually ignorant of race and ancestry.

"You whores dishonor your race," Heinz says. "It is bad enough that you defile your beautiful white skin with tattoos and metal jewelry, and conceal your blonde hair behind unnatural colors, but you also do *this*." He points at the puddle of zombie head twitching on the chair. "You corrupt your pure flesh by this shameful disgusting act."

Gogo snickers again, but then holds her tongue when she sees the fury in his eyes.

"You are Aryan, you should be proud of your race," Heinz told a group of teenagers about his age. They were on the deck of the ship, drinking homemade liquor and lying around when they were supposed to be working in the greenhouses. "You look like a bunch of pathetic mongrels. Your laziness shames your race."

"Shut the fuck up," one of them told him.

Heinz went to the boy who spoke, took the bottle out of his hand and tossed it overboard.

"What the hell did you do that for?"

Four of the boys stood up to him.

"I'm helping you become a proper Aryan," he told them. "Liquor makes you weak."

One of them pushed Heinz. "I'm going to beat the fuck out of you, rich boy. You come in here and tell us how to live? You lived on the island your whole life. What do you know?"

The boys closed in on him.

"I know that you've let yourself become weak and lazy," said Heinz. "I know that you won't be able to lay a finger on me, because all of you have forgotten how to be strong."

One of the boys came at him from behind. Heinz dodged and elbowed him in the stomach. He punched two others in the face and tossed the fourth face-first into the ground. The rest of the boys got up and came after him, but one at a time he knocked them down. When it was over, Heinz was the only one standing. The others lay on the ground, gripping their sore ribs or bloodied faces.

Heinz went to the first of them, towering over him with his blond hair blowing in the ocean wind. The kid cowered beneath him.

"Brother…" Heinz said, holding out his hand to the bloodied kid. "Don't cower like a worm. You are Aryan."

The boy stopped cowering and took Heinz's hand.

As the boy got to his feet, Heinz patted him on the shoulder and said, "Come with me. I will teach you how to be strong."

The other boys stood up and gathered around him. It was the beginning of a new army of the Fifth Reich.

Popcorn notices Heinz is carrying Brick's sledgehammer. Her heart sinks in her chest when she realizes what must have happened to her boyfriend.

"Where did you get that?" she says, pointing at the hammer strapped to Heinz's back.

Heinz glances over his shoulder at it. "I took it from one of those walking corpses."

"That was Brick's weapon!" Popcorn cries. "My boyfriend. Is he okay?"

Heinz frowns. "I'm sorry to say, but your boyfriend has joined the ranks of the living dead."

"I know that," she says. "But was he okay?"

Heinz is confused by the question.

"He's at peace," Heinz says. "I incinerated his remains earlier today."

"You mother fucker!" Popcorn says, getting to her feet.

She holds herself back from charging the guy and ripping out his throat. The submachine gun pointed at her belly holds her at bay.

"You were planning on fucking his corpse like your whore friend, weren't you?" Heinz asked. "It's a good thing I saved you from such blasphemy."

A loud crash out in the hallway causes the two girls to jump. Heinz backs up into the hall, his gun still pointed at the girls. Behind the door to the stairwell, a crowd of zombies have gathered, slamming on the door and shouting. The glass has broken out of the window and three skeletal arms reach through. When they see Heinz in the hallway, the zombies thrash wildly.

"Brains!" the zombies cry.

"Cerebros!" cries a Mexican zombie.

When Heinz recognizes the Mexican zombie, his eyebrows curl with disgust. He marches toward the door, aims the submachine gun through the window slit at the undead Mexican, and fires until the zombie's face is shredded with holes. As he turns away, two figures race across the hall.

"Run," Rainbow yells at Gogo, as the two girls try to escape from the crazed nazi.

Gogo lags behind her friend, trying to put on her clothes as she runs. Heinz fires the machine gun at the ceiling. Because the gun is silenced, the noise isn't intimidating enough to get Popcorn to stop running.

"Don't move, whore," Heinz says.

Gogo stops in her tracks, but continues dressing herself. Heinz goes to her with the barrel of the gun pointed at her face.

"Tell your friend to come out or I'll put a bullet in your head," Heinz says.

Gogo opens her mouth to yell to Popcorn, but instead she pukes all over Heinz's shoes. The puke is a rancid pile of rotten zombie intestines, brains, half-digested flesh, and the head of a zombie dick. Heinz steps back at the offensive smell.

"Call your friend," he says, shifting his face away from the direction of the vomit.

Gogo coughs and gags as she pulls a long intestine from her throat. As it plops on the ground, she spits and wipes green acidic mucous off of her tongue with her fingers.

"Call your friend!"

Gogo looks up at him with disgust, then stands up and does as he says. Popcorn doesn't make an appearance.

"If you don't come out your friend is dead," Heinz says. "I'll give you only three seconds to come out."

Gogo looks up at Heinz's shiny forehead as he points his gun at her.

"One," Heinz says.

Gogo is becoming aroused by the look of his forehead. The way it gleams in the dim lighting. The smoothness of his white Aryan skin. She wants to lick it and rub her body against it.

"Two."

Licking her lips and inching forward, Gogo's eyes go wild with hunger, realizing that it isn't his forehead that's attracting her but the brain inside of his skull. She wants to bite open his skull and pull out his brain. She wants to put it between her legs and fuck the brainstem.

"Three."

Gogo opens her mouth and goes for Heinz, but the nazi shoves the silencer down her throat.

"Don't!" Popcorn cries, stepping into the hallway. "Don't shoot her."

Gogo sucks on the silencer seductively, eying Heinz as if she wants to eat him alive.

When Heinz sees her giving the gun a blowjob, he pulls it out of her mouth and pushes her back.

"Disgusting whore," he says. Then he turns to Popcorn. "Don't try running away from me again. Next time I will fire without warning."

Gogo rubs her breasts and smiles at Heinz. Everything about the nazi is beginning to turn her on. From his uniform to the way he holds his weapon to the electricity flowing through the nerves under his skin. As she rubs her breasts, she feels a stiffness in her chest. She presses her hand to her chest and listens closely, but doesn't hear anything. She no longer has a heartbeat.

"So, we now have only minutes before those walking corpses get through that door," Heinz says. "Help me find a way out of here and I might let you live."

Gogo and Popcorn look at each other. When Popcorn notices Gogo's condition, she winks. They know that Heinz can't kill them if they are already dead.

"Now," Heinz says. "Let's get to work."

Then he leads them down the hallway, away from the undead.

Over the course of a few years, Heinz collected followers among the wretched starving youths of the Fifth Reich. He inspired them to hold their heads up high, to work hard, and believe in the future of the Aryan race. Eventually, his men were practically running the ship. They were the strongest, most skilled members of the Aryan population. They were organized and little by little they improved the living conditions of their brothers.

"I'm taking over the ship," Heinz said to the Captain of the Fifth Reich.

The Captain looked at Heinz. No longer was Heinz a teenaged kid, he was now a fully-grown man and a leader. Behind Heinz, stood a row of his soldiers, armed with shotguns. The Captain stood up from his desk and removed his hat.

"I'm grateful to have you on board," said the Captain. "You have helped discipline and motivate the men. I haven't seen the ship run so smoothly in over a decade."

"So you will relinquish your command?" Heinz asked.

"No," said the Captain.

Heinz nodded at his lieutenant. Then all of his men pumped their shotguns and pointed them at the Captain.

"I beg of you, Heinz," said the Captain. "Our people need food, not war. You don't yet have the experience to run this ship. I'd like you to become my second in command. You can learn the ropes, see what it means to be the leader of this ship before you sit in the Captain's chair. Then you will understand where I'm coming from."

The Captain held out his hand in friendship.

"You are weak," Heinz told the old man. "I would never serve under such a pathetic coward. It is your weakness that allowed this ship to fall into disrepair. It is because of you that your people have fallen into such a pitiable state."

"And you think you can do better?" asked the Captain. "You think you can reshape these people into the Fists of the Fifth Reich?"

"No," Heinz said. "That army died a long time ago. We are now the Hammers of the Fifth Reich. And within five years time, I promise the island of Neo New York will be ours."

Then Heinz turned his back on the old man.

"Don't listen to him," said the Captain. "If you attack Neo New York you will fail. They have superior weapons and a larger military force. If you follow this man you will die."

As Heinz left the room, his men closed in on the ex-Captain. After the chorus of shotgun blasts, Heinz placed the Captain's hat on his scalp. Marching down the hallway with his head held high, whistling Wagner's *Das Rheingold—the Entry of the Gods into Valhalla*.

Heinz takes the girls from office to office, trying to find another way out.

Gogo twitches and holds her stomach as she walks. Popcorn wraps her arm around her shoulder, trying to hold her upright so that the nazi doesn't realize she's infected.

"Are you okay?" Popcorn whispers.

"Hungry," Gogo responds, looking over her shoulder at Heinz. She widens her mouth at him, imagining what it would be like to suck on his fat moist brain.

Although Popcorn never hungers for food, Gogo couldn't be more different. Gogo is indulgent. She is always hungry for food, drugs, and sex. The three are inseparable to her. She finds the act of eating erotic and sensual. Gogo's voluptuous body is as close as any citizen of Copper comes to being fat. Not many people have the money to gorge themselves in the poor quadrant. But with the money she takes in as a stripper and prostitute, Gogo has enough to indulge on rich, greasy foods whenever she wants. She is always either fucking or eating or doing Waste.

Unlike Popcorn, Gogo wants to eat brains. She craves to taste a piece of Heinz's brain. She craves to lay her body in a bed of brains. She craves to lick, suck, and fuck brains all day long.

When she rolls her tongue out of her mouth at Heinz and sucks on the tips of her fingers, Heinz believes the slut is just trying to seduce him into letting his guard down. He has no idea what depraved thoughts are going through her head at the moment. Popcorn yanks her friend forward, trying to get her eyes off of the nazi. If Heinz catches on that the two of them are undead he will surely incinerate them as he did to Brick.

After searching the entire floor, it seems as if the stairwell is the only way out. They either need to barricade the collapsing door or figure out a way to fight through the undead.

"So what are we going to do?" Popcorn asks.

"We fight our way through," Heinz says.

Within five years, Heinz had turned the Aryans of the Fifth Reich into a lean fighting force. Overpopulation had been the problem under the previous Captains' reigns, but Heinz solved that by starting the Population Control Program. His men exterminated all Aryans who proved too weak or too useless to join the Hammers of the Fifth Reich. They also exterminated anyone who disapproved of their methods or seemed disloyal to the commander in chief. He executed many of the breeding slaves, stating that they would have plenty of new breeding slaves after they took Neo New York. It was not the time to raise children. It was the time they answered their calling and finally took what was rightfully theirs.

When he tried to send word to his father in Platinum, Heinz learned that his father had died a few years back. Then he tried to get in contact with other operatives who had infiltrated the island, but the majority of them were no longer supportive of the Fifth Reich. They had become fat and lazy, content with the luxurious lifestyle of Neo New York. They cared more of their own happiness than that of their brothers. They had been dominated by lesser races for so long that it no longer bothered them.

This setback was not enough to dissuade Heinz from his mission. He directed the nuclear-powered aircraft carrier for Neo New

York and went into battle.

"Mein Fuhrer?" said a young soldier to Heinz.

Heinz stopped marching and turned to his soldier. The boy was only twelve-years-old, but he wore his uniform with pride, holding his rifle tightly to his shoulder, standing in line with troops twice his age. Under Heinz's command, children had to pull their weight just as much as the adults. Those who could not pull their weight were put to death. He wasn't willing to waste precious food and water on children who could not work or fight. His men could always make more children later, once they had achieved their goal.

As Heinz looked down on the child soldier, the boy smiled up at him. He was so excited to fight for their cause.

"Yes, soldier?" said Heinz, annoyed that the boy spoke without first asking permission.

"Are we really going to win?" asked the boy. "Are we actually going to live on the island and have all the food we can eat?"

Heinz placed his hand on the child's soldier and smiled.

"Lieutenant?" Heinz asked the man standing by his side.

"Sir?" asked the Lieutenant.

"Have this soldier shot," Heinz said, his smile turning to a frown. "I don't need men who lack faith in our strength. A true Aryan would know that our victory is ensured."

The boy's face deflated beneath his leader, tears filling his eyes. The boy cried out as the Lieutenant grabbed him by the arm and pulled him out of the line. He cried not because his life was about to end, but because he disappointed his leader.

As the gun was fired and the body fell into the sea, Heinz marched down the line to find any other weak-willed soldiers that had to be weeded out. Such men did not deserve the honor of battle.

"We cannot possibly fail," Heinz told himself, over and over again.

Heinz directs the two women to lead the way down the stairwell. The three of them face the door as its metal frame bends inward.

"How are we supposed to fight them with these?" Popcorn asks, holding up a chair.

Heinz wasn't about to hand over any of his weapons to the girls, so he gave them each a chair to fight the living dead with.

"All you have to do is shove them back," Heinz said. "If any of them get past you I will take them down."

Gogo leans against her chair, eying the nazi's body up and down. The hunger builds stronger in her by the second. She's finding the man completely irresistible. Her mouth fills with drool. She's dying to sink her teeth into his moist fleshy brain.

"You know how fucking strong those things are?" Popcorn asks. "Especially when there's so many of them."

"You have no choice," Heinz says. "You do what I say or you will die."

Popcorn groans at him and points her chair at the door.

"Fine," she says. "Let's get this over with."

Heinz gets behind the two girls, pointing the submachine gun at their backs.

"Open it," he says.

Heinz had no idea the military of Neo New York was so large. The aircraft carrier was such a huge vessel that it was seen by the island's Coast Guard from miles away. This gave the island's military leaders plenty of time to put all naval forces into action. By the time the Fifth Reich arrived to the island, the carrier was surrounded by hundreds of ships. Heinz had a thousand men in his army, but the military of Neo New York was two hundred thousand strong. He had the largest ship, but it was not enough to put up much of a fight against his enemy.

"One Aryan is worth a thousand of them," Heinz told his men, his voice shaking as he spoke. "They do not stand a chance against us."

The men looked around at each other, stepping out of line, staring at the battleships approaching them. They instantly reverted back to the small weak wretches they had been before Heinz had become their leader.

"Victory will be ours!" Heinz said. "We are Aryans! We are the master race!"

His words inspired only anger in the men. They now realized that they had been led astray. They had believed in his stupid impossible dream. They had allowed him to take advantage of them. They had killed their friends, their wives, and their children for him, because he convinced them it was for the good of their people. They had believed all of his bullshit and now they were back where they had started.

The Coast Guard warships ordered the aircraft carrier to turn around or they would consider them hostile and attack. The Fifth Reich didn't put up a fight. They turned the ship around and fled into the sea. The nazis didn't stand a chance. Not because they were outnumbered, but because the Coast Guard knew they were coming. The government had long known about the Fists of the Fifth Reich and their plans to attack the island.

It only took a single member of the Brotherhood to ruin their secret plans. An Aryan living in Gold had fallen in love with a Japanese woman, had a family with her, and realized he no longer wanted the Fifth Reich to succeed. After killing two of his Aryan brothers in self-defense, he came forward and explained to the government everything he knew about the Fifth Reich. The government would have sent out their troops right then and there, but they decided the Fifth Reich wasn't much of a threat to them.

After the Aryans returned to their home waters, they put Heinz and his top officers on a boat and sent them adrift with no food or water. Starved and ill, they eventually made their way back to Neo New York. The Coast Guard allowed them to live in Copper with the rest of the white trash, because they knew that these nazis would work well on the Zombie Survival show. Wayne "The Wiz" Rizla paid the Coast Guard well every time they allowed a newcomer with potential into the Copper Quadrant.

With a small band of men and a new life in Copper, Heinz was determined never to give up the fight. He was beaten, but not defeated. He vowed to build a new army of men out of the citizens in Copper. They would rise up and take the island one quadrant at a time and someday Neo New York would become a utopian Aryan nation as it always should have been.

Only one month after he arrived on the island, before gaining a single new recruit, Heinz was gassed in the bathroom of a Filipino she-male whore house. When Wayne Rizla stood over his unconscious body, he chuckled to himself, noticing the line of she-male cum dribbling from the nazi's chin.

When Popcorn opens the door to the stairwell, the zombies spill in. But they don't go for the two punk girls at all, they rush right past them and go directly for Heinz. Heinz wasn't prepared for that. Frozen in shock, confused over why the zombies ignored the girls, Heinz

158

suddenly finds himself surrounded by the living dead. He opens fire on them as they grab at his sleeves.

Popcorn drops her chair and says, "Later, asshole!"

Then she grabs Gogo and pulls her into the stairwell. Furious, Heinz fires a few rounds into the girls' backs, but they do not fall. The bullets hardly faze them. He watches as their pink and green heads disappear into the mob of zombies.

Heinz steps backward, firing into the undead as they fill the room. When the gun runs out of bullets, he drops it on the floor.

"Brains!" the zombies cry, closing in on him.

Heinz closes his eyes and takes a deep breath, allowing the powerful orchestral music of Wagner fill his heart. He feels the blood of a strong Aryan warrior pumping through his veins. He tells himself he must survive, he must win this competition, because there is so much more work to be done.

Just before the zombies reach him, he opens his eyes. Then he digs his hand into his pack and pulls out the severed head of a mechjaw. Like a wet glove, he shoves his fist through the neck of the beast and grabs it by the brain. Then he straps the mechjaw's Gatling gun to his arm.

After he had paralyzed the mechjaw back on the road, Heinz realized that he could use the creature as a weapon. Because it was the dog's brain that controlled its weaponry, all Heinz needed to take was its head and the minigun.

The dog's skinless severed head snarls in the air, as Heinz points it at the zombies.

"I have a Japanese cunt to kill," Heinz tells the shambling corpses. "And you're all in my way."

Then he squeezes the dog's brain and the mechjaw's Gatling gun shreds the zombie crowd into thousands of tiny pieces.

XIU

Far ahead of all of the other contestants, the three merc punks traverse the wasteland. They cross a rail yard in the industrial side of the city, ducking through overturned train cars rusted into the earth. Normally merc punks would never travel through zombie territory at night, but the mercs don't have time to stop for rest. They have to accomplish their mission and get to the helicopter before any of the other contestants.

"Which way?" Zippo asks Xiu, in Spanish.

Xiu takes her homemade metal sunglasses from her eyes and examines the map. Zippo shines his flashlight, tied to his automatic shotgun, over her shoulder so she can see.

"East by northeast for a mile," Xiu says. "Then east. We should get there early in the day tomorrow if we keep moving. Then we should be able to make it to the helicopter before dark."

Behind them, Vine stands on a fallen train car, keeping a look out. The area seems free of the living dead, but he knows not to let his guard down. Standing still, even in a remote area, is always more dangerous than being on the move. Those things always tend to sneak up on you out of nowhere when you least expect it.

Vine watches every structure in the vicinity carefully, especially the fallen train. It looks as if a dump truck had crashed into the train decades ago, causing a pileup. Any one of those overturned train cars could be filled with the undead. Vine eyes each one carefully, watching for movement, and watches the top of the hill on the other side of the rail yard, and watches for other zombies that might have followed them in there.

He does all of this without moving his head an inch, not making a sound. Merc punks know that zombies are attracted to movement and noise. Merc punks are trained as children how to stand perfectly still for hours on end, even in the most awkward positions. Vine's body is contorted in unnatural ways, his limbs bent and twisted, his AK-47 crossing his chest like a crucifix. He's so motionless that he looks more like an abstract steel sculpture than a human being. He does this to camouflage his body against the twisted rusted metal of the wrecked train surrounding him. Blending in with the surroundings is another skill merc punks are taught since childhood. It is something they all are trained to perfect.

Over the last five decades, merc punks have developed zombie survival skills that are unknown to the rest of civilization. They know to cover their eyes with sunglasses or masks, because looking into a human's eyes is the major way zombies can tell the difference between the living and the dead. There are other ways zombies can smell them out of a crowd, but looking into a human's eyes is a sure way to drive a zombie wild with hunger.

They also know how to fight their way through a horde using only a small amount of ammo. They know how to sleep in the same room with the undead, without ever being discovered. They know how to debilitate a zombie in less than a second, using any found object from a rock to a hubcap to a pencil. They know the types of places where zombies are most likely to hibernate. They know how zombies hunt their prey. They know how the zombies think.

Xiu puts the map away. She hydrates herself with a water bottle, just two sips, then pours some water down her face and scalp, and rubs it across her short black mohawk. Zippo sits motionless, awaiting Xiu's command.

Merc punks always move in threes. When they work together, they are no longer three individuals. They are one being. They are one Head and two Arms. In this unit, Xiu is the Head, Vine is the Right Arm, Zippo is the Left Arm.

Xiu does all of the thinking for them. Vine is the fast, quick-striking spearhead. Zippo is the sturdy backup. Ever since they were children, this is how it has been. Once they came together, they were no longer individuals. They were one unit, with Xiu in complete command of their every action and thought. Not just in the wasteland, but every waking moment, even when they were back home, on their ship.

Xiu was not born of merc punk blood. She was adopted into the family nineteen years ago, at age seven. She doesn't remember anything before they found her. Decades after Z-Day, they found her wandering through the wasteland in South America, unarmed, all alone, and behaving as if nothing was wrong in the world.

They didn't call themselves *merc punks*. That's the term Neo New Yorkers gave them. They call themselves *The Mongols*, which was the name of the biker gang that originally started their tribe over 50 years ago. The Mongols are mostly of Hispanic descent, consisting of survivors from the pacific coasts of North and South America. Although many of the original Mongols came from the American biker gang of the same name, most of its members came from gangs of urban South American street punks that were slowly accumulated over the years. These punks were wild and tough, surviving not on the road or on the seas but on their own two feet.

By the time Xiu was adopted by the Mongols, the tribe was over 500 warriors strong. They had a fleet of ships that patrolled up and down the pacific coasts of the Americas. Once a day, ships would drop off three-man units all along the coast. The units would go half a day deep into the wasteland, collect all the resources they needed, then return to the coast to be picked up by nightfall.

They found Xiu in Chile. A unit of Mongols went into La Serena, collecting food and medical supplies, when they came across her casually spray-painting graffiti on the walls as zombies roamed the streets in the area. At seven years old, she was wearing five-inch platform combat boots two sizes too large, three tattoos, a lip ring, and a black and red mohawk.

"Wh-what are you doing, little girl?" The Head of a Mongol unit asked her in Mexican Spanish.

Xiu shrugged and stepped back to examine her painting on the half-collapsed brick wall.

She responded in Chilean Spanish. "Making art."

"Are you all alone out here?" he asked.

She shrugged again. "Yeah."

The Head of the unit held out his hand.

"My name is Carlos. You should come with us."

Xiu never remembers this when she's asked about it. She doesn't remember anything from back then. The Mongols guess that she came from a band of Chilean punks who had survived in the wasteland for several decades all on their own. They aren't sure if she is the only survivor from that group or if she had become separated from them at some point. Either way, they decided to take her with them. Not because they pitied her, but because they were impressed by how a seven-year-old girl could survive in the wasteland all by herself for so long without difficulty. There was also a youth unit within their clan that was in need of a new Head. These Mongols knew this girl had the smarts to be a unit leader.

Vine spends so much time examining each of the train cars for hidden zombies, that he doesn't notice the zombies crawling out of the wrecked dump truck behind Xiu and Zippo.

"Let's go," Xiu says, and turns to face several figures lunging out of the shadows toward her.

There are a dozen of them. All children. The zombies had been hibernating inside of the gravel-filled dump truck for so long that their flesh has become coated in a layer of gravel fused to their rotten flesh.

"Behind you," Xiu yells at Zippo as four more come out behind him.

Xiu throws one of her hand-axes at an undead child coming at Zippo, but the blade just bounces off of its gravel skin.

"Run," Xiu says.

They leap out from the middle of the gravel creatures, and loop around toward Vine. Zippo fires two shells into a zombie in their path, causing bits of stone to fly in the air. The zombie is pushed back, but the blast does no real damage to its body.

Vine drops to the ground and fires his AK-47 at the creatures, slowing them down a bit until his friends get behind him. Then the three continue through the rail yard.

Xiu looks back at the rocky figures lumbering across the train tracks. Stones in their mouths clack together as they try to cry out for *brains*. The undead children come after them, but are too weighed down by their heavy gravel skin to catch up.

"Move out," Xiu says.

As they turn to go up the hill out of the rail yard, they see a horde of zombies assembling above them, drawn to the sound of gunfire. Before they reach the bottom of the hill, they realize that there are hundreds of them up there. The largest mob of zombies they have encountered yet.

"Is there a way around?" Zippo asks.

Xiu shakes her head. "We go through."

Without second thought, Vine dashes forward, ready to cut them a path through the crowd.

"Conserve your ammo if possible," Xiu says in her Chilean accent. "We still have a long way to go."

Xiu has retained her Chilean accent for all these years, and being the dominant member of her unit her two men conformed to her way of speaking and developed the accent as well.

Mongol units are chosen at birth. They are matched up the day they are separated from their birth parents, when they are old enough to walk. These children grow up together, their lives intertwined, as inseparable as conjoined twins. When a unit is matched together, they are immediately assigned their position in the unit: Head, Right Arm, or Left Arm. Sometimes these positions are determined at random, other times they are determined based on their early behavior or the strength of their birth parents. Whoever becomes the Head is the one who decides how their unit behaves, thinks, moves, and reacts. The two Arms completely conform to their Head's ideals, tastes, opinions, and mannerisms, mimicking their leader in every possible way.

"Although you were not born a Mongol," Carlos said, taking young Xiu aboard his crew's ship. "You will become the Head of a Mongol unit."

Xiu nodded, but didn't have any idea what he was talking about. She boarded their ship in her clunky combat boots and scale mail vest, looking around the vessel as if it was a spaceship from another world. The ship was patch-worked together with scrap metal and dozens of different types of wood salvaged from several different sources. It had been repaired and reinforced many times over the decades. The Mongols around her were all grouped into threes, some of them mopping the deck together, some drinking papaya wine together, some sharpening swords together.

Although each Mongol unit was a tight family, all of the units on a Mongol ship were an extended family. They called this extended family their *crew*.

"Hi!" Xiu said to a unit of older Mongols.

They ignored her, drinking wine and playing cards.

"I'm Xiu," she said.

Carlos took her away from their table.

"They won't recognize you while you are an individual," Carlos said. "Individuals are ghosts to the Mongols. You must be joined with your unit before anyone will recognize you. Otherwise you will be ignored."

"You don't ignore me?" Xiu looked up at him and his unit, her chubby round face covered in red spray paint.

"That's because we're doctors," Carlos said. "Part of our job is to heal broken units, so we are allowed to speak to ghosts."

One of the hardest aspects of Mongol culture is when a unit loses a member. Since they act as one being, losing an Arm can be devastating. Some units never recover from that. Severed units are ghosts to the rest of their tribe until a doctor unit can put them back together again. The doctors take broken units and combine them with parts from other broken units, until they are whole again. But these new units never function quite as well as their original units. They are like Frankenstein's monster—body parts from various dead bodies sewn together to form a new being. It sometimes works okay when it is just a Left Arm that is replaced, but a Head is a completely different story.

Zippo and Vine had lost the Head of their unit when they were six years old. The little girl had died of Malaria, leaving her two Arms lost and afraid. They spent their time sitting quietly in the dark together, not speaking or eating, completely unsure how to move or act or speak without their Head telling them what to do.

"I brought you into the tribe to be the new Head for Zippo and Vine's unit," Carlos told Xiu. "They need you more than anything. It is likely they will die without their Head. Without *you*."

"I will save their lives just by telling them what to do?"

"Hopefully. When a new appendage is connected to a body, there is always a chance that the body will reject it. If Zippo and Vine reject you they will likely die."

"Isn't there anyone else who can be their Head?"

"There is one other ghost their age, but he is both a male and a Right Arm. Zippo and Vine require a female Head."

"Can't the Right Arm just become a Head?" Xiu asks.

"It is possible for a Right Arm to become a Left Arm, or a Head to become an Arm, but an Arm has never successfully been able to transform into a Head. Arms spend their entire lives following. They have no idea how to lead."

Carlos' unit brought Xiu to the sick bay, to introduce her to her new Arms. Zippo and Vine are curled together in a corner, staring up at the hospital bed next to them.

"Their Head, Rosa, died here," Carlos said, pointing at the bed. "They haven't moved from that spot since the day of her death."

Xiu crouched down to take a peek at them from under the bed. She saw them cradling each other, wiping each other's eyes even though they were too dehydrated to cry. Zippo looked at Xiu for a second, but the moment his eyes locked on Xiu's they shot right back up to the bed.

"Zippo and Vine are younger than you, by almost two years," Carlos said. "But I think it will be okay, especially with you becoming their Head. They are more likely to conform to an older girl than a younger one."

Carlos took Xiu to the other side of the bed. His two Arms stayed in the back of the room. He positioned Xiu in front of the two boys, blocking their view of the bed. "This is Xiu," Carlos told the boys. "She will be your new Head. She will replace Rosa."

The two boys didn't acknowledge her. They shifted their visions, trying to see around them, waiting for Rosa to come back to the bed.

"The tall skinny one with the long hair is Vine," Carlos told Xiu. "He will be your Right Arm. The short one with curly hair is Zippo. He will be your Left."

"Hi," Xiu said, waving at them.

They didn't acknowledge her.

"Try giving them some water," Carlos said, as one of his Arms handed him a canteen.

Xiu took the canteen and held it up to the boys. "Want something to drink?"

"Don't ask them," Carlos said. "Tell them."

"Drink this," Xiu said to them. "You need water."

"You have to be more forceful," Carlos said. "Command them. Show them you are their boss."

"Drink!" Xiu told Vine, shoving the canteen in his face. "I command you to do as I say!"

Vine didn't respond. Then she tried shoving it into Zippo's face. He too ignored her.

Frustrated, young Xiu punched Zippo in the face.

"Drink it now!" she told him.

Shocked, Zippo stared up at Xiu, blinking. She punched him again. Vine looked over at his Left Arm, wondering what was happening to him. Xiu punched Vine in the face until he stopped looking at Zippo, and started looking at her.

"I'm your new Head," Xiu told them. "And you're going to do as I say from now on. If you don't drink this I'll punch you again."

Then she shoved the canteen in Zippo's mouth and poured it down his throat. After a couple of gags, Zippo gave in and drank the water of his own will. When she brought the canteen to Vine, he accepted it without incident.

"That's not the normal method of getting new Arms to listen to you," Carlos said. "But it seems to have been effective."

"So they'll do everything I say from now on?" Xiu asked, almost excited by the prospect. "Like my personal slaves?"

"Not slaves, Xiu. They will become your Arms. They will become an extension of you."

"But I'll still own them? They'll be mine and they'll do everything I say?"

Carlos nodded. "The ceremony will be tonight. After the ceremonial joining, the three of you will be one unit. One body. Although your bodies will be separate, the three of you will become inseparable from that point on. Three bodies join as one to become the perfect fighting machine."

Xiu nodded and then ordered her new Arms to stand up. They looked up at her, then at each other. Slowly, Zippo and Vine stood to face their new Head. She placed her right hand on Vine and her left hand on Zippo. Then she smiled brightly at them, red bits of spray paint in her teeth. The two boys smiled back, like mirrors.

Xiu has only one throwing axe left, but with her two Arms she doesn't even need a weapon of her own. Zippo and Vine are her weapons. In the middle of the two of them, Xiu directs her Arms to blast out a zombie's knee, leap over a wrecked pickup truck, and slice through a line of undead to get to the sidewalk.

Zippo and Vine are so tuned in to Xiu's commands, that they know what she wants them to do before she even has to tell them. The Mongols call it *unit telepathy*, which is kind of an intuition that Arms develop from following their Head for so long. When Xiu commands them, she feels as if she has tiny invisible strings connected from her fingertips to their brains, as if Zippo and Vine are living marionettes.

Cutting their way through the industrial district, lined with crumbling factories and warehouses, the merc punks are not able to conserve much ammo. There are just too many of those things. These are the kinds of circumstances merc punks are trained to avoid, rather than fight through. And the farther they go into the industrial district, the thicker the mob becomes.

"To that airplane," Xiu tells them.

Vine cuts them a path toward the blackened remains of a Boeing commercial airliner that had crashed into a steel mill long ago. The tail of the plane is missing, so they head for entry to the plane on that side. The rest of the plane leans up the side of the half-collapsed building, like a ramp. When they get to the tail end of the plane, Vine and Zippo hold their ground as Xiu assesses the situation.

"We need to get off of the street," Xiu says. "We're going to have to cross this area from above."

Entering the back of the charred aircraft, they climb the aisle upward toward the cockpit. The mob of zombies try to follow, but as they attempt to scale the slanted passageway they only slide back down across their slimy flesh.

The fuselage rattles as they make their ascent. They balance themselves. Zippo holds Xiu from sliding back into the mob below.

"Keep going," Xiu says, as the building that holds up the plane begins to crumble.

They continue up.

A blackened skeleton sitting in one of the airplane seats nearby turns back and eyes them with black ash-filled sockets. As Vine passes him, the corpse reaches out with burnt twig-like limbs.

"Brains," hisses the zombie.

But the charred undead corpse can't reach Vine. Its seatbelt buckled around its waist keeps it securely fastened to the seat.

When they get to the cockpit, Xiu kicks out the door and the unit jumps out of the plane onto the third floor of the building. Once safely out of the plane, Xiu gives her Arms a smirk. Then, in unison, the three kick the side of the fuselage with enough strength to separate it from the building. The plane rolls down into the street, crushing several zombies below.

Xiu laughs at the destruction they caused, and her men laugh with her. But then the building rumbles and chunks of debris rain down from the ceiling. Sections of the floor break open as the building begins collapsing around them.

"Get to the roof," Xiu says, leaping from a crumbling floor to solid ground.

Zombies come out from the shadows, lumbering toward them, as they head for the nearest stairs. They blast out the zombies' legs, guarding each other's backs, as the structure deteriorates quickly around them.

When they were teenagers, Xiu, Zippo, and Vine were the most un-ruly unit in the Mongol tribe. Raised in the wasteland, Xiu didn't grow up with the traditions of the Mongols. She was used to doing as she pleased, any way she pleased.

They were supposed to be collecting food deep in the Amazo-nian rainforest of southern Columbia, but back then Xiu was easily distracted from her missions. Once she noticed there were zombies wandering through the jungle nearby, she wanted to hunt them down and kill them for fun.

Because they were not to be trusted traveling on their own, Xiu's unit had to be accompanied by a guardian unit. All units are assigned to a guardian unit the day they are formed. This guardian unit be-comes like their unit's parents. The guardian unit raises the young unit, teaches it how to fight, how to scavenge, and accompanies them on missions. A unit is usually separated from its guardians the day the Head of the unit turns thirteen. That's when the members of the unit are considered adults. And though they continue to train with their guardians, they are considered old enough to take care of themselves.

Xiu's guardian unit was the same unit that found her in Chile when she was seven years old, the one led by Carlos.

When Xiu was fifteen, her unit still needed to be looked after by Carlos' unit. At that age, they were one of the weakest, sloppiest, least organized units in the tribe. Her two Arms worked just fine. They did exactly what they were told. Xiu was the problem. She was a trouble-maker. She didn't listen to the Heads of her guardian unit or the other elder units. She did whatever she wanted.

"Let's go," Xiu told her Arms, as they snuck through the trees away from their guardians.

Carlos' unit wasn't watching them. They were busy collecting bushels of wild marijuana into potato sacks. Xiu led Zippo and Vine away from their guardians, through the trees, into the jungle, to hunt down the living dead.

As a youth, Xiu was fascinated by the different kinds of zombies that were out there in the world. She wanted to encounter every kind—from white American zombies, to Mexican zombies, to morbidly obese zombies, to midget zombies. But what she always wanted to find were the zombies from the indigenous tribes of the Amazon rainforest.

When she saw the first of them, Xiu smiled. The zombie stumbled through the trees, covered in mulched vegetation, beetles and grub worms burrowed in and out of its flesh. On the side of its head, there is a wasp nest covering much of its face.

"I get this one," Xiu said, aiming a rifle at the corpse's head.

When she fired, the bullet went through a section of the wasp nest before passing into its brain. The zombie stumbled back, then turned to face Xiu's unit, wasps buzzing angrily around its head. The zombie groaned and stepped forward.

"Now everyone," Xiu said.

And they all shot bullets into the zombie, as it lumbered toward them.

"Xiu!" called a voice from back the way they came.

Their guardian unit had heard the gunshots. Vine and Zippo looked to her for instruction.

"Keep firing," she said, with a mischievous smile.

The bullets didn't take the zombie down, but the three punks weren't interesting in stopping it. They just wanted to use it as target practice. As the zombie came closer, the wasps began to swarm.

Zippo was stung first. He flinched a bit, but kept on firing. Vine was stung by three of them. The bugs left Xiu alone, so she continued firing her rifle. The two boys whimpered as more and more wasps stung them, crawling across their face and down the collars of their shirts. Xiu didn't order a retreat. She continued shooting, giggling at the chunks of mulched flesh exploding from the corpse's body.

"Are we going to leave soon?" Zippo whined, cringing at the bugs crawling on his face.

"No," Xiu said, annoyed that her Left Arm was expressing an attitude different from hers.

The first wasp stung Xiu and she slapped it dead against her wrist, then continued shooting. As the zombie reached them, Xiu had them withdraw a few yards. They walked backwards through the jungle, right into the middle of six more walking corpses that were coming at them from behind, drawn to the sound of gunfire.

Just before one of the corpses grabbed Xiu by the back of her neck, a shotgun blast separated its head from its neck. Xiu turned to see her guardian, Carlos, coming through the woods after them.

"Get down!" Carlos yelled.

Xiu did not get down, so neither did the rest of her unit. They turned and fired on the zombies.

"I said get down!" Carlos ran up to Xiu and yanked her away from the shambling corpses. Then his unit hacked at zombies with axes and machetes, cutting off limbs and heads.

Forgetting about the original zombie that was coming at them, Zippo was grabbed from behind. He thrashed around to free himself form the zombies' grasp, causing the wasp nest to break off the corpse's head and land on his shoulder. Behind the newly exposed flesh, Zippo saw the wasp nest was not just on the outside of the zombie, the wasps had burrowed into its hollowed-out skull and chest. Dozens of wasps flew out of the zombie's hive-like cavities, stinging Zippo in the face and neck.

When Xiu turned around, she was horrified at what was happening to her Left Arm. Little Zippo, barely fourteen years old, was covered in angry wasps, unable to defend himself from the zombie that had a hold of him. She was in too much shock to save Zippo. She was in too much shock to command Vine to save him.

Carlos went in with a machete and chopped the zombie away from Zippo, allowing several wasps to sting him as he pulled the boy to safety. As other zombies poured into the vicinity, the six of them rushed out of the jungle. Xiu cried as Carlos carried Zippo in his arms. The boy wasn't able to walk on his own anymore. When Zippo weakly turned his head to Xiu, he saw that she was crying. This made him cry, too.

Back on the ship, Zippo was treated in the sick bay. He was very upset—not because he was in a tremendous amount of pain, but because Xiu was in trouble.

"You almost got him killed back there," Carlos yelled.

Xiu shrank before him.

"You are a Head," said Carlos. "You have a responsibility to keep your Arms safe. They are not your play things to take advantage of. They depend on you to make the right decisions."

"I'm sorry," she said, tears flowing down her cheeks.

"I don't want you to apologize," Carlos said. "I want you to grow up and take your duty seriously."

"I will."

"I'll believe it when I see it."

"I promise."

From that moment on, Xiu stopped messing around. She stopped thinking only of herself and started focusing on what was best for her unit. After five years of training hard, Xiu's unit went from being the absolute worst unit in the tribe to one of the strongest. She didn't do it for Carlos. She didn't do it for herself. She did it so that nothing bad would ever happen to Zippo ever again.

When they get to the roof, Xiu is surprised to see how many zombies are up there waiting for them. The building rumbles beneath their feet as they scurry across the rooftop.

"This place is collapsing," Xiu yells. "We need to get off of here now."

Zombies spill in from the stairwell behind them. By the time they get to the middle of the roof, they are surrounded. Zippo and Vine go back-to-back, protecting Xiu in the middle. They fire into the crowd with all they've got.

A zombie covered in barbed wire comes at Zippo, but as Zippo fires his shotgun it only clicks.

"It's jammed," Zippo yells.

Xiu throws her last axe at the zombie, cutting through its chest. But the axe gets tangled in the barbed wire, so it doesn't return to her. When the corpse gets to Zippo, he uses the shotgun as a bat and hits the zombie so hard that the barrel of the gun bends a couple of inches, rendering it useless.

When Xiu turns to Vine for help, the roaring AK-47 clicks into silence.

"I'm out!" Vine says, tossing the gun away.

The ground beneath them splinters apart, cracking open under the weight of the mob as it closes in on them. Out of ammo and axes, they stand back-to-back, waiting for Xiu's command. A camera ball floats above them, beeping with anticipation. Miles away, the camera operator sits on the edge of his seat, refusing to blink, determined to capture their deaths on film.

Xiu looks over at Vine.

"It's time," she says.

Vine nods.

Then Zippo and Xiu duck to the ground, as Vine reveals his hidden weaponry. Out of his wrists, two metal hooks appear as he clenches his fists. Then he spins in a circle and in one blink, twenty of the zombies surrounding them are cut in half at the waist. The zombies' upper halves fall to the ground as their legs stumble forward.

Miles away, the operator of the camera ball jumps out of his seat, completely mystified by how Contestant #19 just took out so many zombies within a split second.

"What happened?" asks Wayne "The Wiz" Rizla, peeking over his shoulder.

"I have no fucking clue," says the camera ball operator. "He just spun around and then all of a sudden the zombies were cut in half."

"Rewind it," Wayne says. "Play it in slow motion."

The camera operator rewinds the video. In slow motion, they see the hooks that appeared out of Vine's wrists. When Vine spun around in a circle, the hooks flew almost thirty feet out of his wrists. Connected to each hook is a hair-thin strand of razor-sharp steel wire. The wire cut through twenty of the zombies as Vine spun in a circle. Then, like a yoyo, the wires pulled the hooks back into the merc punk's wrist.

"Holy fuck…" the camera operator says, pushing his glasses up the bridge of his nose.

Wayne smiles. "I'm glad these merc punks volunteered for the show. They have proved themselves to be most interesting contestants."

At the age of 20, merc punks are fitted with mechanical implants. Much of the flesh on their arms are removed to install metal weaponry. These weapons become a part of their body, so that they can always defend themselves, even after they run out of bullets.

"What did you get?" Xiu asked Vine as he came out of the sick bay.

"The wires," he said, showing her the hooks dangling from his bandaged arms. "You?"

Xiu raised her arms at Vine and two foot-long blades burst out of her fists. "Swords." Then she padded her new metal knee-caps. "And jumpers."

They smiled at each other, excitedly. They had been waiting for their implants for a long time. The implants are what define a merc punk. They are sacred. The type of weapon a merc punk gets is a reflection of their soul. Because these weapons are so revered and personal, they are only to be used when absolutely necessary.

Zippo stood silently behind them. When Xiu and vine looked over at him, he blushed.

"Zippo?" Xiu asked. "What about you?"

Zippo lowered his eyes. "I don't like it."

"Tell me."

He sighed. Then he raised his arms, which were now mostly metal. When he clenched his fists and turned them sideways, gigantic razor-sharp sheers emerged from his arms.

"Scissors?" Xiu asked, giggling. "You got the scissors?"

Zippo nodded.

"That is the worst one you could have gotten," she said. "Did they even give you extra leg implants, like my jumpers?"

Zippo sighed again. He raised one leg to them. Another pair of sheers emerged from his ankle.

"More scissors!" Xiu laughed.

Because Xiu thought it was funny, Vine and Zippo thought the scissors were funny, too. But deep down, Zippo felt bad. It was as if they were laughing at his soul.

"Don't tease him," Carlos said, as he came out of the operating room.

The trio quieted down.

Carlos put his hand on Zippo's shoulder. "The shears are a good weapon. If you train hard, they will serve you well." Then a pair of shears sprang out of Carlos' arm. He scratched his chin with it and smiled, then moved on.

After the wires are back in Vine's wrists, Xiu and Zippo stand up. Zombies trample over the halved corpses toward them.

"Zippo," Xiu says to her Left Arm. "Now."

The scissors spring out of Zippo's wrists and cut at the undead, snipping like crab claws. The razor-sharp scissor blades cut arms and sever legs. Then a pair of shears pop out of Zippo's ankle, as he jump-kicks a zombie. The sheers cut through its neck, decapitating it.

Xiu turns to her opponents and crosses her arms. The blades spring out of her fists. With the speed of a samurai, she slashes down the zombies as they run at her.

Zippo stumbles back as the ground quakes below him.

"This place is coming down," Xiu says. "Let's get out of here."

Zippo nods, and wraps his arms around Xiu's waist. With her Left Arm on her back, Xiu bends her knees, then clicks the lever on her metal kneecaps. Her mechanical knees snap up, launching them high into the air. Like a human cricket, she leaps over the street, to the roof of the building next door. When she lands, the suspension in her kneecaps cushion the fall.

Vine's wires slice the heads off the zombies left and right. He cuts down the last one as the floor caves in beneath his feet. He falls through the roof and looks down to see six stories of open space. A horde of zombies staring up at him from below.

Without needing to look up, Vine shoots one of his wires up over the rooftop to the building next door. The hooked end catches a ledge, and Vine reverses directions. He launches up into the air as the wire reels itself back into Vine's wrist, pulling him with it. As he emerges from the building, the structure collapses to the street in an avalanche. When he's completely reeled in, he drops onto the next building's roof beside Zippo and Xiu.

Xiu stares at him.

"Ready?" she asks.

Vine nods.

"Then let's move."

As they turn around, the three merc punks come face-to-face with something they have never encountered before: a pack of mechjaws. There are five of them, on the rooftop, as if they were waiting for them the whole time.

When the dogs growl at them, Xiu freezes. She notices the armaments on the zombie dogs' backs. She sees the look of hunger in their eyes, but she isn't quite sure what to do. They weren't trained to fight mechjaws.

Xiu decides to play it safe.

"Run," she says.

Then she grabs Zippo and leaps into the air, over the dogs, to the roof of another warehouse. Vine shoots a wire at the same building and launches into the air behind them.

The mechjaws open fire. A storm of bullets comes at the merc punks before they make it to the next building, whizzing past Vine's face. As he is pulled through the air, Vine uses his free hand to shoot the other wire at the undead mutts. The hook slices through their storm of bullets and catches one of the mechjaws by the throat.

The dog snarls and thrashes as the hook digs deep into its neck. Once Vine makes it to the next warehouse, the wire from his wrist reels itself in, pulling the mechjaw off of its feet. The mechjaw flies through the air toward them, as Vine's wire reels it in like a fishing line.

Bullets erupt from the dog's minigun as it soars, but while in midair it cannot take proper aim. When the mutt reaches them, Xiu's sword cuts its head off. The dog's body falls to the ground, the head rolling across the roof. Xiu's unit watches the dog's twitching legs, as if it's trying to run while lying on its side.

"What is it?" Zippo asks.

"A hellhound," Xiu says.

Her two Arms nod in agreement.

The mechjaws on the rooftop across the street stand at ledge, their rocket launchers opening up. The merc punks don't see the rockets flying through the air toward them as they stare at twitching dog by their feet. All four rockets hit their target, and the warehouse explodes into a cloud of flames.

The explosion can be seen from miles away, grabbing the attentions of all of the remaining contestants spread throughout the Red Zone.

Rainbow Cat sees the explosion from an office window, as she sharpens her new machete against the sole of her leather shoe. Ever since she killed Bosco, her face has grown colder. She is determined to win this game, no matter what she has to do. She will kill even Junko if she has to. Nothing and no one is more important to her than getting back to Neo New York so that she can get her dead husband's masterpiece published.

Haroon looks up at the explosion from a homemade raft. He drifts down a canal, hoping that it leads to a river, hoping that his raft doesn't fall apart along the way. He built it by tying together a collection of boards and driftwood. As he floats, he prays that he finds *her*. He shines his flashlight on the bank of the canal, hoping to see her standing there, waiting for him. That's the kind of thing he would expect from her. She always knew what he was thinking, what he was planning, what he was going to do next. If he doesn't survive this thing, he prays that he will at least get to see her face once again.

Popcorn looks up at the cloud of flames rising in the distance. She walks down the street, in the middle of a crowd of rancid shambling zombies, dragging Gogo with her. Gogo holds her stomach in agony, groaning, and puking black saliva into the street.

Gogo glares up at the explosion with wild, hungry eyes. She cries, "Brains! Get me some fucking brains!"

Wendy sees the explosion from the balcony of a luxurious downtown hotel, petting the curls in her hair. In her lap, a lawn gnome stares up at her with its red hat and smiling chubby face. She grips it tightly, as if it is the most important thing in the world to her.

Laurence sees the flames rise in the sky over the shoulder of a zombie, while punching its head off of its body. As he charges across the street to another walking corpse, he wonders if anyone got hurt in that explosion. He hopes that whoever is over there got out okay. That is, unless that person happens to be a real scumbag. Then he's glad they got their ass blown up.

Heinz glances over at the explosion through the window of a barricaded studio apartment, then goes back to tidying his things before bed. He hums orchestral music that plays in his head, standing in his boxer shorts, his black swastika tattoo reflecting in a broken mirror. He folds his uniform into a neat stack and organizes his weapons in order of size. He pats the snarling severed heads of two mechjaws propped up on his nightstand. Then he crawls into a dust-caked bed, lying back and sighing with relief.

Nemesis pays little attention to the fire in the distance. She stands in the middle of a high school football field, naked. With her arms spread to her sides, she breathes the air in deeply, her eyes closed, letting the soft breeze press against her bare pale-as-paper skin.

Oro hears the explosion from over his shoulder, but he is too busy trying to make his shot. Within an indoor miniature golf course, he hits a golf ball with his putter. The golf ball goes across the artificial turf, up a ramp, through the windmill, down a hole, comes out the back, and then enters the mouth of a decapitated zombie head. *Hole in one*, Oro says to himself. He smiles on one side of his mouth, then lights up a fresh cigar.

"Shit," Junko says as she sees the explosion in the distance.

"What?" Scavy says.

They are looking out of a window of the white-bricked castle-shaped building downtown, looking at the fire rising in the sky.

"It's those merc punks," Junko says. "It has to be."

"So?"

"If they are all the way over there then that means they are ahead of us by far more than I anticipated. They'll probably get to the evacuation zone sometime tomorrow." She looks Scavy deep in his eyes. "That means we don't have three days to get to the helicopter anymore. We have to get there by midday tomorrow."

"How are we going to do that?"

"I have no idea. Moving around is going to be twice as difficult tomorrow as it was today. It's probably impossible."

Scavy looks down at the sniper rifle in his hands, trying to come up with a plan.

"What if they're already dead?" Scavy asks.

Junko looks back at the flames in the distance.

Scavy says, "All three of them could have died in that explosion. We might not have to worry about them."

Junko takes a deep breath.

"I hope so," she says, "because I'm pretty sure the only way we're going to win this thing is if all three of those merc punks are already dead."

Xiu flies through the air, escaping the explosion, with Zippo gripped tightly to her back. She looks over at Vine as he glides through the air beside her, pulled by his wire. The light of the flames flicker across their sunglasses as they smile at each other in midair.

"We'll accomplish our mission," Xiu tells her Arms. "And there is nothing that will get in our way."

When they get to the street, they run East, toward their goal. The zombies in the area have all been attracted to the flames, so not many of them notice the merc punks as they scurry away.

Xiu's unit passes a parking garage as they head up a freeway on-ramp. Once they disappear down the freeway, an engine whirs into life from within the garage. Headlights flip on. Then a large black truck covered in dried blood pulls out of the parking garage. It slowly weaves through the debris in the road, its engine growling, as it heads up the onramp toward the freeway.

ZIPPO SCAVY POPCORN BRICK

HAROON XIU GOGO HEINZ

ALONZO NEMESIS ORO JUNKO

WENDY BOSCO ADRIANA VINE

LEE RAINBOW CAT LAURENCE CHARLIE

NEMESIS

As dawn begins to crack, Haroon drifts down the canal on his splintered makeshift raft. He's wet, itchy, coated in mud, and tired of trying to keep his balance on the half-submerged floatation device.

He's made it quite a long distance during the course of the night. The few zombies he passed did not even try to come after him. It was so dark out that he was not visible to the living dead from the middle of the canal. But traveling alone in the dark all night has taken a toll on him. For the past six hours, he had been unsure where the canal was taking him, how safe the water was, or how long his raft was going to last.

The blue and pink sky brightening in the East is a comfort to him. Although he's no longer hidden in the darkness of night, he's finally able to see where he's going. He can see the lumps in the brown water are really fallen branches rather than zombies swimming toward him. He can see where the water ends and the algae-coated asphalt wall of the canal begins.

Pulling out his map, his shivering pruned fingers rattle the paper. He's not exactly sure where he is on the map, but he knows that if he keeps going in this direction the canal will eventually empty into a river. He has to find a boat soon. There's no way he can make it much further without one.

As he crosses under a bridge, he sees a fat Rastafarian zombie with oil-caked dreadlocks staggering across the road above him. The zombie goes to the railing and looks down at the raft.

"Brains," the zombie belches down on him.

Black drool sprinkles in the water as Haroon passes underneath. When Haroon comes out on the other side, he hears a splash. The large zombie hits the water, thrashes to keep afloat, and then sinks to the bottom, leaving a coat of green oil on the surface of the water.

Up ahead, a few more zombies on the road running alongside the canal see him coming their way. They shamble toward the water, groaning at him. One of them hops in and sloshes through the thick brown sewage. As Haroon passes, the zombie goes deeper into the water until he's up to his armpits, then dives for the raft. Mere inches from Haroon's ankle, the zombie sinks into the murk and disappears under the surface.

Haroon aims his solar-powered shotgun at the bubbling water as he goes by, just in case the corpse knows how to swim. The zombie doesn't resurface. He goes back to his map. Examining carefully, the river the canal empties into curls north, toward the evacuation zone. If he decides to play the game and go to the helicopter he would have a pretty good chance of making it—a better chance than finding a boat and making it to the ocean. It's not likely that any river will make it out to the ocean. Even if he knew what part of America he's in, he knows nothing of the geography. Still, he doesn't like the idea of playing the game. If he got to the helicopter first that would mean he'd be condemning all the other contestants to death.

But he wouldn't be able to make it out of the Red Zone without help. And since he knows everyone is headed for the helicopter, that would be the best place to meet up with them. They could draw straws to see who gets to go and who has to stay, then together the remaining contestants can figure out how to get off of the continent alive. He would gladly stay behind, especially if *she* is among them. With her by his side, he knows they would be able to make it. All he needs to do is find her.

Her name is Nemy. She doesn't actually have a name, but that's what Haroon likes to call her. The other people in the research facility called her Nemesis, after the project she came from, or Specimen #5. The Nemesis Project was designed to genetically engineer a soldier capable of surviving in the Red Zone. Nemy is the latest model. Completely immune to the zombie virus, sweat that releases a chemical that is repulsive to the living dead, with the eyes of a hawk and the stealth of cat, she is the ultimate Red Zone survivalist. And her offense capabilities are twice that of her defense. There is no better bodyguard you could have while traveling through the wasteland.

Haroon met her when visiting his friend who had recently been transferred to the genetics division. Terry was his closest associate for several years and it just wasn't the same working without him.

"They got you mopping the floors I see?" Haroon asked as he walked into the genetics lab one night.

Terry looked up at his old friend, then continued mopping. "Yep. They couldn't demote me any further than this."

"That's what happens when you blow your boss's finger off."

"It was your fault. I said those shoddy modules you gave me wouldn't work. You should be mopping these floors with me."

"I will if you want me to."

"Serious?"

"Sure."

"Take a mop then," Terry said, rolling the mop bucket over to Haroon.

Haroon went to work, mopping under the work stations across the room.

"How's the shotgun coming?" Terry asked.

Haroon chuckled. "It shoots. Kind of."

"Still got a long way to go, eh?"

"Give me a few years, it'll work."

Haroon mopped down to the hallway and noticed something moving in the corner of his eye. Stepping a bit further into the hall, he discovered a holding cell that contained a woman with long black hair. At first he thought she was a dead body. The woman looked cold and stiff, lying naked in the corner of the cell with paper-white skin and colorless eyes. Once she sat up and looked at Haroon, he jumped back.

"Who is she?"

Terry came over. "That's number five. One of the mad Dr. Chan's creations."

"Is there a one through four?"

"Behind you," Terry said, pointing to four dead specimens in glass cases behind them. Two were stillborn fetuses. One was a deformed three-year-old girl. The last was a skeleton-thin adult. All of them had reptilian features, some with snake teeth, scales, and lizard tails. "The previous versions weren't quite as successful."

"She's part reptile?"

Terry nodded. "You wouldn't think so just but looking at her, would you? Reptiles are immune to the zombie virus, so they spliced her DNA with that of a snake or Gila monster or something like that."

Haroon watched as the woman stood and stepped toward the glass. She looked Haroon in the eyes and cocked her head.

"Put on your clothes," Terry said to her, knocking on the glass. Then he pointed to the white jumpsuit on the bed.

"I don't like them," she said.

Haroon was a little surprised that she could speak. Her voice was a little alien, a slightly higher pitch than a normal female, with a whispery lisp.

"You're going to drive my friend here mad with lust," Terry said, then he turned to Haroon. "She's always taking off her clothes. They say she's built to endure in extreme temperatures, so clothes aren't really necessary to her. Still, the mad doc is a prude and doesn't approve of the indecency."

As the woman walked back to her bed to clothe herself, Haroon realized he couldn't take his eyes off of her body. She wasn't considerably beautiful. She didn't have any curves, her breasts were small, she was a little too thin, a little too muscular, her pale skin seemed almost rubbery, and the vertebrae of her spinal column seemed to stick out of her back so far that they looked like spikes, but there was something about the way she moved and the way her skin glistened in the fluorescent lighting that was alluring to Haroon.

"Don't even think about it," Terry said to him. "She might look like a human, but deep down she is a cold-blooded killer. If you even stepped foot in that cell she'd probably snap your neck in seconds. She'd pick your corpse clean to the bone by morning."

"Has that happened before?"

"Not since she was a kid. But that was only four months ago."

"She's only a year old?"

"Seven months old. They grow up fast."

"Huh."

As Terry went back to the mop, Haroon watched her adjust her jumpsuit. The clothing seemed awkward and uncomfortable to her. She sat on the bed, readjusted the fabric, stood up, readjusted, pulled the sleeves up, put them back down, then she unzipped the jumpsuit and stepped out of it. Haroon laughed. She turned to him and glared with such intensity that he stepped away from the glass. Her inky black eyes looked like that of a snake ready to strike. She didn't take her eyes off of him as he walked out of the hallway, past Terry, and out of the lab.

The canal empties into the river, and Haroon's crude raft barely holds together as he hits a faster current. Haroon was expecting the river to be in a more remote side of the town, but the waterway cuts right through the city. It takes him past an amusement park, where rusty warped roller coasters dangle over the water. The river here is full of debris from the amusement park, including old bumper cars, concession stands, and horses from the merry-go-round. Haroon has to push off of the carnival wreckage to prevent his raft from ramming into anything.

On the side of the river, there is the skeletal frame of a circus tent, the last shreds of tent flapping in the breeze. Haroon sees animal cages and a warped Ferris wheel. Through the bleachers, he catches a glimpse of what he believes to be an elephant. After he floats ten feet, his view becomes blocked by a row of scorched food carts.

Three balls in the water float toward Haroon's raft. At first, Haroon thinks they are more pieces of amusement park junk that has blown into the river, but then he notices that they're floating upstream. When they get close enough, Haroon can tell they are zombies. They are submerged up to their noses, so all Haroon can see are the tops of white skulls and hungry bloodshot eyes. They look almost like alligators stalking their prey as they swim toward him.

Haroon pumps his shotgun and aims it at the first zombie. He was hoping not to have to fire his weapon, but he doesn't have a choice. They are blocking his path and seem to be able to swim faster than he can float.

"Braainns," gurgles the zombie as its head raises out of the water.

Haroon blows off the top of its skull. Its limbs thrash in the water. Haroon shoots off its arm as he passes, just in case it tries to grab for his raft. Then he fires at the other two heads bobbing in the water, blasting them back just enough for his raft to slip past them.

As he feared, the sound attracts more of the creatures. They come out from behind concession stands and the tilt-a-whirl ride. The water splashes all around him as the undead jump into the river. He ignores the ones behind him and focuses his fire on those in his path, the ones capable of reaching him before he can float by. Chunks of green meat spray through the air as Haroon pumps and fires the

184

shotgun as fast as he can.

The ground quakes around him and a rumbling fills the air. Once Haroon hears a shrill trumpet call, he knows what's coming. The zombie elephant crashes through a fallen roller coaster track and dives into the water, trampling human corpses into the brown murk. Its flesh is black and soggy, riddled with pus and sores. The flesh on the left side of its abdomen is missing, revealing the ribcage and rancid organs. From within the creature's stomach, the arms of a zombie clown reach out through its rib bones. Decades ago, the elephant had swallowed a circus clown whole in order to eat its brain, and when the clown had come back to life it found itself trapped permanently within the creature's belly.

As Haroon continues firing at the zombies in his path, he realizes that the elephant is moving too quickly for him to get away. He turns the shotgun on the monstrous animal and aims for its front left leg. He doesn't aim for anything else, just shooting that leg in the exact same spot, hoping to slow it down. Unfortunately, he's not a trained marksman. His shots hit the water, hit its face, and its chest. Only a few hit the leg, but none of them in the exact same spot. If his gun wasn't solar-powered he would have been out of ammo by now. He turns and fires at zombies in front of him, then turns back to the elephant. No matter how many times he shoots it, the creature doesn't slow down.

The zombie elephant's trunk raises and creates a blasting trumpet noise. Green toxic vomit sprays from its trunk in a geyser across the water, barely missing Haroon's raft. He raises his shotgun and aims for its face. Firing six consecutive shots, he blows off the creature's trunk as well as shredding both its eyes. This slows it down, but it keeps plowing blindly forward.

Haroon turns to the zombies in the water ahead and notices a bend in the river. That's his chance. He decapitates a few of the zombies, then paddles with his free hand to take the curve without getting stuck on the rocks along the shore. After the bend, he looks back to see the elephant trampling over the rest of the zombies straight onto dry land. It doesn't change directions, stomping forward into the carnival parking lot at full force.

The second time Haroon saw Nemesis, she was sitting on the bed staring at him in such a way that it seemed as if she was expecting him. He had come to see Terry after the lab was shut down for the night, but Terry was gone. His mop bucket was in the middle of the floor, but he was nowhere to be seen.

But Haroon didn't just come to see Terry. He also wanted to see the reptilian woman again. Ever since he saw her he hadn't been able to get her out of his head. She scared and disturbed him, yet he found her strangely attractive.

He went up to the glass and just looked at her for awhile. She was cross-legged on the bed, topless, eyeing him. After a few moments, she stood up and came to the glass. She put her hand on the door.

"You can come in if you want," she said.

Haroon was surprised to hear her say that. He didn't know how to react.

"It's okay," she said. "I'm not going to hurt you."

She pointed at the door handle. Haroon walked slowly to the glass. He wasn't sure what possessed him to do it, but he went inside with her. She lunged at him and grabbed the door before it closed.

"Don't let it shut," she said, as she held the door open a crack. "You'll be locked in. If Dr. Chan found you in here with me he wouldn't be happy."

Haroon took off his shoe and put it in the door.

"I thought you were trying to escape," Haroon said.

She cocked his head at him, as if she didn't understand the word *escape*.

"Let's get started," she said.

Haroon's questioning face turned into a face of alarm as she crawled onto the bed and pointed her ass at him, as if she wanted him to fuck her doggy style.

"What are you doing?" Haroon asked.

"Aren't you going to have sex with me?"

"What!" Haroon yelled.

She sat upright. "Isn't that why you came here?"

"No, I—"

"I assumed by the way you were looking at me…"

"No, I just wanted to talk. I think you're fascinating. I wanted to learn more about you."

"Oh," she said, perplexed. "That's usually not why people come here."

"I'm sorry, I think I should go." Haroon stepped toward the door.

"No," she said, her hand slapping against the door to keep him from opening it.

Haroon wondered how she got off the bed and across the room so fast.

186

"Don't go," she said. "I'd love to talk. Nobody ever talks to me."

"Okay," he said, his voice shaking a little. "Yeah, that would be good." He smiled at her. She didn't smile back, but cocked her head a little.

Haroon held out his hand.

"My name is Haroon," he said.

She didn't take his hand.

"I don't have a name," she said.

"What do they call you then?"

"I'm from the Nemesis Project so sometimes they call me that."

"I don't want to call you Nemesis. It sounds inhuman." He paused nervously after the word *inhuman*, but it didn't seem to bother her. "What if I call you Nemy?"

She narrowed her eyes at him.

"I'd like that," she said.

But her expression appeared as if she wanted to tear his throat out if he ever actually called her by that name.

Haroon comes to a shop on the edge of the river. Three giant blue letter Rs dangle from an ancient sign, above the words *River Recreation Rental*. On the dock, there are rows of yellow plastic kayaks. The area seems clear of the undead, so he directs his raft to the shore to take a closer look at the boats. If any of them are useable it would be much quicker, safer, and more comfortable than the tied-together driftwood he's been riding.

Dragging his raft into the bushes along the shore, he goes to the kayaks. They look warped and brittle, not very promising. He taps one of them with the tip of the shotgun and the barrel breaks right through, more fragile than paper. Pounding on each one them with his fist, they are all useless. The sun shining on them for several decades has deteriorated the plastic practically to dust.

He looks back at the raft. He really doesn't want to get back on that thing. This kayak rental is probably the best bet he's ever going to get for finding something suitable for water transportation. He knows there's got to be something useable there, somewhere.

Haroon decides his best bet would be to go inside of the shop. Nothing lasts long when its exposed to the elements like this. He walks shotgun-first toward the shop. As the door swings open, Haroon jumps at the sight of a crazed man's face. The man's mouth wide open and snarling. Haroon raises the shotgun, but stops himself from firing. The man isn't a zombie. It is just a life-sized poster of an extreme sports kayaker howling at the top of his lungs as he goes down some wild rapids.

Haroon goes around the advertisement to examine the merchandise. There are some kayaks inside, but not many. Most of them were on display out by the river. He goes to them one at a time, but none of them seem very strong. Just the light from the windows was enough to wear them down. In the storage room, where no light could possibly shine, he finds one last kayak. This one is pink and made for children. He pounds his fist on it. The plastic is still sturdy and seems like it will stay together, at least for as long as he'll need it. He decides to give it a try. Hopefully, his legs will fit inside.

As he drags the pink boat and paddles outside, he runs into three large undead truckers examining his driftwood raft outside, as if they can smell him on it. When they look back at him, Haroon feels almost embarrassed to be carrying the pink kayak. But once the zombies stagger toward him, he runs for the water and dives kayak-first into the river.

Lying across the top, balancing himself with one leg in the water, he paddles out into the middle of the river. The zombies follow him. He squeezes into the opening, but he can't get his legs all the way in. Bending his knees and hunkering forward, he paddles the miniature kayak downstream, away from the splashing corpses of ex-truckers.

Although uncomfortable, the boat is a huge improvement over the driftwood. He can actually control his direction and move several times faster. When zombies hop into the water with him, he easily gets around them and cruises by. He doesn't fire another round of the shotgun until he gets to the edge of the evacuation zone and goes ashore.

Haroon started visiting Nemy on a regular basis. He came to really enjoy visiting her. It was all he had to look forward to every day. Terry had found out about his visits and warned him against it, he said that she's dangerous and not like other humans. He also warned what Dr. Chan would do if he ever caught him in there with her. But Haroon didn't care. He thought it was worth the risk.

The more he visited with her the less she seemed like a genetically-enhanced monster and the more she seemed human. While she at first seemed emotionless and cold-hearted, Haroon began to understand that she did have feelings. She just expressed them in very subtle ways. She never smiled or laughed, but when she expressed joy she did it by narrowing her eyes. When she expressed sadness she widened her eyes. At first, he was scared whenever she narrowed her eyes. Every time he appeared for a visit, her eyes narrowed and he thought she was angry, didn't want him there, and would attack if he came near. But later on, whenever he saw her narrowing her eyes it warmed his heart.

Certain things about Nemy confused Haroon. For instance, she didn't seem to have an ounce of curiosity in her body. She rarely asked him questions about himself and had no interest in learning about the world outside her cell.

"Have you ever even been outside?" he asked.

She cocked her head, confused by what he means by *outside*.

"Don't you want to see the sunlight? The rest of the world?"

She just narrowed her eyes at him, but had no idea what he was talking about. Although she wasn't incredibly interested in hearing about Haroon's life or the outside world, she loved hearing him speak, no matter what they spoke about. She loved having him around.

One day, Haroon sang her a song. The Itsy Bitsy Spider. She had never heard a song before. It didn't interest her in the least.

"Have you ever tried singing before?"

She didn't understand *singing*.

"Try it," he said, and sang the lyrics slowly so she would pick it up.

She said the words, but she didn't sing them. When he gave up trying to teach her, she seemed happy about it. She scooted closer to him on the bed and put her finger in his belly button.

Touch was very important to Nemy. It seemed as if she was desperate for it, craved it. But she touched him in odd ways. Instead of holding hands, Nemy put her finger in Haroon's belly button. Instead of giving him a hug, she pressed her ear against his. He was not sure why she did these things, but he came to accept it.

The first time she put her finger in his belly button, he felt very awkward. He already felt uneasy being around her while she was nude, because he found her increasingly more attractive every time they were together, but it was even more uncomfortable to have her naked body pressed against him while she held her finger in his belly button. Whenever she did it, she just squinted her eyes at him and said absolutely nothing. He learned to deal with it because he understood its her way of showing affection. But her sharp black fingernails often hurt him, and occasionally drew blood. Whenever he couldn't take the pain, he decided it was time to go.

"I'll be back tomorrow," Haroon would say.

And Nemy's eyes would widen as he collected his shoe and left her alone in the cell.

Haroon goes through a parking lot into the evacuation zone. According to the map, the helicopter will pick up the first survivor who gets to the roof of the hospital. With the building just at the end of the lot, all he has to do is get up the stairs and he'd be home-free. If that's what he wanted to do. But he decides to vow to himself right now that he will not take the helicopter. He will wait for others to come. Nemy will make it there, he knows she will. He's not leaving without her.

Inside the hospital, the place looks like a tornado hit. On Z-Day, the hospitals were hit the worst. Everyone took the infected victims of zombie bites to the hospital, then they turned and it was a bloodbath. Haroon can tell the struggle in this building must have been fierce.

He walks slowly, listening carefully to the walls. There aren't any zombies he can see in the lobby, but he's sure there has to be several of them hiding somewhere. He goes straight for the stairs and takes them to the top floor. This level leads to the roof. As his footsteps squeak through the cracked walls, something reacts to the sound. It's a scratchy, gurgling sound. He keeps going. The roof access door is straight ahead. Trying to step softer, it's no use. His shoes keep making nose.

The sound of hoarse whispers comes from a room on the right. With his gun pointed at it, he walks sideways to the door. This entrance is where they would bring in emergency patients by airlift. The door is electronic, so it won't budge open. He tries to pry it open with the shotgun and his flashlight, but they don't work. He'll need to find something else.

The only room nearby is the one that was issuing the strange sounds. If there's anything that can open the sliding doors to the roof, it will be in there. Hopefully, he thinks, it was just the wind coming through an open window.

Haroon moves forward, shotgun leading the way. As he opens the door, he hears another sound. A rumbling, whistling sound. He thinks that one has to have been the wind. It couldn't have come from a human, not even a dead one. Before entering, he looks over at the sign beside the door and wipes the dust from its surface.

It reads: Maternity Ward.

When he looks into the room, he sees a cracked window. A breeze presses against it, causing a rumbling, whistling sound. The room is mostly a mess of overturned chairs and scattered medical equipment, with a mummified human leg on the floor and what looks to be a pile of dehydrated intestines by the sink. On the other side of the room, behind a broken window, there are two rows of hospital cribs.

Looking around the floor, he tries to find a medical tool that might pry open the exit to the roof. Below an overturned chair, he spots some kind of medical tool that looks something like a monkey wrench covered in a film of ancient blood. He moves the chair with the barrel of his shot gun. The tool actually is a monkey wrench. He wonders why somebody might need a monkey wrench in a maternity ward.

As he walks back toward the door, the sound of a baby crying tweaks Haroon's ears. A raspy, piercing baby cry. He turns around. The sound is coming from one of the cribs.

"No," Haroon says. "Please, no."

Three more baby cries issue from the cribs.

"Don't tell me that's for real."

He steps toward the cribs. He doesn't want to, but it's too much for him to accept without seeing it with his own eyes. He's never heard of the virus infecting infants before. It's got to be something else.

When he gets to the first crib, all he sees is a pile of clothing inside, covered in shadows. But then he sees movement. He takes out his flashlight and shines it on the shapeless mound.

When the light hits the baby, a hole opens up in the brown flesh and bawls. Haroon doesn't believe it's really an undead infant. Even though it is crying, it is just a pile of fabric. His mind has to be playing tricks on him. But on closer inspection, he sees that it is an infant. Its arms and legs have molded into the sides of its body, its back fused to the mattress of the bed, its eyes and nose sunken into its hollow skull where half of its brain had been eaten out. It's now just a blob of meat with a crying mouth.

Two more zombie infants begin to cry, and Haroon backs away. He runs out of the room, pries open the exit with the monkey wrench, then runs across the roof to the helicopter pad. He doesn't care about the vow that he made to stay behind. He wants to get out of there. Right now. He isn't even sure if his Nemy is in the contest at all. He can't rely on the hope that he'll find her. He's going home.

Near the helicopter, there's a large wooden plank with a red target spray-painted on it. He goes to that. Below it is a two-way radio and three words written above the target: "Call for rescue."

"Hello?" Haroon says into the radio.

No reply.

"I've made it," he said. "Am I the first one? Or am I too late?"

A camera ball floats down below his shoulder, filming his call.

"Hello?" he cries.

Then a voice comes on the other end. "Congratulations. You're the first contestant to arrive safely. We'll pick you up in ten minutes. Just hold on."

"Ten minutes?" Haroon yells. "Pick me up now, damn it. I want to leave RIGHT NOW!"

But they do not respond. He punches the sign over and yells into the radio.

A figure steps across the roof toward him. When he turns around, his anger freezes on his face. The naked woman comes closer, holding a double-bladed S-shaped sword.

His eyes brightened. It was *her*. It was really her. She was really on the show as he thought. He tossed the radio over his shoulder and stepped toward her. He didn't care about the helicopter anymore. He had *her*. As long as he had her, that's all that mattered. Because he loved her more than anything in this world.

After two months of visits, Nemy and Haroon had fallen in love. They didn't talk much when he came to visit her. They spent their time in bed together, making love, caressing each other's bodies, kissing one another with ferocious passion. Until the day it all ended.

One night, he had not propped the door open with his shoe correctly. The door had closed and he was locked in. Haroon jumped out of bed and went to the glass.

"It's outside," Nemy said, pointing at his shoe on the other side.

He rubbed at the tension building in his forehead.

"Come back to bed." She pulled him to her and pressed their ears together.

Haroon shook her away.

"Do you know what this means?"

She didn't.

"If I get caught in here I'm not going to be allowed to see you again."

Her eyes widened.

Haroon banged on the glass, calling out for Terry. But he knew his friend wasn't there. Terry was disgusted with hearing their love-making and started to clean up earlier, before Haroon got off work. Still, he kept banging on the glass until his fists were red.

"Stop," Nemy said.

He kept banging.

"Stop." She grabbed his fist. Her grip was so strong that resisting was like trying to bend steel. "We still have *now*. We should make the most of it."

Then she wrapped her arm around him and kissed his neck. Tears flowed down his eyes. He wished he had the strength to pull his fist out of her fingers so he could punch the glass one more time, but she pulled his arm down around her body. He released his anger by kissing her with all the power he had in him. He grabbed her around the waist and picked her off the ground, taking her into the bed.

They made love with more passion than they ever had before, because they knew it would likely be their last chance. They tried to put a lifetime worth of lovemaking into a single night, and when all of Haroon's energy was spent they lay together in each other's arms. Haroon's neck pressed against her smooth glistening cheek, Nemy's finger tip snuggled inside of his belly button.

In the morning, Haroon awoke to a knocking on the glass door. When he looked up, there were a crowd of people gathered outside. A group of ten security guards and five doctors. The man in front was Dr. Chan, a hunched over Asian man with small eyes that sunk deep into their sockets. Haroon grabbed his clothes and put on his pants.

"I was wondering how Specimen #5 had become pregnant," said Mr. Chan. "I was worried that she was able to reproduce asexually."

Haroon paused when he heard that, then looked at Nemy. Her eyes narrowed at him.

"I'm sorry," Haroon said, putting on his shirt. "I didn't mean to."

"Didn't mean to what?" Chan asked. "Fuck my specimen?"

Haroon and Nemy stepped out of the bed and went to the door.

"It wasn't my intention to mess with your work. I just—

"Get him out of there," Chan told the security officers. "He's under arrest for committing an act of high treason."

"What?" Haroon cried. "High treason?"

Five of the men came into the cell. Haroon backed away. They surrounded him. The two in front grabbed him and pulled him out of the cell.

"No," Nemy said to Chan.

"No?" asked Dr. Chan, concerned by the disobedient tone in her voice.

"Don't take him from me," she said, with wide eyes. "I love him."

The doctor was not pleased with her statement. "You what?"

"I love him!" she cried.

Haroon looked back. It was the first time she ever put emotion into her voice. A tear was coming from one eye.

Then she jumped at the door and reached her arm through the crack before it closed. She grabbed one of the guards who was trying to take away her love.

"Bring him back!" she cried, then she ripped off the guard's arm.

As she fell back with the severed arm in her fist, the cell door slammed shut and the glass sprayed with blood. The armless guard dropped to the ground, screaming.

"You'll never see him again," said Dr. Chan.

As they dragged Haroon away, he looked back at her eyes wider than they'd ever been. Tears flowed down her face.

"Come back!" she yelled at Haroon. "Come back to me!"

She tossed her bed at the glass and pulled the sink out of the wall.

"We'll see each other again some day," Haroon told her. "I promise."

Nemy dropped to the ground, reaching in his direction with her arms.

"We'll be together again," he yelled, as they took him out of the lab and dragged him down the hall.

And he was right. They are together again.

"Nemy!" he cries.

He runs to her.

He can't stop smiling at the sight of her. They finally found each other. They finally can be together. He doesn't think he even wants to go back to the island. He wants to find someplace else, where they can live alone together for the rest of their lives. Even if they barricade themselves in a building right here in this city, it would be like they were in her prison cell again. Together. Only he would be the one trapped in the cell and she would come and go, to get food and supplies. Then she can have her baby and they can all live together as one beautiful perfect family.

When he sees her face in the light of the low morning sun, she narrows her eyes at him. The same way she always does when she's happy. Tears of joy flow down his eyes. He can't wait to hold her again, make love to her again. He even can't wait until she puts her finger in his belly button until it bleeds.

Something pushes him backward. He balances himself and looks down. A double-bladed sword is sticking through his chest. It is her sword. When he looks up at her, he sees her hand is raised. She had purposely thrown it at him.

"Nemy?" he says, as his blood gushes down his legs and he falls to the ground.

After Haroon had been escorted out of the lab, Dr. Chan looked down at his creation. She was on the ground, tears sprinkling onto her paper-white legs. He shook his head at the mess she had become.

"Have her memory wiped," he said to the doctor next to him. "That asshole destroyed months of conditioning. We're better off starting over from scratch."

"What about the pregnancy?"

Dr. Chan thought about it as he wiped blood from his white tie.

"I'd like to dissect it," said Dr. Chan, then he walked toward the exit. "Have an abortion arranged immediately."

As Haroon bleeds to death on the roof of the hospital, he looks up at the sky. A helicopter flies overhead. A spurt of blood from an artery sprays up into the air. Then he sees his love leaning over him, her pale naked flesh glistening in the light, her eyes no longer narrow.

"At least I got to see you one last time," Haroon says to her. "My beautiful Nemy…"

The woman bends down to him.

"My name isn't Nemy," she says. "It's Nemesis."

Then she rips her sword out of his chest, taking his insides out with it.

ORO

Scavy and Junko wake in an office on the upper floor of the white-bricked castle. The morning sun shines through on Scavy's face. His yellow mohawk mostly flat to one side of his head. He didn't get much sleep during the night. All the screaming and moaning from the zombie crowds outside kept him awake. Junko on the other hand slept like a baby. Curled up under the desk, snoring loudly for hours. He's surprised her snoring didn't attract the zombies outside.

When Junko stands up, she stretches and smile-yawns, as if she just had the best night of sleep in her life.

"How were you able to sleep like that?" Scavy asks.

"Practice," she says. "I slept on the streets of Copper every night until I was capable of sleeping pretty much anywhere, even in the most dangerous sides of town. Contestants rarely get sleep in the Red Zone. Lack of sleep often gets people killed, especially on the third day."

"Good thing for me we don't have to worry about a third day anymore," Scavy says.

"Don't feel so lucky. It's going to be damn near impossible to get to the helicopter before those merc punks unless we find some transportation."

"What kind of transportation can we get out here? Bicycles?"

"Probably not even that. Skateboards maybe, but they would be useless on the street out there even if we knew how to ride them."

Scavy doesn't even know what a skateboard is.

"So what do we do?" he asks.

"Get lucky," she says.

Outside the window, zombies roam the streets. The thickest section of the horde is just below the fire escape they had entered the office from.

"There's too many of them out there," Junko says. "We need to find another way out."

Running down the street, they see a familiar face. Rainbow Cat is dodging through the lumbering corpses, determined to get through to the end.

"Isn't that the hippy chick?" Scavy asks.

Junko examines her carefully. There is a blood-drenched bandage around her neck, but other than that she looks fine. "How is she still alive?"

As Rainbow moves into the middle of the street, she gets surrounded on all sides. The zombies close in on her. One of them grabs her by the dreadlocks from behind and rips her back.

"Well, she's not going to be alive for much longer," Junko says.

Rainbow Cat spins around and flips the zombie over her head. She whips out her machete and severs her captive dreadlock in mid-air. Then she hacks off another's arm and then one of their heads. She leg-sweeps three of them, then cartwheels out of the center of the mob.

"Whoa, shit," Scavy says, smiling. "When'd she get so tough?"

Junko shakes her head. "I knew the bitch wasn't to be trusted. She probably wanted us to think she was a helpless weak little girl this whole time, so we wouldn't see it coming once we got to the helicopter."

A zombie pukes in Rainbow's direction, but she kicks another corpse into its way to block the green toxic spew.

"Rainbow!" Junko yells to her from the fire escape. "Over here!"

Rainbow looks up and sees them. She gives them a one-minute signal with her finger, then roundhouse kicks the puking zombie over a fire hydrant.

"Meet us on the other side of this building," Junko yells.

"I'll be there," Rainbow says.

Many of the zombies break away from the horde and go for Scavy and Junko. They crowd against the wall, but can't reach the ladder to the fire escape.

Scavy looks over at Junko. "I thought she wasn't to be trusted?"

"Yeah, but we need all the help we can get. At least we know where we stand now."

"Are you sure?"

"Just don't turn your back on her."

Junko watches Rainbow carefully as the hippy expertly dispatches zombie after zombie. She wonders if she's made the right decision letting her come with them. That machete she's carrying is new. Junko thinks she had to have gotten it from another contestant, mostly likely stealing it or killing the person in order to get it. Although Rainbow will be useful on their trek through zombie country, Junko's going to have to figure out a way to ditch her before they get to the helicopter.

Scavy and Junko get their equipment together, arm themselves, and prepare to leave the barricaded room. They had not entered through the castle-shaped building, so they have no idea what is in store for them.

"What was this place, anyway?" Scavy asks.

Junko looks at the yellowed papers on the wall and desk. "I believe it's some kind of indoor theme park, designed to look like a castle from the Middle Ages."

Scavy doesn't understand theme parks or the Middle Ages.

"You know, knights, castles, armor, kings, jousting, swords."

Scavy nods. He understands most of those words.

They remove the cabinets blocking the door and enter the hallway. Much of this area is dark, but the end of the hall is illuminated with sunlight. Junko leads them in that direction. When they turn the corner, they enter a glass bridge overlooking a courtyard. Below them they see a Medieval-themed miniature golf course. At the end of the course, on a platform, they see a large vehicle. It is a hand-built flying device, which looks like some kind of bicycle-powered hang glider.

"What the hell is that?" Scavy asks.

Junko puts her hand on the glass and stares solidly at the flying machine.

"I don't know. But I think it might be exactly what we needed."

A man steps out from behind the flying machine, carrying a wrench and spool of wire. He's short, malnourished, and disheveled. His black slacks are brown in the knees. His white button-up dress shirt is ripped up, missing buttons, and covered in grease. His tie is covered in cigarette-burned holes.

"I guess another contestant beat us to it," Scavy says.

The small man wipes the sweat from his brow, then exchanges tools from a toolbox and gets back to work.

"I don't think he beat us to it," she says, shaking her head. "I think he built that thing."

Oro was a genius, or at least that's what he called himself. His father owned the only tobacco farm in Copper. Due to this, his family was one of the most wealthy in the quadrant. Oro, the runt of his father's children, did not want to grow up to be a tobacco farmer like his large older brothers. He had bigger things in mind.

"I am a genius," he would tell his father. "I am not suitable for the life of a mere laborer."

This was always his excuse to get out of doing chores. He was above hard work. He wanted to put his brilliant brain to work on greater things. He didn't have time to waste on his father's business.

"You're a citizen of Copper," his father would say. "The life you have now is the best you're ever going to get here."

"When the world sees my genius they will have to let me into Platinum," he would say. "Then you will understand my greatness."

Ever since he was ten years old, this is what Oro used to say. He had nothing to back up his claims of genius. He was only a kid. He was uneducated and was slow even when it came to doing simple tasks on the farm, but his dream was to one day be recognized as a great thinker. So that's what he spent most of his time doing: thinking. It didn't matter what he was thinking about. He just thought that's what geniuses do.

He spent large amounts of time at the dump. The other quadrants used Copper and the ocean as their dumping ground, throwing out many items that just didn't exist in Copper. Although nothing worked, Oro thought the items in this garbage were wondrous, magical devices. From toasters, to oscillating fans, to remote control cars. These were items you couldn't buy in Copper. He believed the people in Platinum were all great inventors. They all had such strange and wonderful devices there. He thought all of them had been invented by common everyday citizens of Platinum. He wanted nothing more than to become an inventor and live in Platinum with other genius minds.

"You're a simple farmer," his father would say. "Nothing more."

"You will see," said young Oro. "One day you will see my genius."

He spent much of his time trying to prove his genius by inventing new items out of the scraps found in the garbage dump. If he could only invent something worthwhile the citizens of Platinum were sure to allow him to live among them. But most of what he built were useless collections of machine parts that had no use.

His earliest projects didn't do anything at all. They were just crude sculptures that he believed were important inventions. After being laughed at by his older brothers, he focused on inventions that actually did something. He was never more proud of himself than the time he created his first working invention, in his late teenage years. It was a collection of gears and machine parts. When started, the wheels on it would spin. That was all it did.

"That's all it does?" his father asked.

"Yes, but it is self-propelled. Once it starts, it keeps going. It doesn't require fuel or cranking."

"But that's all it does? It's useless."

Oro raised his fists into the air. "It's genius!"

"If you're such a genius then invent me something useful," said his father. "Something I can use on the farm. Then I might actually approve of this hobby of yours."

"That would be easy," he said. "For a genius."

So Oro got to work. He spent day and night trying to figure out what kind of device could be used on the farm. This pleased his father, because Oro was finally taking an interest in farming. Within a year, young Oro understood the technology behind farming more than any of his brothers. He even started pulling his weight around there. His father was proud of himself for finally figuring out how to motivate the young slacker.

But then something happened that surprised his father. Oro had invented something that did actually help his farm. The device was a combine threshing machine which used an upgraded self-propulsion system similar to that of his first working invention.

"It works faster than the old one," Oro said. "But this one doesn't require fuel."

His father and brothers just stared in shock, after seeing the demonstration. It seemed too good to be true.

"The money you save should be quite significant," Oro said.

"This is amazing," his father was nearly speechless. "It's brilliant. It really is brilliant."

"Of course it is," Oro said, smoking a freshly grown cigar. "What else would you expect from a genius?"

He had been wanting to say that for a long time, and it was as satisfying as he imagined. The look of smugness grew on his face with every compliment he received from that day forward. That is, until his father started receiving complaints for the substandard tobacco he had been shipping into the upper quadrants. Using the new device, the machine didn't separate the tobacco plants as efficiently, causing bits of the stalk to mix in with the leaves. This created a harsh, bitter smoke that didn't burn properly. That year's crop had been ruined and most of his clients wanted their money back.

"I'm ruined!" the father yelled at Oro. "I can't believe I actually used something *you* had built. I'm such a moron."

"The design can be improved," Oro said. "I'm a genius. I'll work out the flaws with little difficulty."

"Do you actually believe I'll trust you a second time?" His father grabbed him by the throat, tears of anger in his wrinkled gray eyes. "I've had enough of you. I don't ever want to see your face around here again."

Oro broke out of his father's grip.

"Very well," he said. "I'll leave. I am a genius. I have more important things to build than equipment for your pathetic farm."

"Get out of my sight," his father said.

"I will. You don't deserve one ounce of my greatness."

"Get out!" His father said, hitting his fist onto the useless threshing machine so hard that it sliced open his knuckles.

While his dad was bandaging his hand, Oro gathered his things, swiped several boxes of his dad's favorite cigars, and left home. From that day on, he lived in a shack near the garbage dump, trying to invent something of value. He invented other self-propelled devices. From sewing machines to power drills to motorized roller skates to transportable elevators.

Once a year, an executive from Platinum would come to see his inventions. This man was always looking for new devices that would improve the lives of the citizens of the upper quadrants. He was even willing to check out the devices of some pathetic wretch living in a junkyard with atrocious hygiene and delusions of grandeur. Every visit, the executive would look over each of the items and then shake his head.

"No," he'd say. "None of these interest me."

"But they are genius!" Oro would say. "Each and every one is brilliant. Nobody else could have invented them but me."

"But I can't use any of them," the executive would say. "None of them would be of any use to the people in Platinum. You're going to have to try harder than that."

So Oro tried harder. He built vehicles that did not require gasoline. He created a dehydrator that could preserve meats for years. He invented a one-man airplane that did not require fuel. If he could get just one of these inventions accepted by the executive he would be able to move to the Platinum Quadrant. But none of them were ever good enough.

"I am a genius!" Oro would cry, as the executive returned to the gates of Silver. "Why can't you recognize that!"

"Genius isn't enough," the executive said as he passed through the gates. "I need something that's going to sell."

Oro fell to his knees, exhausted. He had constructed great devices, many which would better the lives of everyone on the island. They were recycled from the waste of the upper quadrants and could easily be mass produced with very little expense. But his ideas were all shot down. Nobody recognized his genius. But he would keep trying. He would fight to his last breath to prove his genius to the rest of the world.

Out of the corner of his eyes, Oro sees the other two contestants on the sky bridge behind him. He doesn't let on that he knows they are there, pretending to be too busy working on his latest creation: the glider-cycle. It wasn't easy getting all the parts together, but it's almost completed. He will be the first one to arrive in the evacuation zone because of this machine. His genius is too great for him to fail.

He steps over to his tool chest and takes it around the back of the glider-cycle, keeping his eyes locked on his work. He stretches and yawns, then slowly places his toolbox on the ground. By the time Junko and Scavy figure out what he's doing it's already too late. Oro jumps for his weapon—a rocket launcher—and aims it at the bridge.

"Nobody's winning this contest but me," he says, as he fires a rocket directly at them.

Oro had a plan from the moment he awoke in the hotel at the beginning of the previous day. He knew he was going to build a vehicle that would ensure his safe arrival to the evacuation zone before anyone else. He refused to team up with any of the other contestants. They were inferior to him. He had no use for lesser minds.

"I deserve to win this more than anyone else," he said to his reflection in a hotel room mirror. "I am a genius. I cannot fail."

But there was one major setback. The weapon he had been given was a rocket launcher. With only seven rockets in his pack, it was not the most useful means of defense. The launcher itself weighed nearly 40 pounds, which wouldn't be that much if each rocket didn't weigh 17 pounds each. Since Oro himself was such a petite man, his pack ended up weighing twenty pounds more than he did. He could hardly even drag the pack, let alone lift it.

When he left the hotel with everyone else, he dragged the large pack one inch at a time until he got past the wall. When he saw the weapon he had been given, he groaned with frustration. He believed the show's producers were playing a very cruel joke on him. They probably thought it would be funny to see such a small man lugging around such a large weapon.

Oro had to ditch all but three of his rockets just so that he could carry it on his back, and even then it was slow going. Luckily, he left on the safer side of the building that was nearly free of the living dead. He left with some innocent-looking young lady named Wendy, who tagged along without his consent.

"I don't need a puppy dog following me around," he told her.

She looked up at him with puppy dog eyes.

"Get lost."

Then he threw rocks at her until she ran away.

After a few blocks, Oro was able to get a shopping cart at a dilapidated grocery store which made wheeling around the rocket launcher much less arduous. He was also able to get several supplies for the machine he planned to build.

He decided not to use the rocket launcher against the undead. That weapon had only one use, to kill the contestants who got in his way. For the zombies, he had only one defense. Since he couldn't run very fast with his shopping cart, he used a variety of chemical sprays on them. While at the grocery store, he grabbed cans of bleach, ammonia, drain cleaner, and bug poison. He grabbed some pepper spray as well, but the aerosol had long left the containers, rendering them useless. He used simple squirt guns to deliver the chemicals, which were still functional even though the cracks in the plastic leaked chemicals over his hands.

As he walked through the wasteland, the zombies came to him attracted by the sound of the cart. But as soon as they approached, he dowsed their eyes with some drain cleaner. Although they were dead, he was still able to disorient them and temporarily blind them long enough to walk by. Whenever there was a horde, all he had to do was combine some bleach and ammonia to make mustard gas and toss a bucket of it in the center of the crowd. It was enough to slow them down.

He continued moving all day, picking up pieces for his machine as he went. Eventually he needed a second cart and that slowed him down even more. By the time he got to the Medieval Times indoor theme park, he found all that he needed. The well-preserved flags of the theme park were just the material he needed for the wings of the glider.

As he closed the gates of the artificial castle, he tossed the last of his mustard gas at the zombies out front. While they shrieked and twitched at the chemicals in their eyes, Oro looked at them and put his finger to his mouth.

"Shhhh," he said. "There's a genius at work."

Then he got started on his flying device.

The brittle glass walls of the sky bridge shatter as the rocket flies through, past the bridge into the upper castle wall. Junko and Scavy dive for the hallway on the other side just before the bridge is engulfed in a cloud of flames.

"Bow to my genius!" they hear the tiny man yell.

Scavy and Junko take the stairwell down to the ground floor. They enter a grand banquet hall designed to look like King Arthur's round table. There are two crippled zombies writhing on the floor. They are wearing the costumes of serving wenches and look to have been beaten with a golf club until all of their bones were broken. Junko and Scavy peek around a wall overlooking the miniature golf course. They get a better look at the flying machine. It is a bit smaller than they had realized.

"What's going on?" Rainbow Cat says as she enters through a broken window.

"Crazy fucker with a rocket launcher," Scavy says.

Rainbow Cat steps over a wriggling serving wench and goes toward them.

"You were awesome out there," Scavy says. "Where'd you learn to do that?"

"Self defense lessons," she says, as she wipes some green slime off of her machete on the bottom of her shoe. "A girl's got to be able to defend herself from scumbags."

Scavy smirked. "Where'd you get that machete?"

Instead of answering the question, she leans against the wall and looks around the corner to see their opponent. Her eyes sparkle when they see his flying machine.

"What's that?" she asks.

"I'm not sure," Junko says. "Some kind of aircraft."

"Can we get it from him?" she asks.

"No," Junko says. "We should get out of here. The explosion is going to attract more zombies."

"But it's worth the risk if we can fly out of here."

"It only looks like it seats one person," Junko says.

"So? At least one of us can use it. We can draw straws."

"Forget it. It's not worth fighting a guy with a rocket launcher."

"We've got a sniper rifle," Rainbow says. "Come on, we can take this guy."

"I said forget it," Junko says. "I wouldn't even know how to fly that thing, would you?"

Rainbow Cat stays silent.

"Let's just get out of here," Junko says, going for the window Rainbow had entered through.

With a loud sigh, Rainbow follows after her.

Oro did eventually invent something worthy of getting him into the Platinum Quadrant. It wasn't his flying machines or home recycling devices that satisfied the executive. It was a football alarm clock.

"This is it!" said the executive. "This is what every man in Platinum needs!"

It wasn't even a real invention. It was just something Oro slapped together for fun and he hadn't even planned to present the item to the executive. He didn't even know what a football was for.

"Are you sure you don't want this water filtration system? It turns salt water into fresh water."

"No, no," the executive shook his head. "I'd have no luck selling that. Now this," he held up the football clock, "this I can sell."

205

Oro was a bit disappointed that his winning invention took him only a few minutes to shove together, whereas his other projects took months.

"A football alarm clock…" The executive's face brightened with excitement. "Genius. Pure genius."

It was the only time he felt bad to be called a genius.

When he moved into Platinum, it was not at all as he hoped. The people there weren't geniuses. Most of them seemed dumber than his low class father. They were a bunch of fat, spoiled, lazy morons. He couldn't stand any of them. His football alarm clock sold well though, and he was able to live a comfortable life for a while. And more importantly, he was finally given the respect he rightly deserved.

He got used to the good life. He spent his time on the golf course or at the public swimming pools. He smoked cigars and drank purple martinis on rooftop bars overlooking the sea.

"Ahhh," Oro would say. "The life of a genius…"

But the good life didn't last. Oro couldn't produce another invention as stupid as the football alarm clock and his funds ran out. He was quickly thrown back to Copper, back to his old way of life. The executive stopped making his annual visit to the junkyard. Oro thought he was doomed to stay there for the rest of his life.

Then Oro came up with a plan. While he lived in Platinum, he had seen the first season of Zombie Survival on television. If he could volunteer to go on the show and win then they would move him up to the Silver Quadrant. He would also have a passport to Platinum and could try to sell some new inventions there. He would then come up with the most ridiculous, superfluous inventions possible. He already had plans for creating pedicure slippers, giftwrap cutters, laser-guided golf clubs, and the baconator, which was a cooking device that could infuse any type of meat with the taste and texture of fried bacon. All he had to do was win the contest and he could live the rest of his life in luxury.

But just getting on the show wasn't as easy as he expected. He had met with Wayne "The Wiz" Rizla at a bar in downtown Copper. He heard the rumor that if you knew an interesting contestant for the show you'd be rewarded greatly. He had the perfect contestant for him.

"So who's this contestant you have in mind?" Wayne said.

"Me," said Oro.

Wayne squinted at him. He rarely got volunteers. "You? Why would I choose you for the show? There's nothing special about you."

"I am a genius," Oro said.

Wayne continued as if he didn't even hear him. "Look at you. You're a shrimp. You have no muscle, no agility. You're ugly, so there's no sex appeal there…"

"But I'm a genius!" Oro stood up in his chair. "I would survive longer than any contestant you could ever find. Perhaps I'm not the strongest, fastest, or most attractive contestant, but I can outwit anybody. You have never met an intellect as impressive as mine before."

Wayne laughed. Oro slapped the smile off of his face, then found several guns pointed at his chest.

"Put me on that show and I'll show you what kind of genius I am," Oro said, stubbing out his cigar on the producer's plate.

"Fine," Wayne said. "I'll put you on."

Wayne waved at his men and they took Oro by the elbows. Then he said, "I could use another easy kill anyway. Not enough early bloodshed and the viewers get annoyed."

A few weeks later they gassed him at his shack by the garbage dump. He saw them coming and greeted them at the door.

"Are you ready?" one of them asked.

"A genius is always ready," was his response.

Oro knows that he can win this contest, as long as he can protect his glider-cycle. He knows where the intruders are hiding. He had seen a girl with blonde dreadlocks peeking her head out from the entrance to the banquet hall.

"You can't hide from a genius," Oro says, pointing his rocket launcher at the wall they are hiding behind.

He fires the rocket at the wall, knowing the explosion will kill everyone on the other side of it. The wall crumbles in the fiery blast. On the other side, through the window, the trio of intruders run across the street, safe from the blast. They survived, but at least he scared them away.

The explosion causes more damage than Oro had expected. After the inner wall goes down, the outer castle wall soon follows. Through a ten foot opening through the pile of debris, the walking dead enter Oro's sanctuary.

"Get back," Oro says to the scab-encrusted corpses.

Oro grabs his putter and stomps toward the zombies. He hits one over the head so hard it collapses to the ground.

"I don't have time for your interruptions," he says, slamming them left and right with his gold club. "I am a genius. I require solitude."

"Brains!" the zombies cry.

"Exactly," he says.

As he beats the zombies back with his club, he recognizes that the scabbed-over skin of one of the zombies looks a lot like bacon. It's like all of its skin had been put into his future invention, the baconator. This gives him an idea for marketing it to the executives: "Even brains can be baconized!"

Oro continues to daydream as he fights the dead. He doesn't kill any of them. Once they fall down, they just get right back up, but he keeps swinging at them one at a time without tiring. He's got the adrenalin of his fantasies to fuel him. He's got a bright future to think about.

"I am a genius," he says to the undead. "You can't possibly defeat me."

As Oro clobbers them one at a time, another contestant passes by the castle outside. It is Heinz. He stops for a moment to look at Oro fighting back the mob of zombies. Then he moves on.

Heinz doesn't mind the small white man when there's a Japanese bitch that needs to be killed. He can see her just down the street, running through the wandering dead. He's almost got her. He imagines how her flesh will smell when he burns her alive.

SCAVY

"We're being followed," Junko tells Rainbow and Scavy, as she chainsaws a zombie's head down the middle.

Scavy looks back.

"Don't look back!" Junko yells. "We've got to lose him somehow."

"Who is it?" Rainbow asks.

A camera ball floating over her head zooms in on the conversation.

"I don't know." Junko leads them farther down the road. "One of the less friendly contestants, I'd say. We should move faster."

They pick up the pace, but the zombies crawling out of the surrounding buildings make it difficult to get away. They can't dodge them, so they have to hack their way through corpse after corpse. This slows them down. Even worse than that, because they are doing all the zombie killing, their pursuer is able to move down the street quickly without the need to fight the already-incapacitated undead.

"He's gaining on us," Rainbow Cat says.

They turn around to see Heinz charging toward them, burning the few zombies left standing with his flame thrower. Junko tries to avoid going face-to-face with any of the lumbering dead, but they just keep coming. A zombie with a newspaper beard grabs her by the chainsaw arm. She fires her 9mm into its head but the small bullets just barely hold it back from biting into her wrist.

Heinz reaches into his pack and pulls out the two mechjaw heads. He straps them to his arms. Then opens fire. The trio use the zombies as cover, but the corpses' flesh is so thin and liquidy that many bullets pierce through and whiz past Junko's shoulder.

Rainbow Cat hacks the newspaper zombie with her machete until it lets go of Junko. The three of them duck for cover inside of an old apartment complex.

Scavy knocks back a zombie with his spear as it comes in from the street, then he stares back at Heinz. The large nazi makes a pretty big target, especially with those clunky tanks of fuel strapped to his back. If only he could get a better shot at him. Bullets tear into the bricks near Scavy's head and he falls back.

"You two keep going," Scavy tells Junko. "I'll deal with this guy."

"Are you serious?" Junko asks.

Scavy holds up his sniper rifle. "I can take him. I'll go upstairs and find a good vantage point. All you have to do is lure him down the street until he gets past me, then I'll get him from behind."

"It's a bad idea splitting up," Junko says.

"I can do this," Scavy says.

Junko stares him in the eyes, assessing him. She doesn't like the idea of leaving him behind, even if he does end up taking down the nazi. Even though he's an incompetent slacker, she's learned she could trust him. Maybe not trust him enough to competently watch her back, but trust him enough not to stab her in the back. Which is more than she can say about Rainbow.

"Okay," Junko says. "But you catch up to us as soon as you can. Don't get yourself killed."

Scavy flips the safety off of his rifle. "Don't worry about me."

Junko and Rainbow Cat stand up and prepare themselves to run.

"I'm going to fuck his ass up and shit."

Junko nods, then the two girls take off running. Bullets mince the asphalt by their feet, as the two girls weave past the shrieking undead.

Scavy looks back at his opponent, to evaluate how much time he has to prepare. The nazi is only twenty yards off, blasting his Gatling gun, the mechjaw head growling against his fist. Then Scavy runs for the stairwell, to find a good sniper's nest on an upper floor.

Scavy was a worthless, low life, conniving, thieving, drug-dealing, vandalizing, good for nothing punk. But when it came to his friends, he always had their back. If anybody fucked with one of his own he didn't let them get away with it.

Gogo was the one he regularly had to back up. She was a self-centered whore and a complete bitch, with a mouth that often got her into a lot of trouble. Whenever she didn't like someone, she let them know. She didn't care who they were. If a customer in her strip club pissed her off while she was dancing she had no problem spitting on them, kicking them in the head, or even farting on them when she had her dancing bare ass pointed directly in their face. This would often lead to her coming home with a black eye or a bloody nose. Scavy never let a single asshole ever get away with doing that to her, even if she sometimes deserved it. He'd find them and leave them bruised and broken in an alley somewhere.

One time Gogo fucked with the wrong guy. It was Domino, the leader of the largest street gang in Copper. They were called the Diamonds and they had twelve times the man power of any gang in the quadrant. Scavy's gang didn't have a name. He thought gang names were pretentious, and there was no gang name more pretentious than the Diamonds. Scavy hated the Diamonds stupid gang name, and their stupid matching leather jackets with the word *Diamonds* on the back spelled out in artificial diamond studs. Scavy already hated them just for that, but then Domino gave him a much bigger reason to piss him off.

Gogo often slept with the men she danced for, but only if they paid well and she thought they looked fuckable. Domino was a large, balding, scarred-up, punk who Gogo did not find the least bit fuckable. But Domino wanted her, and he thought he deserved to get whatever he wanted.

"Listen, bitch," he grabbed her by the arm as she walked toward the dance floor. "I know you just fucked that scrawny kid over there. If you can fuck him then you can fuck me."

Gogo just laughed in his face and called him a limp-dick slob. Then she started her dance. While she was on stage, Domino gave her looks of intimidation. When she leaned into him, teasing him with her breasts to show him up close what he's never going to get, Domino whispered in her ear. "I'm going to fuck you whether you

211

like it or not."

Then Gogo grabbed a cigarette from his ashtray and put it out in his eye. He shrieked and jumped back. Gogo seductively bit her lip at him, as her body curved to the music on the stage. Domino clenched a fist and came at her, but the bouncers grabbed him before he could get on the stage. The punk and his crew were escorted out of the club.

But before he left, he yelled back to Gogo, "Your ass is mine, bitch."

After the club was closed, the bouncers offered to escort Gogo home, but she said she'd be fine. She could take care of herself. That is, until Domino and four of his men jumped her on her way home. They put their hands on her mouth and pulled her into an abandoned slaughter house. There, they beat her until she was in too much pain to fight back, then they took turns raping her. With a switchblade, Domino cut a slit down the center of her lips, then kissed her. She spit blood in his face. Then he headbutted her until she was out cold.

Gogo arrived at Scavy's place naked and crying. It was the first time he'd seen her in such a fragile, hysterical state. He cleaned her up and put her to bed. She didn't stop crying until she was asleep.

"I'm going," Scavy told Popcorn. "Look after her."

"Shouldn't you wait for Brick?" she asked, as she washed the blood from Gogo's tattered clothing in the sink.

Scavy shook his head. "That guy is out there basking in satisfaction right now."

Opening the drawer of his dresser, Scavy dug through his cache of weapons. There were knives, guns, and railroad spikes, but Scavy decided to go with his old standby: a crowbar. When he was really pissed off at somebody, he used a crowbar on them.

"I want to beat that satisfaction off his face while it's still there."

Even though Scavy has just met Junko, he considers her his friend, just as much a friend as Gogo or Brick. She's earned his respect, proved herself to be one tough chick, and Scavy thinks of himself as a brother to anyone he respects. That's why he's willing to do this for her. Plus, he's been wanting to use his sniper rifle on some asshole ever since he got the thing.

On the fifth floor of the apartment complex, Scavy takes his position. Heinz has gotten a bit further ahead than the punk had expected, but not nearly far enough ahead to get out of his range. A camera ball floats over Scavy's shoulder, another is filming Heinz. Scavy swats the camera ball away like a fly as it gets too close to his face. When he looks into the scope of his sniper rifle, it's out of focus. He adjusts the scope, but only seems to blur his vision even more.

"Fuck!" Scavy says, trying to figure out his aim.

Meanwhile, Heinz gets further away. If Scavy doesn't figure it out soon the nazi will be too far out of range, then Junko and the hippy will have to deal with him on their own. Scavy continues working on the scope, but just can't get it focused right.

"Damn son of a bitch!" he says, slamming his fist down on the rifle.

A man steps out of the intersection and blocks Heinz's way. Scavy recognizes the man. It is Laurence, the vagrant who had handed out the bags back at the hotel. Only, the guy looks a lot different now. His body is made of gold-plated steel, glimmering in the mid-morning sunlight.

Laurence stands there, in Heinz's way, his hands on his hips.

"Shooting women in the back as they're running away," Laurence yells at the nazi. "The T-2000 don't think that's very friendly behavior."

Heinz stops his pursuit, staring at the golden metal man with a confused expression. The dog heads on his hands snap and snarl in Mr. T's direction.

"Mr. T's gonna have to teach you a lesson in manners," then he punches his metal fist into the palm of his other hand.

Heinz opens fire on Mr. T, but the bullets just ricochet off the cyborg's chest. Mr. T roars as he rips off a chunk of the building next to him, then lifts it over his head. The piece of brick wall is the size of a dumpster.

"Here's a gift for you," Laurence says, tossing the enormous piece of wall at the nazi. "Courtesy of Mr. T."

Heinz ducks out of the way and the chunk of debris explodes against the cement wall behind him. Then he continues firing. Scavy adjusts the scope, not sure whether Laurence is on his side or if he's got to shoot down the both of them. He's able to see Laurence through the glass, letting it out just a bit to zoom off of his chest.

Heinz's Gatling gun runs out of ammo, so he drops the mechjaw into his pack and raises his left arm. The mechjaw on his left arm isn't connected to a Gatling gun. It's connected to a rocket launcher. Heinz squeeze's the dog's brain and the rocket shoots from his fist. It hits Mr. T square in the chest and the enormous cyborg flies back, through a wall, into an old bank building. The explosion creates an avalanche, and three stories of the building cave in on top of the T-2000.

"Fuck…" Scavy says, as he witnesses the nazi take down the cyborg. He wonders if going up against Heinz is such a good idea. If a bulletproof Mr. T with a robot body isn't strong enough to defeat him how does Scavy have a chance?

Heinz waits for the dust to settle, to make sure the T-2000 will not be getting up again. Once he is satisfied, he turns to the direction Junko was headed for and continues on his hunt.

Scavy lifts the sniper rifle to his shoulder and peers through the scope, aiming for the gas canisters on the nazi's back. The aim is dead center. Scavy knows that he only has one shot at this. If he misses he's dead. He takes a deep breath.

When Scavy pulls the trigger, the kickback slams his shoulder hard, jerking back his arm. The bullet hits the street in front of Heinz, missing by over five feet.

"Damn it," Scavy says, rubbing his bruised shoulder.

Heinz turns around, slowly, and looks up at Scavy. Then he aims his mechjaw rocket launcher at the window and fires.

When Scavy caught up to Domino and the other Diamonds who raped Gogo, they were doing Waste in the back of a broken down van. He crept up alongside the graffiti-coated vehicle, and heard Domino's low grunting voice and laughter coming from the other four in his crew.

"Smell my finger," he could hear Domino say. "I still got the scent of her sweet cunt on me."

"Get that out of my face," another said. "That shit is rank."

The others laughed.

Their conversation only pissed Scavy off more. He gripped his crowbar tightly, fantasizing about how it will feel to bash Domino's face in with it.

When the first of them stepped out of the van to take a leak, Scavy broke his kneecap with the crowbar. The guy fell face-first into the street.

"What the fuck?" Domino said.

Scavy jumped in the back of the van and smashed the closest asshole in the mouth. Blood and teeth splashed across the backseat. Then he lowered the crowbar into another's forehead, knocking him out with a loud metal *clunk*. Scavy leapt out of the back of the van before the other two could grab him.

Domino pulled out his switchblade and came out of the van after him. As the knife darted toward his throat, Scavy swung the crowbar. It made contact with Domino's knife-hand, breaking three of his knuckles. The switchblade flew across the street.

The other punk grabbed Scavy from behind, but quickly found a crowbar in his eye. Scavy turned around and beat him repeatedly, smashing the crowbar against his face, his chest, and his arms that waved out for mercy. When Scavy looked back, Domino was running away. His four men were either out cold or writhing in pain.

"You're dead, asshole," Domino yelled back at Scavy from the far end of the street. "Your whole crew is dead."

The punk lying in the street with a dislocated kneecap went for a gun in his coat. When Scavy saw the gun pointed at him, he clicked his heels together, triggering a switchblade that emerged from the toe of his right boot. With his boot-knife, he kicked the punk in the stomach five times, stabbing him in his guts, until the bloody piece of shit dropped his gun.

Then Scavy picked up the pistol and shot the other three until they stopped moving.

Heinz' rocket hits the wall below Scavy's window, taking out the front of the building. The blast knocks Scavy back across the room. When he gets to his feet, Scavy can hardly balance himself. There's a piercing ring in his ear and the taste of blood leaking from the roof of his mouth. He retrieves his rifle and staggers back to the window. He doesn't realize his face is charred black, nor does he realize a piece of debris has impaled his side.

The flames in the burning window cover his view of Heinz, but Scavy aims the rifle through the smoke and fires again. The bullet is several feet off target.

Out of rockets, Heinz tosses the dog head and pulls out his flame thrower. He approaches the entrance to Scavy's building. Riding the adrenalin of being blown off of his feet, Scavy keeps firing. He gets off two more rounds, but shooting vertically at a moving target isn't a manageable task for a poor shot with a mortal wound. Heinz enters the building unscathed.

The camera ball filming Heinz floats in the doorway below Scavy, hovering in one place as it zooms in on the nazi's back. Scavy's bloody teeth open in a smile as he puts his eye in the scope. He aims directly at the center of the camera ball, holds his breath, then fires.

The explosion takes out the entire block, blowing out the first floor of the apartment building, as well as the first floors of every building on the block. Scavy jumps back and dives over a bed, as the flames rise into the air and engulf room. When the air is clear, Scavy lifts his head and laughs.

"Checkmate, motherfucker!" he cries.

Most people assume Scavy is as dumb as a rock, but he's actually a lot smarter than he looks. Although uneducated, he's got a natural intelligence. He's quick-thinking, clever, and a born strategist. Chess was a game he loved to play, and he never lost a game in his life.

When Brick met up with Scavy and saw the four dead bodies of Domino's men lying in the back of the van, Scavy was already working on a plan.

"Oh, shit," Brick said, checking for a pulse on any of the fallen gang members. "Why the hell did you have to kill them?"

"I got a little carried away," Scavy said. "They pissed me off."

"Do you know what that means? Domino isn't just going to let you get away with this." Brick looked around, making sure the street was clear. "We have to go to war now. With the fucking Diamonds of all gangs!"

"They asked for it. If they would have left Gogo alone this never would have happened."

"Gogo would have been fine," Brick said. "She's a fucking whore."

Scavy got into Brick's face. "How can you say that? She's your girlfriend."

"I know it's bullshit what happened to her," Brick said. "But you're going to end up getting all of us killed."

"Not if we get them before they get us," Scavy said.

"Are you kidding? They outnumber us twenty to one *and* they have more firepower. We wouldn't stand a chance."

"It doesn't matter how big their gang is," Scavy said. "We just have to get clever. Outsmart them."

Brick shook his head. Scavy had never seen the big guy so worried. The reason Scavy became friends with him in the first place was because the guy never backed down even when the odds were against him.

"Trust me," Scavy told Brick, placing a hand on his shoulder. Then Brick grunted and gave him a nod. "Help me take their jackets off. I have a plan."

The plan was simple. Although the Diamonds were the biggest street gang in Copper, they were not the top dogs in the quadrant. The local drug lord, Tim Lion, had a much more powerful crew behind him. Domino was a mere cockroach in comparison to Tim Lion. So Scavy, Brick, and a couple of their friends decided to dress up as members of the Diamonds gang using the jackets they took off of the dead bodies of Domino's friends. Then they robbed a drug shipment that was headed into Silver. Let everyone see the Diamonds jackets they wore. Then they dropped off the drugs on the porch of one of the Diamonds' hangouts.

When Tim Lion got wind of what the Diamonds had done, he sent his men after Domino. With the drugs in his backyard and all of the witnesses of the robbery, Domino had little chance of proving his innocence to the drug lord. Scavy had fucked him good.

As the smoke clears in the room, Scavy stands up and feels the tightness in his hip. He looks down to see the piece of shrapnel in his side and all the blood soaking his clothing. Because he can't feel any pain, he realizes that the wound must be even worse than it looks.

"Fuck me," Scavy says, then wheezes out a laugh.

Something shoots him in the back. A fiery pain at the base of his spine. He rubs the wound and lifts up his fingers to reveal a layer burnt skin. He turns around to the camera ball floating in the room with him. It shoots another laser at him. He jumps over the bed, but the blast gets him in the thigh.

He knew it was against the rules to fuck with the cameras, but he thought the punishment for that was the self-destruction of the cameras. Having other camera balls attack him with lasers was not something he had anticipated.

Scavy tosses a blanket over the camera, grabs his naginata spear, and runs out of the room. The camera ball blasts blindly through the sheet as Scavy closes the door on it. Out in the hall, he sees that all the movement is causing his wound to rip open even more. He needs to pull out the metal but worries that it's the only thing keeping the blood in his body.

As he steps carefully down the stairs of the apartment complex, Scavy comes face-to-face with Heinz. Not only did the nazi survive the blast, he had come out of it without a single scratch on him. Scavy nearly topples over in shock at the sight of the guy, standing there with his flame thrower pointed at him.

Scavy freezes. His sniper rifle is aimed at the ground. He's not sure if he can raise it up in time to shoot the nazi before he's eaten alive by flames. But Heinz doesn't fire. He too is frozen in his place as he examines what Scavy has on.

"You are a member of the Fifth Reich?" Heinz asks him.

Scavy looks down at the clothes he wears. The uniform he had gotten off of the sculpture of Adolf Hitler in the wax museum is similar to that of Heinz. They have matching swastika armbands. Scavy decides his best course of action would be to play along.

"Yeah," Scavy says.

"You must be one of the operatives positioned in Copper. I had no idea there was another Brother in this competition."

"Yeah, me too."

Heinz notices the look of hesitation on Scavy's face. He can tell the punk has no idea what he is talking about.

"Why would you help that Japanese cunt you were with?" Heinz's tone becomes more aggressive. "A true Aryan would have not allowed her to live so long."

Scavy considers lying and telling him that he was just playing Junko the whole time, and he planned to kill her once she proved useless to him, but he respects the woman too much for that. He'd rather go sniper on flame thrower than sell her out like that.

The camera ball blasts its way out of the apartment on the floor above them. Scavy realizes he's trapped on both sides: the camera ball hovering down the staircase and Heinz pointing his flame thrower, convinced the punk is an imposter with no right to be in that uniform.

Scavy always finds himself between a rock and a hard place. It's almost as if such situations seek him out. When Tim Lion and his men hit Domino's hangout, after killing a good portion of the Diamond crew, he allowed Domino to explain himself. Lion had no clue why Domino would be stupid enough to try to get away with stealing his merchandise, so he was curious.

"How could you be so stupid?" Tim Lion said, pointing his index finger at his head.

Then, somehow, Domino convinced Tim Lion that Scavy set him up and that he had nothing to do with it. Domino mentioned his four dead men with missing jackets. There were four men who hit Lion's shipment. The packages of Waste were left on the porch unopened. Nobody in their right mind would leave all of that on a porch unless it was Scavy sneaking in at night to frame him. All the pieces fit together. Lion believed him.

So then Scavy in his crew not only had the Diamonds after them, they also had Tim Lion coming for their heads.

"This is even worse," Popcorn yelled at Scavy. "We're all dead for sure."

"Not necessarily," Scavy said. "We've already taken out half of Domino's men without a single casualty. I'd say we're doing pretty good."

"But what about Tim Lion?"

"Lion has no idea who we are. If we can just take out Domino then Lion wouldn't know how to find us."

"But he'll find out eventually. The guy practically owns this quadrant."

"Let's just focus on one problem at a time."

No matter how dire the situation seemed, Scavy had optimism. He knew there was always a way around a problem. He just had to figure it out.

With his fingers tapping on the sniper rifle, Scavy decides to just go for it. He's going to shoot the guy. Perhaps he will get burned, but it's possible he can kill the nazi before the fire kills him. As long as he doesn't miss, he can take the guy out.

"The Japanese girl is smart," Scavy says. "A lot smarter than you."

This infuriates Heinz more than Scavy was expecting.

"You went after me and let her get away," Scavy continues. "Dumb move. I'm not letting you out of here alive."

Heinz laughs. "Brave talk, for an insect."

Scavy chuckles with him, exposing his charred bloody teeth. Then Scavy raises the sniper rifle and fires.

The Diamonds knew that the only way to make peace with Tim Lion was to bring him Scavy's head on a platter, so Scavy didn't have to hunt down Domino. He just had to wait for the prick to come to him. Domino didn't know exactly where Scavy lived, but he knew the side of town he hung out in. Scavy, Brick, and the rest of his crew were known to hang out in the Southeastern park by the shore. It wasn't exactly a park, it was a wide open piece of land that was once a junkyard, where citizens of Copper often dealt drugs, got drunk, got into fights, played chess, ate lunch, and just hung out. Scavy and his crew were often seen patrolling the park like bulldogs. It was the first place Domino was going to check.

"I'll hang out here, by myself," Scavy said to his crew. "When they see me that'll bring them out into the open. I want the rest of you to get them from behind."

"That's it?" Brick asked. "That's your plan? It sounds like suicide."

Scavy smiled. "All my best plans sound like suicide."

Scavy gets off a round with his sniper rifle, but Heinz gets him first. The flames engulf Scavy with such force that he drops the rifle as it's fired. The bullet misses Heinz completely. Unarmed and coated in fire, Scavy thrashes around, trying to put the flames out as he is burned alive. With each flame that Scavy puts out, Heinz covers him in several more.

Then Scavy stops thrashing around and jumps at Heinz, grabbing tightly around the waist. It catches Heinz on fire and they shriek in each others' ears as they burn together.

"I told you I'm not letting you out alive," Scavy yells at him.

Heinz screams, "You're going to get us both killed!"

Then Scavy tears the hose out of a gas canister on Heinz's back and breaks away from him. Heinz whips his arms around, trying to get the tanks off his back as the leaking gas catches fire.

Scavy dives for cover, just before the explosion. He jumps out of the stairwell into the third floor hall, then rolls on the ground until he puts the fire out on his clothes. His face is charred black, his mohawk burned off, and uniform melted to his flesh, but he's still standing. He gets up and staggers back into the stairwell to retrieve his weapons. Grabbing his naginata spear, he sees Heinz looking up the stairs at him in anger. Although half-burnt, the nazi was able to get the tanks off before they exploded.

As Scavy grabs his spear from the steps, Heinz pulls out the double-fisted sledgehammer.

"I'm going to squash you like the vermin that you are," Heinz says, as he swings the hammer.

The hammer smashes into the stairs by Scavy's feet. The punk uses the chance to swing the blade of the spear at Heinz's head, but Heinz catches it with his free hand.

"Not good enough," Heinz says.

Scavy pulls the spear out of his grip, slicing open the palm of the nazi's hand. Then he ducks as the floating camera ball comes in from behind, blasting its lasers at the punk. The particle beams pass over Scavy's head and hit Heinz in the chest. Not enough to kill him, but enough to throw him back.

Scavy takes off running—in a hopping, limping, getting-blood-all-over-the-place kind of way—down the hallway of the third floor. Heinz chases after him. Scavy dodges into an apartment, then jumps down a hole to the second floor. As Heinz enters, he doesn't see Scavy looking up at him from the floor below. Scavy drives the spear through the hole, into Heinz's leg. The blade cuts through the calf muscle, scraping across his fibula bone. Heinz screams at the pain, then roars at the punk. He lowers the hammer down at the spear, breaking it in half.

Scavy laughs up at Heinz and flips him off. Then Heinz puts his blowgun to his lips and shoots a poisoned dart into Scavy's forehead. The punk's laughter cuts off as he sees the dart sticking out from between his eyes. He pulls it from his skin and examines it slowly, as if in a daze, then tosses it aside.

"What the fuck was that?" Scavy's voice is soft and shaky.

Heinz laughs as he pulls the spear blade out of his leg.

"Fuck," Scavy says, then takes off down the hall, before the camera ball hovering behind Heinz's shoulder can take a shot at him.

Domino and his men did catch up to Scavy in the park, but he brought more men with him than Scavy had anticipated, three times as many. They also brought guns. When they surrounded Scavy, the punk just smiled at him, waiting for his men to jump him from behind. But his men didn't come.

Scavy's smile faded when he realized his crew had ditched him. "Fuck."

"Fuck is right," Domino said, then punched him in the face.

The poison sets into Scavy quickly. His face is the first thing to go numb, mouth dangling wide open. Then his arms go limp, dangling by his sides as he staggers down the hall. When he trips over a piece of debris, he can't get himself back up again. He kicks his legs around, but without the use of his arms he can't move.

Domino's men took turns punching Scavy in the face and stomach, as the others held his arms behind his back. They bloodied his nose and broke his lip. He drooled blood down the front of his shirt, then looked up and scanned the edges of the park for his friends. He couldn't see them anywhere.

Domino grabbed Scavy by the mohawk and twisted his head up to yell in his face. "Why the fuck did you jump me and my men the other night? Do you have a death wish or something?"

Scavy spit blood. "You started it."

"What?" Domino kneed him in the face.

"You raped my friend, Gogo. You shouldn't have done that."

"All of this is over that worthless fucking whore? Is she your girlfriend or something?"

"She's a friend," Scavy said. "You don't do that to one of my friends and get away with it."

Domino laughed. "You're going to die just because I fucked your stupid bitch whore of a friend. You're the stupidest motherfucker I ever met."

Heinz laughs when he sees Scavy lying in the middle of the hall, paralyzed. He limps over to the punk and hovers over him, pointing one fist of the sledgehammer at his face.

"You're a white man," Heinz says to Scavy. "Why would you sacrifice yourself to save some worthless Japanese cunt? You should be wearing that uniform with pride, as a true Aryan would."

"Fuck you." The words are mumbled as they stumble out of Scavy's dead lips.

"Call her a whore one more time," Scavy threatened Domino.

Domino laughed at him.

"What?" Domino asked. "You still trying to be a tough guy?"

Scavy spit again. "You don't fucking call my friend a whore."

Domino stared him in the eyes and annunciated every word loudly in Scavy's face. "She is a worthless, filthy, rotten cunt whore and she deserved everything we did to her."

As Domino raised his fist to punch him again, Scavy clicked the heels of his shoe. Before impact, Domino's fist went limp as Scavy kicked him in the throat. The blade of Scavy's boot-knife pierced through the bottom of Domino's jaw, up through the roof of his mouth, and into his brain.

The Diamonds just stood there, staring at Scavy's foot in their leader's neck. Then Scavy's men attacked. Brick drove a truck into the park, roaring across the littered beach. In the back, the rest of Scavy's men fired bullets into the Diamonds gang, taking them down before they could get off a single shot. The Diamonds dropped Scavy and took off running. Some of them got away, others didn't. The ones who stayed behind to fight were the first to fall.

As Scavy pulled his boot-knife out of Domino's head, Brick came up to him and patted him on the back.

"You're late," Scavy said to him.

"We needed to find a vehicle," Brick said. "They aren't easy to come by on short notice."

"One minute longer and I would have been dead."

"Yeah, but you pulled through, as always," Brick said.

"I just got lucky," Scavy said.

"Now it's time for you to die," Heinz tells Scavy, gripping the double-fisted sledgehammer. "If you were proud of your Aryan heritage you wouldn't be dying for that insignificant Japanese cunt right now."

Scavy spit blood at him. "Call her a cunt one more time."

"I'll call that cunt whatever I damn well—"

Scavy clicked his heels together, and the switchblade emerged from his right boot as he kicked the nazi in the chest. But Heinz catches him by the ankle less than an inch away from his uniform. He bends Scavy's foot back.

"You're an idiot," Heinz says to him. "You bring shame to the master race."

Heinz drops the sledgehammer, puts his hand into his pack, and into a mechjaw's neck. Although the mechjaw's minigun is out of ammo, its teeth are still as sharp as ever.

"I don't think I'll kill you," Heinz says. "You deserve much worse." He brings the snarling head of the mechjaw toward Scavy's ankle, below the boot-knife. "I'm going to turn you into one of those things out there." The dog head snaps at Scavy's flesh. "You'll spend all eternity as a disgusting, disgraceful living corpse."

Scavy kicks him in the calf, breaking his spear-wound wider. Heinz releases Scavy's leg, and the punk kicks his boot-knife through the mechjaw's face.

Heinz steps back, clenching his wrist below the dog head. He slips his hand out of the mechjaw's neck and tosses the growling head over his shoulder. Then he pulls off his glove. Examining his hand, he sees his blood mixing with the dog's green zombie slime. The boot-knife had gone through the mechjaw's head, through the glove, and into Heinz's fist, infecting him with the zombie virus.

Looking at Scavy with distress, Heinz holds his hand, shivering in fear.

"You infected me?" Heinz says.

Scavy sneers through his drooping lips. "Checkmate, motherfucker."

Anger flashes across Heinz's face. He retrieves the double-fisted sledgehammer from the floor. The poison has now paralyzed all of Scavy's body, so the bleeding, burnt up punk just laughs up at the nazi. He chuckles at him as loudly as he can, as Heinz lifts the sledgehammer, aiming for Scavy's head.

Domino was dead. The Diamonds no longer wanted to fight a war against Scavy. Then Tim Lion was found dead in his club one morning, murdered by a lone mysterious assailant.

"Tim Lion's dead?" Brick said to Scavy. "Are you serious?"

"That's what they say," Scavy said, lighting a cigarette.

"You're the luckiest motherfucker on the planet. I can't believe you got away with it."

"I think I've got a guardian angel," Scavy said.

Just before Heinz lowers the sledgehammer into Scavy's skull, something hits the nazi in the back of the head. His neck breaks, his body goes limp, and then he falls to the floor. Scavy looks up to see a guardian angel standing over him. A golden, glimmering guardian angel named Mr. T.

"You forgot this," Mr. T says, then tosses the twisted casing of a rocket at Heinz's chest.

Scavy smiles in a daze as his guardian angel picks him up and carries him down the hall. A particle beam is fired at Scavy, but his guardian angel blocks it with his elbow, then swats the camera ball out of his way.

"Hang in there," says the guardian angel. "The T-2000 knows how to fix you up. You'll be back on your feet in no time."

When Mr. T looks down at Scavy, he sees tears of blissful joy on the punk's face, as if Scavy is looking at the most beautiful angel in all the heavens.

ZIPPO

The three merc punks arrive at their destination: the city's art museum. A fortified white building covered in brown hop vines.

Xiu says, "Let's get in, get what we need, and get out."

Her Arms nod their heads and get to work, prying open the barricaded entrance. Zippo uses his claw-hands to cut through the boards and vegetation. Vine uses his wires to rip open the doors. Clouds of dust billow out of the shadowy interior as the merc punks enter.

"The client wants as many as we can carry," Xiu says. "But most importantly we need to get the masterpiece. He said we'd recognize it by the red dress."

Her Arms get straight to work, searching the museum for the works of art they were hired to retrieve. Many of the paintings in the museum have been destroyed by moisture and UV rays entering from the cracks in the ceiling. Some of the works of art are so faded that the images are completely unrecognizable, worthless.

Zippo finds one that is still mostly intact. A picture of two little girls gathering acorns. He pulls it off the wall and wipes a layer of dust from the surface.

"That's not one of them," Xiu tells him over his shoulder. "The ones we are looking for are different. Unique."

Zippo smiles and gazes at the little girls in the picture. Xiu wraps her arm around his waist and peers longingly into the image from behind Zippo's shoulder. They put the picture back onto the wall, then press their foreheads together as they take one last look at the girls gathering acorns.

The day Xiu, Zippo, and Vine became a unit was the day that they were married. In Mongol culture, the ceremony that brings three children together into one unit is also a bond of matrimony. Merc punk units are all threesome relationships. They share the same bed as a trio, they mate as a trio, and they raise children as a trio—until their children are old enough to join their own trio.

When the Head of a unit reaches the age of twenty-three, they can decide whether or not to take time off to breed. They have another chance at age twenty-five, and at age twenty-seven. Xiu wanted to have a child. Even though she would not be able to raise it for long, she still wanted to produce young. Zippo and Vine also wanted to have children badly, because it was what their Head wanted. So Xiu put in a request to enter a breeding period.

During a breeding period, merc punks don't have to go on missions or do much work of any kind. They get to stay on their boat and spend their time trying to get pregnant. These are the happiest days in a merc punk's life.

The first time Xiu's unit made love, they were all very awkward. Because a unit is trained to think and act as one being, sex is more like masturbation.

"Ummm…" Xiu giggled as they sat naked on the bed together, in a circle. They were already completely familiar with each other's bodies, yet intimacy on this level was new to them. It was mysterious, exciting.

Zippo was the most awkward of the three. As an Arm, he is not supposed to have desires and feelings of his own. He is supposed to put all of his attention into mimicking his Head's feelings and desires. Arms are trained to empty their minds of their own thoughts and fill them with the thoughts of their Head. They see their bodies as puppets for their Heads, and their consciousnesses as mere spectators that view everything from above the action.

However, Zippo sometimes finds himself with desires of his own. He is in love with Xiu, more in love with her than any Arm is supposed to love their Head. Sometimes he wants to hold her in his arms, kiss her with all of his passion, but if Xiu doesn't order him to do these things he's not allowed to. He just has to wait for the moment to come, when she commands him to do so.

Zippo was on the bed, shaking with the thought of being able to make love to Xiu for the first time. He knew that Xiu saw it only as if she was just making love to herself, but he couldn't stop the feelings from flooding in. He waited patiently for Xiu to order him onto her body.

Xiu smiled at her Arms and giggled. It was as if she didn't know where to begin. They had all been waiting so long for this moment that they could hardly believe it was finally happening.

Zippo visualized strings connected to the end of Xiu's fingers as she reeled him toward her body. She giggled as she had him lick her left breast, suck her cocoa-colored nipple into his mouth, rub his hands down her tobacco-scented chest. She leaned back and put her hands behind her short black mohawk, as her Arms followed her telepathic commands. Vine kissed the right side of her neck and ear, as Xiu's strings pulled Zippo's tongue further down her body, over her belly button, to her inner thighs.

Merc punk threesomes are not quite the same as a normal threesome relationship. When units have sex, it is always the two Arms having sex with the Head. The two arms never make love with each other. Some units are bisexual, but these are only in the cases where the Head and one of the Arms are of the same gender.

Xiu widened her mouth as she masturbated herself with her Arms. She gave herself oral sex with her Left Arm as she rubbed her breasts with her Right Arm. Then she laid back and brought her Left Arm's penis inside of her.

The moment Zippo felt his Head's warm insides, he knew that he was already going to have an orgasm. If he could only pause for a moment he wouldn't pass the point of no return, but he couldn't stop unless she commanded him to. "I'm going to come," Zippo said.

"Don't," Xiu ordered, moaning beneath him. "Keep going."

Zippo tried to do as he was ordered, but it was the first time he had ever had sex. He couldn't prevent himself from ejaculating before she ordered him to do so. When she felt his penis become soft inside of her, Xiu's face filled with shock. Her Left Arm had disobeyed orders.

"Get off of me," she said.

She pulled his strings and moved him to the far side of the bed, then continued masturbating herself with only her Right Arm.

It is common for a Head to prefer one Arm over the other during sexual intercourse. In bisexual units, the Head might prefer one gender over the other. Or a Head might just find one Arm more sexually attractive, or one Arm might perform better in bed.

Zippo tried not to cry as he was left out of the lovemaking. He wasn't allowed to be sad if Xiu wasn't sad. He wasn't allowed to be jealous of the Right Arm. He was not allowed to look away as Xiu masturbated herself without him.

When a Head prefers one arm over the other, the unit would be considered either Right-handed or Left-handed. Zippo had always thought that Xiu's unit was ambidextrous, until they started to make love. Then he discovered that her unit was actually Right-handed. Although he was supposed to have no feelings of his own, this hurt Zippo deeply. He loved her so much. He couldn't bear the thought of her preferring Vine over him, even if it was just a little bit.

They come to a chained door upstairs. After searching the entire museum, this is the last door they haven't searched. Zippo cuts the chain with his right scissor-arm, and the chains clank against the floor.

"Let's go," Xiu says, as Vine kicks the door open.

Inside, the room is a vast hall. It had been designed for special exhibits, and there was no exhibit more special than the works on display here.

Xiu enters first, going toward a sculpture in the center of the room.

"This is it," she says.

The sculpture raises its head and looks at her.

"Brains..." it says.

The piece of artwork is a zombie that had been torn apart and re-assembled into a twisted abstract sculpture, with steel bars woven through its flesh. The ribcage opened like butterfly wings, a black fist in its chest in place of a heart. A living, writhing piece of art created out zombie flesh.

There are dozens of them, abstract sculptures made out of the flesh of the living dead. Along the walls, there are paintings, also composed of undead tissue. Each one still shifting and wheezing, permanently frozen inside of their frames.

"Get as many as you can carry," Xiu says. "We need to get them to the helicopter before dark."

Her Arms nod at her, pulling sheets and twine from their bags, to wrap up the valuable works of art.

Their client is the grandson of a man named Gunther von Hagens, the inventor of plastination. His grandfather was a controversial anatomist known for his *Body Worlds* exhibits, which blurred the line between science and art. He used the bodies of the dead, fixed with a formalin, dissected into unusual forms, dehydrated and gas-cured. This would preserve the bodies, shaping them into grotesque and fascinating works of art.

After Z-Day, Gunther von Hagens had found himself trapped in the United States, in the very city where this season of *Zombie Survival* is being filmed. Fifty years ago, he barricaded himself in an art museum and slowly went mad. Whether he admitted it to the public or not, Gunther was an artist and human flesh was his medium. Having found himself trapped in the middle of the zombie wasteland surrounded by the living dead, with an infinite amount of time on his hands, he decided to continue his work, but this time he used the flesh of the living dead.

His sanity had left him on Z-Day, when the sculptures in his *Body Worlds* exhibit had come to life. The sculptures had become infected by the first zombie he had seen, staggering through the science museum and puking green vomit onto his sculptures. The zombie was only freshly turned and security thought it was just a crazed drunk. They escorted it out of the exhibit and the crowd of bystanders turned their attention back on the exhibits.

The first sculpture to come to life was the infant inside of the pregnant woman sculpture. A man saw it moving in there, wiggling. He leaned in for a closer look, then the pregnant woman came to life, bit into his skull, and ripped out his brains with her plasticized teeth.

The crowd ran screaming as the exhibits came to life. A zombie split into three sections on top of a horse trampled through the crowd. A running male zombie with its muscles sprayed out like fans grabbed a woman from behind, weaved his rope-like muscles around her torso, then ripped her throat out. A soccer-playing exhibit staggered through the crowd with his soccer ball glued to his forehead. A paper-thin slab of an obese man gurgled on top of a table.

When he saw his specimens come to life, Gunther von Hagens fell to the ground, bawling. He looked over at his wife and saw blood spraying from the top of her head. A skinless corpse dangling from the ceiling by wires had torn the scalp off of her head. As he watched his wife shrieking, blood coating her dress, Gunther began to scream.

The zombie dangling from the wires looked over at him, chewing on his wife's scalp. The sight made Gunther scream louder. This made many of his sculptures turn their attentions on him. They staggered toward him. Gunther found himself surrounded by his specimens. A basketball player growled behind his back, a male and a female joined at the crotch pulled themselves across the floor, a chess player with an open skull cried for his brains.

Gunther ripped an umbrella from the hand of one of his exhibits and used it to push his way through the walking dead. He grasped his shrieking wife by the wrist and ran out of there, through the chaos of Z-Day, and barricaded himself inside of the art museum.

This is where he spent the next decade of his life, constructing new works of art out of the flesh of the undead. Eventually, he was discovered by a band of soldiers scavenging the wasteland, and brought back to an outpost outside of town. He re-married, had children, and those children moved to the island of Neo New York. But his works of art were left behind.

His grandson hired the merc punks to retrieve his work from the museum, as many pieces as they could carry. The rumors of his grandfather's work were spread wide through the Platinum Quadrant. He knew they would become popular gallery pieces. All he needed to do was hire some merc punks willing to go there. Unfortunately, merc punks didn't travel that far into the Red Zone, they only went on missions near the coasts. That is, until he told the Mongol tribe about the *Zombie Survival* television show. He told them if he could get a merc punk unit on the show, he would reward them handsomely. Of course, only one of them would be able to come back alive.

"But make sure to get the one with the red dress," Gunther's grandson told the merc punks the night before their mission. "That was his masterpiece."

"Red dress?" Xiu asked.

"You'll know it when you see it," he said.

Xiu stares at Gunther's masterpiece on the wall, a 4' x 5' painting using the flesh of a woman wearing a red dress. It was Gunther's first wife. After she had become infected and turned into a walking corpse, Gunther decided to turn her into the most beautiful work of art he could create. He knew that she never wanted to become one of his sculptures, but it was the only way he could be with her and be safe from infection. She would not become an ordinary sculpture, though. She would become his masterpiece. Like the Mona Lisa, Gunther's wife was transformed into artistic nobility within the frame.

"Mission accomplished," Xiu says, as she takes the woman down from the wall, wraps her in a sheet, then ties her in twine.

The woman in the painting rolls her eyes into Xiu's direction, her lips tremble, begging for mercy.

"Let's go," she tells her Arms. "The helicopter is only an hour away. Forty minutes if we hurry."

Her two Arms nod at her. Zippo doesn't nod very excitedly. He doesn't want to hurry to the helicopter. He wants their mission to last forever.

Xiu's unit sees this as a suicide mission. Even if they succeed, they will not be able to return home as a whole. Xiu will have to leave her two Arms behind. Mongol units are always willing to sacrifice themselves for the good of the tribe. The money that would be made if this mission is successful is enough to feed their tribe for a very long time.

After three months into the breeding period, Xiu learned that she was unable to have children. No matter how many times she had sex with her Arms, she could not conceive. This was crushing to her unit. It was what they wanted most in the world. Then Xiu's unit was volunteered for this suicide mission. Because her unit was unable to reproduce, they were considered expendable by the Mongol tribe.

Zippo didn't want to go on the mission. Even though Xiu was proud to be of service to her people, Zippo couldn't help but disagree with her.

"I don't want us to go," Zippo said to his Head, the day before the mission. "I don't want to lose you."

Xiu kissed him on the head. Even though he surprised her with his disobedience, she decided not to punish him.

The thought of leaving them behind was horrible to her. She would rather stay in the Red Zone and die with her Arms than return home without them. There was a part of Xiu that hopes their mission will fail.

"We will always be together," Xiu said, rubbing his curls out of his eyes. "Even after we die."

"In Heaven?" Zippo asked.

"Yes," she said. "On that day we will be combined into one body, together as we were meant to be, for all eternity."

Zippo laid his head on her breast, a tear rolling from his eye, as she stroked his dark curly hair. Then she saw Vine ready to move out, so she got up and dropped Zippo face-first into the side of the bed frame.

They arrive outside of the hospital with the paintings shifting on their backs.

"This is it?" Vine asks.

"This is it," Xiu says.

They pause there for a moment, staring at the crumbled asphalt ground. None of them are ready to part ways. Zippo trembles at the thought of losing Xiu. When she departs, they will just be two empty shells, severed limbs lying on the ground, waiting to be eaten by ants.

"Good journey," Xiu tells Vine.

She wraps her arms around him and kisses him on the cheek. Zippo wishes she was hugging him instead of Vine. Because the unit is Right-handed, she decides to say goodbye to her favorite Arm instead of both of them. He wishes he could feel what Vine is feeling as Xiu cries on his shoulder. He wishes he would have been a Right Arm instead of a Left Arm.

When Xiu lets go of Vine, she turns to Zippo. His mouth widens in surprise as she embraces him as well.

"Good journey, Zippo," she says, her hot tears dripping down his neck.

Then she grabs him by the face and kisses him deeply. She holds him with all of her strength, releasing all of her love into him through her lips, her tears running down his cheeks.

When she stops kissing, she looks Zippo in the eyes. She tells him she loves him in the telepathic way Heads communicate with their Arms. Although Xiu's unit is Right-handed, it is only because Vine is the stronger warrior of the two and a better partner in bed. But in Xiu's heart, she loves Zippo the most of the two. Zippo was her little sweetheart ever since they were kids. She has always loved Zippo. Leaving him is the hardest part of their separation.

"I'll finish the mission," Xiu says, her voice cracking. "Our death won't be for nothing."

Then she takes the paintings from Zippo and Vine, and straps them to her back. She bends down and clicks her jumper kneecaps on. Then she nods at her Arms in a last quick goodbye. They nod back.

Xiu's mechanical kneecaps launch her into the air, up to the roof of the hospital. Zippo looks up at her as she flies, his lips curling into a smile. Although they are separating, it fills his heart with warmth to know how much she loves him. He watches her for every last second, not blinking, enjoying his final view of the woman who was his wife, his mind, his voice, his all.

He wants to yell up at her, tell her he loves her for the first time. He has never told her he loves her, because she has never ordered him to do so. In order to tell her this, he would have to speak with his own free will. He would have to do something he wasn't ordered to do. Even though it is against everything he has been taught, he decides to do it. He has to.

As Zippo opens his mouth to tell Xiu he loves her, a glimmer of light flashes into his vision. Then blood sprays into the sunlight. Xiu's body falls to the earth in two separate pieces.

When the two Arms see their Head's body on the ground by their feet, they don't know what to do. Without her to give them commands, they are just dead limbs.

Zippo looks up at the roof of the hospital to see Nemesis standing there, her white naked body blocking out the sun. She holds out her hand and her double-bladed S-shaped sword returns to her.

"You fucking bitch," Zippo yells at the genetically engineered super soldier. "I'm going to kill you!"

Zippo climbs up the cracked wall with his scissor-hands, then leaps at Nemesis. He swings his shears at her, clipping at her cold lizard flesh.

Xiu is not commanding Zippo, but he believes that she is. There are thoughts and commands filling his head, telling him what to do. He assumes they are Xiu's thoughts, giving him orders telepathically from beyond the grave. He doesn't realize that the thoughts are actually his own.

Nemesis swings her sword at Zippo, but he catches it in his claw and tosses it aside. The voices in his head are telling him to kill this creature, to avenge the woman he loves. He cries out Xiu's name as he jump-kicks into the air, foot-scissors widening toward the woman's paper-white neck.

A memory flashes into Zippo's head. Since his head has always been filled with Xiu's thoughts, he had completely forgotten the memory until now.

It was a time when they were still kids. They were training in the Red Zone at night. Their mission was to learn how to sleep in the same vicinity as the undead.

While surrounded by zombies, they weren't supposed to be talking to each other, but Xiu rarely did as she was told. She covered them with a blanket and lit a flashlight.

"I want to show you something," young Xiu told Zippo.

She whispered as quietly as she could so she wouldn't wake Vine or attract the undead.

Little Zippo sat up and faced her.

"I made them," Xiu said, as she pulled out two tiny dolls. One of them had blonde hair and the other short dark hair, both of them wearing dirty black dresses.

"Someday we are going to have children just like these," Xiu said. "Two little girls. One with blonde hair and one with black. I want you to be the father of the one with black hair."

Zippo smiled at the little doll. Its face crudely drawn with charcoal.

"I want you to keep it," Xiu whispered. "Protect her for me."

Zippo nodded and took the doll. He held it firmly in his arms to keep it safe. His previous Head had never given him anything before. He had never heard of a Head giving an Arm a gift like this, especially not a precious toy.

"Let's play," Xiu said. "Let's pretend they are our babies and we have to take care of them."

Zippo nodded excitedly. Then she kissed him on the lips. He blushed and looked up at her pretty round face.

"You're the daddy," she said. "And I'm the mommy."

Zippo straightened his back, pretending to be a strong confident father.

"You can break the rules," she said. "You don't have to do everything I say when we're playing."

"Okay," Zippo said, though he wasn't sure how to play without being given commands.

After a few minutes of playing mommy and daddy, they heard a zombie groaning somewhere nearby. Xiu turned off the light and pulled Zippo down, giggling at herself for being so mischievous. She shushed Zippo as they hid from the zombie, her arms wrapped around his body, still cradling their babies in their arms. Zippo could feel her smiling as her lips were pressed against his neck.

As the memory flashes through his mind, Zippo can still feel Xiu's smile against his neck. He closes his foot-shears around Nemesis' neck, tears filling the insides of his goggles.

Nemesis grabs Zippo by the ankle. She twists his leg, breaking it in three different places, and drives his foot-shears into his own chest.

Zippo falls to the ground. His body goes limp as the blades of his scissors cut through the outside of his heart. As he dies, he watches the clouds drifting overhead. Within the clouds, he hears Xiu's soft, sugary voice. She gives him one last command.

"Come to me," she orders him.

Vine stands next to Xiu's body, awaiting her orders. She doesn't give them to him. She is long dead. Like he did as a child when he lost his first Head, he just stands there, not able to think or act on his own. But an Arm's job is to intuit his Head's command before she even has to give him one. If she were alive, Vine would know exactly what she would tell him to do.

"Finish the mission," she would say.

Nemesis drops down from the roof next to Vine. He looks over at her as she steps across the living works of art toward him, spinning her sword like a propeller by her side.

"Finish the mission."

Nemesis swings her sword at Vine.

"Finish the mission."

A wire springs out of Vine's wrist, knocking the sword back. Another wire shoots out of him and hooks onto the roof above. Before Nemesis can attack again, Vine is pulled through the air to the top of the building. He runs across the roof and shoots his wire to the next building, then swings across. He shoots his wire at the next building, swings to that one, then the next building, and the next building, until he gets far away from the woman who killed two-thirds of his body.

As he flees, Nemesis stands above Xiu's corpse, watching as the merc punk swings from rooftop to rooftop. She does not follow after him. That wasn't what she was ordered to do.

It was Dr. Chan who approached Wayne Rizla about getting Nemesis on *Zombie Survival*.

"She's ready to be field tested," said Dr. Chan. "I want to get her in the middle of the Red Zone."

Wayne smirked at the tiny man leaning on his desk. "No thanks."

"What do you mean?" asked Dr. Chan. "She would be perfect for your show."

"She would be boring," Dr. Chan said.

"But she's nearly invincible. Nobody would survive as long as she would."

"That's the problem," Wayne said. "It would be too easy for her to win. Where's the drama? Where's the excitement? She's immune to the virus, zombies don't find her edible, she's fast, she's a perfect killing machine. Do you know how boring it will be to see her get all the way to the helicopter in half a day completely unharmed? The show would be over before even a quarter of the contestants were killed. No thanks."

"But the government won't give me the funding to airlift her out there myself," said Dr. Chan.

"Not my problem."

"There's got to be a way," the doctor said. "I'm telling you, she would be very fascinating to your audience." He thought for a minute. "Maybe if we gave her a handicap?"

"A handicap?" Wayne asked, straightening himself up from his chair.

"What if she had the weakest weapon or something like that?"

Wayne shook his head. "She's still invincible. No, it would have to be something else…"

Wayne stroked his goatee as he thought about it.

"How about this…" Wayne said. "Her handicap is that the helicopter won't pick her up until all the other contestants are dead."

"But what if she gets to the helicopter first?" asked Dr. Chan.

"Then she'll just have to wait there and kill off any contestant who comes to her… until she's the last one."

Dr. Chan nodded. "I think this would work just fine."

"Better than fine," Wayne said. Then he smiled. "It will be golden."

WENDY

Scavy wakes up to the sight of Mr. T looking down on him.

"Almost lost you there," says the cyborg.

Scavy sits up. He's in a hotel bed, in the cleanest room he has seen since he arrived in the wasteland. He's wearing only boxer shorts, with his torso and head wrapped in bandages.

"It's lucky you were hit with that poisoned dart," Laurence tells him. "The toxin slowed your heart rate and the bleeding. If it wasn't for that you would have bled to death before the T-2000 could fix you up."

Scavy rubs his wound. "Did we get him?"

Junko nods. "You're a lucky son of a bitch."

Scavy looks out the window, the sun is getting low in the sky. "How long have I been out?"

"Too long," Junko says. "With all the sterilization, we're several hours behind schedule."

"But it was worth it to get you back," says Mr. T, handing Scavy his sniper rifle and some new clothes. "We're gonna need all the help we can get."

Scavy looks at the clothes they have picked out for him. Musty-smelling khaki pants with a red and white striped polo shirt.

"This is all you could find?" Scavy asks, frowning at his clothing.

"I think you'd look pretty cute in that shirt," Mr. T says, giving him a big, frightening smile.

Scavy isn't sure whether Mr. T is coming on to him or if he's just so comfortable with his sexuality that he doesn't fear calling another guy *cute*.

Rainbow paces impatiently behind them. "Are we ready? Let's go."

Scavy stands. He's able to walk just fine, but light-headed and in quite a bit of pain.

"I'll be ready in a minute," Scavy says, holding his side. "We got a plan for getting there faster and shit?"

"Yeah," Junko says. "But it's not going to be easy, and we're not sure it's even going to work."

"It's probably impossible," Rainbow Cat says.

"What are you two fools talking about?" says Mr. T, waving their comments away. "With the T-2000 on the job, ain't nothin' impossible."

They explain the plan to Scavy. While the punk was out, Junko had come across a group of smart-cars on the freeway. If they can get to those then it is possible that they can drive to the evacuation zone. But there is a problem. The smart-cars have become infected with the zombie virus.

Smart-cars were invented a few years before Z-Day. They were state of the art solar-powered vehicles with organic implants. The vehicles were designed so that they could drive themselves. Because they were fitted with human brains, grown in a lab, the smart-cars were basically living beings. They could think, feel, communicate, and even love. Unfortunately, they could also become infected by the zombie virus.

When Z-Day struck, even the smart-cars were not safe from the hordes of zombies. They were cornered, ripped open, bitten, infected, and joined the ranks of the living dead. And because they were created to last forever, without requiring fuel or much repair, many of the smart-cars are still around, patrolling the zombie wasteland.

Junko had seen undead smart-cars on Zombie Survival in the past, but contestants had never tried to ride them before. They were always run over by them if they got too close, then the vehicle would futilely try to eat their victim's brains. Because they do not have mouths—normally fed a protein fluid inserted through a slot on the dashboard—eating brains was not possible.

"The problem is," Junko says. "They will attack us on sight. Even if we manage to get inside one of them, we have no idea how we'll control it."

Many smart-cars weren't even fitted with steering wheels. Their insides look similar to the backs of limousines. The brains of the smart-cars were programmed to be experts at driving. It was said that using a smart-car was the safest way to travel. That is, until they turned into mindless brain-hungry zombie cars.

Junko, Scavy, Rainbow, and the T-2000 walk down the freeway through the city, keeping a look out for the smart-cars. The undead vehicles are no longer in the same spot that Junko had last seen them in. They'll have to seek them out.

"They could be long gone by now," Rainbow Cat says.

"We'll find them," Junko says.

The four contestants cross a freeway overpass, scanning the interstate below. The road stretches for miles, overgrown with weeds so thick it's like a brown forest dotted by hundreds of wrecked rusted-out vehicles.

A section on Mr. T's robot body opens and a pair of small binoculars come out. They raise themselves up to Mr. T's eyes, then he scans the distance.

"The T-2000 don't see nothin' out there," says Mr. T.

The other four of them stare up at him, surprised to see the binoculars attached to the inside of his chest.

"What else can you do?" Junko asks.

The binoculars fold themselves back into his body.

"Well," Mr. T says, "the T-2000 wasn't designed to look pretty. The doctor who built this body designed it for missions near the outskirts of the Red Zone, and so it's been equipped accordingly."

"Got any weapons hiding in there?" Scavy asks.

"All the T-2000 needs is Brick and Mortar." Mr. T holds up his two fists. "Those are the names of Mr. T's fists."

"Why do you call them Brick and Mortar?" Rainbow asks.

"Because they're tough like brick and mortar," Mr. T says.

"But your fists are made out of steel," Rainbow says. "Isn't steel stronger than brick?"

Mr. T pauses. He scratches his chin.

"Hey," Mr. T says. "Mr. T never thought of that before. You've got a point." He thinks about it a bit more. "But Mr. T's fists can punch through brick and mortar, so maybe the names make sense after all."

"If you say so," Rainbow says.

He doesn't like her snarky tone.

"Mr. T *does* say so."

Ahead, the party of four come across a horde of zombies crowded in a circle, gathered around something.

"What's that?" Rainbow asks.

"Not sure," Junko says.

Mr. T uses his binoculars.

"It's strange," Mr. T says. "The center of the mob is wide open, as if something is holding them back."

Getting to higher ground, they look more carefully. In the middle of the mob, there is a girl lying on the street. The zombies are after her, but something is keeping them from getting to her. It's as if there is a twenty-foot barrier around the girl, but nothing looks to be there. There's no railing or glass stopping them. It's as if an invisible wall protects the girl.

"She's one of the contestants, isn't she?" Rainbow asks.

"She *was*," Mr. T says. "Look."

His binoculars shift over to Rainbow and she looks through to see blood on the pavement by the girl's face. She's dead.

"I don't remember her," Junko says. "What was her name?"

"Wendy," says Mr. T. "I'm surprised she lasted as long as she did. Back at the hotel, she was a sorry sight."

When Wendy awoke back at the hotel, she was so frightened she couldn't speak to anybody. Perhaps she could have joined some-body's team if she had spoken up, but she couldn't get the words out. When she saw Oro escaping out of the side door, she followed after him, but he wouldn't let her follow for very long. She was on her own.

The weapon they had given her wasn't exactly a weapon. It was a lawn gnome. She assumed it had to have been a mistake, then she assumed it had to have been a cruel joke. She wondered what she was supposed to do with it. Smash zombies over the head with it? Poke them with the pointy red gnome hat? The weapon assigned to each contestant was supposed to match that person's fighting capabilities. She didn't understand how they could think she would be capable of fighting off hordes of zombies with a ceramic gnome.

"I don't need a weapon to fight them," she said to herself. "My greatest weapon is my faith in Jesus."

Religion was rare on the island of Neo New York, especially in Copper. But Wendy was a devoted Christian. Her mother and her mother's mother were all dedicated to the faith. They had passed down their only remaining copy of the bible to her. It was a book that guided her through her life.

"You have to go to school," her mother told her. "I don't care what those bullies did to you."

Young Wendy looked up at her mother. Her eye swollen and black. An agonizing pain in her privates.

"But they'll hurt me again…" Wendy cried.

Her mother handed her the precious family bible.

"Have faith in Jesus," she said. "He will protect you from the heathens."

"But he didn't protect me yesterday…"

"That's because you didn't have strong enough faith!"

Wendy looked down at her scabby knuckles.

"Okay?" her mother said.

"Okay," Wendy said.

Wendy's school wasn't really a school. There were only five students who were taught by a lady from the back of the porch outside of her shack. Three of the students were her children. She taught the other two students for a small monthly fee from their mothers.

Unfortunately, the school wasn't on the best side of town. Wendy was often attacked on her way to and from school, by teenaged gang members or angry old men, who wanted inside of her. She could have tried to sneak through the back streets to get away from them, but her mother told her all she needed was faith and nothing could harm her. But every time, no matter how much she believed Jesus would deliver her from harm, she was raped by different attackers. Sometimes she was even assaulted more than once in a day. When she would arrive home, her mother would have no pity for her.

"It's because you lack faith," her mother would say, and if Wendy ever argued back she would be beaten.

She grew up and got a job in a soup kitchen, but her problem never changed. She was still attacked on the street. Her frail body and cowering posture made her a perfect victim. Predators seemed to be drawn to her. Every day, she believed with all her heart that Jesus would protect her. Some days she would get away with no harm done to her, other days she would come home with a ripped dress and a black eye. The last man who attacked her had a white suit and a white goatee. The next day, she awoke as a contestant on *Zombie Survival*.

In the zombie wasteland, Wendy knew that she had to believe in Jesus more than she ever had in the past. She had to have faith so no harm would come to her.

As she walked down the street in the Red Zone, she moved with confident strides. She did not take a safe route, because she believed that would show a lack of faith. She went straight toward the goal. With all her heart, she believed Jesus would save her. With all her heart, she knew no zombie would lay a hand on her body.

Wendy didn't have her bible on her, nor her crucifix. This worried her at first because her mother had always told her that carrying a holy symbol or being in the presence of the bible would increase her faith. These things would give her power, but she had none. This worried her greatly.

When she encountered the first zombie, her faith was put to the test. A zombie was standing in her way, growling, calling out for her brains. She paused for a moment. Without a holy symbol, she wasn't sure if her faith would be strong enough. So she closed her eyes and put all of her soul into her faith. She visualized the beautiful magnificence of Jesus. She let him into her heart, filled herself with his love, and knew that he would let no harm come to her. She kept on her path, marching directly toward the living corpse.

Then something miraculous happened. As she approached the corpse, the creature got out of her way. It cowered before her, trembling at the might of the holy spirit filling her soul. She smiled as she moved on. For once in her life, her faith was strong enough to protect her. When she looked down at the lawn gnome, she discovered she did have a holy symbol in her possession. A blob of brown paint in the gnome's coat looked exactly like a crucifix. She hugged the gnome close to her body. She knew that Jesus had come to her in the form of a lawn gnome.

Then she came across a large mob of zombies. They barreled through the street toward her. As she arrived to them, they moved aside, opening a path for her to go through.

"You were right, mother," Wendy said to the heavens. "All I needed was faith."

She walked all day with no incident. She didn't run into any other contestant. Every zombie cowered before her faith. She knew she would be the winner of the contest, because she had Jesus on her side. At night, she bunked down in a hotel room, without even locking the door. She held her gnome tightly to her heart.

"You'll save me, Jesus. I know you will."

"Wait here," says Mr. T. "The T-2000 will be right back."

The others stay back as Mr. T goes down toward the zombie mob. A camera ball floats after him. He punches his way through the crowd until he enters the open circle. The zombies don't follow him within. Junko, Scavy, and Rainbow come in for a closer look. Mr. T examines the girl's body, digging through her pack. He tosses the pack aside and takes a lawn gnome lying by the girl's side. He lifts it up, inspecting each side of it. When he moves it toward the zombies, they back away. He moves away from the dead girl, back toward the others. As he moves, the open circle moves with him.

"What is it?" Rainbow asks.

Junko squints her eyes. "I don't know, but whatever it is the zombies won't go near it."

As Mr. T moves far enough away from Wendy's body that the invisible perimeter no longer protects her, the zombie horde pounce on top of her. They screech with excitement, rolling over one another, as they tear apart her flesh to get to her brain.

When Mr. T arrives to them, they all stand within the protective barrier. Zombies quickly surround them. Scavy, Junko, and Rainbow Cat stand back-to-back, aiming their weapons at the shambling corpses. But the zombies keep their distance, they do not attack.

Mr. T holds up the lawn gnome.

"They did it..." he says.

"What?" Junko asks, looking back and forth between the gnome and the undead.

Mr. T explains, "The doctor who built the T-2000, he developed a technology that could keep zombies at bay. Mr. T guesses those scientists in Neo New York got it up and running."

Junko takes the gnome from him. A camera ball overhead zooms in on it.

Mr. T continues, "Inside this little guy, there's a device that emits a sonic wave that the zombies just can't stand." Mr. T takes back the device and bounces it in his metal hand. "This one's emitting a pretty low frequency, so it only holds them back a dozen feet or so. But with a more powerful emission this thing could hold back at least a square mile, or even protect an entire city."

"This technology could save the world," Junko says.

"If those suckas bothered to use it," he says. "Mr. T don't think those fat cats in Platinum care about saving the world at the moment. They're more interested in their own well-being. The only thing they care to use it for is as a mere toy on this vile television show."

"So we can use this to get safely to the helicopter?" Rainbow asks. "And even if we don't get to the helicopter, we can still use it to get out of the Red Zone, can't we?"

"The T-2000 isn't sure how long the power supply will last," says Mr. T. "If it's solar powered then it will last all the way to the coast, but that's doubtful. It'll likely only last for a few days. Maybe less."

"Knowing Wayne," Junko says. "It will likely be less."

"So if this thing protected that girl from the undead…" Rainbow asks, looking back at the mound of corpses attacking Wendy's body. "Then what killed her?"

Wendy had made it a third of the way to the evacuation zone. Mobs of zombies followed her, surrounded her, but they could not touch her. She believed her faith in Jesus was protecting her, but the power that held the zombies back was really a device hidden inside her lawn gnome.

Then Wendy came across a pack of mechjaws. They growled at her from a distance. When the girl saw these hellhounds, snarling and gnashing their teeth at her, she did not fear.

"Have faith," her mother's voice said in her head. "And Jesus will protect you."

Wendy had faith. She marched forward, directly toward the mechjaws. Then the Gatling gun on one of their backs whirred in a circle. Bullets sprayed into her body. She looked down at the holes in her chest, blood dribbling down her blue dress. Then she fell back into a pool of her own blood.

As she lay dying, she looked up at the clouds. Tears drained from her eyes.

"I'm sorry, mother," she said to the sky. "My faith wasn't strong enough."

The mechjaws growled at her from the distance.

Her last words were, "My faith was *never* strong enough." Then the gnome rolled from her limp hands.

"Her body was riddled with bullet holes," says Mr. T. "I think those cyborg zombie dogs got to her."

"We have to be careful," Junko says. "This thing might protect us from the zombies, but it doesn't protect us from the mechjaws."

Mr. T grunts in agreement. "And we should watch our backs. A pack of those things might still be in the area."

The other three nod their heads at the cyborg.

Mr. T gives them a thumbs up.

Then he gets run over by a truck.

The SUV-sized zombie smart-car plows through the zombie horde, slams into Mr. T, taking his body across the field with it. The lawn gnome flies out of Mr. T's hands, soaring through the air alongside severed zombie body parts. It lands several yards away, on the other side of the mob.

Junko, Scavy, and Rainbow Cat suddenly find themselves in the middle of the zombie horde without protection. The zombies fill the open space between them.

"Go for the gnome!" Junko yells.

The Japanese woman's chainsaw arm roars into life. She slashes her way through the corpses, taking off limbs and heads. Behind her, Rainbow Cat swings her machete, chopping at the limbs coming in from the back. Scavy stays between them, using the butt of his rifle to push the corpses back.

Mr. T opens his eyes to find himself several yards away from everyone else. He's lying in the dirt, watching the zombie SUV tearing across the field. It curves around, then speeds toward him.

As he gets halfway to his feet, a mob of corpses tackle him. They pull his machine body to the ground, piling on top of him, as the vehicle barrels toward them.

Mr. T looks up at a zombie on his chest. It chatters its teeth and shrieks in his face.

"Brrrraaaainnns!!" the zombie cries in a high pitched voice.

The zombie bites down on Mr. T's head, but it's teeth can't break through his skin.

"You can't bite through Mr. T's head, fool!" says Mr. T.

Then he headbutts the zombie in the face.

"Mr. T's head's not made of metal," he says. "But it might as well be."

He headbutts the zombie again, so hard it breaks open the creature's skull.

Junko chainsaws her way through the crowd. Once she breaks through, she spots the lawn gnome across the field.

"That way!" she cries.

Scavy and Rainbow Cat follow close behind, as she runs through the field. Scavy limp-hops as fast as he can, trying not to rip open his wound.

Once they're all out in the open, they see the vehicles flying at them. Four more smart cars race through the field, picking up clouds of dust. Rainbow Cat leaps out of the way, as a small black smart-car races by, narrowly missing her.

"The gnome isn't going to help save us from those," Scavy yells.

"Let's get to it anyway," Junko responds.

As they continue on, Junko looks back at Mr. T. He's under a pile of zombies, over a dozen thick, with the zombie SUV charging right for him.

The zombies hold Mr. T down, biting at his metal body, yanking on his limbs. Even with his cyborg strength, he can't lift himself up. The sound of the zombie SUV fills his ears, as it comes closer, only a few car lengths away.

"Think you can keep down the T-2000?" Mr. T asks the zombies growling in his face. "Think again!"

Long metal spikes spring out of Mr. T's arms and torso. Then the rows of spikes spin in opposite directions, like a meat-grinder. All zombie flesh touching his body becomes pulverized. Zombie muscles are grated apart, hands split down the middle, skin strips away like shredded paper, bones break, meat liquefies.

Mr. T leaps to his feet and roars, mangled corpses flying over his shoulder. As the zombie SUV slams into him, the T-2000 turns and punches the front of the vehicle.

The T-2000 stays in one spot, but the SUV crumples inward. As if it had hit a pillar of steel, the vehicle folds itself around Mr. T's fist, metal twisting, the back wheels flying up into the air. When Mr. T removes his fist, the SUV whirs and gurgles. His fist had gone all the way through the engine, rendering it useless.

Junko grabs the lawn gnome, then brings it to Scavy and Rainbow Cat. They turn to Mr. T and see the other four smart-cars roaring toward him all at once.

Mr. T leaps over the first one, fifteen times higher than an average human can jump, then lands on the next car's hood, crushing it into the dirt.

"How much does he weigh?" Rainbow asks.

By the look of the front of the vehicle, flattened all the way to the earth, Mr. T's robot body must weigh at least a ton.

As the next vehicle comes at him, he grabs it by the bumper and tosses it upward. The vehicle flips twice in the air and lands on its side behind him.

"Think you got what it takes to take on the T-2000?" he yells at the remaining vehicles.

He swats at another car with the back of his hand as it passes. The vehicle spins around in circles, rolling over the zombie horde, throwing bodies into the air.

"I didn't think so," he says.

As the last smart-car comes at him, he jumps out of the way, then grabs it by the back bumper. He holds it into place, the wheels spinning in the dirt.

"Come on," he yells at the other three.

Junko, Scavy, and Rainbow Cat run across the field toward him. They go to the doors of the smart car. As they approach, its wheels move faster, as if it's trying to get away from the device within the lawn gnome.

Junko breaks a window with the side of her chainsaw and unlocks the door. They jump inside. Her mouth drops open as she notices there is no dashboard in the vehicle, no steering wheel, no controls. There are just two long seats along the sides of the interior. This one wasn't meant to be driven by anyone but the car itself.

"What do we do?" Rainbow asks. "How are we supposed to drive this thing without a steering wheel?"

"Just get in," Junko says.

After they enter, Mr. T works his way along the side until he gets to the door. Then he hops in. The smart-car speeds away, driving in the opposite direction. They hold onto their seats as it drives up onto a street and flies down the road, weaving between rotten husks of old automobiles.

"It's out of control!" Rainbow cries. "We're going to crash!"

Scavy looks at the direction they're going in, then looks at the lawn gnome.

"It's trying to get away from this," he says, pointing at the gnome.

"Well, we just can't get rid of it," Rainbow says.

Scavy grabs the gnome from Junko's hands.

"No," he says, "but we can use it to direct this thing and shit."

He aims the gnome at an angle, and the vehicle turns, heading in the correct direction. Then he hands it back to Junko.

"Just hold it in the opposite direction you want to go," Scavy says.

Junko moves the gnome to the left side of the car and the vehicle turns right, then she brings it to the other side of vehicle and it turns left. When she holds it in the middle, it goes straight.

"See?" Scavy says. "If the thing is trying to get away from the gnome we can control where we want it to go."

Junko gets the hang of how it works.

"Good job," she says, smiling at him. "I'll take it from here."

Scavy smiles back through his blackened teeth, then pulls out the map to act as navigator.

"Ahhh," Mr. T says, leaning back in the comfortable luxurious seats. "It's about time the T-2000 got a little rest."

He sits back to enjoy the ride.

Rainbow Cat is too on edge to enjoy the ride. She stares anxiously through the window. At the speed they are moving, they are all likely to be killed if they crash. She tries out the seatbelts, but the buckles fall apart in her hand.

Outside of the window, Rainbow sees something flying in the air. It is a man in a small flying machine, peddling it like a bicycle, gliding through the air.

Oro looks down on the smart-car from his glider-cycle, peddling casually, in no real rush.

"You will not get there faster than I," Oro says to the vehicle. "I am a genius. You don't stand a chance against an intellect as grand as mine."

Gogo and Popcorn arrive at the field littered with broken smart-cars and mangled zombies. They had been watching from the overpass, but didn't get there in time to join their friends. They go to one of the vehicles that still runs, lying on its side.

"Help me push this over," Popcorn asks her friend.

"Brains!" Gogo says.

"We're going to try to help them, not eat their brains," Popcorn says, as they push the vehicles onto its wheels.

When they get into the car, they aren't sure how to drive the thing. Gogo leans toward the dashboard of the car.

"Brains," she says to the zombie car.

The car starts its engines and begins to drive.

"Did you just talk to the car?" Popcorn asks.

"Yeah," Gogo says. "If we lead it toward brains it will go wherever we want."

Gogo pukes up green slime on the floor of the vehicle.

"That's sick, Gogo!"

"I really fucking need some brains," Gogo says, wiping the gunk from her face with her arm.

"We'll be there shortly," Junko says, while directing the zombie car with the lawn gnome. "Be ready for those merc punks. They are going to be a lot tougher to deal with then the zombies."

Scavy nods and loads his sniper rifle.

"So who gets to go on the helicopter?" Scavy says. "If we all do make it there in one piece."

Junko pauses. It's a conversation she was hoping to avoid.

"We draw straws," says Mr. T. "It's the only way."

Junko thinks about it for a minute, then sighs.

"I'll agree to it only if everyone else agrees," Junko says. "But everyone has to agree to the outcome no matter what happens. The three losers will have to give their life to protect the person who gets the longest straw."

"Well, the T-2000 agrees to those terms," says Mr. T. "It's the only way that's fair."

Scavy puts his rifle in his lap.

"Fuck, why not," Scavy says. "I'm in. If I don't pull the long straw I'll still support the winner. You got my word." He looks down at his hands, then looks up with a smile on the side of his mouth. "The three of you deserve to get out of here more than I do, anyway."

There is a long pause before Rainbow Cat speaks up. All of them look at her, wondering what she's thinking.

"Okay," she says. "I agree, too."

"You sure?" Junko says.

"Yes."

"You promise you won't disregard who pulls the long straw the second you see the helicopter?"

"I Promise!"

Junko takes a deep breath. "Okay. Well, let's do it." Then she turns to Rainbow. "Let me see your knife."

Rainbow pulls the dagger out of her bag and gives it to her. Junko grabs one of Rainbow's dreadlocks and cuts it off.

"Ow!" Rainbow cries, holding her head.

Junko tosses Scavy the dagger and the dreadlock.

"Cut that into four pieces," she says. "Each one bigger than the last. We are going to create a hierarchy. If the person with the longest piece of hair gets killed or infected, the person with the next longest piece of hair takes their place. If something happens to that person then the next one in line gets to go. And so on."

Everyone understands. Scavy begins cutting up the dreadlock.

"That way, there's still hope for all of us," she says. "We can still work as a team."

Rainbow draws the shortest dreadlock.

"What the fuck?" Rainbow cries. "I can't be the last in line! I need to get back to the island. I *need* to!"

"Fair is fair," says Mr. T.

"But you don't understand," Rainbow says. "This isn't about me. It's about my husband's work. He's the greatest novelist of our time. If I'm not the one who makes it back to the island his masterpiece will never be published!"

"You agreed to the rules," Junko says. "There's no backing out now."

"But—"

"No buts," Mr. T says. "It was a fair draw. Mr. T is third in line, and you don't hear him whining about it, do ya?"

Rainbow keeps quiet as Mr. T raises his voice. Her face becomes flushed. Junko pulls the second longest piece of hair and thinks nothing of it.

When Scavy is left with the longest piece of hair, his face lights up.

"What?" he says. "I got the longest! No shit!"

"We've got your back," Mr. T says.

"But I don't deserve this," Scavy says. "I think Junko should take it. I'm just a fucking scumbag loser."

"You're not a loser to me," says Mr. T. "I saw you take out that nazi fool all by yourself. In my opinion, you're a first class hero."

Mr. T smiles bright white teeth at Scavy.

"I'll trade you," Rainbow says. "You said you don't deserve to go, so give me the long straw. You can have the short one."

Scavy doesn't want to give her his straw.

"Fine," she says. "Junko can take the long straw and I'll take the second longest. How about that?"

Scavy thinks about it. Though he likes the idea of giving Junko the long straw, he would rather not give Rainbow the second longest.

"No trades," Mr. T says. "We all agreed before we drew. This is the lineup. No matter what, we got to stick with that, or else none of us will get home."

"I agree," Junko says.

Scavy puts the lock of hair in his pocket and nods his head. After an intimidating stare from Mr. T, Rainbow nods her head as well.

VINE

Vine stands on a rooftop overlooking the hospital. He sees Nemesis, standing on the roof of the hospital as still as a statue. She is naked, her cold white skin glimmering in the sunlight as the sun peeks out from a sheet of gray clouds, her long black hair flowing in the breeze.

His hands shake as he stares at her. Vine doesn't know exactly what he's going to do. He's lost without Xiu and Zippo. He knows Xiu would want him to finish the mission. He has to kill the woman with the paper-white skin, reclaim the artwork, and wait for the helicopter to arrive. But he's not sure he can fight without Xiu telling him what to do.

There was only one time in his life that Vine was in a similar situation. In his early twenties, Vine had become separated from Xiu and Zippo in a city along the Mexican coast. He was all alone and had to make it back to the ship by himself.

At first, he couldn't even walk on his own. He was just a dead severed limb. Then zombies started to come for him.

"Cerebros!" they said.

He still couldn't move. If he had Xiu he could have cut them all down with his wire in less than a second, but operating his wires was difficult for him. It was always as if she was the one operating his wires for him. But then something happened. When the zombies got too close, his survival instincts clicked in and without thinking about it he cut down every last zombie on the street.

He looked at his hands. He was able to move them. He tried his feet. He was able to move them, too. That's when he realized it was possible for him to move on his own, without the commands of his Head.

But as he crept through the city, he still had problems using his own thoughts. That is, until he channeled Xiu's voice. He found that if he pretended his thoughts were really Xiu's thoughts, he could move on his own. Perhaps he wasn't as efficient of a soldier without his Head, but he was still capable of defending himself.

Zombies ran at him from left and right. His wires darted out of his wrist, cut off their heads, then came back. He shot a wire at a zombie pig, hooked onto its snout, spun around, and tossed the pig face-first into a wall.

Although he did not feel at all whole, he was still a competent zombie-killing machine. He cut his way through the streets, down to the beach, and was picked up by the closest ship. When he met with Xiu again, she rested her forehead against his chest. His thoughts emptied from his head, her thoughts filled it up. From that moment on, he had no need to think on his own. Until now.

Vine focuses his thoughts, attempts to bring back the method he used years ago. He tries to imagine his thoughts are really Xiu's commands. If he focuses hard enough, envisioning Xiu by his side just out of view, he will be able to complete his mission.

Just as Vine launches his wire at the next building and swings toward the ground, he sees a black vehicle barreling across the weed-coated parking lot, heading straight for the hospital.

"There it is," Junko says, as they drive across the parking lot to the hospital. "We need to get onto the roof."

As they race toward the hospital, the vehicle shows no signs of slowing down.

"So how do we stop this thing?" Scavy asks.

Junko looks at him. "I was hoping you had some ideas."

"I didn't think that far ahead," Scavy says.

The wall of the hospital closes in on them.

"Jump!" Mr. T cries, opening his door and rolling out into the street.

"Oh, fuck," Rainbow says.

Scavy grabs the hippy and they roll out of the car across the fractured asphalt, scraping up her elbows and knees.

When it's Junko's turn, she waits for the last minute. When she moves to the side of the vehicle with the lawn gnome, the car swerves. This slows it down enough for her to jump out safely. The car slams through the wall of the building, causing an avalanche of bricks. The entire front of the hospital collapses onto the smart-car, nearly knocking Junko off her feet as she retreats.

Mr. T is helping up Scavy and Rainbow when Junko arrives to them. They are engulfed by a cloud of dust from the building, filling their lungs with grit, blinding them. Junko waves the dust away from her face and tries to focus.

"We need to move," Junko says, hacking up bits of rubble. "That crash is going to attract a lot of zombies."

"But aren't we safe from them with the gnome?" Rainbow asks.

"Not if the battery runs out," says Mr. T.

The sound of screaming zombies echoes in the distance. Coming from every block surrounding the hospital, the undead are on the run, forming together into the largest horde of the undead they have yet faced. Beyond the parking lot, a tidal wave of zombies flows in their direction.

"Here they come," Junko says, holding the gnome tightly to her chest.

As the dust settles, they see a lone figure standing on top of the rubble: A nude woman with a double-bladed sword.

"Who's the bitch?" Scavy asks.

"Is she another contestant?" Rainbow asks.

Junko squints her eyes, then shakes her head.

"I don't think so," she says. "If she was a contestant she would have taken the helicopter and gotten out of here already."

Nemesis stares at the four contestants, determining which target she should take down first. The large man with the metal body is obviously the strongest. If he is eliminated the others will have little chance of survival.

Mr. T jumps between the woman and his friends, as Nemesis tosses her curved double-bladed sword at them. He reaches out to grab the weapon on the air, but it cuts off the little finger on his left hand. The blade continues spinning through the air, curving across the parking lot, and returns to Nemesis' hand. Mr. T looks down at the sparks fizzling from the remains of his finger. He clenches a fist.

He looks up at her. She leans on one leg, her head cocking to the side.

"That's how you say hello?" Mr. T yells at her. "Let the T-2000 show you the proper way to greet somebody."

Mr. T charges her. His steel feet crush the asphalt beneath him, rumbling the earth with every step he takes. As he runs, his legs move faster and faster. He holds out his fist into a cannonball flying directly for her head. But once he arrives, Nemesis flips into the air and lands on the other side of him. His fist crashes into the building, knocking another section of wall into the street. He turns around and charges her again.

As the T-2000 stomps toward her, she comes at him. In a flash, she zips across the pavement, too fast for Junko and the others to see. The blade of her sword passes over Mr. T's fist and hits him in the neck.

Mr. T looks down at the blade below his chin. It didn't cut him, frozen in place. He isn't sure why she stopped herself. She could have sliced his head from his metal body right there.

Then Mr. T sees the merc punk standing in the distance, over Nemesis' shoulder. Vine has his arm elevated, pointed at the reptilian woman, his wire wrapped around her sword.

Then Mr. T gives her a big smile, as the merc punk pulls back on the wire, ripping the sword from the woman's hands. The sword flies over Vine's head, landing on the far side of the parking lot.

With his other hand, Vine launches his second wire, swiping it toward both of the two contestants. Mr. T leaps twenty feet up to dodge the wire as it slices through the air. Nemesis just stands in place. Without moving her feet, she bends her waist all the way back, in a perfect L-shape, as the wire passes over her. Then she flips out of the way, as Mr. T comes back to the earth fist-first. His metal knuckles cause a crater to open up in the asphalt beneath him. When he looks up, he sees the horde of zombies closing in on them.

"Get to the roof," Mr. T yells at Junko. "I'll handle these two."

Junko doesn't hesitate. She grabs Scavy, Rainbow, and the lawn gnome, and races toward the building.

Going through the crumbling hospital, Junko, Scavy, and Rainbow Cat make their way up to the roof. They go for the two-way radio.

"We have to call for the helicopter," Junko says.

She walks carefully along the edge of the roof to the two-way radio. A section of the roof had collapsed when the car crashed into the side of the building. The ground could fall out on her at any moment as she works her way to the communication device.

"We're here," Junko says into the radio. "Come pick us up."

Rainbow Cat looks out over the roof as the parking lot fills with the living dead. They surround the building on all sides, a sea of molten flesh. As a camera ball hovers over Junko's shoulder, a voice comes on the other side of the radio.

"We can only pick up one of you," says the voice.

"I know that," she says. "Just come pick one of us up."

"Wait right there," says the voice. "The remote helicopter will be there in ten minutes to pick *one* of you up."

"Hurry up!" Junko cries.

She tosses the radio to her feet and returns to the others. Scavy is on the other side of the roof, examining a dead body.

"Who is it?" Rainbow asks, as they gather around him.

"That Haroon guy," Junko says. "It looks like the strange woman killed him."

Scavy bends down and picks up the solar-powered shotgun.

"What's that?" Junko asks.

"Some kind of homemade shotgun," he says.

"Let me use it," Rainbow says.

Scavy shakes his head. "It's mine now."

Rainbow gives him a dirty look as they move to the helicopter pad.

"Okay," Junko says. "We have ten minutes to hold up here. Hopefully the gnome has enough juice in it to keep them back that long."

Peering over the roof, they can already see dozens of the undead entering the hospital from every entrance.

"They don't know we're on the roof," Junko says. "With luck the helicopter will get here before they find us."

Scavy nods, then looks up into the air. From above, they see Oro circling the rooftop in his flying machine.

As the zombies engulf Nemesis, Vine, and the T-2000, they no longer have space to fight each other, and turn their efforts toward the living dead.

Vine spins in a circle, both wires shooting out at maximum length, and cuts down thirty zombies. Sixty severed legs stand on the ground surrounding him, like freshly mowed blades of grass.

Metal spikes rotate on Mr. T's body, as he shreds and punches his way through the horde. He picks up a zombie by the leg and swings it around like a bat, clubbing the undead out of his way as he moves closer to his opponents.

Nemesis doesn't bother with the walking corpses. They ignore her, passing her by as if she's one of them. She retrieves her double-bladed sword, and ducks down into the crowd, like a snake waiting for its chance to strike.

From his glider-cycle, high in the gray cloudy sky, Oro looks down at the contestants on the rooftop.

"Those simpletons will not be victorious over me," Oro says. "My genius is almighty. My genius is supreme."

He aims the rocket launcher at them.

"My genius is absolute!"

Then he fires.

The trio on the roof scatter as the rocket comes toward the helicopter pad. The explosion knocks them off of their feet and blows another section of the roof away.

Scavy rolls over and aims his sniper rifle at the aircraft.

"That was a cheap shot," Scavy says, as he looks into the scope.

He fires and blows a hole in Oro's wing the size of a quarter. Scavy fires again, then again. As he hears the bullets tearing into the wings of his glider-cycle, Oro pedals it away from the rooftop, circling back toward the city.

"Shit," Junko says, helping Rainbow Cat to her feet. "That explosion is going to lead the entire horde up here."

Scavy switches from sniper to shotgun.

"Prepare yourself," Junko says.

In the small section of roof that remains, they go back-to-back.

Popcorn and Gogo drive into the parking lot of the hospital, staring at the massive horde of the living dead surrounding the building. When the car can no longer move within the mob of zombies, Gogo opens the door and jumps out.

"Hey!" Popcorn yells. "Where are you going!"

"Brains!" Gogo yells, pushing her way through the crowd. "I'm going to eat their fucking brains!"

"No!" Popcorn yells. "Get back here!"

Popcorn jumps out of the smart-car and chases after her zombie friend, but she quickly loses her in the mob.

"If she hurts Scavy," Popcorn says, "I'm going to cut off her fucking head."

Then she continues on, toward the hospital.

Nemesis goes for Vine. As the merc punk cuts down a row of undead, leaving himself open, she tosses her double-bladed sword at him.

When Vine sees the weapon spinning toward him, he launches his left wire at it, catches it in the air. Then he spins in a circle, whipping the sword back in her direction. Zombie torsos are sliced into halves as the wire circles toward Nemesis. She ducks out of the way, narrowly missing the blades of her own sword on the end of Vine's wire.

The wire continues cutting through the zombie crowd, green and black fluids splashing into the air. It hits Mr. T. Catching the central handle of the sword with his steel fist, Mr. T looks over at the merc punk.

"We should be fighting her," he yells at the punk. "Not each other."

The merc punk pulls the wire, ripping the sword out of Mr. T's grip, cutting a gash into the gold plating of his hand. When he looks at his gold-stripped palm, Mr. T's eyebrows curl.

"Now you've gone an made Mr. T mad," he says.

The horde of zombies spill onto the rooftop. Junko places the lawn gnome on the ground between them, and revs up her chainsaw arm.

"We've only got a few minutes left to wait," Junko says. "Let's just hope the roof can hold the weight of all those zombies."

"You mean this whole place can collapse if they get too close?" Rainbow Cat says.

"Let's try to hold them back as far as we can," Junko says.

Scavy raises the solar-powered shotgun and unleashes a barrage of blasts onto the crowd. He doesn't realize the gun has nearly unlimited ammo, but he fires as if deep down he knows it does. Zombie meat splatters across the roof with each shot. With every body that topples over, it holds back three more trying to get through.

As Mr. T clobbers zombies out of his way to get to Vine, Nemesis flies through the crowd and punches him with an open-handed palm. Mr. T's face lights up in surprise as he finds himself flying backward into the side of the building.

Mr. T's body becomes immersed halfway into the brick wall of the building. He leans his head forward and shakes the powdered brick out of his mohawk.

"Damn," he says. "That bitch is strong."

Running so fast she looks as if she's teleporting, Nemesis flies at him. She stops right in front of his face, staring at him with her cold black eyes. Then she raises her hand back, with her fingers pressed together in the shape of a snake, as if she is going to drive her fingertips all the way through to the back of his skull.

Stuck inside of the brick wall, Mr. T can't protect himself. He just watches as her fingers come toward him.

No matter how many times he fires, even with unlimited ammo, the zombies get closer to Scavy. They surround the perimeter, pushed back by the gnome's sonic wave. The ground below them begins to crack.

"Fuck," Junko says. "The roof isn't going to hold us for much longer."

The sound of the helicopter fills their ears. They look up and see it coming across the city buildings toward them.

"There it is!" Rainbow cries.

Scavy continues firing the shotgun, only glancing up for a second to see how close it is.

The helicopter hovers over the hospital for a few moments, but finding no place to land it continues on.

"Where's it going?" Scavy cries.

The helicopter flies low over the parking lot, over the horde of zombies, and finds a clearing on the far end of the street. Then it slowly descends.

"We have to get you over there," Junko says.

Scavy nods, then continues blasting.

As Nemesis drives her fingers toward Mr. T's face, Vine shoots his wire at her. Nemesis' arm is severed at the elbow and rolls down Mr. T's chest. Then Vine shoots his second wire and it hooks onto her bony spine. She flies backward through the air, as Vine's wire reels into his wrist. Then he spins her in a circle around him, the razor-sharp wire decapitating zombies as he twirls her through the air.

"Now throw her against a wall," Xiu's voice tells Vine. Vine nods and aims her flying white body toward the wall of the hospital.

As the reptilian woman is thrown toward him, Mr. T breaks out of his brick encasing and says, "Time to play a game of bitch base-ball."

Mr. T flexes a fist and charges forward. Like a tetherball, he punches Nemesis in the chest. Her eyes widen as her torso caves in around his fist, blood spraying from the sides of her ribcage. Her body flies off of Vine's wire, over the zombie horde, and rolls across the pavement.

"Homerun for the T-2000!" says Mr. T.

A camera ball watches Nemesis' body as it lies still on the ground, blood pooling beneath her. The camera zooms in on one side of her ribcage. The ribs are split open in a messy crevice below her armpit. She isn't breathing.

On the other side of the camera, miles away from the Red Zone, Dr. Chan watches Nemesis from the *Zombie Survival* control room.

Wayne "The Wiz" Rizla comes up behind the doctor and pats him on the back.

"Looks like your ultimate soldier wasn't good enough after all," Wayne says.

He laughs in the doctor's face, then takes a bite of a chocolate cruller.

The hospital rumbles as the roof begins to collapse under their feet. Junko falls to her knees, nearly landing on her chainsaw. Scavy holds his balance, continuing to fire his shotgun at the reaching limbs.

Rainbow Cat looks down at the lawn gnome behind them. Then she looks back at the other two contestants. Their attentions are elsewhere. Rainbow decides to take advantage of the opportunity.

As Junko gets to her feet, she doesn't see it happen. Rainbow grabs the lawn gnome, then charges into the zombie crowd. By the time Junko notices, it's too late.

"Stop her!" Junko cries.

Scavy fires at Rainbow's back, but the zombies close in behind her. Without the lawn gnome holding them back, the zombies fill in the gap, staggering toward the two unprotected contestants.

The zombies open up a path for Rainbow as she charges through the horde, the lawn gnome under her arm like a football. Her dreadlocks flop through the air, leaping over crippled zombies that can't get out of her way fast enough. When she goes through the doors into the hospital, she looks back to see Junko and Scavy aren't chasing after her. They are back-to-back, shooting and slashing at the undead closing in on them, the ground cracking wider at their feet. Rainbow smiles at the sight.

I did it, she thinks to herself. *I'm going to win. I'm going to get to the helicopter, get back to the island, and then the world will finally get to see the great masterpiece of Charles Hudson. The greatest writer of our time. My husband.*

Droplets of rain sprinkle over Nemesis' white naked skin. A thunder-cloud moves in, drizzling on the horde of zombies. Her eyelids flash open, and she stares into the camera ball with her cold black eyes.

On the other side of the camera, from the control room of *Zombie Survival*, Dr. Chan shakes his head at Wayne "The Wiz" Rizla.

"It's going to take more than that to defeat her," says Dr. Chan.

Wayne shoves the rest of his chocolate cruller into his mouth and goes to the monitor. He sees Nemesis standing up. Her crushed ribcage expands, the split down her side disappears. Then she raises her severed arm, which is growing nerves and tissue. Wayne's eyes light up as she grows a completely new hand.

"Like a lizard's tail," says Dr. Chan, "she can grow new limbs, only a million times as fast. Her regenerative powers surpass all living creatures on this planet."

"Fuck…" Wayne says, coughing up bits of donut.

"She is nearly invincible," says Dr. Chan.

Vine sees the helicopter landing on the far side of the parking lot, as raindrops trickle onto his head. He removes his goggles to see more clearly.

"Now's your chance," Xiu's voice tells him. "You can use your wires to get there before the other contestants. But first you need to get the works of art. You must complete the mission."

Vine cuts away a row of zombies with his wire. Then he scans the edge of the hospital for the paintings.

"There they are," says Xiu's voice.

Vine sees them on the ground, next to his Head's corpse. "Use your wires to get over there."

Raising his left hand up, he shoots a wire at the roof of the hospital and is pulled up into the air.

As he soars above the shambling corpses, Xiu's voice tells him, "You don't have much time. Grab the paintings and get to the helicopter."

Nemesis throws her double-bladed sword at Vine as he flies toward the building. The blade hits his left arm, cuts it off at the elbow. Vine falls. He watches as his left arm continues on without him, pulled by the wire up to the rooftop.

Before Vine's body falls, Nemesis races through the undead, catches her sword as it boomerangs back to her, and then slices the merc punk through the midsection just before he hits the ground.

Nemesis turns her attention to Mr. T. She runs through the parking lot, flying at him like a bullet. Mr. T sees her coming. He charges at her.

"Time for round two," Mr. T yells.

Corpses tumble from their path as they plow toward each other. Mr. T's feet crush the ground with every step. Nemesis runs so fast her flesh becomes a white blur.

Mr. T throws his punch, with all of his weight behind it. Nemesis catches his punch, thin white claws wrapped around his golden knuckles, then she buries her sword deep into his metal chest. Sparks explode between them, oils and wires spill out of his abdomen.

"Think that's enough to stop Mr. T?" yells the cyborg.

As his mouth is open, Nemesis spits a green fluid down his throat. She rips out her sword and watches as he falls to his knees, choking, holding his neck in his metal hands.

Her black eyes glare at him as he curls into the mud, beneath the pouring rain.

"You see?" Dr. Chan says to Wayne, from the control room. "She's invincible. There's nobody who can stop her now."

Wayne looks carefully at the cyborg contestant as he writhes on the ground. "What is that she sprayed in his mouth?"

"A concoction I brewed up," says Dr. Chan. "It is a mixture of snake venom and a hyper-accelerated variety of the zombie virus."

"Zombie virus?"

"Yes," the doctor smiles. "Specimen #5 isn't just part reptile. She is also part leopard, part hammerhead, part spider, and part zombie."

"Part zombie…" Wayne says, staring at the screen.

"She can only infect a human using her venom," says the doctor. "But it moves faster through the nervous system and creates a more powerful zombie."

Wayne turns his head slowly to the doctor. "Why on earth would you give her such an ability?"

"I gave it to her…" The doctor looks back at the producer. "So that in any combat scenario…" He pauses to steal one of Wayne's chocolate donuts. "She would always win."

As Junko and Scavy battle the zombies back-to-back, the roof below them finally gives way. It breaks open, dropping half of the undead down to the level below. The ground beneath Scavy goes with it and he falls.

With one arm, Junko catches him by the wrist.

Scavy looks up. "What are you doing?"

"You drew the long straw," Junko says, holding him with her left arm. With her other arm, she chainsaws the zombies coming in from behind. "You need to get to the helicopter."

The zombies on the floor below reach up for Scavy's boots. He kicks the skeleton hands away. Then looks back up at Junko.

Scavy shakes his head. "Fuck the straws. Let me go. You have to catch up to that hippy bitch before she gets away."

"Not a chance," Junko says, pulling him up with all of her strength. "I'm going to make sure you're the one who gets on that helicopter. We had a deal."

As she pulls Scavy up by her left arm, a zombie grabs her chainsaw. It bites down into her wrist. She screams out and nearly drops Scavy, as a chunk of meat is pulled out of her arm. She thrashes the chainsaw until it cuts the zombie away from her.

"Let me go," Scavy says.

But it's too late for her to back out now. She continues pulling him up. Another zombie bites into her shoulder. Another bites her on the thigh. Junko squints her Asian eyes tightly to resist the pain, as she gets the punk back onto the roof. Once he's safely on his two feet, Scavy turns around and cuts the zombies away from her in one clean stroke. Scavy fires his shotgun at them, blasting their knees out of their legs.

When Scavy looks over at Junko, he sees the bleeding wounds on her body.

"You've been bit?" Scavy asks.

Junko's face grows solemn. "It's okay. You're the one who drew the long straw. Let's get you to the helicopter."

Scavy can see a look of disappointment behind her eyes. Even though she wasn't planning on getting on the helicopter while Scavy was alive, he can sense that she had really wanted to go. She had a mission to go back to the island and take her revenge on Wayne "the Wiz" Rizla. Now she would have to stay back, and let Wayne get away with sentencing human beings to death for the sake of amusement, for the sake of money. Scavy knows this is why she is disappointed. She had told him all about what she would do if she won the contest.

"Junko," he said to her, looking her seriously in the eyes. "Don't worry. If I'm the one who gets back to Neo New York I won't let that motherfucker get away with this anymore. I'll kill his ass and shit. For you."

Junko smiles at him, like he's a kid who just said the cutest thing. Then she kisses him on the cheek, in the one spot that isn't horribly burned.

"Let's get you on that helicopter," she says.

Then she revs her chainsaw arm and cuts them a path through the zombie horde.

Mr. T squirms on the ground as the virus pumps through his blood and circuitry. Fat green veins pulse up his neck and face. His eyes become bloodshot. He looks over at Nemesis as she walks slowly toward the hospital.

"Mr. T's down," says the cyborg, as he pulls himself to his feet. "But that don't mean he's out."

Nemesis turns and whips her sword at him. Mr. T catches in midair. Then breaks it in half against his knee.

"Enough with the toys," he says. "The T-2000's not playin' anymore."

He charges her and leaps into the air. Before he reaches her she flies at him, and kicks him in the chest. He flies across the parking lot, smashing through the zombie crowd. Torsos explode on impact, spraying black goo into the air, as Mr. T's metal body hits the undead.

Wiping zombie guts from his eyes, Mr. T gets up and charges again. This time when Nemesis kicks him, he grabs her by the leg and smashes her against a smart-car as it drives toward the hospital.

Then he tosses her across the parking lot, through the undead masses.

Vine crawls across the ground, holding in his guts as blood and intestines spill out of his deep wound. When zombies come at him, he gets up on one knee, and using his one remaining arm he shoots the wire through their heads. The zombies stagger after him as he crawls, crowding up around him.

"You have to get to the paintings!" Xiu's voice cries. "You must complete the mission! Or it will all have been for nothing!"

He pulls himself to his feet and slices down a row of zombies. Then he sees Nemesis's body fly over his head into a light pole.

Junko and Scavy run through the hospital corridors, looking for Rainbow Cat. Through the missing section on the side of the building, they see Rainbow two levels below.

"I'll get her," Junko says.

She jumps down to the level below, then jumps down to the next level below that. Scavy covers her, blasting zombies with his solar-powered shotgun as they spill out of hospital rooms.

Junko drops down behind Rainbow Cat. She sees her running down the hallway with the gnome under her arm, her deadlocks whipping through the air like medusa snakes. A camera ball floats directly behind her. Junko charges the hippy.

As she catches up to her, Junko grabs the camera ball from the air and slams it into the back of Rainbow's head. Sparks scatter from the camera ball as it wobbles away from Junko's hand. Rainbow hits the ground, fumbling the lawn gnome. It rolls across the floor of the hospital waiting room.

Rainbow turns and swings her machete at the Japanese woman. Junko jumps back, revs her chainsaw.

"You ready to rumble, bitch?" Junko says, her chainsaw roaring against her arm.

"I *need* to get to the helicopter," Rainbow says. "It's more important that I get back to the island."

Junko swings her chainsaw at Rainbow. The hippy blocks it with her machete, then kicks Junko in the stomach to knock her back.

"My husband's manuscript *must* be published," Rainbow says.

Zombies fill the waiting room. Junko grabs one and tosses it at Rainbow, but the hippy chops it open with her machete, then kicks it back to Junko.

As Junko chainsaws off the zombie's arms, Rainbow gets back into the circle, protected from the living dead. After Junko follows her into the circle, the zombies crowd around them.

"Ever see a sumo match?" Junko says, looking at the surrounding zombies. "Don't get pushed out of the circle."

Then Junko charges Rainbow, spinning her chainsaw at her. Rainbow is forced back, toward the edge of the circle, zombie arms reaching out to her. One of them grabs a dreadlock.

Held in place, Rainbow can't duck as Junko's chainsaw slashes across her chest. Her shirt breaks open, revealing a bloody gash that drips down her stomach.

Rainbow cuts off her dreadlock with the machete, then elbows Junko in the face, breaking her nose. Junko stumbles back into the zombie crowd. They bite into her shoulder. She rips herself away from their grips, then chainsaws their arms off.

"You're already infected," Rainbow says. "Why do you even bother?"

Junko wipes away the blood draining from her nostrils.

"I'm not doing this for me," Junko says. "Scavy is the one who's supposed to get on that helicopter."

They face each other, moving sideways along the perimeter of the circle. The zombies growl at them like a roaring crowd.

"Brains!" they cry.

Junko swings her chainsaw and Rainbow kicks it off of her hand, over the top of the crowd.

"You're trying to stop me so you can save that worthless punk?" Rainbow says, as she brings her machete down on Junko's back.

The machete cuts through Junko's tank top, carving a strip of red down her back. Junko falls to one knee.

"I'd rather save him than a stuck-up bitch like you," Junko says.

Mr. T charges through the rain as Nemesis gets up off the ground. She grabs a zombie by the arm and throws it at the cyborg. Mr. T catches it in midair.

"Show a little respect for the dead," says Mr. T.

271

Then he rips the zombie in half and tosses the pieces aside.

He rumbles the muddy earth as he races across the lot toward her. She runs at him, her claws spread out to her sides. When they collide, Nemesis buries her arm deep into Mr. T's torso. Then Mr. T grabs her by the arm. He smiles with big bright teeth. Then he stomps on her foot.

The massive weight of his robot body crushes her foot into pulp. She shrieks like a banshee in his ear.

"Sorry about that," he says. "Mr. T's not the best dancer. Always stepping on ladies' toes."

She twists his arm, picks his massive body up over her tiny figure, and slams him to the ground. Then she drives her knee into his crotch, shattering the metal casing.

Mr. T looks down at the crushed metal between his legs. He doesn't feel a thing. Although the body of the T-2000 is equipped with fully functioning sexual organs, they did not come with the ability to feel pain. Mr. T laughs at her.

As he laughs, Mr. T doesn't see the attack coming. Nemesis opens her mouth, dislocating her jaw like a snake, stretching it so wide that she can fit the cyborg's head between her lips like a lollipop. She goes to bite into his skull, but Mr. T dodges. Her teeth catch the strip of hair on his head. She takes a chunk out of his mohawk.

When she spits the clump of hair out of her mouth, Mr. T's forehead wrinkles with anger. She has just fucked up Mr. T's mohawk. *Nobody* fucks with Mr. T's mohawk.

"You shouldn't have done that," says the T-2000, feeling the hole in his mohawk. "Now you've really gone and made Mr. T mad."

She goes to punch him through the skull, but he punches back at her. Their fists collide. Nemesis' hand pops, bursting into a soupy mess, on impact with Mr. T's robot fist. His knuckles break all the way through her arm, then punches her in the face. She rolls off of him.

Mr. T gets to his feet and roars. He grabs her bony spine and tosses her high into the air. Before she lands, Mr. T punches her back up into the air, over the zombie crowd. Then he charges after her and punches her again, across the parking lot, through a light pole.

When Mr. T catches up to her again, he grabs her around the neck and picks her up off the ground.

He says, "I pity the fool who messes with the T-2000!"

Then he smashes her face into the street. Her skull explodes. Reptilian brains splash across the pavement. The rest of her body flops down into the gore, twitching, coiling up like a snake with its head cut off.

Mr. T collapses on the ground next to her, the virus taking over his nervous system, sparks shooting out of his abdomen. He lets out a big sigh, as rain pours down on his face.

In the distance, he sees the clouds opening up and a bit of sunshine coming through. A rainbow arches across the sky.

"You know..." he says to Nemesis' corpse. "Mr. T never did like the rain. The cold winds, the gray skies. Too depressing. But rainbows..." He squints his eyes at the rainbow. "Mr. T likes rainbows."

He smiles at the sky as his metal hands drop to the side of his golden robot body.

Dr. Chan's eyes can't leave the monitor as he sees Specimen #5's brains splattered across the pavement.

"Invincible, huh?" Wayne says, then he laughs.

Dr. Chan straightens his tie and stands up. Then he leaves the room.

Scavy blasts his way into the waiting room to find Junko and Rainbow Cat fighting in the middle of a circle of zombies.

Rainbow slashes twice at Junko, but the Japanese girl dodges. Then the hippy roundhouse kicks her in the face. Junko staggers back.

"Junko!" Scavy says.

The Japanese woman looks back at him.

"Kick her ass!" he yells, pumping his fist.

Rainbow Cat runs at Junko with the machete while her attention is turned. As the machete lowers down toward her head, Junko dropkicks the hippy, sending her flying back into the zombie crowd.

"Wait!" Rainbow cries, as the zombies grab her by the arms.

The living corpses bite down into Rainbow's flesh. She shrieks.

"You can't," she screams. "No!"

Junko grabs the gnome and runs toward Scavy, leaving the hippy completely unprotected. The zombies close in on her.

"You fucking bitch!" Rainbow screams, as muscles peel out of her skin between zombie teeth.

Junko gets to Scavy, bringing him into the circle of protection. He grabs her up into his arms.

"That was awesome," he says.

Junko pushes him away.

"Don't touch me," she says. "I'm infected."

Scavy steps away.

"Now," she says, "we need to get you to the helicopter. Let's go."

They take off down the hallway.

As the zombies sink their teeth into her flesh, Rainbow Cat fights back. She elbows them in the face, chops off their arms, and thrashes out of their grips.

After she gets free, she slashes her way through their bodies until she breaks out of the crowd and runs down a hallway. She grabs a floating camera ball and charges down the corridor.

"It's not over yet," she says. "I can still do it. I can still make the world love Charles Hudson again."

Junko and Scavy exit the hospital, out into the pouring rain. They see the helicopter on the other side of the parking lot and run toward it.

"Come on!" Junko yells at Scavy as he limps too far behind. "We're almost there!"

Scavy picks up the pace.

As the zombies separate out of their way, Gogo emerges from the crowd.

"Brains!" Gogo shrieks.

She pukes green vomit at them. It sprays across the barrier protected by the gnome, and splashes Scavy in the face.

Scavy cries out and falls to the ground. The vomit burns through his neck and cheek, melting into his bloodstream. He can taste it in his mouth. Junko doesn't see it happen. She keeps moving with the lawn gnome in her hands. As Scavy's legs leave the barrier, zombies grab him by the feet.

Junko stops when she hears his screams. She turns back to see

Gogo biting into the backs of his knees, tearing into the nervous tissue. Other zombies try to get a bite, but Gogo pushes them back.

"Mine!" Gogo says. Then she gorges on Scavy's flesh, savoring every nerve ending against the tip of her tongue, too gluttonous to share with the other zombies.

Popcorn breaks through the crowd and kicks Gogo away from him.

"What the fuck, Gogo!" she yells.

She blocks all other zombies as Scavy crawls back into the circle, falling into Junko's lap as she bends down to him. At the edge of the circle, Popcorn punches Gogo until her conscience comes back. Gogo sees Scavy lying there with bloody legs, the flesh on his face and neck burning red.

"I'm sorry…" Gogo says to Scavy.

Scavy doesn't even look at her. She looks over at Popcorn.

"I didn't mean to…" she says to Popcorn.

Then Gogo runs away, out of the crowd, toward the hospital.

Popcorn looks at Scavy as if it's her fault. She wants to hold him, make him feel better, but the noise filling her head when she gets too close to the perimeter of the circle is too much for her to bear. It's like thousands of needles stabbing her in the brain.

Junko holds Scavy in her arms, looking down on his burnt face. With all the rain pouring down on them, Scavy doesn't notice the tears rolling out of her eyes.

"So does Laurence get the seat on the helicopter now?" Scavy asks.

Junko scans the parking lot until she sees Mr. T, smashing his way through the horde. When she gets a look into his empty white eyes, she can tell he is no longer among the living.

"No," she tells Scavy, shaking her head. "He's infected, too."

Scavy looks over at the T-2000. The cyborg zombie smashes everything that moves, rumbling the earth beneath his feet.

"Fuck…" Scavy says. "Zombie Mr. T…"

Then he looks up at Junko. "So now what?"

Junko looks back at the helicopter. Then looks around to make sure none of the camera balls are close enough to hear.

"Plan B," she says. "One of us will still get to that helicopter. We'll get back to the island of Neo New York. Then unleash the virus on those fat cats in the Platinum Quadrant, starting with that mother-fucker Wayne Rizla."

Scavy smiles. "That would be punk as fuck. Sounds like a plan."

Junko lifts him to his feet, but he screams and drops down to the ground.

"I'm not going to get anywhere like this," Scavy says. "You go. I know you can do it."

Junko nods at him.

"Okay," she says. "But I'll leave the gnome with you."

"Take the shotgun," Scavy says. "This thing is awesome."

She pushes back the barrel of the gun.

"No, keep it," she says. "You can cover me."

"Okay." He nods, then smiles. "Give them hell and shit."

She stands up.

"I will," she says. "…and shit."

She smiles brightly as she revs her chainsaw, then runs into the crowd toward the helicopter.

Scavy looks back at Popcorn and says, "I love that woman!" Then he turns back to Junko, firing his shotgun at the zombies in her path.

Vine cuts his way through the zombies to the hospital and tries grabbing the artwork with his one arm, but he can't get it onto his back. A zombie comes at him and his wire slices it in half down the middle.

"Make sure to get the masterpiece," says Xiu's voice.

Vine leaves all of the artwork except for the masterpiece. It is light enough for him to strap it to his back with only his right arm. One at a time, he straps a few more of them to his back.

"That should be enough," says Xiu's voice. "Now get to the helicopter before it's too late."

Vine looks over at the helicopter across the parking lot.

"Don't let our deaths be for nothing," says the voice of his Head.

Zombies explode left and right, as Junko runs toward the helicopter. On the other side of the parking lot, she sees Mr. T running alongside her, staring at her with raging hunger. He slams corpses out of his way as he tries to cut her off before she gets to the aircraft.

Junko swings her chainsaw like a ballerina as she runs, jump-spinning in the air and slashing zombies into halves. Scavy blasts those that come in behind her, throwing them back into a cloud of meaty chunks.

Halfway there, Junko sees something coming down from the sky. It lands between her and the helicopter, safely away from any of the living dead.

Scavy sees it from his seated position. His mouth drops open as he recognizes what it is.

It's Oro's glider-cycle.

Oro steps out of his glider-cycle and walks casually over to the helicopter.

"Just in time," he says, wiping dust from his shirt.

He looks back to see Junko running toward him from the distance.

"Didn't you know?" he says to her figure across the parking lot. "Geniuses always win."

He snickers as he steps up into the helicopter.

The aircraft has no cockpit, as it is computer-controlled. The inside of the craft contains only one seat. Oro sits down in it. He puts his last cigar into his mouth and lights it up. Takes a puff, then laughs loudly.

"Of course I would win," he says. "I am a genius. I *deserved* to win!

He chuckles as he sucks on his cigar. Then he looks over to his right and sees zombie Mr. T staring back at him, only a few inches from his face. The cigar falls out of Oro's mouth.

"Gimme them brains, fool!" yells the zombie T-2000.

Oro screams as he is ripped out of the aircraft and dragged across the ground.

"But I'm a genius!" he cries. "You can't eat my brains!"

"Quit yo' jibber jabber," says zombie Mr. T.

Then he bites into his skull and eats his brains.

Vine rushes toward the helicopter with paintings strapped to his back. He slices through rows of zombies, blood draining down his side, his intestines uncoiling out of his belly.

"You have to get there!" Xiu yells. "Get close enough to use your wire!"

Vine trips over his own intestine and falls to the ground. He slashes the oncoming zombies as he gets up and continues on.

Junko runs past Mr. T to the helicopter. She glances over at him as he tears into Oro's brains with his big bright teeth. He growls and thrashes at the brains like a mad dog.

Cutting down the last zombie in her way, Junko boards the helicopter. She collapses against the seat. Her head leaning back against the metal casing, catching her breath.

As the helicopter lifts off, she turns off her chainsaw and looks down at the chaos below. The aircraft ascends high into the sky.

Below her, she can see Scavy sitting safely within the circle, protected by the lawn gnome. He waves at her, pumping his shotgun into the air.

She waves back. The motion causes blood to spray out of the zombie bites on her arm, sprinkling into the air, mixing with the falling rain.

Vine sees the helicopter flying above the hospital.

"There's still time!" yells Xiu's voice. "Do it!"

Vine launches his wire and it hooks onto the helicopter's landing skid. He is pulled into the air, reeled upward. His insides spill out, raining on the corpses below, as he flies through the sky, getting closer to the aircraft.

"Finish the mission!" Xiu's voice cries. "You can do it!"

When he reaches the helicopter, he climbs up into the cabin. Junko's eyes light up in shock when she sees him standing there. She tries to start up her chainsaw, but can't get it going. It's finally out of gas.

With his one arm, Vine pulls the artwork from his back and tosses it into Junko's lap. Then he pulls the mask from his mouth.

"Tell her in English," says Xiu's voice.

It has been a long time since Vine has spoke English, so it takes him a while to get the words out.

"Give these to the son of Gunther von Hagens," he tells her.

She slowly nods at him. "Okay…"

Then he lets go of the helicopter doorway, drops backward, tumbling into space without his wire to catch him.

"You did it," Xiu's voice tells him, as he falls through the air, staring up at the helicopter. "You accomplished the mission. We didn't die for nothing."

A smile grows on his lips and tears flutter from his eyes, watching the helicopter get smaller and smaller as he falls away from it.

Scavy hollers in excitement as he watches the helicopter flying over the buildings. He waves his shotgun into the air.

"You did it!" he cries. "Fuck yeah!"

Behind him, Popcorn covers her mouth as she giggles with joy.

"Those bastards aren't going to get away with it!" Scavy cries. "Teach them a lesson you beautiful badass bitch!"

He laughs out loud.

Then he pumps his shotgun into the air.

"Anarchy! Anarchy! Anarchy!"

But the smile fades from his lips as he sees the rocket flying up from the ground toward the helicopter.

"No…" Scavy says in a soft whisper, as the rocket hits the helicopter.

The aircraft erupts into a ball of fire and falls from the sky.

As he falls, Vine sees the helicopter exploding in the air above him. His eyes close, the tears raising into the air.

"I failed," Vine says to the voice in his head. "It was all for nothing…"

When his body hits the ground, his brain splatters across the horde of hungry undead.

Scavy can't look away from the fire in the sky. He can't believe it just happened.

"Let's go, Scavy," Popcorn tells him.

"...what happened?" he says.

He puts his hand into his face.

"Let's just get out of here," Popcorn says. "You don't want to spend your last moments as a living human at this hospital. Come on."

Scavy lifts himself to his feet, using his sniper rifle as a crutch, and follows his ex-girlfriend out of the parking lot, to find a good place to die.

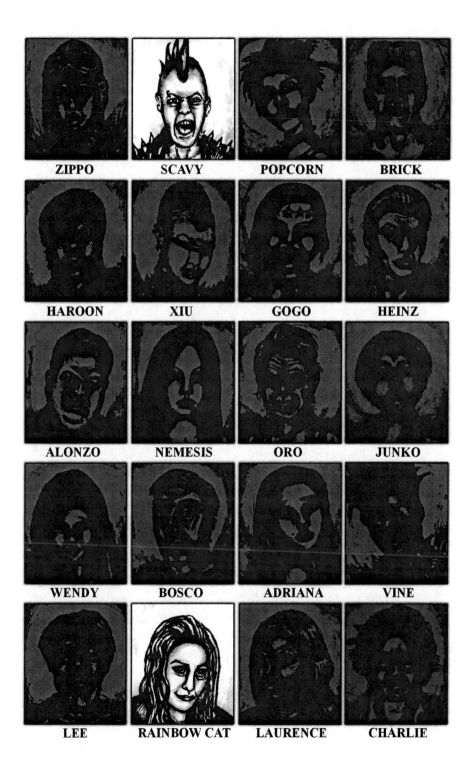

ADRIANA

Wayne "The Wiz" Rizla chuckles to himself as he watches the helicopter explode repeatedly on his monitor. He rewinds and zooms in
on Junko's face, to see her expression as the rocket hits.

"BOOM!" he yells, as it explodes.

He laughs louder.

"Did you have something to do with that, sir?" asks his assistant,
a mousy woman with too-short hair and too-large glasses.

He looks over at her and whispers, "Of course I did."

He scans the room for anyone paying attention, then curls his
finger at her to draw her in closer. She goes to him.

"Here's a secret," Wayne says.

He switches monitors to a different camera, then zooms up on a
mechjaw with a rocket launcher on its back.

"You see this little doggy?" he says. "These things were built by
the government of the USA sometime before Z-Day. Hell, they were
the things responsible for Z-Day. Back then, the government would
send orders to the dogs via satellite."

He looks at the girl with anticipation.

"And?" she asks.

"*And* I figured out that how to hack into that satellite," he says.
"The mechjaws were following my commands the whole time!"

"You rigged the game?" she asks.

He shushes her, looks around the room, then leans in closer. "No, I just gave them a little nudge and sent them in the right direction. Those mutts would have sat around doing nothing otherwise."

"But you had a mechjaw blow up the helicopter?"

Wayne blows a puff of air at her through his white goatee. "That's because Junko was on it. I couldn't let *her* win. That would be stupid."

"Why would it be stupid?"

He waves away her question. "The government doesn't want anybody winning the contest anyway. It was hard enough convincing them to allow *one* person to win *once*. They don't want anyone from Copper moving up to the higher quadrants."

"Then why do you bother offering them a prize?"

"Because the audience loves it when the winners get a prize. Otherwise, the contest would be just a tad bit too cruel for them."

"So the show's not too cruel as long as there's a chance that the lone survivor might get a prize?"

Wayne doesn't like her tone. He frowns at her.

"Why don't you get me some more coffee, okay?" he asks, then goes back to his monitor.

She nods. As she turns, she catches a glimpse at a picture on Wayne's desk. She does a double take, then looks closer at the image. It is of a young girl, about fourteen years old.

"Isn't that one of the contestants?" she asks, picking up the picture.

"Hmmm?" Wayne says, glancing over from his screen. "Oh, yeah. The little prostitute." Then he goes back to the monitor.

"Why do you have a picture of one of the contestants framed on your desk?"

"Hmmm?" he asks again, as if he has no recollection of the conversation. "Oh, yeah. She was my daughter."

The assistant's face widens at him as he goes back to watching Junko explode over and over again. She isn't sure if he's joking or not. How could Wayne seriously put his own daughter on the show?

Adriana was the daughter of Wayne "The Wiz" Rizla from a previous relationship. She never knew he was her father. Her mother never told her about him.

Wayne was married to a wealthy woman who held a powerful seat in the Platinum courts. He had married her for the money, but because she was so much older than him he really wasn't interested in her sexually. Instead, he had a series of affairs with various women on the side. One woman he had an affair with had become pregnant. She wanted him to divorce his wife and raise the child with her. He refused.

When she threatened to go to his wife with the information, Wayne used his influence to get her sent to the Copper Quadrant where she would have no contact with his wife whatsoever. Several years later, his wife died and he inherited the money. That's when he began to wonder what had ever happened to the woman he had impregnated. He was curious about whatever became of this woman and his daughter.

He tracked her down, but realized he was too late. The woman was already dead, raped and killed. A common death for a beautiful fragile woman in the Copper Quadrant. But he discovered that his daughter was still alive. She was working as a prostitute on the worst side of town. The idea that his daughter was a prostitute was not surprising to him, but it made him feel a little ill inside. He decided he might want to get her out of this life, bring her back to the Platinum Quadrant.

When he first met his daughter, she was a scrawny young girl just barely through puberty. She had been turning tricks since she was nine.

"Hello, little girl," Wayne said to her, smiling in her bright blue eyes. "What's your name?"

"Adriana," she said.

Wayne brushed her dark red hair out of her eyes.

"That's a pretty name."

"Do you want a blow?" she asked. "Or a fuck? If you want it in the ass it will be double because I've got a colon infection."

He stepped back.

"No," he said. "I didn't come for that. I wanted to tell you—"

"You can't talk to me unless you pay," she said.

"Okay, I'll pay for your time," he said. "I just want to talk."

"Whatever," she said.

After he paid her pimp, she took him into a small bedroom with a leaky roof and a mattress stained with brown menstrual blood.

"I wanted to tell you," he said. "I'm your—"

She pulled off her shirt and took off her pants. Wayne stared at his daughter's body. It seemed very familiar to him, yet alien. Her bony ribs popping out of her pale skin reminded him of his own body, when he was a child.

When she went to him to take off his pants, Wayne grabbed her hands.

"I'm your father," he said.

"Okay," she said. "If you want to role play I can do that..."

She took off his pants. He was surprised to see that he had an erection. The idea of having sex with his daughter was exciting him, and the idea that she didn't know who he really was excited him more.

"I want you to call me daddy," he said to her, a big smile forming in his white goatee.

She knelt down, grabbed his penis with her small bony fingers, and looked up at him.

"Okay, daddy," she said, widening her baby-soft lips.

"Now," he said, breathing deeply. "Daddy wants to feel the back of your throat."

For the next year, Wayne Rizla became Adriana's best customer. He would have sex with her in every way he could possibly imagine, always demanding she treat him as if he was her father. She never had a clue that he was really her father, that it wasn't just a sick game. Wayne relished the thought of it, every time he came inside of her.

Then Wayne came up with the idea of putting Adriana on his show. He had put many of her prostitute friends on the show before. The idea of seeing his daughter as a contestant on *Zombie Survival* excited him sexually. It turned him on knowing that she never knew he was her father, never knew he was the reason she was sentenced to death. It was all his little secret. His and his alone. That is, until his assistant asked him about it.

"Is she really your daughter?" Wayne's assistant asks.

"Yes," Wayne says. "It's a pity she didn't last very long..."

The assistant puts down the picture and rushes to get her boss his coffee.

"Here's to a great season everyone!" yells the director of photography, popping open a bottle of sparkling wine. "The best one ever!"

The camera crew cheers and holds out their glasses to catch the bubbling wine. Wayne gets up and peeks out from behind his desk.

"What are you all doing?" he yells. "It's not time to celebrate."

"But the show's over," says the director. "The helicopter blew up."

"There's still a couple of survivors out there," Wayne says.

"But they're all infected," says the director. "They're basically dead."

"The show's not over until each and every one of them is dead," Wayne says.

"Okay…" the director says, frowning. "Everyone, back to work. Let's film the final contestants as they turn into zombies…"

As the crew go back to their monitors, the director shakes his head at the producer.

"It's going to be worthless footage," he tells Wayne. "There's nothing more boring than watching infected contestants turn into zombies."

"Not necessarily," Wayne says.

Wayne turns and goes back to his desk. He brings up the program he used to connect with the satellite system.

"I'll just have to send the dogs after the scraps," Wayne says to himself. Then he sends the order through the satellite to the mech-jaws, commanding them to hunt down and destroy the final contestants.

Rainbow Cat is locked in a hospital room, sitting on the floor in the corner. Behind the door, dozens of zombies try to break through. They slam against the frame, trying to tear it down, screaming out for her brains.

In front of her, a camera ball films her face. It hovers in the air, in the position she had placed it. She had brought the camera ball into the room with her for a reason. She has something to say to the people in the Platinum Quadrant.

"My husband was Charles Hudson," she says to the camera. "He was a contestant on this show, as you surely already know. He was the greatest writer on the island. Perhaps the greatest writer who ever lived. I brought him on the show so that you would pay attention to him again. After his publisher went out of business, he wasn't able to get any more work out there for his audience to read."

She pauses to wipe away her tears.

"In our home, in the drawer of his desk, is a copy of his last manuscript. The greatest novel he's ever written. A masterpiece. This novel *must* be published. It is probably the most significant work of art of the past fifty years. I believe this with every ounce of my soul. I believe it so much that I was willing to sacrifice my own husband's life, as well as my life, in order to bring this book to your attention."

The door begins to split down the middle. Zombie fingers poke through the crack. Rainbow's eyes widen and she begins to shake. She doesn't have much time.

"Whoever is watching this," she continues at a much faster pace. "If you're a publisher or somebody with a lot of money who wants to invest in publishing this book, you must send somebody to Copper to retrieve the manuscript. You must publish it. I swear it will be worth it. Every one of you watching, I beg you to read it. I promise it will be the greatest book you will ever read in your lives. *Please*, I beg you. Publish his book."

The door breaks open and the zombies spill in.

"Publish his book!" she shrieks.

Then, as she stares into the camera, she notices something off. The lens of the camera is missing. A tiny spark pops out of the top. She was so busy worrying about her message, that she didn't pay attention to which camera ball she had grabbed. She took the one that Junko had slammed into her head. It's broken. It hadn't been filming anything she had just said.

Rainbow Cat looks up in a panic as the mass of zombies crowd around her.

Scavy and Popcorn walk down a street together, fifteen feet apart. Scavy limps along, using his rifle as a cane. The gnome is in his free arm with the solar-powered shotgun strapped to his back. Whenever a zombie comes near, he pulls up the shotgun and blasts out its legs. Then Popcorn kicks its face into the ground until it shuts its mouth.

"How are you feeling?" Popcorn asks.

Scavy shrugs. "In a lot of pain, I guess. Gogo sure fucked me up."

"Sorry about that," Popcorn says.

"It's not your fault," he says.

They walk silently for a bit.

"How about the virus?" she asks. "Are you starting to crave brains yet?"

He shakes his head. "No. I'm hungry, but not for brains."

Another silence.

"She wouldn't have made it, you know?" Popcorn says.

"Who? Junko?"

"Yeah." Popcorn brushes her pink hair from her face. "They would have taken her out before she made it back to Platinum. I'm sure they're pretty cautious about that kind of thing."

Scavy nods. "I know… Still, I would have preferred not to know for sure."

"Yeah…" Popcorn says. "I guess not."

They stop. Scavy sits down on an iron bench and looks out at the wasteland around them.

"Ever think we'd end up dying out here?" he asks.

"Who's dying?" she says, sitting on the street across from him. "We're going to live forever. As zombies."

"You ever imagine something like this would happen to us?" Scavy asks.

Popcorn smiles.

"Strangely," she says, "this is exactly how I imagined we'd end up. Just you and me. Alone in a destroyed city. Though I always figured we would have been the ones to destroy it."

Scavy laughs.

"It could have been worse," he says. "We could have grown old together. Got married. Had kids. Worked on the docks for shit pay."

"Ewww…" Popcorn says.

Then they sit in silence for a while, staring at the pink and orange light reflecting from the clouds on the horizon.

Rainbow Cat leaps to her feet and holds out her machete.

"I have to find another camera," she says. "Where's another camera!"

Gogo pushes her way through the zombies and lunges at Rainbow. The hippy stabs her through the chest, between her breasts. Gogo curves her body as if dancing on the stage of her old strip club, pulling the handle of the machete out of Rainbow's hands.

As Rainbow tries to punch and kick her way through the crowd,

Gogo grabs her around the throat and rips her head off. The zombies swarm her corpse as it hits the ground.

Gogo runs out of the room with Rainbow's head, away from the other zombies. She cracks the head open like an egg, then tastes her first bite of fresh brain.

"Oh, hell *yeah!*" she moans, her eyes rolling in absolute bliss.

Gogo sits down, cross-legged, like a little kid eating her favorite sugary cereal. Using Rainbow's skull as a bowl, Gogo chows down, scooping the brains out with her fingers and slurping them up with her tongue.

As Scavy and Popcorn continue down the road, they run into a pack of mechjaws. Four dogs growl at them, aiming their weapons at Scavy's head.

"Fuck," Scavy says. "This little gnome won't protect me from them."

"Hand me a gun," Popcorn says. "Let me help."

Scavy tosses her the sniper rifle, then lifts his shotgun.

"Let's do this and shit!" Scavy yells, as the mechjaws open fire.

He fires his shotgun repeatedly, blowing one of them into three pieces. Bullets pierce his shoulder, but he keeps firing. He only has a few moments as a living human, so he might as well go out in a blaze of glory.

Popcorn shoots the sniper rifle, hitting the one with a rocket launcher. When it explodes, it takes out the other two with it. Their flesh flies up into the air and rains down on them.

"That was fucking awesome!" Scavy says to her, as chunks of meat splat on the ground between them.

As Popcorn smiles back at him, she sees another mechjaw coming up from behind.

"Think fast!" she cries.

She jumps into the circle, resisting the intense pain emanating from the lawn gnome, and blocks Scavy's back.

The mechjaw fires its Gatling gun, shredding her body with bullets. Her pink clothing tears open, revealing dozens of red holes. When the dog's gun runs out of bullets, Popcorn drops to the street. Scavy lifts his shotgun and blasts the dog until it no longer has a head or any front legs.

Scavy leans down to Popcorn. He lifts her head into his lap.

"You okay?" he asks.

"I can't move," she says. "I think I'm dying."

"You can't die," Scavy says. "You're a zombie and shit."

She smiles up at him.

"I saved your life out there, big brother," she says, raising her hand to his cheek. "Or at least what's left of it..."

"You should have let it get me," he says. "It might have saved me the pain of becoming a zombie."

"No pain..." she says. "I feel no pain..."

"Are you doing alright?" he asks.

"Kiss me," she says.

"Huh?" He becomes confused by the funny look she's giving him.

"One last kiss..." she says, rubbing her finger down his lips. "From my ex-boyfriend."

"Okay..." he says.

He leans in to kiss her, while pulling her up to his face by the back of her neck. As their lips touch, Popcorn's hand drops against his lap. Her body becomes limp. He sits up.

"Popcorn?" he asks, shaking her. "What happened?"

She doesn't move.

He shakes her again.

"Popcorn?"

Nothing.

"It can't be..." he says.

She's dead.

No longer undead, she's become a normal lifeless corpse.

"What the hell just happened?" the director asks Wayne from the control room, pointing at Popcorn's dead body on the screen.

Wayne smiles.

"The device doesn't only act as a repellent for the undead," he says. "It's also a cure for the zombie virus."

The director's eyes widen.

"Are you serious?" asks the director. "Where did you get this thing?"

"I have my connections," Wayne says.

"I didn't even know such a thing existed."

"Nobody does," Wayne says. "It's top secret. Nobody on the island is supposed to know about it."

"Then how did you get it?"

"I pay my spies well." Wayne dips a chocolate cruller into his coffee. "I had this prototype built specifically for my show. Those fat cats who run this island are probably shitting their pants now that this has been aired. By the end of the day, I bet every last person on the island, even the wretches in Copper, will know about this device."

"But why do they keep it a secret?" asks the director. "Do you know what's possible if we used this on a grander scale?"

Wayne wipes chocolate icing from his white goatee.

"The world would be saved," he says. "We could move back to the mainland. Rebuild society. Everything would be as it once was."

"Exactly!"

Wayne gives him a smirk. "But why would they want to do that? They are fat and happy where they are. With this device everyone would leave the island. They would be out of power. Without the citizens fearing the undead, and the big mighty government there to protect them, where would they be? This device is the most threatening thing to their way of life. The most threatening thing they ever could have imagined… a cure."

"So you put it on the show so everyone would find out?" asks the director. "To save humanity? To give us all a better future?"

"Hell no!" Wayne says. "Fuck humanity! I did it because those bastards pulled my funding. The show was going to be cancelled. After all my hard work trying to prove this show was worth its budget, they decided they would cancel it no matter how well it went. And they did it the day before production!"

Wayne chugs his coffee and then tosses the cup across his desk.

"I'm no hero," Wayne says. "I just wanted to piss those fuckers off."

The director falls out of his seat as the door to the control room breaks open. Twenty armed men charge in, filling the room. They aim their guns at each member of the crew. Wayne slowly raises his hands for the soldiers.

"Go ahead and arrest me," Wayne says. "There's nothing you can do to stop it. The damage has already been done."

"We're not here to arrest you," says one of the armed men, raising the barrel of his machine gun to Wayne's face.

Blood splashes against the picture of Adriana on Wayne's desk, as the armed men open fire.

Scavy figures out that the device in the lawn gnome is also a cure for the zombie virus. That is why Popcorn died on him. Once she had become human again, the bullets in her chest and brain ended her life.

Now he knows that he himself is safe from the virus. He will not join the ranks of the living dead. As long as he has the gnome, he is immune.

Sitting behind the wheels of a smart-car, one that could be operated manually, he lets out a big sigh. It's going to be a very long journey. He wishes the brain inside of the smart-car could drive him toward the coast, but its organic material within the dashboard didn't survive the gnome's cure.

Mr. T opens up the passenger door and sits down next to him.

"Ready to go?" he asks.

Scavy tried to save as many contestants as he could with the gnome, but in the end he could only save Mr. T. The large cyborg was the only one in a good enough condition to survive the cure.

Mr. T looks closely at Scavy's freshly bandaged wounds. The cyborg had removed the bullets from the punk's gunshot wounds and stitched up the zombie bites in his legs.

"How's the shoulder doing?" Mr. T asks. "You gonna be okay to drive?"

"Yeah," Scavy says. "If I can stay awake and shit."

Mr. T slaps him on the back.

"Then get a move on, fool!" he says. "We've got a world to rebuild!"

Scavy shifts the gear out of park and hits the gas. With a solar-powered car, a solar-powered shotgun, and the cure for the zombie virus, Scavy and Mr. T drive off, into the setting sun, toward a brighter tomorrow.

THE END

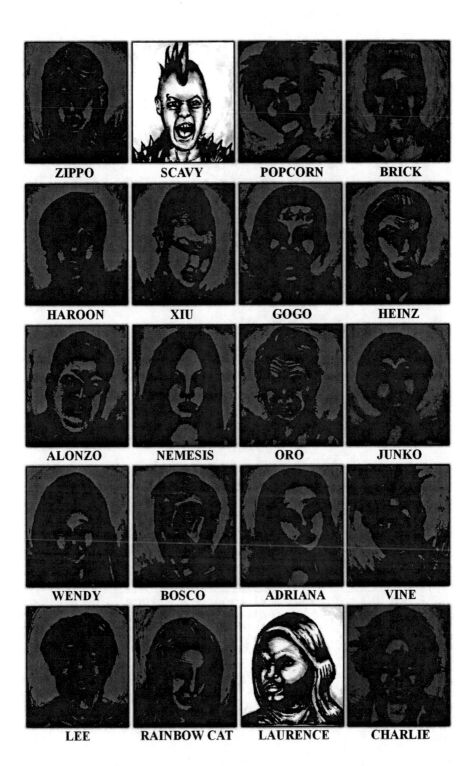

ZIPPO   SCAVY   POPCORN   BRICK

HAROON   XIU   GOGO   HEINZ

ALONZO   NEMESIS   ORO   JUNKO

WENDY   BOSCO   ADRIANA   VINE

LEE   RAINBOW CAT   LAURENCE   CHARLIE

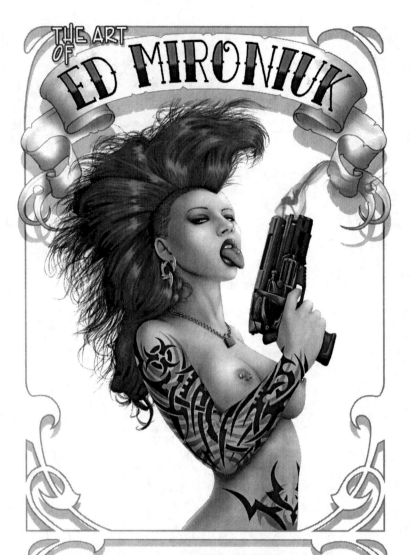

ABOUT THE AUTHOR

Carlton Mellick III is one of the leading authors in the new *Bizarro* genre uprising. Since 2001, his surreal counterculture novels have drawn an international cult following despite the fact that they have been shunned by most libraries and corporate bookstores. He lives in Portland, OR, the bizarro fiction mecca.

Visit him online at **www.carltonmellick.com**

Bizarro books

CATALOG   SPRING 2010

Bizarro Books publishes under the following imprints:

www.rawdogscreamingpress.com

www.eraserheadpress.com

www.afterbirthbooks.com

www.swallowdownpress.com

For all your Bizarro needs visit:

WWW.BIZARROCENTRAL.COM

Introduce yourselves to the bizarro genre and all of its authors with the Bizarro Starter Kit series. Each volume features short novels and short stories by ten of the leading bizarro authors, designed to give you a perfect sampling of the genre for only $5 plus shipping.

BB-0X1
"The Bizarro Starter Kit"
(Orange)

Featuring D. Harlan Wilson, Carlton Mellick III, Jeremy Robert Johnson, Kevin L Donihe, Gina Ranalli, Andre Duza, Vincent W. Sakowski, Steve Beard, John Edward Lawson, and Bruce Taylor.

236 pages $5

BB-0X2
"The Bizarro Starter Kit"
(Blue)

Featuring Ray Fracalossy, Jeremy C. Shipp, Jordan Krall, Mykle Hansen, Andersen Prunty, Eckhard Gerdes, Bradley Sands, Steve Aylett, Christian TeBordo, and Tony Rauch.

244 pages $5

BB-001 **"The Kafka Effekt" D. Harlan Wilson** - A collection of forty-four irreal short stories loosely written in the vein of Franz Kafka, with more than a pinch of William S. Burroughs sprinkled on top. **211 pages $14**

BB-002 **"Satan Burger" Carlton Mellick III** - The cult novel that put Carlton Mellick III on the map ... Six punks get jobs at a fast food restaurant owned by the devil in a city violently overpopulated by surreal alien cultures. **236 pages $14**

BB-003 **"Some Things Are Better Left Unplugged" Vincent Sakwoski** - Join The Man and his Nemesis, the obese tabby, for a nightmare roller coaster ride into this postmodern fantasy. **152 pages $10**

BB-004 **"Shall We Gather At the Garden?" Kevin L Donihe** - Donihe's Debut novel. Midgets take over the world, The Church of Lionel Richie vs. The Church of the Byrds, plant porn and more! **244 pages $14**

BB-005 **"Razor Wire Pubic Hair" Carlton Mellick III** - A genderless humandildo is purchased by a razor dominatrix and brought into her nightmarish world of bizarre sex and mutilation. **176 pages $11**

BB-006 **"Stranger on the Loose" D. Harlan Wilson** - The fiction of Wilson's 2nd collection is planted in the soil of normalcy, but what grows out of that soil is a dark, witty, otherworldly jungle... **228 pages $14**

BB-007 **"The Baby Jesus Butt Plug" Carlton Mellick III** - Using clones of the Baby Jesus for anal sex will be the hip sex fetish of the future. **92 pages $10**

BB-008 **"Fishyfleshed" Carlton Mellick III** - The world of the past is an illogical flatland lacking in dimension and color, a sick-scape of crispy squid people wandering the desert for no apparent reason. **260 pages $14**

BB-009 **"Dead Bitch Army" Andre Duza** - Step into a world filled with racist teenagers, cannibals, 100 warped Uncle Sams, automobiles with razor-sharp teeth, living graffiti, and a pissed-off zombie bitch out for revenge. **344 pages $16**

BB-010 **"The Menstruating Mall" Carlton Mellick III** - "The Breakfast Club meets Chopping Mall as directed by David Lynch." - Brian Keene **212 pages $12**

BB-011 **"Angel Dust Apocalypse" Jeremy Robert Johnson** - Meth-heads, man-made monsters, and murderous Neo-Nazis. "Seriously amazing short stories..." - Chuck Palahniuk, author of Fight Club **184 pages $11**

BB-012 **"Ocean of Lard" Kevin L Donihe / Carlton Mellick III** - A parody of those old Choose Your Own Adventure kid's books about some very odd pirates sailing on a sea made of animal fat. **176 pages $12**

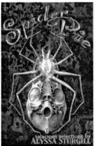

BB-013 **"Last Burn in Hell" John Edward Lawson** - From his lurid angst-affair with a lesbian music diva to his ascendance as unlikely pop icon the one constant for Kenrick Brimley, official state prison gigolo, is he's got no clue what he's doing. **172 pages $14**

BB-014 **"Tangerinephant" Kevin Dole 2** - TV-obsessed aliens have abducted Michael Tangerinephant in this bizarro combination of science fiction, satire, and surrealism. **164 pages $11**

BB-015 **"Foop!" Chris Genoa** - Strange happenings are going on at Dactyl, Inc, the world's first and only time travel tourism company.

"A surreal pie in the face!" - Christopher Moore **300 pages $14**

BB-016 **"Spider Pie" Alyssa Sturgill** - A one-way trip down a rabbit hole inhabited by sexual deviants and friendly monsters, fairytale beginnings and hideous endings. **104 pages $11**

BB-017 "The Unauthorized Woman" Efrem Emerson - Enter the world of the inner freak, a landscape populated by the pre-dead and morticioners, by cockroaches and 300-lb robots. **104 pages $11**

BB-018 "Fugue XXIX" Forrest Aguirre - Tales from the fringe of speculative literary fiction where innovative minds dream up the future's uncharted territories while mining forgotten treasures of the past. **220 pages $16**

BB-019 "Pocket Full of Loose Razorblades" John Edward Lawson - A collection of dark bizarro stories. From a giant rectum to a foot-fungus factory to a girl with a biforked tongue. **190 pages $13**

BB-020 "Punk Land" Carlton Mellick III - In the punk version of Heaven, the anarchist utopia is threatened by corporate fascism and only Goblin, Mortician's sperm, and a blue-mohawked female assassin named Shark Girl can stop them. **284 pages $15**

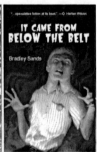

BB-021 "Pseudo-City" D. Harlan Wilson - Pseudo-City exposes what waits in the bathroom stall, under the manhole cover and in the corporate boardroom, all in a way that can only be described as mind-bogglingly irreal. **220 pages $16**

BB-022 "Kafka's Uncle and Other Strange Tales" Bruce Taylor - Anslenot and his giant tarantula (tormentor? fri-end?) wander a desecrated world in this novel and collection of stories from Mr. Magic Realism Himself. **348 pages $17**

BB-023 "Sex and Death In Television Town" Carlton Mellick III - In the old west, a gang of hermaphrodite gunslingers take refuge from a demon plague in Telos: a town where its citizens have televisions instead of heads. **184 pages $12**

BB-024 "It Came From Below The Belt" Bradley Sands - What can Grover Goldstein do when his severed, sentient penis forces him to return to high school and help it win the presidential election? **204 pages $13**

BB-025 **"Sick: An Anthology of Illness" John Lawson, editor** - These Sick stories are horrendous and hilarious dissections of creative minds on the scalpel's edge. **296 pages $16**

BB-026 **"Tempting Disaster" John Lawson, editor** - A shocking and alluring anthology from the fringe that examines our culture's obsession with taboos. **260 pages $16**

BB-027 **"Siren Promised" Jeremy Robert Johnson & Alan M Clark** - Nominated for the Bram Stoker Award. A potent mix of bad drugs, bad dreams, brutal bad guys, and surreal/incredible art by Alan M. Clark. **190 pages $13**

BB-028 **"Chemical Gardens" Gina Ranalli** - Ro and punk band Green is the Enemy find Kreepkins, a surfer-dude warlock, a vengeful demon, and a Metal Priestess in their way as they try to escape an underground nightmare. **188 pages $13**

BB-029 **"Jesus Freaks" Andre Duza** - For God so loved the world that he gave his only two begotten sons… and a few million zombies. **400 pages $16**

BB-030 **"Grape City" Kevin L. Donihe** - More Donihe-style comedic bizarro about a demon named Charles who is forced to work a minimum wage job on Earth after Hell goes out of business. **108 pages $10**

BB-031 **"Sea of the Patchwork Cats" Carlton Mellick III** - A quiet dreamlike tale set in the ashes of the human race. For Mellick enthusiasts who also adore The Twilight Zone. **112 pages $10**

BB-032 **"Extinction Journals" Jeremy Robert Johnson** - An uncanny voyage across a newly nuclear America where one man must confront the problems associated with loneliness, insane dieties, radiation, love, and an ever-evolving cockroach suit with a mind of its own. **104 pages $10**

BB-033 "Meat Puppet Cabaret" Steve Beard - At last! The secret connection between Jack the Ripper and Princess Diana's death revealed! **240 pages $16 / $30**

BB-034 "The Greatest Fucking Moment in Sports" Kevin L. Donihe - In the tradition of the surreal anti-sitcom Get A Life comes a tale of triumph and agape love from the master of comedic bizarro. **108 pages $10**

BB-035 "The Troublesome Amputee" John Edward Lawson - Disturbing verse from a man who truly believes nothing is sacred and intends to prove it. **104 pages $9**

BB-036 "Deity" Vic Mudd - God (who doesn't like to be called "God") comes down to a typical, suburban, Ohio family for a little vacation—but it doesn't turn out to be as relaxing as He had hoped it would be... **168 pages $12**

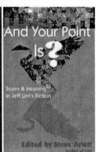

BB-037 "The Haunted Vagina" Carlton Mellick III - It's difficult to love a woman whose vagina is a gateway to the world of the dead. **132 pages $10**

BB-038 "Tales from the Vinegar Wasteland" Ray Fracalossy - Witness: a man is slowly losing his face, a neighbor who periodically screams out for no apparent reason, and a house with a room that doesn't actually exist. **240 pages $14**

BB-039 "Suicide Girls in the Afterlife" Gina Ranalli - After Pogue commits suicide, she unexpectedly finds herself an unwilling "guest" at a hotel in the Afterlife, where she meets a group of bizarre characters, including a goth Satan, a hippie Jesus, and an alien-human hybrid. **100 pages $9**

BB-040 "And Your Point Is?" Steve Aylett - In this follow-up to LINT multiple authors provide critical commentary and essays about Jeff Lint's mind-bending literature. **104 pages $11**

BB-041 **"Not Quite One of the Boys" Vincent Sakowski** - While drug-dealer Maxi drinks with Dante in purgatory, God and Satan play a little tri-level chess and do a little bargaining over his business partner, Vinnie, who is still left on earth. **220 pages $14**

BB-042 **"Teeth and Tongue Landscape" Carlton Mellick III** - On a planet made out of meat, a socially-obsessive monophobic man tries to find his place amongst the strange creatures and communities that he comes across. **110 pages $10**

BB-043 **"War Slut" Carlton Mellick III** - Part "1984," part "Waiting for Godot," and part action horror video game adaptation of John Carpenter's "The Thing." **116 pages $10**

BB-044 **"All Encompassing Trip" Nicole Del Sesto** - In a world where coffee is no longer available, the only television shows are reality TV re-runs, and the animals are talking back, Nikki, Amber and a singing Coyote in a do-rag are out to restore the light **308 pages $15**

BB-045 **"Dr. Identity" D. Harlan Wilson** - Follow the Dystopian Duo on a killing spree of epic proportions through the irreal postcapitalist city of Bliptown where time ticks sideways, artificial Bug-Eyed Monsters punish citizens for consumer-capitalist lethargy, and ultraviolence is as essential as a daily multivitamin. **208 pages $15**

BB-046 **"The Million-Year Centipede" Eckhard Gerdes** - Wakelin, frontman for 'The Hinge,' wrote a poem so prophetic that to ignore it dooms a person to drown in blood. **130 pages $12**

BB-047 **"Sausagey Santa" Carlton Mellick III** - A bizarro Christmas tale featuring Santa as a piratey mutant with a body made of sausages. 124 pages $10

BB-048 **"Misadventures in a Thumbnail Universe" Vincent Sakowski** - Dive deep into the surreal and satirical realms of neo-classical Blender Fiction, filled with television shoes and flesh-filled skies. **120 pages $10**

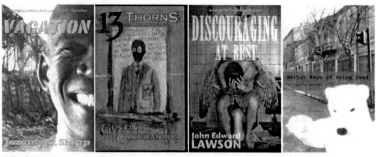

BB-049 "Vacation" Jeremy C. Shipp - Blueblood Bernard Johnson leaved his boring life behind to go on The Vacation, a year-long corporate sponsored odyssey. But instead of seeing the world, Bernard is captured by terrorists, becomes a key figure in secret drug wars, and, worse, doesn't once miss his secure American Dream. **160 pages $14**

BB-051 "13 Thorns" Gina Ranalli - Thirteen tales of twisted, bizarro horror. **240 pages $13**

BB-050 "Discouraging at Best" John Edward Lawson - A collection where the absurdity of the mundane expands exponentially creating a tidal wave that sweeps reason away. For those who enjoy satire, bizarro, or a good old-fashioned slap to the senses. **208 pages $15**

BB-052 "Better Ways of Being Dead" Christian TeBordo - In this class, the students have to keep one palm down on the table at all times, and listen to lectures about a panda who speaks Chinese. **216 pages $14**

BB-053 "Ballad of a Slow Poisoner" Andrew Goldfarb Millford Mutterwurst sat down on a Tuesday to take his afternoon tea, and made the unpleasant discovery that his elbows were becoming flatter. **128 pages $10**

BB-054 "Wall of Kiss" Gina Ranalli - A woman... A wall... Sometimes love blooms in the strangest of places. **108 pages $9**

BB-055 "HELP! A Bear is Eating Me" Mykle Hansen - The bizarro, heartwarming, magical tale of poor planning, hubris and severe blood loss... **150 pages $11**

BB-056 "Piecemeal June" Jordan Krall - A man falls in love with a living sex doll, but with love comes danger when her creator comes after her with crab-squid assassins. **90 pages $9**

BB-057 **"Laredo" Tony Rauch** - Dreamlike, surreal stories by Tony Rauch. **180 pages $12**

BB-058 **"The Overwhelming Urge" Andersen Prunty** - A collection of bizarro tales by Andersen Prunty. **150 pages $11**

BB-059 **"Adolf in Wonderland" Carlton Mellick III** - A dreamlike adventure that takes a young descendant of Adolf Hitler's design and sends him down the rabbit hole into a world of imperfection and disorder. **180 pages $11**

BB-060 **"Super Cell Anemia" Duncan B. Barlow** - "Unrelentingly bizarre and mysterious, unsettling in all the right ways..." - Brian Evenson. **180 pages $12**

BB-061 **"Ultra Fuckers" Carlton Mellick III** - Absurdist suburban horror about a couple who enter an upper middle class gated community but can't find their way out. **108 pages $9**

BB-062 **"House of Houses" Kevin L. Donihe** - An odd man wants to marry his house. Unfortunately, all of the houses in the world collapse at the same time in the Great House Holocaust. Now he must travel to House Heaven to find his departed fiancee. **172 pages $11**

BB-063 **"Necro Sex Machine" Andre Duza** - The Dead Bitch returns in this follow-up to the bizarro zombie epic Dead Bitch Army. **400 pages $16**

BB-064 **"Squid Pulp Blues" Jordan Krall** - In these three bizarro-noir novellas, the reader is thrown into a world of murderers, drugs made from squid parts, deformed gun-toting veterans, and a mischievous apocalyptic donkey. **204 pages $12**

by Tom Bradley

BB-065 **"Jack and Mr. Grin" Andersen Prunty** - "When Mr. Grin calls you can hear a smile in his voice. Not a warm and friendly smile, but the kind that seizes your spine in fear. You don't need to pay your phone bill to hear it. That smile is in every line of Prunty's prose." - Tom Bradley. **208 pages $12**

BB-066 **"Cybernetrix" Carlton Mellick III** - What would you do if your normal everyday world was slowly mutating into the video game world from Tron? **212 pages $12**

BB-067 **"Lemur" Tom Bradley** - Spencer Sproul is a would-be serial-killing bus boy who can't manage to murder, injure, or even scare anybody. However, there are other ways to do damage to far more people and do it legally... **120 pages $12**

BB-068 **"Cocoon of Terror" Jason Earls** - Decapitated corpses...a sculpture of terror...Zelian's masterpiece, his Cocoon of Terror, will trigger a supernatural disaster for everyone on Earth. **196 pages $14**

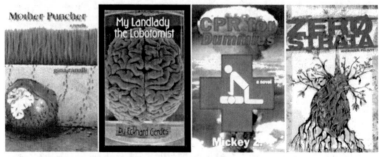

BB-069 **"Mother Puncher" Gina Ranalli** - The world has become tragically over-populated and now the government strongly opposes procreation. Ed is employed by the government as a mother-puncher. He doesn't relish his job, but he knows it has to be done and he knows he's the best one to do it. **120 pages $9**

BB-070 **"My Landlady the Lobotomist" Eckhard Gerdes** - The brains of past tenants line the shelves of my boarding house, soaking in a mysterious elixir. One more slip-up and the landlady might just add my frontal lobe to her collection. **116 pages $12**

BB-071 **"CPR for Dummies" Mickey Z.** - This hilarious freakshow at the world's end is the fragmented, sobering debut novel by acclaimed nonfiction author Mickey Z. **216 pages $14**

BB-072 **"Zerostrata" Andersen Prunty** - Hansel Nothing lives in a tree house, suffers from memory loss, has a very eccentric family, and falls in love with a woman who runs naked through the woods every night. **144 pages $11**

BB-073 "The Egg Man" Carlton Mellick III - It is a world where humans reproduce like insects. Children are the property of corporations, and having an enormous ten-foot brain implanted into your skull is a grotesque sexual fetish. Mellick's industrial urban dystopia is one of his darkest and grittiest to date. **184 pages $11**

BB-074 "Shark Hunting in Paradise Garden" Cameron Pierce - A group of strange humanoid religious fanatics travel back in time to the Garden of Eden to discover it is invested with hundreds of giant flying maneating sharks. **150 pages $10**

BB-075 "Apeshit" Carlton Mellick III - Friday the 13th meets Visitor Q. Six hipster teens go to a cabin in the woods inhabited by a deformed killer. An incredibly fucked-up parody of B-horror movies with a bizarro slant. **192 pages $12**

BB-076 "Rampaging Fuckers of Everything on the Crazy Shitting Planet of the Vomit At smosphere" Mykle Hansen - 3 bizarro satires. Monster Cocks, Journey to the Center of Agnes Cuddlebottom, and Crazy Shitting Planet. **228 pages $12**

BB-077 "The Kissing Bug" Daniel Scott Buck - In the tradition of Roald Dahl, Tim Burton, and Edward Gorey, comes this bizarro anti-war children's story about a bohemian conenose kissing bug who falls in love with a human woman. **116 pages $10**

BB-078 "MachoPoni" Lotus Rose - It's My Little Pony... *Bizarro* style! A long time ago Poniworld was split in two. On one side of the Jagged Line is the Pastel Kingdom, a magical land of music, parties, and positivity. On the other side of the Jagged Line is Dark Kingdom inhabited by an army of undead ponies. **148 pages $11**

BB-079 "The Faggiest Vampire" Carlton Mellick III - A Roald Dahl-esque children's story about two faggy vampires who partake in a mustache competition to find out which one is truly the faggiest. **104 pages $10**

BB-080 "Sky Tongues" Gina Ranalli - The autobiography of Sky Tongues, the biracial hermaphrodite actress with tongues for fingers. Follow her strange life story as she rises from freak to fame. **204 pages $12**

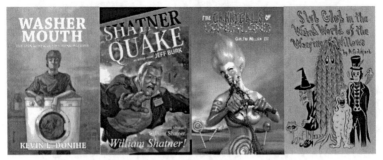

BB-081 **"Washer Mouth" Kevin L. Donihe** - A washing machine becomes human and pursues his dream of meeting his favorite soap opera star. **244 pages $11**

BB-082 **"Shatnerquake" Jeff Burk** - All of the characters ever played by William Shatner are suddenly sucked into our world. Their mission: hunt down and destroy the real William Shatner. **100 pages $10**

BB-083 **"The Cannibals of Candyland" Carlton Mellick III** - There exists a race of cannibals that are made of candy. They live in an underground world made out of candy. One man has dedicated his life to killing them all. **170 pages $11**

BB-084 **"Slub Glub in the Weird World of the Weeping Willows" Andrew Goldfarb** - The charming tale of a blue glob named Slub Glub who helps the weeping willows whose tears are flooding the earth. There are also hyenas, ghosts, and a voodoo priest **100 pages $10**

BB-085 **"Super Fetus" Adam Pepper** - Try to abort this fetus and he'll kick your ass! **104 pages $10**

BB-086 **"Fistful of Feet" Jordan Krall** - A bizarro tribute to spaghetti westerns, featuring Cthulhu-worshipping Indians, a woman with four feet, a crazed gunman who is obsessed with sucking on candy, Syphilis-ridden mutants, sexually transmitted tattoos, and a house devoted to the freakiest fetishes. **228 pages $12**

BB-087 **"Ass Goblins of Auschwitz" Cameron Pierce** - It's Monty Python meets Nazi exploitation in a surreal nightmare as can only be imagined by Bizarro author Cameron Pierce. **104 pages $10**

BB-088 **"Silent Weapons for Quiet Wars" Cody Goodfellow** - "This is high-end psychological surrealist horror meets bottom-feeding low-life crime in a techno-thrilling science fiction world full of Lovecraft and magic..." -John Skipp **212 pages $12**

BB-089 "Warrior Wolf Women of the Wasteland" Carlton Mellick III
Road Warrior Werewolves versus McDonaldland Mutants...post-apocalyptic fiction has never been quite like this. **316 pages $13**

BB-090 "Cursed" Jeremy C Shipp - The story of a group of characters who believe they are cursed and attempt to figure out who cursed them and why. A tale of stylish absurdism and suspenseful horror. **218 pages $15**

BB-091 "Super Giant Monster Time" Jeff Burk - A tribute to choose your own adventures and Godzilla movies. Will you escape the giant monsters that are rampaging the fuck out of your city and shit? Or will you join the mob of alien-controlled punk rockers causing chaos in the streets? What happens next depends on you. **188 pages $12**

BB-092 "Perfect Union" Cody Goodfellow - "Cronenberg's THE FLY on a grand scale: human/insect gene-spliced body horror, where the human hive politics are as shocking as the gore." -John Skipp. **272 pages $13**

BB-093 "Sunset with a Beard" Carlton Mellick III - 14 stories of surreal science fiction. **200 pages $12**

BB-094 "My Fake War" Andersen Prunty - The absurd tale of an unlikely soldier forced to fight a war that, quite possibly, does not exist. It's Rambo meets Waiting for Godot in this subversive satire of American values and the scope of the human imagination. **128 pages $11**

BB-095 "Lost in Cat Brain Land" Cameron Pierce - Sad stories from a surreal world. A fascist mustache, the ghost of Franz Kafka, a desert inside a dead cat. Primordial entities mourn the death of their child. The desperate serve tea to mysterious creatures. A hopeless romantic falls in love with a pterodactyl. And much more. **152 pages $11**

BB-096 "The Kobold Wizard's Dildo of Enlightenment +2" Carlton Mellick III - A Dungeons and Dragons parody about a group of people who learn they are only made up characters in an AD&D campaign and must find a way to resist their nerdy teenaged players and retarded dungeon master in order to survive. 232 **pages $12**

BB-097 "My Heart Said No, but the Camera Crew Said Yes!" Bradley Sands - A collection of short stories that are crammed with the delightfully odd and the scurrilously silly. **140 pages $13**

BB-098 "A Hundred Horrible Sorrows of Ogner Stump" Andrew Goldfarb - Goldfarb's acclaimed comic series. A magical and weird journey into the horrors of everyday life. **164 pages $11**

BB-099 "Pickled Apocalypse of Pancake Island" Cameron Pierce A demented fairy tale about a pickle, a pancake, and the apocalypse. **102 pages $8**

BB-100 "Slag Attack" Andersen Prunty - Slag Attack features four visceral, noir stories about the living, crawling apocalypse. A slag is what survivors are calling the slug-like maggots raining from the sky, burrowing inside people, and hollowing out their flesh and their sanity. **148 pages $11**

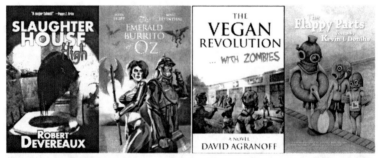

BB-101 "Slaughterhouse High" Robert Devereaux - A place where schools are built with secret passageways, rebellious teens get zippers installed in their mouths and genitals, and once a year, on that special night, one couple is slaughtered and the bits of their bodies are kept as souvenirs. **304 pages $13**

BB-102 "The Emerald Burrito of Oz" John Skipp & Marc Levinthal OZ IS REAL! Magic is real! The gate is really in Kansas! And America is finally allowing Earth tourists to visit this weird-ass, mysterious land. But when Gene of Los Angeles heads off for summer vacation in the Emerald City, little does he know that a war is brewing...a war that could destroy both worlds. **280 pages $13**

BB-103 "The Vegan Revolution... with Zombies" David Agranoff When there's no more meat in hell, the vegans will walk the earth. **160 pages $11**

BB-104 "The Flappy Parts" Kevin L Donihe - Poems about bunnies, LSD, and police abuse. You know, things that matter. **132 pages $11**

ORDER FORM

TITLES	QTY	PRICE	TOTAL

Please make checks and moneyorders payable to ROSE O'KEEFE / BIZARRO BOOKS in U.S. funds only. Please don't send bad checks! Allow 2-6 weeks for delivery. International orders may take longer. If you'd like to pay online via PAYPAL.COM, send payments to publisher@eraserheadpress.com.

SHIPPING: US ORDERS - $2 for the first book, $1 for each additional book. For priority shipping, add an additional $4. INT'L ORDERS - $5 for the first book, $3 for each additional book. Add an additional $5 per book for global priority shipping.

Send payment to:

BIZARRO BOOKS
C/O Rose O'Keefe
205 NE Bryant
Portland, OR 97211

Address

City   State   Zip

Email   Phone

CPSIA information can be obtained at www.ICGtesting.com
Printed in the USA
LVOW10s1953301015

460458LV00019B/429/P